C

is a philosophy gra
a short-story writer,
art of computer programming. He wouldn't mind
being a wizard, but you can't get a grant for that
sort of thing nowadays.

He lives in Essex with a human and five
non-humans, and is writing a sequel
to *Wizard's Brew*.

By the same author

THE MAN WHO STOLE THE FUTURE

Chris Fox

WIZARD'S BREW

The Humour Club
H.001

Aspire Publishing

An Aspire Publication

First published in Great Britain 1998

ISBN 1 902035 011

Printed and bound in Great Britain by
Mackays of Chatham Plc, Chatham, Kent.

Typeset in Palatino by Kestrel Data, Exeter, Devon.

Cover design by Gary Long

Aspire Publishing – a division of XcentreX Ltd.

For Jeanie (who provided moral support
and endless coffee) and Sebastian
(who sat on the keyboard
and purred)

Chapter One

In the small and stony bay below the little village of Fishcake, the sea was coming in.

It had been coming in (and indeed going out) at that same spot for several million years, and it did it pretty well, which was not surprising after so much practice. It had a varied repertoire of tidal movements at its disposal, from the slow, leisurely sweep to the headlong froth-laden rush. It was an expert at all of them. There wasn't much you could tell that particular stretch of water about doing its job. As seas went, it was a professional.

Today, though, it was having a problem with a large rock.

The sea grumbled to itself as it heaved the rock a yard or so towards the shore, and then sighed in exasperation as the rock fell back almost as far when the sea paused for breath. It had been trying to get this damned rock out of its hair for several hours, but to no avail. Every time it landed the rock on the beach and tried to hurry away, the wretched thing got caught in a back-current and rolled out into open water again.

The sea was good at its job, but it wasn't a great thinker. It didn't know why it was so important to get the rock to shore; it just knew that it was, and it was doing its best to oblige. It knew the rock had to get ashore, because the rock had told it so.

The sea didn't question the fact that the rock had told it something. It didn't even question the fact that the rock floated, which was fairly unusual behaviour for rocks. It wasn't used to thinking about rocks at all. It was used to flowing over them, or round them, or battering itself against them in a frenzy (which generally gave it a headache). None of this had given it much of an understanding of what rocks were really like. Rocks were annoying, usually because they got in the way of a nice smooth artistic ebb and flow and made it all messy. This one was just more annoying than usual, and in a slightly different way.

The sea retreated a few yards from the beach, got squarely behind the rock, and gathered itself for one final heave.

The business with the floating rock had started some hours earlier, though the sea wasn't to know this.

It was early morning. On the windswept beach, a lone figure in a grey robe was pointing at the sea and chanting. A group of men in ragged clothes stood behind him, watching dourly and occasionally muttering to one another.

The chanting figure raised a long straight piece of wood, ebon-black and carved with curious runes, and waved it in what he hoped was a convincingly arcane gesture. To all appearances, he was a wizard. Appearances can be deceptive, but in this case they were fairly accurate. To be totally accurate, he was a *probationary* wizard.

A more violent wave of the staff caused the wizard's hood to fall back to his shoulders, revealing a shock of black hair and a youthful face wearing a nervous expression.

Huw Llewellyn Tiberius Germanicus Jones (his father

8

was Welsh and his mother Roman) was twenty-two years old, and this was his first professional post since leaving the Academy of Magic in Anglesey. It was also going to be his last, but he didn't know that.

Huw Jones's career thus far had not been distinguished. He had been in the bottom class in his year, in every subject from Elemental Runes to Advanced Necromancy, and after seven painful years had graduated without honours, and with the lowest possible pass mark. He had taken the job of Wizard-in-Residence in Fishcake because it was either that or work for King Piddle of Pittenweem, who chewed off cats' heads and strangled his servants if they spilt the wine.

This was Huw's first big task: to conjure up the large catch for which the villagers of Fishcake had been waiting for the past three months. They were starving and desperate, and if he didn't deliver the goods, they were going to tie rocks to his feet and drop him into the deepest part of the bay. He knew this because they had explained it to him carefully while staring at him with mad, hungry eyes.

He glanced anxiously at his spectators. They were still staring at him, evidently unimpressed with his performance so far. Huw licked his lips. What was it he had been told by his final-year tutor, the one with the expensively-cut pin-striped robe and the pointy hat trimmed with silver? Oh yes. 'Always perform your spells with élan – with panache. It impresses the punters.' *That's the trouble,* thought Huw sadly. *I've searched through the Wizard's Starter Pack supplied by the Academy, and there are plenty of eyes of newt and toes of frog, but not a single élan or panache. Perhaps the Academy stores were out of stock.*

One of the watching men, a tall rawboned fellow with red hair and a manic squint, seemed to be having a mild altercation with his mates. After a few muttered

9

exchanges, he detached himself from the others and ambled across to Huw with a gait reminiscent of James Stewart.

'How's it going, friend?' he said amiably. He fixed Huw with his right eye, while the left examined the acne scars on the side of the speaker's nose.

'Er – fine, thanks,' said Huw, wishing fervently that the man would go away. 'Not long now. Should be getting a bite soon.'

'Good on you,' said the rawboned fellow. 'I allus said you was all right. The rest of 'em – he jerked a thumb at his companions, twenty yards distant – 'they don't have no faith in you. They reckon you're a green, wet-eared novice with no more magic in you than a flat-eyed flounder. They say you should've bin packed off back to Anglesey the first day you come.'

'Oh,' said Huw. His confidence, which had been at rock-bottom for several days, took a nosedive through the remaining strata to the magma of depression beneath.

'That's what *they* say. But what *I* sez is, give the lad a chance. Even if he does look like he don't know which end of a wizard's staff is which.'

Huw glanced hastily at his staff. No, it was all right – he *was* holding it by the right end. Not that he was likely to get it wrong, because the staff was the most expensive money could buy, the Excelsior Demongrabber, manufactured by Grimsdyke & Co. of Camelot, and it had five little grooves for the fingers and thumb at one end. Huw's parents had bought it for him as a reward for getting into the Academy. The Excelsior Demongrabber also had inlaid brass hinges so that it could be folded up, and its own hand-tooled dragon-skin carrying case, on which were engraved the words *To our darling Huw from Mummy and Daddy with all our love.*

Huw's fellow-students had noticed this on the first day, and for the next seven years his life had been hell.

'Very kind of you, I'm sure,' he said.

'Let the young 'un do his stuff, that's what I sez. He's got to learn. We all got to learn.' The red-haired man closed his right eye very slowly, while the left continued to take an inventory of its owner's nasal pock-marks. Huw gazed at this apparition for several seconds before realising that what he was witnessing was a wink.

'Er – yes. Quite so.'

'Mind if I stand here and watch?' asked the red-haired man. 'Only I allus wanted to be a wizard meself. Tried it once, but I couldn't get the hang of the Latin. Why's it in Latin, anyway? Why not Gaelic, or Saxon?'

'Well . . . It always has been in Latin,' said Huw, aware that this was a rather feeble reply.

'Don't seem much of a reason to me,' said the other. 'Still, it's your racket not mine. Don't mind me. Just you carry on.'

He smiled a gap-toothed smile at Huw, and moved closer, so that there was scarcely a yard between them. His breath drifted across Huw's face. It smelled of salt water, sour ale and old haddock.

Huw swallowed, and tried to refocus his attention on the spell. With a sudden surge of panic, he realised that he couldn't remember it properly. He had stayed up half the night memorising it, and now it was slipping away from him. What's more, he had left the grimoire in his hut. Too late to go back for it now.

Full of foreboding, he raised his staff again and silently groped for the next phrase.

'. . . O sea, give up your treasures to us who are waiting here on the land. . .'

He was pretty sure that was okay. But what came next?

'. . . O great ocean, yield up the thing you have held imprisoned for so long in your depths . . .'

That didn't seem quite right. The Latin words had become vague in his mind. He had a nasty feeling he was making some of them up.

'. . . we who have waited hungrily for its awful return . . .'

That was definitely wrong, but the red-haired man was breathing several years' worth of fish suppers in his nostrils, and he couldn't concentrate properly.

'. . . we who have waited for the reawakening of the ancient power that was thought to have died long ago . . .'

It was all going horribly wrong. A cold sweat broke out on Huw's face, and the staff shook in his hand.

'I likes a nice bit of magickin',' said the red-haired man conversationally. 'Very comforting, it is. Makes you feel someone understands what's going on.'

Not me, whispered a desperate voice inside Huw. *I don't have the faintest idea what's going on.*

'. . . come hither! come hither! come hither! come NOW!'

Huw's voice rose to a crescendo, cracked like unseasoned wood, and tailed away in a croaking whisper.

The summoning was complete. But what, exactly, had he summoned?

There was a long pause, while the villagers gazed expectantly at the churning waves as if they hoped to see a shoal of herring come swimming up out of the sea and commit suicide on the sand at their feet. When nothing happened, they looked back at Huw with expressions of deep cynicism.

'Tomorrow morning,' said Huw, finding his voice with difficulty. 'First thing. Tomorrow morning, first thing, take your boats out in the bay, and – and – and you'll see what the sea has brought in for you.'

The villagers stared at him hollowly. Then they turned and trudged away up the beach, heading back to their cold cottages and empty larders.

'You showed 'em,' said the red-haired man, squinting at Huw cheerfully.

'Did I?'

'Sure. Tomorrow morning. Then we'll all see what you've done for us.' The red-haired man smiled his gap-toothed smile, and set off after the others.

Huw sighed unhappily. Folding his staff in three, he put it back in its case and began the long post-conjural plod back to his tiny hut on the outskirts of the village.

Soon the beach was empty of everything but seagulls and crabs.

Out of sight of the watchers on the shore, deep down at the bottom of the bay, a large rock began to shift slightly in the mud.

It took most of the day for the rock to work its way up through the accumulated mud and barnacles of a thousand years. At around midnight it rolled onto the edge of the beach and stuck there, wedged in a hollow between two sand-dunes.

The stars were out in a black sky, and the beach was a chilly and barren place. No-one was about. They were all half a mile away, huddled in their cottages, drinking. What they were drinking was the local brew, a lethal concoction of fermented seaweed. Some of the other coastal villages made the ubiquitous seaweed into laver bread. The people of Fishcake hated laver bread, and preferred to use the seaweed to produce a liquid that would get them crab-sidling drunk, so that they could forget their hunger. They had been drinking for hours, and the process was pretty far advanced.

In one of the cottages, the red-haired man was embroiled in a ferocious argument with two of his neighbours.

'What I sez is,' said the red-haired man, in a voice that was beginning to lose the distinction between vowels and consonants, 'th' boy done OK. Must've done, 'cos he's a trained wiz. Neither of you's a trained wiz. I'm not a trained wiz. No-one in Fishcake is a trained wiz, 'cept him. You got a trained wiz, you got proper magickin'. Stands to reason.' He nodded several times, and stared blearily at the side of his nose, where the acne scars seemed to have grown into pits of Grand Canyon proportions.

'Codswallop,' said one of his neighbours, a thickset man with a huge purple wart on the end of his nose. As the blood pulsed through the wart, it alternately lit up and subsided, like a neon sign in a Soho back-street.

The third man, who was considered very deep because he hardly ever said anything, sniffed.

'Snot,' said the red-haired man indignantly. 'Snot codswallop. Strue. I bet if we went down to th' beach right now, we'd find lossa fish. Lossa fish. Allovertheplace. Betcha.'

'Garn,' said the man with the wart, and took a defiant swig of his seaweed.

The deep thinker sniffed again.

The red-haired man drained his tankard with a flourish, put it down on the table at his elbow, and said in a louder voice, 'Awright. Awright. Lessall go down to th'beach. We'll see. Lossa fish. Betcha. OK?'

'OK,' said the man with the wart. 'But there won't be any. No fish. Nonatall.'

They stood up unsteadily and faced one another, red-faced and breathing heavily.

'We'll all go,' said the red-haired man, swinging his

arm round in a grand gesture. 'Th'whole village. Ev'ryone. Lossa fish for ev'ryone.'

The man with the wart grinned. 'Awright. But there won't be no fish.'

'*Lossa* fish!'

'*No* fish!'

The two of them swayed like trees in a high wind. With a great effort, as if uprooting himself, the red-haired man swung his legs round and headed for the door. The man with the wart followed, chuckling.

Sniff. The deep thinker levered himself out of his chair. He was feeling slightly miffed, because they hadn't asked him what *he* thought. That was the trouble with being a deep thinker. People assumed that you were too busy thinking about the curvature of space or the military strategy of Alexander the Great to ask your opinion about ordinary things like fish. Which was a pity, because he would have liked to explain his hypothesis.

No fish, or lots of fish?

The deep thinker gave a deep smile. Easy-peasy.

There would be no fish. Probably. Although there might be a lot. Either there would be fish, or, alternatively, and on the whole more likely, there wouldn't. That was *his* hypothesis, and it was a good hypothesis, because it covered the known facts, and all the possibilities.

The deep thinker sniffed in a deep and meaningful way, and staggered out into the street after his friends, bumping into both door-posts as he went.

The red-haired man was lurching from house to house, banging on the doors and shouting incoherently about fish and wizards. Doors opened in his wake and faces, red and blotched from the consumption of too much seaweed, peered out.

To a drunken man, the company of other drunks, especially those who are shouting incoherently, is irresistible. Soon the red-haired man, the man with the wart and the deep thinker were leading a gaggle of inebriates down the windy path to the beach.

Overhead the stars winked at one another as if they were in on a joke that the villagers knew nothing about.

In his tiny and isolated hut set apart from the rest, Huw Jones was dreaming. He was also smiling. It was a very pleasant dream.

He was standing on the platform at the Academy of Magic in front of a vast audience of his fellow-wizards. They had just elected him to be the youngest Arch-chancellor in the Academy's history.

His mother and father were there. His father stepped forward and shook his hand. 'Well done, Huw boy. I always knew you would be a success. And I'm sorry the staff we bought you was no good. You can get a proper one now.'

Huw was pleased that his father had apologised, but he wanted to make him squirm a little. 'You do realise, Dad, that for seven years I've been known as the Taff with the naff staff? How are you going to make it up to me?'

His mother smiled tenderly at him, and held out a large basket with a cloth over it. 'Here, son,' she said. 'You can have what's in this basket.'

She lifted the cloth off. The basket was full of fish.

Huw began to twitch uneasily. The dream was starting to go wrong. They should be showering him with gold and things. Why were they offering him fish?

'I don't want all these fish,' he said. 'I don't like fish. Can't I have gold or jewels or something?'

His tutor stepped forward. He was frowning. 'You made a mess of the spell, Huw. You summoned the wrong kind of fish. These fish are no good. Look.'

Huw stared at the fish in the basket. They were rotting before his eyes and giving off a foul stench.

'It isn't my fault,' he protested. 'It was the red-haired man. He put me off.'

'Don't blame the customer,' said his tutor. 'How often have I told you, Huw? The customer is always right.'

'It's the Latin,' said Huw desperately. 'I get mixed up with the Latin. If it was in Gaelic, or Saxon . . .'

His tutor shook his head disapprovingly. 'This is a right wizard's brew[1], Huw. What are you going to do, Huw?'

'I dunno,' said Huw unhappily.

He woke then, and sat up in bed, breathing heavily. There were noises in the distance, beyond the hut – unsettling noises, like people shouting, or possibly screaming. As he listened, the noises died away, and there was only the wind blowing fitfully under the door of his hut.

He got out of bed, put his wizard's robe on over his nightshirt, and went out into the cold, starry night. He stumbled down the stony path to the beach, and stood looking around.

The surface of the beach glistened. Here and there, white things glinted among the stones. Shells, probably.

Huw shivered. The sea rolling in under the stars was a grey and unattractive prospect. The wind ruffled his hair, tasting of salt. And something else. He wrinkled his nose.

Blood? How could the wind taste of blood?

He took a few tentative steps over the pebbles, stumbled, and almost fell. The pebbles were very slippery.

---

[1]Wizard's Brew: a cock-up, or unholy mess. The name comes from a traditional beverage made by wizards. The recipe is secret, but is believed to involve sulphur, raw alcohol and old potato peelings.

He bent down and touched them. They felt slimy – an unpleasant feeling.

He took another step, and kicked something that made a light clacking noise. He looked down at his feet.

A bone. Long, thin, mostly white, but with dark fragments of gristle clinging to it.

There was another of the white things a few yards away. He stepped over to it, walking carefully so as not to fall on the treacherous pebbles.

Another bone.

He looked around wildly. What had happened here? Where were the villagers?

Some yards away, a dark, round shape was lying among the dunes. Beside it lay a second. He walked over to the two objects, treading carefully on the slippery pebbles.

They were rough hemispheres, hollow, and taller than himself. The outer surfaces were encrusted thickly with barnacles and mud. A dreadful stench emanated from them, an odour of something ancient and rotten. Huw gagged, and held his hand over his nose.

The jagged edges of the hemispheres looked as if they might fit together. If so, they would make a rough sphere, like a large hollow rock. The inner surfaces glistened, and a trail of slime ran away from them across the beach.

What sort of thing, thought Huw, *leaves a trail of slime?*

He heard a noise behind him. It sounded a bit like someone sucking a drink through a straw.

He turned.

Five yards away, a *thing* was lying on the beach. It might be some sort of creature, but if so, it was certainly the ugliest Huw had ever seen. There was no definite head, but from the end of the creature nearest to Huw grew a pair of long stalk-like things, which waved slowly to and fro. At the end of each stalk was a pale, globular eye. Below the eye-stalks was what might be a mouth, an irregular lipless slit.

The body glistened, with the same sheen as he had seen on the pebbles. There were suspicious-looking lumps under its skin, as if it had recently swallowed a partly-chewed meal.

It looked for all the world like a giant slug.

A giant slug, thought Huw, and shuddered. *What have I done?*

The answer was horribly clear. He had summoned something monstrous from the depths of the sea, and it had eaten his clients. This was not a good start to his career as a wizard.

Huw forced open his mouth, which had gone very dry, and said hoarsely, in his best Latin, 'Evil creature, I conjure you to obey me. I conjure you by the sun, by the moon, by summer and by winter—'

The slug opened its narrow mouth and hissed. Then it moved. It oozed towards him over the stones, much quicker than anything resembling a slug had any right to move.

Huw's voice died in his throat. He tried to think of a useful Latin phrase, but his mind was blank. For once in his life, he really wished he had brought the Excelsior Demongrabber with him.

He opened his mouth wide in order to scream, but the slug's mouth was also open, and he found that there wasn't time.

Morning came. If the weather had had any feelings at all, it would have been a sad, misty sort of day, in keeping with the tragedy that had befallen the village of Fish-cake.

It wasn't. It was a warm, bright, cheerful day. The sun

beamed down happily on the bone-strewn beach and the silent village with its swinging doors and empty street. Little clouds skipped unfeelingly through a blue sky. Birds sang. What they sang is not recorded, but it was probably something catchy and mindless, the sort of song that drives a cat to commit murder[1].

In Fishcake, there was only one cat. Yesterday there had been five, but during the night the slug had oozed up the village street and met four of them on the way. They weren't much of a meal, but after a thousand years without food, the slug was very, very hungry. It wasn't about to turn anything down, even something that arched its back and hissed.

The slug oozed out of the village and on into the countryside. It was watched, round-eyed, by the remaining cat, which was crouching behind a chimney-stack. Even when the slug had vanished over the horizon, the cat stayed on the roof. The danger wasn't necessarily over. The giant slug might have gone, but suppose it was being pursued by a giant blackbird?

The slug was heading inland. It felt stiff and sore, which is not surprising after a thousand years squashed into the smallest possible space. It was also very angry. It wanted *revenge*. Revenge for having been shrink-wrapped in granite cling-film for an entire millennium without so much as a by-your-leave. Revenge against the ones who had imprisoned it.

[1]The real reason cats murder birds is because they can't stand their taste in music. Cats hold midnight soirées in each other's back gardens at which they perform complex atonal pieces by Webern and Schoenberg. In the morning they are trying to catch up on their sleep, and they don't like being woken up by some feathered cretin singing 'Chirpy Chirpy Cheep Cheep' on a branch outside the window.

There had been a great warrior, tall and yellow-haired, with a sharp, shiny spear. The slug had fought the warrior and lost. This had been humiliating. Then the warrior and his friends, who were also tall and yellow-haired, had driven the slug into the rock's tight, airless stone prison, and sealed it in. This had been painful. After that there had been a thousand years of continuous hunger and cramp, which hadn't been much fun either.

The slug seethed with fury at the memory. That particular warrior was unlikely to still be around, but there would be others. Warriors. Wizards. Kings. People who thought they owned the place, that they could do what they liked. Humans, and humanlike creatures. Bipeds. Vertebrates.

Just because they have legs and a backbone, and I don't, thought the slug, *is no reason to treat me like a second-class citizen. It's discrimination, that's what it is. Molluscism. Invertebratophobia.*

Well, now I'm going to get my own back on them all. Bipeds. Humans. Things with legs, warm-blooded and crunchy. Yummy.

Hunger and revenge. Two powerful motivating forces.

Revenge and hunger were nice, simple things. Nothing fancy, nothing complicated. You caught up with your enemy, and you ate him. No worries.

But there was something else. A stray memory, something that didn't quite fit. It was lodged in the back of the slug's mind, like the grit that drives an oyster to spend weeks slaving over a hot pearl when all it really wanted was a quiet snooze in the mud.

It hadn't been as simple as that. Not a mere knockabout fight with a muscle-bound warrior and his spear. *He wasn't just an ordinary warrior,* said a nagging voice in the slug's mind. *And you're not just an ordinary slug. You were doing something, just before the warrior and his spear interrupted you. Something important.*

But what, exactly?

The nagging thought was like an itch. It wouldn't go away, and the slug didn't know how to scratch it. At the moment it was just irritating, but in time it would probably produce something as monstrous and unexpected as a pearl.

The slug undulated through a small wood and into a field full of sheep. The sheep looked up, saw and smelled the slug, and bleated in vague, woolly-headed panic.

There were several minutes of carnage, followed by a strong smell of mutton. Then the slug smashed through the hedge on the other side of the field and oozed on its destructive way.

It was getting stronger. The more it ate, the stronger it got. Soon it would be strong enough for anything.

In the distance, it could see a thatched roof poking above the surrounding greenery. Smoke came from the chimney. The slug vaguely remembered what thatched roofs and chimneys meant. They meant people. Crunchy bipeds. Food.

Revenge.

Swiftly and almost silently, it approached the isolated cottage.

Chapter Two

'Strawberries! Get your luverly strawberries here, only fifteen pence a pound!'

'Fish! Wet fish, dry fish, slightly damp fish! All less than a month old!'

'New potatoes! Old potatoes! Fossilised Roman potatoes!'

In Cheapside – which, as its name suggests, was not the most sought-after part of Camelot – the usual business of the day was in full swing. Cheapside was a narrow thoroughfare, generally congested with stalls, barrows and donkey-carts from which the street-vendors bawled their wares and haggled desperately to avoid being swindled by the Camelot housewives, who were a canny lot. The Camelot Tourist Office described Cheapside as having "character", which was a euphemism for tuneless street-vendor's shouts and the insistent smells of half-rotten fruit, over-ripe fish and fly-blown joints of meat.

Meanwhile, above the heads of the milling crowds, a dwarf was leaning out of an attic window and trying not to sniff the air.

The dwarf's name was Hergrim, and like all dwarfs, he had come originally from the far, bleak land of Dwarfheim. Dwarfheim was famous as the land where (1) a dwarf could become fabulously rich by mining gold in the deep caverns under the earth, and (2) all the women had beards. For some reason which dwarf-women could never understand, most male dwarfs declined the chance of fabulous wealth in Dwarfheim and took jobs abroad as wood-cutters and black-smiths, where they generally married the first beard-less woman below average height who would have them.

This did not mean, however, that they always liked the places they ended up in. Hergrim did not care much for Camelot. He regarded it as dull and parochial, and had been heard to refer to it disparagingly as "a city of sweaty shopkeepers".

Quite often, though, he just found it boring.

'Damn this city,' he said aloud, screwing his face up into a scowl. 'Nothing ever *happens* here.'

'Strawberries!' called the voice below. 'Get your slightly bruised but nevertheless totally scrumptious strawberries here! Get your luverly str . . . omigawd!'

The fruit-seller suddenly fell silent.

Hergrim was slightly puzzled by this. It took a lot to silence a Camelot market-trader. Cutting out his tongue would be a necessary first step, followed by sticking his head in a bale of hay. Even that might not work. Camelot street-traders were reputed to shout their wares in their sleep.

The dwarf leaned further out of the window and wrinkled his nose. Was it his imagination, or did the street smell worse than usual? It hardly seemed possi-ble, and yet . . .

Below his window, someone screamed. There was a crash, and a shout. A donkey hee-hawed in panic.

'What on earth—?' muttered the dwarf.

Further disturbing noises followed. Banging doors. More shouts. Donkeys' hooves clattering on cobbles. The crash of a market stall falling over.

He leaned out to try and see the street, but the overhang of the building was too great.

'Something's happening down there,' he said to himself. 'Some kind of disturbance.'

A curl of smoke drifted up past his window and into his nostrils. He coughed violently. The smoke was sulphurous, acrid and hot. It was also bright green.

'Something is definitely going on,' he murmured. 'I'll go and take a look.' Seizing his battle-axe from its place in the corner, he descended the stairs and flung open the front door.

The street was in chaos. People were running here and there shouting incoherently. Market stalls lay with their legs in the air like huge dead cockroaches. Fish and apples and loaves of bread lay strewn across the cobbles. Green smoke billowed everywhere.

Then the smoke drifted apart, and Hergrim saw what all the fuss was about.

Coming up the street was a dragon. It was bright green, about ten feet high, and walked with a curious waddling gait, as though unusually light on its feet. Dragons traditionally breathe fire, but this one was puffing out clouds of green smoke.

Alongside it, hobbling on one sandalled and one bare foot, came a thin, white-haired man in a grey robe.

The dwarf relaxed. All was suddenly made clear. 'Gwydden the Abstruse,' he murmured. 'I might have known.'

Despite his white hair and beard, the thin man looked surprisingly young. He looked like a poverty-stricken wizard – which is exactly what he was. Hence the white hair: most wizards' hair went white early, due to messing about with powerful magical substances.

The wizard was carrying a length of rope with a noose at one end, and was clearly trying to lasso the dragon. As Hergrim watched, he made a dismal attempt at it; the rope fell short of the dragon's head, slid down its flank and dropped to the cobbles.

The thin man tried again. This time he scurried ahead of the dragon, whirled the noose, and flung it over the dragon's head. But as he did so, he slipped on a barrow-load of spilled apples and fell, directly in the path of the dragon's taloned feet.

Hergrim acted instinctively. Charging forward, he swung the axe with all his strength at the dragon's neck.

BANG!

The dragon exploded like a punctured balloon. Hergrim found that he and the man at his feet, the house-fronts and pavements, the stall-holders and customers, and most of the fruit, fish and meat, were covered in bright green, evil-smelling slime.

The man in the grey robe got up slowly and looked down at his green-spattered clothes.

'Oh dear,' he sighed. 'More laundry bills.' He looked up, saw the dwarf, and smiled ruefully. 'Hullo, Hergrim. Haven't seen you for a while. I seem to have caused rather a mess. Of course it would have been better if you hadn't used your axe . . .'

'I was trying to save your life,' said the dwarf crossly. 'Another few seconds and that dragon would have been on top of you.'

Gwydden laughed. 'It wouldn't have mattered. It wasn't a real dragon.'

'Obviously,' growled Hergrim, wiping some of the green goo from his tunic and sniffing it with distaste. 'I hope this stuff comes off.'

'Use hot water and plenty of washing-soda,' Gwydden advised. 'I always do.'

Hergrim raised an eyebrow. 'You've been doing a lot of this recently, have you?'

'On and off. I've been trying to make a dragon—'

'*Make* a dragon?'

'Yes, for a month now, but it's a tricky spell. You need a hundredweight of toadstools, a gallon of firedrake essence, five hundred tubes of oil paint – any colour will do, I just happen to like green – and you boil them together in a cauldron for thirteen hours at gas mark 6, until—'

''Ere, you,' growled a voice. 'Wotcher mean by it, spreadin' this 'orrible green gunge over me pork chops?'

The dwarf and wizard turned to see a huge and menacing figure looming over them. He was evidently a butcher, though his red-and-white apron was now liberally spattered with green blobs. Behind him an angry crowd had gathered. To Hergrim's eyes they looked very much like a lynching party.

The wizard seemed oblivious to the dangerous situation he had created. He smiled at the butcher winningly. 'Ah, hello. I'm Gwydden of Anglesey, your local GP – Geomantic Practitioner. Private consultations any time, special reductions for OAPs. Sorry about the mess, but you see, when someone disrupts a spell, as happened just now, the Intrinsic Monad, or as one might say in layman's language the universal substrate, is no longer confined within its accustomed boundaries, and consequently—'

A large paw descended from the sky and seized him by the collar.

'Wot I want ter know,' said the butcher, shaking the wizard like a rabbit, 'is wot abaht compensation?'

An angry murmur of assent rose from all sides.

'I'm awfully sorry,' squeaked the wizard, 'but I don't have any money.'

'Indeed?' The butcher nodded slowly. 'In that case we'll 'ang yer from the nearest lamp-post. Eh, neighbours?'

Raucous approval greeted this suggestion. Hoisting the wizard off his feet, the butcher strode across the street to where an ancient iron pillar, surmounted by a battered lamp, flowered from the pavement like a rusty weed. The horizontal bar below the lamp bore a disconcerting resemblance to the business end of a gibbet.

'All we need nah is a rope,' said the butcher. 'This'll do, I reckon.' He plucked from Gwydden's hand the noose with which the wizard had pursued the dragon. 'All ready fer the 'angman,' said the butcher with a vast leer. The crowd laughed and whistled, and shouted various things which were complimentary to butchers and derogatory to wizards.

The butcher looped the rope around the wizard's scrawny throat and began tightening the noose.

There was a sudden disturbance among the onlookers. A stocky figure with a red beard pushed his way to the front. In his hands he cradled a double-headed axe.

'Butcher,' said Hergrim, 'release that wizard.'

The butcher looked at the dwarf, who was only half his height. Then he looked at the axe, which was large and wickedly sharp. For half a minute, while the crowd held its breath, he stood still with his brow deeply furrowed, as if calculating some long and difficult sum. Then, reluctantly, he loosened the rope and put the wizard down on the pavement.

'Perhaps you will allow us to pass,' said Hergrim to the crowd. 'And if anyone is unwise enough to try and follow us . . .' He distorted his face into what he hoped was a psychopathic grin, and moved the axe suggestively.

Faced with Hergrim's axe, the onlookers seemed to lose their stomach for a lynching. They dispersed, muttering, and busied themselves with salvaging their scattered wares. Last to give up was the butcher, who glowered after the retreating pair for a long time before slowly bending to retrieve his chops and sausages from the gutter.

As Hergrim led Gwydden into his front hall and bolted the door behind them, he heard the fruit-seller calling out, 'Rare green-spotted strawberries! Exotic fruit, all the way from the South Seas! Only thirty pence a pound while stocks last!'

Camelot street-traders, Hergrim reflected, were not the sort of people to be put off the serious business of earning money by a little thing like an exploding dragon.

They climbed the stairs to Hergrim's garret, where Gwydden flopped into a moth-eaten armchair.

'Those Philistines!' he said indignantly. 'They don't deserve to have a Master of the Secret Art living in their midst. I should have turned the lot of them into toads.'

'So why didn't you?'

'Oh well.' The wizard shrugged. 'You know how it is. One can't always remember the right spell for the occasion. And some of these incantations are so complicated . . .'

'Nothing complicated about cold steel,' said the dwarf. 'Everyone understands that.' He went to a cupboard and took out two tankards and a large brown bottle.

'What I really hate about Camelot,' the wizard went

on, as he watched Hergrim pour two pints of Frigga's Revenge[1], 'apart of course from the bad drains, and the all-night goblin rave parties, and the really criminal price the local apothecaries charge for a simple bottle of chimaera's blood – what I really hate is the dullness, the complacency, the – the—'

'Boredom?'

'In a word, yes.'

'A city of sweaty shopkeepers.'

'Well, exactly. This business with the dragon, now. That's typical of the sort of mindless opposition I've had to put up with. If it's not someone shoving parchments through my letterbox complaining about the smells from my laboratory, it's some petty official from the Camelot Housing Department telling me I can't keep gryphons without a licence. It was only a baby one, too.'

'You sound as if you need a holiday,' Hergrim suggested, handing him a tankard. 'Somewhere away from Camelot. Somewhere rural and peaceful and quiet.'

Gwydden rolled his eyes up and squinted at the dwarf. 'What I need is an adventure. Huh! Fat chance.' And he took a gloomy swig of Hergrim's beer.

The slug was hungry. Several hours had passed since it had found the cottage, and the benefits of that rather insubstantial meal – one stringy old man, one stringy old woman and a budgerigar – had worn off. Since then, it had found nothing worth eating.

It had been oozing wearily through scrubland for

[1]Brewed for export in Dwarfheim by sour-tempered unmarried dwarf-women, who put all sorts of unmentionable things in it to give the male dwarfs who had deserted them terrible hangovers. On the label, in crabbed, vicious dwarf-runes, it said: *Probably the worst lager in the world.*

hours, and it was deeply unimpressed with the part of the country in which it found itself. Things had definitely gone downhill in the last thousand years. The only living things it had seen for a long time were gorse, heather, and small birds who flew away screaming in terror as it approached. Nothing worth eating at all.

All the while, behind the ever-present hunger for food, were the two nagging thoughts: revenge, and the odd feeling that there was some unfinished business somewhere.

It began to get dark. Stars appeared overhead. The slug dragged its empty belly over a low rise.

A few hundred yards away, a little yellowish light flickered against the dark ground – the light of a campfire.

Something stirred in the slug's memory. Something about fires and human beings. Where you got one, you generally found the other. And human beings meant food, and possibly the descendants of the spear-wielding warrior from so long ago.

Gathering its famished strength, the slug started to undulate across the ground towards the little yellow light.

'Well, now,' said the fat wizard in a scathing tone, 'here's another fine mess you've got us into. We're lost. I said we would be, and I was right. You're hopeless, Stan, do you know that? Hopeless.'

'Yes, Ollie,' said the thin wizard sadly. 'I know I am.'

'Well, just so long as we've got that straight. Now let's have some food. I'm ravenous.' Wizard Third Class Olaf Hardicanute rummaged in the smaller of the two sacks that lay on the ground beside them, and produced a string of sausages and a long brass fork. 'Here – grill these, will you?'

Wizard Third Class Dyrstan Laurelbush obediently put two sausages on the toasting-fork and held them over the flames of the little camp-fire. After a while, the sausages began to swell. The thin wizard gazed into the flames, and sighed despondently. The toasting-fork drooped lower, so that the flames licked round the sausages, which crackled and began to blacken.

'Don't burn them, you nitwit,' said the fat wizard crossly. 'Here - let me do it.' He took the fork and continued to grumble while he cooked the sausages. 'What did you have to lose the map for, anyway? We could be anywhere between Anglesey and Camelot – or up in Scotland, for that matter. Can't you do anything right?'

The thin wizard pulled at his thinning hair in a distracted way, and his face took on a doleful expression like a spaniel which has been told that nobody loves it. 'I'm sorry, Ollie,' he said miserably. 'I didn't know there was a hole in my tunic. Shall I go back and look for the map again?'

'Tcha!' said the fat wizard. It was a satisfying sound, so he repeated it. 'Tcha! What's the point of going back? You could have lost it anywhere in the last twenty miles. It'll have blown away by now. The trouble with you, Stan, is that you haven't any brains.'

The thin wizard's mouth drooped at the corners. 'I know. My father didn't have any either. They opened his skull when he died, and there was nothing inside but an empty space and an IOU. Turned out that one of his classmates at the Academy had borrowed his brains while he was asleep as a practical joke, and forgot to put them back. For forty years he went round with only air in his noddle, and no-one noticed.'

The fat wizard pursed his lips disapprovingly. 'Lack of

green matter[1] is no excuse. You should have held onto the map. How are we going to get this load of stuff to Camelot if we don't know we're on the right road?' He gave the other sack, which was large and bulging, a disrespectful kick. The sack made a metallic rattling noise.

'I don't think you should do that, Ollie,' said Stan, looking worried.

'Stupid old sack,' said Ollie, giving it another kick. The sack tinkled in a way that was tuneful but perhaps not entirely reassuring. 'Why do we have to do this sort of work anyway? Fancy two qualified wizards having to peddle magical trinkets to earn a living. It's not dignified.'

'It's the only work we could get,' the thin wizard pointed out. 'No-one will let us do any actual *spells* any more.'

'And whose fault is that?' demanded the fat wizard. 'Who ruined every spell we ever tried? Like the spell to get rid of rats that caused a plague of white mice? Or the spell that was supposed to turn lead into gold, and instead turned the Duke of Llanberis's castle into Gorgonzola? Gorgonzola, forsooth! I don't even *like* Gorgonzola! And what did you say to the Duke, as he stood looking at his castle and contemplating the fact that his ancestral home now smelled like a gigantic sweaty foot?'

Stan's face had gone crumply, like a wet paper bag. 'All I said was, "Never mind, my lord, at least the mice will have something to eat".'

'Tcha!'

[1] A wizard's brain is not like the brain of an ordinary person. An ordinary human brain contains grey matter (nerve cells) and white matter (nerve fibres). Wizards' brains similarly contain grey and white matter, but they also contain green matter, which is much more mysterious and is where the magic goes on. You could think of it as a sort of squishy kryptonite.

There was an unpleasant silence, broken only by an unhappy crooning noise from Stan and the sound of two sausages frizzling to a frazzle.

'What was that?' said the fat wizard suddenly.

'What was what?'

Ollie peered suspiciously into the darkness. 'I thought I heard a noise.'

The thin wizard's misery was replaced by apprehension. 'Ooh, Ollie! What sort of noise?'

'A sort of sucking noise. Like something oozing. Yes, definitely an oozing, sucking kind of a noise.'

'Ooooh, Ollie.' Stan's expression would have made Stephen King green with envy. 'Ollie, I'm frightened.'

Sssssssssh.

'All right, Ollie, I'll try to be quiet. You don't have to shush me.'

'I didn't shush you.'

'Oooooooh, Ollie . . . !'

Beyond the fire, something dark and shapeless reared up against the sky.

Sssssssssssshh!

'Quick,' said the fat wizard in sudden desperation, 'the staff. Where's the staff?'

'I don't know!' wailed Stan. 'I thought you had it!'

'It's in the sack!' shouted Ollie. 'I remember, I put it in the big sack.' He fumbled at the neck of the sack. 'Why won't this open? Stan, you didn't! You didn't!'

'I did, I did! I closed it with a binding spell!'

'Which one? *Which one?*'

'*I can't remember!*'

'Well, here's another fine mess you've—'

Sssssssssssh-GLNKGH.

The slug burped as the two wizards went down. Then it ate the sausages, both the two burnt ones and the remaining raw ones. It oozed onto the fire, snuffing it out with a hiss.

The darkness closed in. The slug liked the darkness. It lifted its eye-stalks skyward, stared at the stars, and gave a soft hiss.

One of the humans had been satisfyingly large. With luck, it wouldn't need to eat again for several hours.

But they had tasted funny. Not like the villagers, and the old man and the old woman. More like the other one, the one on the beach it had eaten last of all, the one in the grey robe. A strange taste. Something about the insides of their heads . . .

Not that it mattered. They were just food, that was all.

But food with a sort of *power* inside it. Not strong power, like the warrior with the shiny spear long ago, or his tall, yellow-haired companions, the ones with fire in their fists and diamonds in their eyes. But *like* that, only weaker.

The slug's mind oozed around these thoughts for a while. Then its eye-stalks drooped, and it slept. Down in its stomach, its juices got to work on Stan and Ollie.

And the slug dreamed . . .

There were stars in the sky then, too. Not the same stars: it was a different land, and the constellations were different. They did not twinkle, but glared steadily with a harsh, cold brilliance.

The land was barren and treeless. Nothing grew on its wasted surface, where a stale wind blew thick grey mist over the land at all times of the year.

There were no animals, or birds, or insects. It was a dead land, ruined beyond reclaiming. Grey slug-like creatures roamed the land, perpetually hungry. Long ago, they had fed that hunger by devouring the other creatures that originally shared the land with them. Now the other creatures were gone, and all that kept the slug-like beings alive was magic.

35

In all that desolate monotony, there was only one feature of note: a tall, misshapen tower, which rose from the ashes and dust, and resembled one end of a bone, long and thin with a bulbous top. It had no windows, and only one door, a wide, round opening at ground level.

In the bulbous top of the tower was a large depression. It looked like a socket in which something might rest. But if so, whatever should be in the socket was missing.

.As dawn came, a thrush sang on a nearby gorse bush.

The slug woke. It lifted its eye-stalks and stared at the sky with its pale, globular eyes.

The dream.

It had had the dream before, countless times during the long imprisonment in the hollow rock. Each time before, it had woken, tried to change position in its suffocatingly narrow bed, failed, burned with rage and resentment for a while, and then drifted off to sleep again. Each time it forgot the dream, only to dream it over again the next time.

It had never before recalled the dream on waking.

Now it knew something it had not known before. The dream was not a dream at all. It was a memory.

A grey land, sterile and lifeless.

Home.

The slug let its eye-stalks droop again. It missed the dead land, and wanted to get back there. If it went to sleep, perhaps it would have the dream again.

Perched on a sprig of gorse, the thrush cocked its head on one side and scrutinised the great slug.

Amazing. He'd been catching slugs all his life, but this was the first one he'd seen in a giant economy size. How many breakfasts would you get out of a thing that big?

Gosh.

He might never have to look for another slug again. All he had to do was perch on its head, stab it with his beak, straight into the brain, and then drag it away . . .

. . . or perhaps he and his mates could drag it away . . .

. . . or they could hire a few dozen eagles to drag it away . . .

. . . or maybe they could peck chunks off it, and store them until needed in . . .

. . . what?

. . . their nests? mud? ice?

Ice. Hmm.

Pity it wasn't winter. There was no ice about at the moment.

Oh well. Nice thought while it lasted.

The thrush gave it up, and flew away to look for an individual size meal. *Giant economy slugs?* he thought. *Nah. It'll never catch on. They haven't worked out the after-sales aspects.*

Inside the slug, green matter from the brains of three wizards had been thoroughly absorbed. Some of it was now finding its way into the slug's own brain, where it was beginning to cause some interesting changes.

Unaware of this, the slug slept on, while the sun rose, traversed the sky, and sank.

None of this, of course, was supposed to have happened.

A thousand years earlier, in the plain around the hill on which Camelot castle now stood, there had been a battle between two armies to decide who was going to make executive decisions affecting the islands of Britain for the next few centuries. One army consisted of tall, yellow-haired, blue-eyed warriors, who were in fact Celtic gods and goddesses (the good guys). The other consisted of the Fhomoire, a race of horribly misshapen, deformed, malevolent demons with unbelievably disgusting skin conditions (the bad guys)[1].

The battle had been won by the gods, who had immediately driven the Fhomoire back into the land of Lochlann from which they had come, which could only be reached through the back of a chest of drawers. (They had tried the more traditional wardrobe, but some of the Fhomoire were a very awkward shape.) They had then locked the chest and thrown away the key. Then they had thrown away the chest, by sending it into another dimension. No point in taking chances.

When they head-counted the Fhomoire as they sent them into exile – no easy task, since most of the Fhomoire didn't have heads – they found they were one short. It transpired that one of the Fhomoire, called Archon, had slipped away unnoticed into the deep forest that surrounded the plain. After a long pursuit, he was eventually caught, imprisoned in a rock, and flung into the depths of the sea.

The incident is recorded in the ancient *Boke of ye Daemons*, in the appalling spelling that was unfortunately so common in those days:

Yt was ye noble and powerfull warrior Lugh who drove ye loathely creature ynto yts hollowe prysonne. Wyth stronge magicke he robb'd ye daemon of yts memorie, so that henceforthe yt shoulde appere even unto ytself as a mere beeste. He then forc'd ye Fhomoire ynto ye confinynge rocke, whych he and hys helpers then seal'd and flungge into ye oceane. Never

---

[1] In case this equation of beauty with goodness and ugliness with evil appears politically incorrect, it should be noted that the Fhomoire's deformities were caused by dabbling in magic, not by things they couldn't help such as a calcium-deficient diet in the womb or unbalanced hormones.

agayne will this hydeouse monster preye upon ye ynnocent of ye islandes of Brytaine.

Like many pundits down the ages, this one was over-optimistic.

Chapter Three

The morning after is proverbially an unpleasant reminder that you enjoyed yourself too much the night before. If what you were drinking the night before was Frigga's Revenge, the morning after is also a reminder that dwarfs, who are famed for their skill with iron, have constitutions forged from the same metal, and that if you try to drink as much as they do, you will subsequently regret it.

Gwydden the Abstruse, professional wizard and amateur drinker, opened his eyes. He immediately said, '*AAARGH!*' and closed them again, unable to cope with the supernova which seemed this morning to be standing in for the sun.

'How are we today?' said Hergrim, breezing in out of the kitchen.

'Uurrrghhh,' was Gwydden's considered reply.

'Not feeling too good? How about some black coffee?' Gwydden nodded. '*AAAAAAARRRGHHHH!!!*'

'You shouldn't nod,' said the dwarf. 'It just makes it worse.'

Gwydden shut his eyes tight and whimpered.

An hour later, after a breakfast of black coffee and raw egg in Worcester sauce, he was starting to feel a bit better.

'Where are you living these days?' the dwarf enquired.

'Same as always – Housebreaker's Alley.'

'I'd better see you home. Come on.'

After traversing several narrow streets, Gwydden and Hergrim entered a dingy and unprepossessing quarter of the city. Ancient grimy buildings leaned against one another like winos seeking mutual support. In the shadows moved a selection of dubious figures whose general air of down-at-heel furtiveness suggested that it might be wise to keep clear of them. Outside many of the buildings hung the green lamps of cheap apothecaries, dealers in love potions, and the less respectable sort of consultant sorcerer. They had come, in fact, to the notorious Green Light District.

Hergrim wrinkled his nostrils as a pot-pourri of acrid fumes drifted into them from a hundred back-street laboratories.

'I'm surprised the Camelot Environmental Health Officer doesn't close all these places down and have them demolished,' he observed. 'They must breed disease like an open sewer.'

Gwydden, who was feeling a lot better now that he had the familiar noxious air of downtown Camelot in his lungs, bridled. 'Not true. You won't find a rat within five streets of here – not a live one, anyway.'

'Then what's that?' The dwarf pointed to a small dark shape scurrying along the side of a building.

As if in answer, the small dark shape halted and turned its sharp little face towards them. Hergrim saw two cold, pale eyes staring into his own. An odd feeling stole over him. His arms and legs seemed to have disappeared, and he was floating in a bath of icy water. He didn't seem to care about anything any more. He was drifting into sleep . . . drifting . . .

Gwydden said something in a rasping, sibilant voice.

The creature squeaked defiantly and vanished down a grating.

Hergrim felt himself coming slowly back to life. 'What was that?' he managed to say eventually.

'Basilisk,' explained the wizard. 'Turn you to stone as soon as look at you. Lots of 'em living in the sewers round here. They're the main reason why the rats don't get a look in. Here we are – my lodgings.' He pointed down the dingiest of several alleyways.

They picked their way through a litter of broken retorts, grimy scraps of parchment covered with half-legible writing (unsuccessful spells, according to Gwydden) and various charred and slimy objects whose origins were unguessable. Eventually they stood under a sign that said:

Gwydden of Anglesey, M.A.
Wizard for Hire
Anything Magical Considered

Hergrim had seen this sign many times before. This morning, however, there was something else – a piece of parchment nailed to the door. Hergrim took it down and read its contents aloud.

'The wizard Gwydden is hereby evicted from these premises following various breaches of local bye-laws, including:

  —distilling "Wizard's Brew" in unlicensed premises
  —entertaining demons at unsocial hours
and, most recently,
  —allowing a synthetic dragon to wander the streets without proper supervision.
Signed,
  Merlin Ambrosius, Royal Wizard in Residence,
  on behalf of His Imperial Majesty, Uther Pendragon Rex.'

Hergrim tried the door. It was locked. 'Looks like you'll have to find some new lodgings,' he observed.

Gwydden stood with his mouth open, staring at the closed door. Suddenly he lurched forward and began beating at the panels with his fists. 'Lemme in!' he shouted. 'How dare you lock me out! I live here! Merlin!'

Hergrim pulled him away from the door. 'Steady on. Merlin isn't here, he's up at the castle.'

The wizard swung round, his face flushed and angry. 'Then I'll go to the castle and turn *him* into a synthetic dragon. Gimme that.' He seized the eviction order from Hergrim's hand and marched away up the alley.

'Odin's armpit,' growled the dwarf. 'What does he think he's doing? Merlin will make mincemeat of him – literally, I shouldn't wonder.' He sighed. 'I suppose I'd better go after him. He'll probably need rescuing again.'

He turned, and started to retrace his steps distastefully among the rubbish of the alleyway.

Camelot castle, viewed from the outside, was not a thing of great beauty. The National Trust would have thought twice before putting in an offer to preserve it. It was a lumpy building, which squatted on the top of Camelot Hill like a toad on a compost heap. At dusk, the silhouette of the turrets and battlements against the red sky looked like a badly made set of false teeth. Architecturally, it was slightly less attractive than Battersea Power Station.

Gwydden was not thinking about architecture, or indeed about false teeth, as he toiled his way up the hill to the castle gate. He was thinking about Merlin. He was remembering the first time they had met, at the Anglesey Academy of Magic, and that practical joke Merlin had played on him with the self-emptying inkwell. He was remembering the competition to

43

become Head Boy, and how he and Merlin had been neck and neck until Merlin had 'accidentally' knocked over Gwydden's tripod, spilling red-hot firedrake essence on the examiner's foot. He was thinking about two careers, one leading to fame and wealth and a secure position as Royal Wizard, while the other . . .

'Here, you,' said a peremptory voice. 'You in the moth-eaten grey dressing-gown. State your business.'

Gwydden's eyes slowly came back into focus. He had arrived without being aware of it at the castle gate, and a burly sentry was standing in front of him, holding a pikestaff in the recommended position[1].

'What did you say?'

'State your business,' the sentry repeated stolidly.

Gwydden drew himself up in a dignified manner. He hadn't really been listening, but he had the idea that somebody had just referred to his wizard's robe as a dressing-gown, which showed a lack of respect for his calling. 'Tell Merlin I wish to see him at once,' he snapped.

The sentry raised a supercilious eyebrow. 'And what makes you think the Lord Merlin will want to see a skinny old scarecrow like you? On your broomstick, or I'll sling you in the dungeon with the rats.'

The wizard's eyes narrowed. He pointed at the sentry, and began to mutter in Latin.

[1]There are three basic positions for a pikestaff, depending on the status of the person the sentry is confronting at the time; they are known as the *If it wasn't a court-martialling offence I'd like to stick this right up your arrogant nose, sir* position, the *Come on, punk, make my day* position, and the *Hold still while I pull it out, it's your own fault for running at me with that drawn sword* position. The sentry facing Gwydden was using the second, but was quite prepared to move to the third if the situation demanded it.

At that moment a hand seized his conjuring arm by the elbow.

'Don't you think you're in enough trouble,' panted Hergrim, pulling Gwydden round to face him, 'without turning the royal soldiery into toads?'

'It's no worse than he deserves,' the wizard said sulkily.

'I daresay, but—'

'I am a qualified wizard, and a fully paid-up citizen,' said Gwydden loudly. 'All I want are my rights. Am I not to be heard? I demand to be heard!'

'I imagine most of Camelot can hear you at the moment,' said a voice above their heads.

They looked up. Forty feet above them, a head was protruding from the wall. It had long white hair and a white beard, and looked rather like Gwydden's, but with fatter cheeks and a more prosperous air. It wore a silver circlet and a superior expression.

Seeing Merlin's head, Gwydden hopped up and down with rage. 'You!' he shouted. 'Come down from there! I demand to see you! I demand that you listen!'

'I am listening,' came the curt reply. 'Please be brief. I am rather busy at the moment.'

Gwydden brandished his fist in apoplectic fury. 'You overpaid hedge-wizard! What right have you to lock me out of my lodgings?'

'I have the rights vested in me as King Uther's Deputy Head Bureaucrat,' Merlin said coolly, 'and if you can't pursue your absurd Pygmalion hobbies without causing a public nuisance, you must go and practise them elsewhere. Now go away, please. I have some *real* magic to attend to.' Merlin's head withdrew into the wall.

Gwydden picked up a stone and threw it at the spot where Merlin had been. 'Why are you picking on me?' he yelled. 'Why is it just me you're evicting – a rival wizard? It wouldn't be professional jealousy, by any chance?'

Merlin's head reappeared, this time looking amused. 'Me, jealous of you? Don't be absurd. Why would I be jealous of a second-rate illusionist like you?'

'Hah!' Gwydden snorted. 'Prove it! Prove you're not just evicting me out of jealousy!'

'How?'

'By evicting someone else, of course!'

'Very well.' There was a momentary pause, and then a piece of parchment floated out from the wall and drifted to the ground. Hergrim picked it up and read it.

In view of his association with a notorious undesirable, i.e. Gwydden of Anglesey, the dwarf Hergrim is hereby ordered to remove himself from Camelot within 24 hours.

'Satisfied?' said Merlin sarcastically, and vanished once more into his tower.

Hergrim turned a withering eye on Gwydden. 'So now you've got me evicted as well. Thanks a bunch.'

'Oh, you hate Camelot anyway,' said Gwydden. 'Come on. I've had an idea.'

Twenty minutes later they were standing outside the window of Camelot Estates & Rentals Ltd., a dingy shop on the corner of Cheapside and Washerwomen's Row. Hergrim strained to decipher the flowery lettering, and even more flowery descriptions, surrounding the wildly flattering charcoal sketches on the placards inside.

'Des. res. in quiet avenue on scenic west side of Camelot,' he read. *'Own outside privy, en suite dungeon and archery butts. Nine hundred pounds.'*

'Daylight robbery,' said Gwydden indignantly. 'I've seen those new developments on the west side – hardly room to swing a cockroach. Anyway, we need somewhere outside the city, and outside Merlin's jurisdiction.'

'How about this?' Hergrim pointed to a yellowing card tucked away in a corner. *'Bijou cave in unspoilt forest situation. Sleeps one in moderate discomfort. No amenities whatever. Ideal bachelor pad for hermit.'*

'Be sensible, will you? This is no use – I'm getting eyestrain trying to read Gothic script through two-inch thick glass. Let's see what they've got inside.'

Behind the counter, a sharp-faced man in a greasy smock looked up and eyed them in a calculating way as they went in. 'Good morning, gents. Smyrk's the name, Zephaniah Smyrk. How can I help you?'

'I'm looking for a house,' Gwydden said. 'Somewhere inexpensive, and preferably away from the city.'

'Certainly, certainly.' Mr Smyrk rubbed his hands together until Hergrim felt sure they would burst into flames. 'Just let me consult my file of properties.' He delved under the counter and brought out a huge leather pouch stuffed with bits of parchment. 'Now – what price had you in mind?'

The wizard opened a pouch at his belt and consulted the contents. 'Anything up to nine pounds, two shillings and a groat.'

The estate agent's expression became disdainful. 'Dear me. I'm afraid you won't find anything to buy at that price. How about a property to rent? I have one here that should be right up your street.'

From the very bottom of the pouch, he pulled out an ancient brown parchment. He blew the dust off it, smoothed out the creases and laid it reverently on the counter. 'There you are, sir. Feast your eyes on that.'

The dwarf and wizard bent over the parchment. It bore a sketch of an idyllic-looking rustic thatched cottage surrounded by trees.

'It looks very nice,' said the wizard wistfully. 'I've always rather fancied a little place in the country. How much is the rent?'

'Only ten shillings a week,' said Smyrk. 'A real snip.'

'That seems remarkably cheap,' said Gwydden in surprise. 'Not much more than I was paying for my lodgings in Housebreaker's Alley.'

'Don't touch it, Gwydden,' said Hergrim, eyeing the estate agent narrowly. 'There's got to be a catch. I bet it's riddled with dry rot.'

'No dry rot, no wet rot, no fungi of any kind, I assure you. I have the owner's personal guarantee,' smiled the estate agent.

'Who is the owner?' asked the wizard.

Mr Smyrk turned the parchment over, and pointed to what was written on the back:

The Earl of Redbrush, Redbrush Hall.
Apply to Mrs Tod at the Hall for key.
Three weeks' rent payable in advance.
All breakages must be paid for.

'The Earl of Redbrush, eh?' Gwydden was visibly impressed. 'Well, if the aristocracy are involved, I suppose it must be OK. All right, I'll take it.'

'A wise decision, if I may say so.' The estate agent beamed greasily, like the sun rising out of an oil-slick. 'I'm sure you'll find it a delightful place. Just ask at the Hall for Mrs Tod, and she'll take care of you.'

'Yes, I'll bet she will,' murmured Hergrim, as they left the shop. '*All breakages must be paid for.* Sounds to me as though Mrs Tod may be a bit of a dragon.'

'At least she won't be green,' answered the wizard. 'Now, how do we get to Redbrush Hall?'

*   *   *

Redbrush Hall, the only stately home in the Forest, had been there longer than anyone could remember. Originally it must have been a Roman villa, and the lower storey, constructed of red brick and with graceful arched windows and doors, still had something of the sunny Mediterranean about it. But someone had recently extended the building, adding two incongruous wings and an upper storey, all built of grey, Gothic stone. The resulting effect was of an armoured giant sitting on the shoulders of a red-bearded dwarf; a top-heavy, slightly menacing appearance.

A cluster of chimneys rose from the centre of the roof, and attached to one of these was a flagpole. The flag that fluttered from it bore a distinctive design. On a pale green background was painted a hairy, reddish-brown object: a fox's brush, the symbol of the Earls of Redbrush.

The Redbrush family had occupied the Hall for generations. In the family's heyday, there had been hunts, and balls, and raucous parties. On summer nights the windows blazed with yellow light, and laughter and singing filled the quiet glades, keeping the forest creatures awake long past their bedtime.

Now, however, Redbrush Hall was cold and mostly empty. The dark windows were never opened, and the only light seen by the forest animals was the occasional flicker of a candle in the window of a scullery near the back of the west wing. In this scullery, and one or two damp rooms above it, lived the two remaining residents of the house: Mrs Tod, the sister of the last Earl, and the gardener, Macpherson.

A rush of wind sent the open scullery door crashing against the dresser that stood behind it. Mrs Tod looked up sharply from her embroidery, pulling her woollen shawl closer around her shoulders.

'Macpherson! Close that door, if you please, before I catch my death!'

The gardener staggered across the threshold, bearing a mountainous load of firewood which he dumped in the corner of the room with a rumbling clatter that made Mrs Tod start in her seat and utter a tut of annoyance. Turning ponderously to the door, he closed it and stood with his back to it, slowly brushing the dust and fragments of wood from his hands.

' 'Tis unseasonably chilly this afternoon, ma'am,' he remarked.

'Ah, you noticed that, did you?' returned Mrs Tod, in a tone of icy sarcasm. 'I thought perhaps you hadn't, since you left the door wide open.'

'I noticed,' was the reply. 'Though I've known far colder, ma'am, aye, raw nights of skirling gale that'd tear the skin frae your back and leave your backbone bare to the elements.'

'Really.' Mrs Tod sounded unimpressed. 'That would be in Scotland, I suppose.'

'Aye, in bonny Scotland.' There was the hint of a tremor in the gardener's voice. ''Tis only north o' the border there's real weather. Ice and blizzards and floods and hail. Real weather a man can get his teeth into.'

'Well, perhaps for the benefit of a pampered Sassenach like myself, you'd deign to put a couple of logs on the fire,' said Mrs Tod with heavy irony. 'You may like to sit in the scullery with icicles dangling from your nose, but I don't care for it.'

Macpherson scratched his head among the wiry bristles of his red hair, and gazed intently at his employer. 'I dinna see any icicles on your nose, ma'am. A wee dewdrop, mebbe, but no icicles.'

'Don't be impertinent,' snapped Mrs Tod. 'Dewdrop

indeed! Put those logs on the fire, before I freeze to death.'

'Aye, verra weel, ma'am.'

The gardener bent down and rummaged among the pile of logs, while his employer surreptitiously took a small handkerchief from her sleeve and wiped the end of her nose with it.

'What are you doing down there?' she demanded. 'What's taking you so long?'

Macpherson slowly straightened up and looked at her over his shoulder. 'I was looking for the apple branches, ma'am.'

'Apple branches? What do you mean, apple branches?'

'I found three apple branches in the Forest,' the gardener explained. ''Tis a pleasant thing to burn, an apple branch. I thought 'twould sweeten the air in this scullery.'

This remark struck Mrs Tod on a nerve. 'What's wrong with the air?' she demanded. 'I keep this scullery spotless. It's you, with your muddy boots and your sweaty shirts, that's the only unpleasant-smelling thing round here.'

Macpherson's bushy red eyebrows drew together in a frown. 'Weel, ma'am, I dinna deny there may be a smell of honest toil aboot me. But that's no' the smell I detect in this scullery.'

Mrs Tod carefully laid down her embroidery – a sampler bearing the words *Peace and love be in this house* – and looked at Macpherson coldly over her pince-nez. 'And what smell do you detect in this scullery, pray?'

The gardener hesitated. He was not bent on revolution, lacking the temperament of a Wat Tyler or a Jack Cade, but having gone so far, his Scottish pride forbade him to retreat. He stuck out his bony jaw, and said resolutely, 'Overcooked brussels sprouts, ma'am.'

Mrs Tod's jaw fell in astonishment. Then she closed her mouth firmly with a snap. Finding that this was not enough to express her displeasure, she said, 'The trouble with you, Macpherson, is that you don't understand English cooking.'

'The trouble wi' me, ma'am,' was the gardener's somewhat melancholy reply, 'is that I understand it a muckle deal better than ye do yersel'.'

Mrs Tod's eyes narrowed.

This friendly conversation could have gone on for hours (on most evenings it did, there being not much else to do in Redbrush Hall). At that moment, however, there came an urgent knocking at the door Macpherson had just closed.

'Someone at the door, Macpherson,' said Mrs Tod, with the air of a boxer delivering a knockout punch.

'Aye, ma'am.' Macpherson opened the door and stood gazing out.

'Well, who is it?' demanded the lady of the house.

' 'Tis a tall thin man in grey, and a wee one wi' a red beard, ma'am.'

'What do they want?' asked Mrs Tod, her tone suggesting that whatever it was, they were pretty unlikely to get it.

'Och, I dinna ken, ma'am.'

'Well, ask them, you buffoon.'

'Aye, ma'am.'

There was a murmur of subdued voices.

The gardener turned a face filled with extreme surprise to his employer. 'They *say*, ma'am,' he reported, in a tone of some disbelief, 'that they wish tae rent the cottage.'

'Oh!' Mrs Tod could not hide her own surprise.

'Aye, the cottage.' The gardener's face took on a grim

expression, such as John Knox might have assumed if approached by a lady of the night. He did not approve of Mrs Tod's renting out part of the ancient Redbrush estate for monetary gain, especially in view of the state of the cottage. He came from a line of peasants who had been forced to pay rack-rent prices for draughty hovels in wind-scoured Scottish glens, and his sympathies were definitely with the tenant.

'Well, don't keep them standing on the step,' said Mrs Tod sharply. 'Let them in, let them in!'

Macpherson stepped back, and the two visitors entered. They looked round the scullery.

'Very nice,' said the taller of the two, smiling the all-purpose vacant smile adopted by visitors since time immemorial. 'Now then, my man – could you tell Mrs Tod we're here, please?'

'She's straight before ye,' said Macpherson gruffly. He did not care for being addressed as "my man". 'Can ye no' see her?'

The two visitors looked baffled.

'Er—' said Gwydden, looking all round the room.

'I'm over here,' said the lady of the house coldly. She had had to put up with this kind of thing before, and she always found it infuriating.

With a start of surprise, Gwydden realised that the old blanket, shawl and sampler draped with apparent carelessness on a chair in the corner had someone inside them. He recollected himself, and bowed to Mrs Tod.

'How do you do, madam. I'm Gwydden of Anglesey, a practitioner of the ancient and respected art of wizardry, and this is Hergrim son of Harr, a dwarf of unimpeachable reputation. Forgive me for not seeing you as we came in. The estate agent didn't tell me you were a – a—'

53

'A vixen,' said Macpherson with a grim smile. 'Aye, she's a vixen. The Earls of Redbrush are foxes, ye ken, and Mrs Tod is the Earl's sister.'

'The word "vixen" is not considered polite these days,' said Mrs Tod, with a sniff. She rearranged her skirt to conceal the end of her bushy red tail, which was peeping out, and adjusted the pince-nez balanced on her long fur-covered nose. 'We prefer to be referred to as "lady foxes".'

'I beg your pardon,' said Gwydden. He had not been the one to use the offending word, but Mrs Tod was glaring at him as if he had, and he felt compelled to apologise for Macpherson. 'A lady fox, of course – and a very charming lady fox, if I may say so.'

'You may say so if you wish,' said Mrs Tod, 'but I won't lower the rent because of it.'

'Er – no, of course not.' The wizard looked momentarily confused. 'If it's not too much trouble, could you show us to the – er—'

'Macpherson,' said Mrs Tod, in a businesslike tone, 'show these two persons to the cottage. You may show them the portraits on the way, if they are interested. And,' she added, as the three of them turned towards the inner door of the scullery, 'make sure they pay three weeks rent in advance.'

The inner door closed.

'A wizard and a dwarf, indeed,' muttered Mrs Tod. 'Riff-raff. But what is one to do? There are so few *respectable* people these days. Breakages galore, I'll be bound.' Shaking her head ominously, she turned her attention back to her sampler.

'Aye, she's a hard woman, there's nae doot aboot it,' said Macpherson mournfully, as he led the wizard and dwarf along stone corridors that smelt fusty and damp with disuse. 'She leads me a rare dance, I'm telling ye. Nothing I do is right for her. Either the wood's too damp, or the fire's too hot or too cold, or the lettuces frae the garden are eaten by caterpillars, or the sheets on her bed are no' properly aired, or . . .' He sighed deeply, and left the inventory incomplete, as if suggesting that it might go on indefinitely. 'There are times a-plenty when I wish I hadna left the bonny glens o' Scotland.'

'Why did you?' Hergrim asked, not so much out of politeness as out of professional interest, as between fellow-exiles.

'Och, 'tis a lang tale, and muckle boring. I'll tell ye aboot it one evening when we've naething better tae do.'

'If it's as boring as that,' said the wizard, 'I should think we'll always have something better to do.'

The gardener shook his head. 'There's niver anything much tae do in Redbrush Hall. There used tae be parties an' the like. Och, but these days there's niver anything like that. *She* wouldna pay for it.' He jerked his head in a gesture of contempt towards the scullery they had just left.

'So there's no Earl at present,' said Gwydden.

'Aye, that's the sad truth. He's gone awa' tae a better place. Gone tae Arcadia, if ye understand me.'

'I'm sorry to hear it,' said the wizard. 'Was his departure . . . expected?'

'Hah!' The gardener threw his head back in a scornful laugh. 'Expected, aye, ye could say so. I expected it long afore it happened. *She* drove him tae it. She made his life a misery, and then one day he jist went, wi'out warning. Aye, the last heir of the Redbrush line. 'Twas a tragedy. But he's at peace now, the puir fox.'

'Very sad,' said Gwydden, nodding in what he hoped was a sufficiently sombre manner. 'Very sad indeed.'

Next moment they turned a corner, and came into a wide hall with a high ceiling. The walls were hung with riding crops, mantraps, rabbit-snares, garottes, pig-stickers, and other pleasant accoutrements used in the noble and gentlemanly sport of hunting. Several oil paintings filled the remaining spaces. On one wall, above a huge fireplace, were pictures of hunting scenes, with foxes dressed in pink coats sitting on very small horses[1] and chasing after desperately fleeing rabbits. On the opposite wall hung a row of portraits. Macpherson stopped in front of the first, which was blackened with age, and showed a fierce, white-whiskered fox in a dark, green-stained jacket that might once have been pink. In one paw he carried a hunting-horn, and in the other he held a dead rabbit by the ears.

'The first Earl,' murmured the gardener in an awed tone. 'Attila Redbrush the First. 'Tis said he killed three hundred rabbits in his time. Died when his horse ran under a hawthorn bush and left him skewered to the branches. A true fox o' the old school.'

Gwydden and Hergrim followed the gardener in respectful silence as he passed slowly along the line of portraits, describing the subject of each. Finally he stopped at the last in the line, which showed a young, sensitive looking fox reading a book.

[1]The Earls of Redbrush rode the smallest breed of horse ever seen, the Shetland Whippersnapper. These were incredibly fast, and there was only one method of catching them. A bow-legged man would stand facing the charging horse, which would run under his legs, gleefully thinking *By Pegasus, these humans are stupid* – only to find that behind him stood a knock-kneed man with a net. The whole remarkable business is described in detail in *Memoirs of a Rabbit-hunting Fox*, by Siegfried Redbrush the Third.

'The last Earl,' said Macpherson sadly. 'Too guid for this world, the puir soul.'

He shook his head dolefully, and led them on, down further corridors, until finally they came to a huge iron-studded door. Macpherson spent some time wrestling with the bolt, and finally threw the door wide to reveal a kitchen-garden lined with rows of vegetables.

'Here we are,' he said, throwing his chest out in evident pride. 'Here's ma wee garden. What d'ye think? Bonny, eh?'

The wizard and the dwarf made suitably polite and admiring noises. The garden was well-stocked with lettuces in particular – but over towards the east wing, the lettuces seemed to grow smaller and smaller, until finally there was nothing but bare earth.

Hergrim pointed this out enquiringly, and the gardener sighed.

'Aye, the east wing,' he said. 'Things dinna grow weel close tae the east wing. 'Tis a dour, unhealthy place. A few o' the family tried to live there, but they soon gave it up.'

'Why?' asked the dwarf.

The gardener's voice sank to a whisper. 'They all grew sick – or mad. The rooms are always dank an' cold, nae matter how ye build fires tae heat them. 'Tis a rare an' terrible mystery. There's something there that's . . .' He lowered his voice to inaudibility, and gave two or three significant nods.

'That's what?' asked Gwydden.

'I think he means it's haunted,' said Hergrim.

'Oh, that's just superstition. Come now, Macpherson, you don't believe in ghosts, surely?'

The gardener's bushy brows came together in a fierce glare. 'Suppose *you* try tae grow a lettuce under the wall

57

o' the east wing, an' then tell me there's nae such thing as a ghost.'

'Well,' said Gwydden, feeling that there were several logical steps missing in this argument. 'Er—'

'Have you been in the east wing yourself, Macpherson?' asked the dwarf, grinning mischievously.

The Scotsman's face went very pale. 'Aye, once,' he said hoarsely. 'Niver again. Niver again.' He turned away, muttering to himself, and made a great business of examining two or three nearby lettuces.

'Superstitious rubbish,' muttered the wizard. 'I'll bet it's just bad plumbing. I remember one of the corridors at the Academy was supposed to be haunted, and in the end we discovered that – Hey, what's the matter?'

Macpherson had apparently spotted something in the garden. With a loud oath in his native Gaelic, he rushed back into the Hall, and emerged a moment later carrying a crudely-fashioned blunderbuss.

'Wee varmints!' he shouted. 'Leave ma lettuces alone, ye wee furry thieves!' He let off his gun with a loud bang, and rushed away between the rows of lettuces, gesticulating wildly.

'Mad,' said the wizard, staring after him. 'He's bonkers.'

'No, he isn't,' said Hergrim, pointing. 'Look there.'

Beyond the lettuces, three small shapes could be seen scampering away, hotly pursued by the furious Macpherson. They were brown, with white tails and long ears.

'Rabbits,' said the dwarf. 'The traditional quarry of the Redbrush family – and of their servants too, apparently. If Macpherson shoots one, perhaps we can have stewed rabbit for supper.'

'I just wish he'd give us the key to this wretched

cottage,' said the wizard. 'I'm dying for a sit down and a strong cup of tea.'

Despite appearances, a rabbit's life is not all sex and carrots. (Carrots are sometimes in short supply.) Rabbits have many enemies, including foxes, badgers and sabre-toothed tigers, though the last of these are less of a problem than they used to be. Mother Nature has designed rabbits to fulfil a specific role in the scheme of things – i.e., to be pursued by bigger animals and, where possible, made into pies. They therefore have long ears (to hear you coming), long legs (to run away from you) and a highly visible white tail (to give you something to shoot at – Mother Nature is noted for her sporting instincts).

On the edge of Redbrush Park, three small brown figures were loping through the undergrowth. Their names were Flopkin, Mopkin and Cottonseed, but they viewed themselves as the crack commandos of the local warren, and preferred to be called the Magnificent Three.

Flopkin was in charge. Mopkin was carrying the spoils (two lettuce leaves). Cottonseed, the smallest, was at the back, watching for predators – or, more often, whingeing.

'All I'm saying,' said Cottonseed plaintively, 'is that two lettuce leaves isn't much for an afternoon's work. It won't go far among a whole warren, will it?'

'Listen, Cottonseed,' said Flopkin, stopping so suddenly that Mopkin ran into him, 'is it *my* fault that Macpherson came out of the Hall at just the wrong moment, with his gun loaded, and that we were in the open at the time?'

'Well, Flopkin, old man,' said Mopkin slowly. He was a large, ponderous rabbit, with a direct approach to things which would have got him beaten up several times a day if he hadn't been so big. 'It *is* your fault that we were in the open, I think. Don't you think so, Cottonseed?'

'Yes, I do,' said Cottonseed, after making sure that Mopkin was between him and Flopkin. 'We should have approached the kitchen-garden from the south-west, where there's more cover. But *you* took us round by the south-east. *You* said the lettuces there were smaller and easier to push back to the warren. *You* said—'

'Pipe down, you little squirt,' Flopkin said angrily, 'or I'll tie your ears in a knot and hang you from the nearest bush.'

Cottonseed put his tongue between his front teeth and blew a raspberry.

There was a scuffle as Flopkin tried to attack Cottonseed, Cottonseed tried to hide behind Mopkin, and Mopkin tried to pinion the others' paws behind their backs. At the end of it they were all lying in a heap, breathing heavily.

'Well,' said Mopkin, 'I don't think that achieved very much.' He got to his feet. After he had removed his heavy bulk, Flopkin was able to stand up.

Lastly, and rather shakily, Cottonseed stood up. 'I'm going to tell my mum about this,' he said, in a trembly voice. 'When I joined the Magnificent Three I was promised adventure, excitement and extra lettuce. Instead I get shouted at and sat on. I resign.'

'You can't,' said Flopkin. 'You're a conscript.'

'Don't care,' said Cottonseed defiantly.

'I say,' said Mopkin, picking up something crushed and dirty from the ground, 'someone's rolled on these leaves. No-one's going to want them now.'

There was a glum silence.

'All right,' said Flopkin at last. 'Back to Macpherson's garden. Let's try again.'

'Here we are,' said Macpherson. 'This is the cottage. What d'ye think of it?'

The wizard and the dwarf stood with their mouths open, the power of rational speech having temporarily deserted them.

Imagine a stone pigsty which the pigs have left in disgust because they can't bear to live somewhere so squalid. Imagine a thatched roof like a badly-made toupee owned by an unusually slovenly scarecrow. Imagine doors and windows that bear the same relation to the straight line and the right angle that the Eurovision Song Contest bears to a prelude and fugue by J.S.Bach[1]. Imagine a garden so overgrown with weeds that an oak tree would have a hard time getting itself some elbow room. Imagine that all this is topped off with a warped and twisted chimney from which blue smoke is writhing upwards into the grey afternoon sky, and that the smoke, as it writhes and dissipates into the air, spells out over and over again the word BOGHOLE.

Hergrim at length managed to find his voice. 'How,' he asked, 'does it do that?'

'Och, the previous tenant was a witch,' said the gardener. 'It was her way of telling Mrs Tod what she thought o' the place. Come on – there's a path somewhere over here tae the left.'

They plunged into the jungle of weeds, temporarily leaving the daylight behind. After a dark and tortuous journey among half-visible vegetable monstrosities, of

---

[1]The first Eurovision Song Contest, back in 1956, was won by a song called *Refrain*. Regrettably, the organisers failed to take the hint.

which giant hogweed seemed to be the smallest and most friendly-looking, they came to a warped and decayed door. Above the lintel, carved into the stone, were the letters EB.

'What does that mean?' the wizard asked suspiciously, thinking it might be a spell he had temporarily forgotten.

'That's jist the builder's initials. They do that tae advertise.' Macpherson forced the door open with a squeal of tortured hinges. 'Though why anyone would want it known 'twas them that built this calamity beats me.'

The dwarf and wizard followed Macpherson into the cottage, feeling sure that at any rate the inside must be an improvement on the outside.

They were wrong.

'Here ye are,' said the gardener, in a tone of gloomy relish. ''Tis damp, draughty and cold, the chimney pours smoke into the living-room, the beds are full o' fleas, an' there are rats everywhere. I hope ye'll be verra happy. I'd help ye tae settle in, but tae be pairfectly frank I canna stand the place, so if ye'll excuse me, I'll be awa' back tae the Hall.'

He went out, dragging the protesting door shut behind him. The dwarf and wizard heard him slashing his way back through the Amazonian garden.

'Well,' said the wizard, looking round the interior of the cottage.

'Well indeed,' said the dwarf. 'Ten shillings a week. That estate agent obviously saw you coming. *All breakages must be paid for*. Can you see anything that isn't broken already?'

Gwydden let his gaze wander over the furnishings. There were three chairs, none of which had a full complement of legs. The settee had a hole in the seat through which the springs were visible. The fireplace was filthy, but not as filthy as the kitchen-range that stood next to it. A drop-leaf table stood against one wall: both its leaves had dropped off, and lay on the floor beside it.

'It could be worse,' said the wizard.

Hergrim turned to look at him. 'How, exactly?'

'Well . . .' Gwydden looked round for inspiration. Finding none at floor-level, he looked up. 'At least the roof looks okay.'

There was a sudden clap of thunder overhead. The weather, which had been deteriorating all day, had finally decided to stop messing about and do the thing properly.

A spot of rain splashed on the table. It was followed by another, and another.

'We need a bucket,' said the dwarf.

'It's only a little hole in the roof,' said the wizard cheerfully. 'There's no great problem about fixing a hole in the roof.'

'True enough,' said the dwarf. 'The hole that bothers me is the one in your head. Ten shillings a week – ye gods!'

'I'm sure it'll be very cosy once we've got a few things sorted out,' said Gwydden stiffly. 'I expect to be very happy here.'

'You always were an optimist,' the dwarf said sourly. 'Come on, then. Let's start by lighting a fire. With any luck the place will burn down, and then we can go and live somewhere warmer, drier and more comfortable.'

'Such as?' Gwydden enquired in a frosty tone.

The dwarf thought for a moment. 'How about the inside of a dragon's stomach?' he suggested.

Chapter Four

The slug had slept for a whole day. This is not unusual
for slugs, which are pretty late risers on the whole –
hence the term 'slug-a-bed'. In this case, however, it had
more to do with the changes at work in the slug's brain
than anything constitutional.

The slug raised its eye-stalks and stared at the sky
with its pale, luminous eyes. The stars were out again,
but were thinking of getting a bit of shut-eye themselves. A chill breeze blew over the scrubby moors, and
the birds were still tucked up in bed, dreaming. One
thrush was having a really mind-boggling dream about
slug steaks and something called a *refrigerator*, but he
would forget about it when he woke up.

The slug considered.

It felt somehow . . . different. More alive.

No, not more alive. More *intelligent*.

The slug suddenly understood what had changed. *It
knew its own name.*

Archon, it thought. *I am Archon. That's who I am. And
I'm not an it; I'm a he. I am one of the Fhomoire.*

*The Fhomoire. The practitioners of Grey Magic, which gives
us immortality.*

And it also gives us the ability to change shape.

*Shape-shifters. Yes. I'd forgotten that part. I can change my
shape into anything I like. Anything at all. Assuming, of
course, I can remember how.*

So what shall I be?
Let's start with a dragon.

Archon concentrated. His slug body shimmered for a moment, as if a heat-haze surrounded it. Then it vanished, dissolving into air. The air swirled round and round in a vortex as sub-atomic particles danced round each other in time to some unheard quantum music of the spheres.

It lasted for a few seconds. Then the music stopped, and the particles all rushed to sit down in the nearest quantum chair.

Archon looked down at his new body. It was *like* a dragon's in some ways, being red and hard and metallic, and the concept of flames was definitely in there somewhere. But he had to admit that, to be honest, a fire-engine wasn't really the same thing as a dragon.

He closed his pale, luminous headlamps, thought hard, and tried again.

After half an hour, he felt he had re-learned the basics. He could change into almost anything in three seconds. He was still prone to a certain fuzziness round the edges, as if some of the quantum chairs had been removed while the music was playing and a few of the particles were left with nowhere to sit, but it was definitely coming along.

He now felt spoiled for choice. When you can be any shape in the universe, it is difficult to choose which one to assume on a permanent basis.

One option was the slug-shape. That was certainly good for catching and eating things, but it had bad associations. Imprisonment. Warriors with shiny spears. No, he would rather be some other shape for the time being.

Of course, there was always his *real* shape – or, to be more accurate, *lack* of shape. After all, why not?

He vanished. Three seconds later, he reappeared in his true Fhomoire form.

Compared with the Fhomoire in their real shapes, Cthulhu the Great would have been about as frightening as Winnie-the-Pooh.

The thrush woke, yawned, put his wing over his beak to hide the yawn, and got out of bed. He strutted a little way into the gorse, and then performed a few loosening-up exercises, as he did every morning. Left wing out, left wing in. Right wing out, right wing in. Bend to touch the talons.

He straightened up, flew to the top of the nearest gorse bush, and surveyed the landscape.

AAAAARGH!!

What in all the feathered hells was *that*?

The thrush stared, paralysed, at the demonic horror that stood among the heather a few yards away. Then he fell off the gorse bush in a dead faint.

Archon looked thoughtfully at the spot where the thrush had been sitting.

Yes, he mused, *now I remember. That used to be a typical reaction. Perhaps I'd better save my true shape until I really need it. What else could I try?*

Ah, yes.

The air swirled briefly.

A naked man crouched among the gorse.

Ow!

Archon stood up sharply. Clearly he was going to have to be more careful.

Not bad, though. A bit tight under the armpits, but I expect I'll get used to it. And I can always introduce a few variations – a different face, for instance. Now – there was something else you had to have with this shape. Clothes, that

66

was it. What about the clothes those two I ate last night were wearing?

No, I ate their clothes as well. Bother.

I wonder what's in these two sacks?

Archon fumbled with the neck of the smaller sack. He wasn't used to having fingers yet, and it felt like trying to pick a lock with a hairpin held between five bananas. Even so, the sack seemed more resistant to his attentions than mere clumsiness could account for. Then he remembered the two wizards talking about a binding spell.

Archon smiled.

Spells were less of a problem to the Fhomoire than to humans. The Fhomoire were themselves magical, and could therefore suck the magic out of an enchanted object into themselves, as laid down in McFinagle's Law of Magical Attraction[1].

Archon touched the sack, and the magic of the binding spell flowed into him. The sack was now just an ordinary sack. He untied it and tipped out the contents. They consisted of two sausages, a street-plan of Camelot, and a long woolly vest knitted for Stan by his mother.

The shape-shifter put Stan's vest on, and ate the sausages. Then he opened the larger sack.

This contained Stan and Ollie's stock-in-trade. Apart from Ollie's staff (which, being a demon, Archon didn't need), they were mainly low-grade specimens of the Art Magical. Stan and Ollie had not been senior enough in the wizards' hierarchy to be allowed to sell really

---

[1]If the sucker contains less magic than the suckee, the same process works in reverse. The hapless sucker is reduced to a coating of slime all over the object, which some other sucker has to clean off.

powerful artefacts. Most of the objects in the sack could be classified as wizards' party tricks. They included:

The Miniature Sea Monster – Drop Him in Your Aquarium and Watch him Eat the Goldfish!

and

The Perpetually Drinking Vampire – Attach It to an Artery and See It Bob Up and Down!

and

The Ragnarok Showstopper – The Twilight of the Gods on your Coffee Table – End the Party with Apocalypse!

Kids' stuff, thought Archon, and brushed them aside impatiently.

There was one thing, however, that made him pause. A mirror. Just an ordinary hand-mirror, with a mother-of-pearl border round the glass and along the handle. On the back were inscribed the words *A Souvenir from Anglesey*.

Archon studied his human face in the mirror. Yes, a mirror had definite possibilities. You can do amazing things with mirrors, if you know how.

If you go *through* a mirror, you get into mirrorspace, which is the wizards' equivalent of hyperspace. Knowing where you are in mirrorspace is a bit tricky, because all maps are reversed; inexperienced wizards sometimes get lost, and emerge in Catford instead of Katmandu. But as Archon was aware, mirrorspace links up all the mirrors in the universe, which can be very useful if you want to get somewhere in a hurry.

And I do need to get somewhere, thought Archon. *I need to find the thing I hid a thousand years ago. Using mirrorspace, I should at least be able to get close to it.*

Slipping out of Stan's vest, Archon metamorphosed once more into his slug-shape, oozed into the mirror, and was gone.

* * *

On a nearby gorse bush, a thrush came to a decision.

Giant economy slugs – demonic horrors – nude men – what was the place coming to? This used to be a nice quiet bit of moorland, where the most exciting thing you were likely to find was a dead sheep.

The thrush spread his wings and flew off. He had a cousin who lived in a village on the coast, who was always bragging about how much better the worms and slugs tasted in his part of the world. It didn't sound likely, but it had to be better than this.

Three hours later, the thrush and his cousin were happily gorging themselves on fat juicy slugs, snails and worms in the deserted village of Fishcake.

An hour after *that*, they were both eaten by the last cat in Fishcake, which had finally plucked up courage and come down, ravenous, from the rooftop.

The grass on the other side of the hill may well be greener, but you should always check that there isn't something with teeth and claws crouching in it.

In his study in the highest tower in Camelot castle, Merlin was sitting in an armchair, gazing at a large mirror. It was a magic mirror, capable of seeing into the far corners of England, but at the moment Merlin was using it for a more important purpose. He was admiring himself.

'Mirror, mirror on the wall,' he murmured, stroking the silky strands of his long white beard (carefully brushed a hundred times each morning and night), 'who is the most accomplished wizard of them all?' This didn't scan, but Merlin was not much interested in poetry. He smiled at his reflection and answered his own riddle. 'Me, of course. Who did you think?'

He smirked briefly at himself. Then he picked up his favourite grimoire, *Fearful Spells for Irate Wizards*, and thumbed through its pages. There was plenty of scope here. He could conjure up anything from a giant flesh-eating troll to an ice age, if he wanted to. Some of the more drastic spells bore a warning in heavy black runes: *Caution! Not to be attempted by the inexperienced!* Merlin shook his head sadly. He knew of several wizards who had over-estimated their own abilities, and embarked on spells which they later found they couldn't control. Some had died screaming. Some, less fortunate, were still screaming, but hadn't yet died.

Merlin, who was breezily confident of his ability to control anything, scanned a few of the more disastrous spells with a gourmet air. Then, with a sigh, he tossed the grimoire aside. He was bored, that was the trouble. He wanted something to entertain him.

His gaze returned to the mirror. At the moment it was showing its default display, a slowly moving pattern of coloured blobs.

Merlin considered. He had frequently used the mirror to spy on ('monitor' was the word he used himself) people and their doings in various parts of Britain. Suppose he turned it further afield – to places he had never looked at before?

He waved an imperious hand, and uttered a command in the debased Celtic dialect which was the only language the mirror (being Welsh) understood. A few green swirls washed across the mirror's surface. A landscape appeared – ice-covered mountains under a brilliant blue sky.

'Somewhere in the far north, I guess,' Merlin decided. 'No signs of life. Let's try again.'

He waved his hand, and the ice mountains dissolved away, and were replaced by a barren vista of sand-dunes under a burning yellow sun. A line of camels wandered slowly by in the distance. Camels, however, were not especially interesting. Merlin waved his hand for a third time.

The landscape in the mirror suddenly vanished. A face, grey and amorphous, with two pale globular eyes on stalks, peered into Merlin's own.

'Where did that come from?' muttered the wizard uneasily. 'A repulsive-looking thing – it looks positively malevolent. A good job it can't see me. Although from the way it stares at me, you'd almost think that – hey!'

The slug in the mirror was no longer in the mirror. With an unpleasant sucking noise, it oozed out through the glass and onto Merlin's carpet, rather like Alice in Tenniel's illustration to *Alice Through the Looking-Glass*, except that the slug wasn't wearing Victorian clothes, and the furnishings in Merlin's study didn't include a smiling clock[1].

Merlin stared round-eyed at the grey horror that was squatting on his carpet. It occurred to him that this would be a very good time to think of a spell.

Merlin had, of course, taken part in many duels of wizardry in his time – most of them in a Camelot night-club called *The Pink Goblin*, where he sometimes went on Saturday evenings to watch certain rather dubious cabaret acts[2]. The lowliest acolyte was liable to fancy

---

[1] Merlin did have a clock in his study, but it was a grandfather clock, i.e. a clock made from his grandfather. His grandmother made it from her husband's bones shortly after he died. She used to say that the old buzzard hadn't given her the time of day when he was alive, but he damned well would now he was dead.

[2] Such as Deirdre the Delectable Dryad, Nadine the Naughty Naiad, and a number of other young (or, more often, heavily made up) ladies with similar names. I'm afraid Merlin was what is technically known, in the jargon of clinical psychology, as a Rather Sad Person.

himself as the world's greatest wizard after a few drinks, and Merlin had lost count of the number of slurred challenges to sorcerous combat he had received in *The Pink Goblin* from young men sporting wispy beards and faces runically engraved with acne. He usually rendered them unconscious with a spell so swift and unexpected that they barely had time to open their grimoires and discover that they had accidentally brought volume 12 of *Grimsdyke's Compendium of Sorcery* instead of volume 13. (Volume 13 was entitled *Killing Spells for Taking On Succubi and Sorcerers*. Volume 12 was called *Kitchen Spells for Making Succulent Sauces*. It was an easy mistake to make, but that wasn't much consolation if you were facing the top wizard in England and your only weapon was a recipe for Thousand Island Dressing.)

Archon, however, was a Fhomoire, and therefore an entirely different proposition. Also Merlin couldn't be expected to remember the best spell to use against an enemy who was supposed to have vanished from the earth a thousand years earlier.

It was all over in a matter of seconds.

As the grey slug oozed menacingly towards him across the floor, Merlin tried to think of the best incantation to use in a situation like this. His mind stayed resolutely blank. As the slug got nearer, he quite uncharacteristically panicked, and shouted out the first spell that came into his head.

He stared down at the bowl of Thousand Island Dressing that had materialised in his hand.

It occurred to him, just as the slug reached him, that his position as top wizard was in serious jeopardy.

There was a brief scuffle, and then Merlin screamed, which was something he hadn't done for years. Then there was silence.

Archon stayed still for a moment in the middle of the floor, waving his eye-stalks and examining his new surroundings. Satisfied that there were no further immediate threats, he vanished. For three seconds, the quanta in that particular bit of space ran frantically here and there for no particular reason, rather like the England football team. Then the unheard music stopped. In place of the slug, a tall, white-haired man in a pointy hat and a black robe stood in the centre of the floor. Apart from a slight fuzziness around the edges, he looked very much like Merlin.

Archon examined his new shape in the mirror.

'Good,' he murmured. 'Very good. That should fool them all - for the time being.'

Behind him, on the bench in the corner of the study, a tiny figure was jumping up and down and waving its fists.

'Fiend!' it cried, in a tiny, virtually inaudible voice. 'Monstrosity! How dare you treat Merlin Ambrosius like this! Restore me to my proper size at once, or there'll be trouble!'

The shape-shifter pointed a finger at the tiny gesticulating figure, which immediately froze in mid-gesture.

'There,' said Archon. 'Now you won't be able to work any magic, until someone un-enchants you.'

He picked up the doll-like figure, popped it into a drawer in Merlin's desk, and turned the key.

As Merlin was beginning his ill-fated explorations using the magic mirror, King Uther was several floors below, in the Great Hall. He had the room to himself. Spread on the table in front of him were assorted pens, parchments, inkwells, india-rubbers, official seals, unofficial seals, sealing wax and pieces of string. To all appearances, he was engaged in issuing edicts and proclamations.

Actually the edicts Uther was writing were more in the nature of a hobby. He was snatching a precious half-hour in which to indulge his favourite pastime.

Uther Pendragon, King of England and several other bits and pieces of the British Isles, was planning his abdication.

As he got older, Uther had got rather tired of being King, a job which seemed to consist mainly of sitting on an uncomfortably hard throne, wearing an uncomfortably heavy crown, and doing things because other people expected you to, rather than because you wanted to yourself. In recent years he had thought more and more about abdicating – though in fact it was quite impossible for him to abdicate, because the Saxons and the Scots and the Picts and the Welsh and the Irish would all immediately tear each other to pieces and plunge the kingdom into chaos. But there was no reason why he couldn't *pretend* to abdicate, by secretly writing long and florid abdication decrees that were never destined to be issued.

He licked his pen-nib and dipped it in the third ink-well from the right. There were seven inkwells altogether, each containing a different ink. The laws of England were extremely complex, and it was important that all royal decrees were written in an appropriate colour. Death sentences, for example, were normally written in black. Once, many years ago, Uther had carelessly signed a batch of death sentences in red, which the axeman had taken as an instruction as to how he should despatch his victims. Usually after the executions a man from the Camelot Cleansing Department stepped forward and gave the axeman's block a ceremonial wipe with a damp cloth. On that particular morning, they had had to hose down all the neighbouring streets.

The third inkwell from the right contained gold ink. It was generally reserved for joyful proclamations such as the birth of an heir to the throne, or the conquering of a particularly troublesome enemy. Or in Uther's case, abdications.

Uther carefully put pen to parchment, and began to write.

Whereas I, Uther Pendragon Rex of England, have decided to devote my sunset years to gardening and the breeding of a new strain of ornamental basilisk . . .

It was at this moment that Merlin screamed. Uther's hand jerked violently, and a large gold blot splashed onto the page.

'Bother,' said Uther. He put his pen down and stared at the ceiling.

The scream had come from the direction of Merlin's study. Perhaps he should go and see what had caused it.

He chewed his moustache doubtfully. If Merlin had screamed, then something must have frightened him. Anything capable of frightening the top wizard in England was not something Uther cared to meet in a hurry.

On the other hand, he was the King, and if something was going on in his castle, he ought to look into it.

Some unregal part of him was inclined to argue with this, but Uther had been a king for most of his life and was used to dealing with such internal rebellions. Getting up stiffly, he went out of the Hall and climbed the stairs.

When he reached Merlin's door, he put his ear to the panels and listened. At first he thought he could hear nothing. Then he thought he could hear something. Then he knew he could hear something, and he wanted to run back down the stairs.

Slither – slither – slither. The sound was coming

towards the door. It was like someone dragging a body: a slimy, blood-covered body, as of someone newly murdered. He took a shaky step backwards.

The door opened, and a figure in a black robe stood looking at him.

'Ah – Merlin,' said Uther nervously. 'There you are. Jolly good. I thought I heard a – but perhaps I was wrong. Are you – I mean, is everything all right?'

The figure in the black robe smiled – at least, Uther supposed he was smiling, though that baring of the teeth could equally well have been a snarl. 'Everything is going according to plan, thank you.'

'Oh, good.' Uther backed slowly down the stairs. 'Glad to see you're – I mean, that everything's – yes. Well. See you at dinner, perhaps.'

'Perhaps.' The figure in black closed the door. Uther heard slither, slither, slither going away on the other side of the panels.

The old king slowly descended the stairs until he was once again in the Great Hall. He sat down and stared at the abdication papers.

That had been Merlin, hadn't it?

Of course it had. Who else could it have been?

Everything is going according to plan. What plan? A plan to do what?

Who could tell what devious plans Merlin might have in mind? Probably they were nothing to do with the well-being of Uther's kingdom.

The fact was, he had never known what Merlin was up to, and he was too intimidated by the wizard to ask. He would just have to hope that Merlin knew what he was doing.

With a sigh, the King of England picked up his pen, dipped it once more into the inkwell, and carried on writing.

. . . of ornamental basilisk, which . . .

He stopped writing, and stared at the parchment. Then he picked up the inkwell and peered into it.

One by one, he picked up the other inkwells and examined the contents of each. He frowned in perplexity.

All the inks were the same colour. They had all, for no apparent reason, turned grey.

Having disposed of Uther, Archon closed the door of the study and all the windows. He didn't want to be disturbed for some time. There was work to be done. Work that had been uncompleted for a thousand years.

First, however, there were precautions to be taken.

'There are evidently still wizards in this land,' the shape-shifter murmured to himself, 'and I am out of practice at magic. I took this wizard by surprise. Others may be harder to overcome. I must protect myself. I need a spell – a spell of concealment.'

His eye wandered idly round the study, until it came to rest on a row of grimoires neatly arranged on a bookshelf halfway up one wall. The shelf had no brackets, and if a modern observer could have seen it, he would have assumed that it was held up by concealed screws. In fact, however, it was held up by magic. Contrary to appearances, the shelf was not holding up the grimoires: it was the grimoires that were holding up the shelf.

The shape-shifter, who perhaps knew this, waved his hand, and the leftmost grimoire floated across the room and landed in his lap. He opened it, and read the first spell:

For the Removal of Unsightly Facial Hair

The shape-shifter, who could grow and remove hair

at will, not to mention scales and tentacles, impatiently turned the page.

The next spell was more promising:

The Separable Soul

Being a spell to conceal the wizard's soul in a secret place: whereby the prudent wizard, setting forth upon a dangerous enterprise, may protect himself from an enemy's magic.

Excellent, thought Archon. *Just what I need.*

He ran his finger along the lines of writing, and read the entire spell out loud. The words were written in silver ink, but as Archon's finger passed over them, they faded from silver to grey.

Having finished the spell, Archon put the grimoire back on the shelf and went out of the study, slithering as quietly as he could manage.

When being King got too much for Uther, as it often did, there were various places he would slope off to for a bit of peace and quiet. They weren't as good as a real abdication, but they were the best he could do. There was the bar-parlour at *The King's Head*, for example, a pub of which he was the patron (there was a portrait of him on the sign outside); there were the dungeons, where he often went for a chat with the prisoners, who had their own inverted and refreshing view of the world; and there was the castle garden, where he could potter about looking at the roses and chrysanths and doing a bit of weeding.

Today, what with Merlin's scream and the ink mysteriously turning grey, abdicating had been spoilt somehow, so he wandered down to the garden to talk to the woman who looked after the hens.

The hen-woman was called Boadicea. Her mother had also been called Boadicea, and so had *her* mother, all the way back to the most famous Boadicea of all, the Dear Old Queen herself, in whose glorious reign there had been so much pillaging, looting, bloodletting, burning of Roman villas, and general high spirits. If the Romans had not come along and interrupted the right of descent, the hen-woman would have been Queen of Britain. Uther derived obscure comfort from this fact. The hen-woman was the only person in the kingdom who he felt really understood his problems, although the landlord at *The King's Head* was a fairly good substitute.

The hens ran about in the garden pecking at worms, bits of gravel, chrysanthemum seeds, and anything else they could find. They were all extremely fat and healthy, and the hen-woman collected their eggs each morning and took them to the castle kitchen. There was also a rooster, but he was seldom in evidence, since he spent most of his time dozing on top of the castle wall.

In the afternoons Boadicea generally sat in the doorway of her small hut, smoking her pipe, while Uther wandered about the flower-beds and chatted to her whenever he came within range. It was a pleasant, timeless, relaxing place, and Uther was grateful that no-one ever came to disturb him while he was in it.

Or they hadn't, until now.

Uther straightened his back, which was aching a little, and dropped the little bunch of weeds he had collected onto the bigger heap he had accumulated earlier. He watched the familiar figure in its black cloak and pointy hat advancing along the gravel path, and sighed.

'Hello, Merlin,' he said. 'Did you want me?'

The shape-shifter did not reply at once. He was trying to muffle the slithering noise, which was still faintly audible when he walked. It was due to post-quantum shift ghosting, an unavoidable side-effect of shape-shifting – rather as if a shadow of the original shape followed the new shape for a while. If he concentrated hard, he could block it out, but then the fuzziness round his edges got worse. This, of course, was exactly as predicted by von Klaptrapp's Law of Badly-Behaved Particles, which states that in any event involving quantum changes, all particles which are not told exactly where to stand will organise themselves so as to cause as much mischief as possible[1].

'Er, no,' said Archon, after a moment. 'No, I wasn't. I was looking for – er—' His gaze wandered vaguely towards the hen-coops, and then settled on Boadicea.

Boadicea took her pipe out of her mouth and wiped a drop of spittle from her moustache. 'Good morning to 'ee, sir wizard. What may the greatest wizard in the land want with a poor old woman of no importance?' Boadicea spoke mildly, but her sharp eyes were fixed on the wizard's face with a suspicious gaze. She had never cared for the wizard, considering that he gave himself airs.

'Ah – good morning, ma'am,' said Archon, endeavouring to be bright and friendly. 'I wonder if I might – ah – look inside the hen-coops for a moment.'

Boadicea's eyebrows tried to come together in a

---

[1]Physicists have been slow to realise that quantum uncertainty is due to particles not doing what they are told. Most particles behave fairly well – protons, neutrons and electrons, for example. But there are some real troublemakers. These include the so-called 'hard particles', such as croutons (which rose to the top of the primordial matter-soup in the early days of the universe), futons (which sank to the bottom) and mekons (big green particles that beat up defenceless quarks when no-one is looking). Hard particles avoid detection in the laboratory by hiding behind other particles when a microscope is pointed in their direction.

frown. Since they were already joined together, what resulted was a hairy explosion above the bridge of her long, hooked nose. 'Why?'

'Er – why?'

'Aye, master wizard - why? Why do 'ee want to poke about in my hen-coops?'

'Oh.' Archon thought furiously. 'Well, I wondered if you might have an egg or two. I'm hungry, you see.'

'I took a dozen eggs to the kitchen this morning,' said the hen-woman, 'and I see no reason, master Merlin, why 'ee can't go and ask the cook to boil one for 'ee, like everyone else. What be 'ee going to do? Eat un raw?'

The shape-shifter, who ate everything raw if he possibly could, laughed uneasily. 'No, no, of course not. Yes – yes, I'll go to the kitchen. Capital idea, capital.' He turned and stumped off up the garden, slithering so quietly that neither Uther nor Boadicea heard it.

One of the hens, however, looked up as he passed and stared at him with her head cocked on one side. Her name was Rosemary Featherbrain, and the other hens regarded her with awe because she could sometimes tell that gravel was inedible without picking it up and trying to eat it. She watched the receding shape-shifter for a moment, wondering why he reminded her of both a fox and a worm at the same time. Finding no answer, she gave it up and went back to her chrysanthemum seed.

'Well, Uther,' said the hen-woman, replacing her pipe between her teeth, 'what do 'ee reckon that was about?'

'No idea,' said the King, gazing after Archon. 'It's not like Merlin to go looking for food. He generally sends a message down to the kitchen.'

'Well, now,' said the hen-woman darkly, 'there be other strange things happening these past few days. I've seen omens in the droppings.'

Uther looked puzzled. 'In the what?'

'The hen-droppings. I looks at them every morning. Some people reads the stars, and some reads tea-leaves. I read droppings. They make patterns in the straw.'

'Ah.' Uther nodded wisely. 'And what have the droppings been saying?'

'Dark forebodings,' said the hen-woman, her voice sinking into a low monotone. 'The kingdom be under threat. Doom and destruction wait in the coming days. Ancient evils awake and swarm across the land. Powers be thrown down, and worse powers rule in their place. Misery and despair be the lot of every man, woman and child.'

'Oh dear,' said Uther uneasily.

'And it'll rain by Thursday,' said Boadicea, taking her pipe out of her mouth and knocking the ashes out against one of her hobnailed boots.

Uther looked up at the sky, which was blue and cloudless.

'Do you really think so?' he said.

At the darkest hour of the night, as the whole of Camelot lay sleeping, and Boadicea lay snoring under her rough woollen blanket on the floor of her hut, a dark shape emerged from the highest window of the castle and began to ooze down the castle wall, leaving a trail that glistened faintly in the starlight.

The giant slug reached the foot of the wall, oozed across the castle garden to the hen-coops, and then changed into the Merlin-like figure in black robe and pointy hat.

Archon reached deep inside his cloak – so deep, in fact, that he seemed to be reaching right inside his own ribcage. He drew out something that shone with a faint grey light, like a will o' the wisp. Bending down, he reached inside one of the hen-coops. When he with-drew his hand, it was empty.

Archon changed shape once again into a slug. He moved back to the wall and began to ooze up the stones.

Finally he reached Merlin's window, and disappeared inside.

Rosemary Featherbrain woke feeling unsettled. She had had a most unpleasant dream, all about a big grey lump of gravel that grew legs and chased her round the garden. She was relieved to find that it wasn't true.

The warm, familiar scent of hen-droppings sur-rounded her. She clucked quietly to herself, and got up to inspect the egg she had laid yesterday.

There it was, round and brown and slightly speckled, just like all her other eggs. Soon the hen-woman would come and collect it. Rosemary had always vaguely resented this, but that was, after all, the way of things, you laid an egg and a big hairy woman smelling of tobacco came and took it away. That was how it had been since time immemorial. No point getting cross about it.

Except that this morning, for some reason, Rosemary felt different.

She scratched a little in the straw, and put her head on one side, contemplating the new egg. It looked the same as every other egg she'd laid, but somehow she knew it wasn't. It had a strange feel to it. Something drew her to it, made her feel that she must protect it at all costs.

She knew, suddenly and without any doubt, that she was not going to let that hairy old hen-woman take this one away.

Rosemary gathered up her feathers and settled back

on the egg. That hen-woman – what right did she have to take someone else's egg? If she wanted eggs, let her lay some herself.

Later on that morning, Boadicea presented herself at the castle kitchen. She was carrying a basket of eggs as usual, but her right hand was crudely bandaged with a torn bit of blanket.

'Been in a fight?' asked the castle cook, as he took the basket. Boadicea had a reputation for getting into brawls. The previous Saturday night, after three large gins, she had knocked the captain of the castle guard and two of his toughest soldiers out cold.

'One of my hens,' explained Boadicea. 'Pecked me when I tried to collect her egg. Odd – she's usually a placid old thing.'

'Under the weather, mebbe,' said the cook.

Boadicea glanced up at the sky, which once again was cloudless blue.

'Mebbe,' she said. 'At any rate, there'll be thunderstorms soon.'

Back in Merlin's study, Archon was using the magic mirror to survey the local countryside. Eventually the mirror showed what he was interested in – a tangled green profusion, the interior of a dense forest.

'There,' he muttered. 'That was where I hid it. A thousand years ago.'

In the mirror, the trees swayed gently in a breath of wind. The shape-shifter leaned closer.

'It must still be there. But where, exactly? I shall have to go there, and search. It may take time. In a thousand years, much will have changed.'

There was something partly visible among the trees – an extremely squalid cottage, with a sagging roof and a chimney from which smoke poured repeatedly, spelling out the word 'BOGHOLE'.

'It must be somewhere close to that cottage,' murmured Archon. 'I guess that's the place to start looking.'

The cottage had taken a deal of cleaning and tidying, but it was now reasonably habitable. The hole in the roof had been mended, you could sit on the chairs without them collapsing, and the kitchen-range was capable of producing food that didn't taste too badly of soot.

Unfortunately, that meant that Gwydden no longer had any excuse not to start work.

He stood at the cottage window, looking across the garden towards the dense mass of the Forest beyond. Both the garden and the Forest looked peaceful and inviting under the unbroken blue of the sky.

He had to admit that Hergrim had worked wonders in the garden. Three-quarters of it was cleared, and although what was now visible in place of the dense jungle could hardly be called a lawn, at least it was no more than ankle high. Some of it even consisted of grass.

At this precise moment, Hergrim was making full use of the area he had cleared by lazing in the middle of it on an old deck-chair they had found in a corner of the cottage. He was somewhat casually dressed in bright yellow shorts and a pale green tunic. He had taken his boots off, and his bare feet were stretched out in front of him. His eyes were closed, and his beard rose and fell in peaceful somnolence.

Gwydden sighed. It would be nice to be out in the sunshine like Hergrim, half-listening to the wood-pigeons cooing among the distant trees, catching up on the gossip in the latest issue of *Wizard's Weekly*. Instead of which he was stuck indoors, proofreading an article for *The Learned and Academic Symposium of Pure and Applied Magic*, a publication which was about as racy as a snail on crutches.

He turned back into the room and scowled at the papers on the table. The article was called "Shape-shifting: is it Real Magic, or just cheating?", and he would be reasonably well paid once he had checked it, provided he could stay awake that long.

He sat down reluctantly at the table, stifled a yawn, and continued to read.

'It has been suggested by other learned contributors to this excellent and scholarly journal—'

'Get on with it, you creep, and stop sucking up to the editor,' Gwydden muttered.

'—that in ancient times the power of shape-shifting was possessed by the race of demons called the Fhomoire. This, however, must remain unproven, since the evil Fhomoire all perished long ago, and will never trouble the world again . . .'

A sudden noise made the wizard jump. 'Oh, it's just a book. Fallen out of the shelves. Funny – I'm sure I didn't dislodge it.' He picked the book up and stared at the open page, which contained a mere four lines of spidery and faded print. 'What's this?

Whenne ye shapelesse one awaykes,

Ande from ye towere olde eville creepes,

Goe sunnewyse from ye welle, and finde

Ye grove wherein ye grene godde sleepes.

What on earth is this book?' He turned the volume over and examined the spine. 'Oh, I should have known. *Ye Prophecies of Nostradimwit.* Load of old cods-wallop. I didn't know I had a copy of this.' A sudden thought struck him. 'Oh rats.' He turned to the fly-leaf. A piece of paper was stuck inside it, on which was written the following:

Property of the Library, Academy of Magic, Anglesey

UNDER NO CIRCUMSTANCES MAY THIS BOOK BE REMOVED FROM THE LIBRARY PREMISES!
Signed: Trimblus Pedanticus, Librarian

'Oh well,' Gwydden said to himself. 'I shall just have to send it back anonymously. I don't expect anyone's missed it. No-one takes Nostradimwit seriously any more.'

He turned the book over and glanced again at the page with the verse on it. Then he drew in a sharp breath, and exclaimed involuntarily. The four lines of antique script had disappeared. The page on which they had been printed was completely blank.

Chapter Five

Hergrim squinted up at Gwydden sceptically from his deck-chair. 'Gwydden, are you making this up?'

'Of course not,' said the wizard indignantly. 'First there was a verse written on the page, and then, when I looked again, there wasn't. See?' He brandished the blank page in Hergrim's face.

'All right, keep your shirt on.' Hergrim wiped his sweaty forehead with an even sweatier hand. 'What's the explanation?'

'Well.' The wizard shuffled his feet, evidently embarrassed. 'There's an old saying – load of superstitious nonsense, mind you, I wouldn't give it any credence, not in this day and age – that when a prophecy of Nostradimwit is about to be fulfilled, the person chosen to fulfil it will read it, and the prophecy will then vanish.'

The dwarf raised his eyebrows. 'A bit inconvenient, isn't it? What if you want to refer to it later, to see if you're doing the right thing?'

'You're supposed to remember it,' said the wizard.

'Ah. And can you?'

'Can I what?'

'Remember it.'

'I don't know. Let me see . . . *Whenne ye eville one awaykes* . . . No, that's not right. *Whenne ye creepinge one* . . . No. Oh dear. I can't remember it at all.'

The dwarf folded his arms. 'Jolly good. Does it matter?'

Gwydden shrugged. 'Probably not. We had to study Nostradimwit at the Academy, but no-one takes any notice of his prophecies these days. Anyway, if I can't remember it, it's just too bad, isn't it?' He sniffed the air. 'Hergrim, there's a terrible smell in this garden.'

The dwarf nodded. 'I think there's something rotting over in that far corner – the bit I haven't cleared yet. I'll have a go at it this afternoon.'

'Okay.' Gwydden sniffed again. 'It's pretty bad, whatever it is. Smells like a dead animal, or worse.'

Hergrim yawned. 'Don't worry. I'll get the axe out again after lunch. At the moment I'm having a well-earned rest.'

'So I notice,' said the wizard drily. He turned and went back into the cottage.

The dwarf closed his eyes and settled down for another few minutes.

Two hours later, Gwydden was sitting once more over his proofreading, although since his eyes were shut and he was snoring, he probably wasn't working at maximum efficiency.

Hergrim stomped into the cottage, sweat pouring down his face. 'I've found it.'

The wizard woke up with a start. 'Found what?'

'The source of the bad smell. Come and see.'

They went out into the garden, and Hergrim led the way to the darkest, most overgrown corner of all. Broken stems lay on all sides where Hergrim's axe had been at work.

Gwydden stared around at the plants. 'I've never seen hemlock as big as this. Or thistles. Or – what are those huge things with white tops?'

'Dandelions, I think,' said the dwarf. 'The plants in this corner of the garden are very strange. They're all huge, but they look unhealthy, somehow – spindly and deformed. Look at these.' He picked up a handful of the tall dandelion stems. They were a sickly grey colour. 'What could cause that, d'you reckon?'

'I don't know.' Gwydden's hand had gone automatically to his nose. 'The smell round here is dreadful. What's causing it?'

'This.' Hergrim pointed at a hummock like a small burial mound. 'I think it might be a well.'

The wizard became agitated. 'A well? Are you sure?'

'Looks like it. Why?'

'Because that verse I read mentioned a well, I think. Only I still can't remember it.'

Hergrim pulled a handful of withered and deformed branches away from the hummock. Underneath was a stone wall. 'Yes, I was right. A circular wall – must be a well. And someone's capped it with a large stone.'

'Why would they do that?'

'To stop people falling in, I expect.'

They stared at the well. It was about six feet in diameter, and looked very ancient and weathered. The stone wall and the capstone were discoloured with dead moss and lichen.

Gwydden leaned over the well, sniffed, and backed away hurriedly. 'Ugh! That's where the smell's coming from - probably through gaps in the mortar. Perhaps an animal fell in and died.'

'Nothing could have fallen in there,' said Hergrim. 'That capstone hasn't been moved for years.'

Gwydden again leaned over the well, being careful not to breathe in this time. 'Is it my imagination, or is there writing on this capstone?'

They peered at the weathered and defaced stone.

'It isn't writing,' said Gwydden eventually. 'It's a drawing of some kind, etched into the stone. Looks like a circle with radiating lines.'

'It's an eye,' said the dwarf suddenly. 'The circle is the pupil.'

The wizard squinted at the carved lines. 'Possibly. Yes, it could be an eye.'

'Of course it is,' said the dwarf. 'The question is, what does it mean?'

'Why should it mean anything? Perhaps it's just decoration.'

Hergrim snorted. 'Ah, of course. The famous staring eye motif, as found on all disused wells of the Lower Microcephalic period. Yes, I should have realised.'

The wizard looked at him suspiciously. 'Are you being sarcastic?'

Hergrim favoured him with a crooked smile. 'Just a touch, maybe. Look, if someone goes to the trouble of capping a well with a huge great stone, and then goes to the further trouble of carving an eye on the well, and meanwhile inside the well there's something that smells as bad as *this* well does, you can bet your life the eye is a warning of some kind. It's trying to tell us that whatever is inside this well is not to be tampered with.'

'Possibly,' said the wizard, sounding unconvinced. 'Anyway, we'll know when we uncap it, won't we?'

Hergrim stared at him. '*Uncap* it? Are you mad? Haven't I just presented a watertight argument for *not* uncapping it?'

'Possibly.'

The dwarf folded his arms and stuck his beard out. 'What is it about you wizards, eh? Can't you leave things alone? Must you always be sticking your magestaffs in where wise men fear to go? If you open that well, you'll regret it.'

The wizard opened his mouth to speak.

'And if you say *possibly* again,' said the dwarf, 'I'll give you an extremely close haircut with my axe.'

'I was going to say that I'll regret it if I *don't* open it. Where's your curiosity, Hergrim?'

'Curiosity killed the wizard[1],' said Hergrim. 'Look, I have a suggestion to make. Why don't you see if you can find out about the well first, and *then* open it, if you still feel like risking your neck?'

The wizard nodded reluctantly. 'Okay, if you insist. The library in Anglesey has the biggest collection of magical books in the country – I'll see if they have any information.'

'Good. That should keep you out of trouble for a while,' said Hergrim. 'It'll take you several days to get to Anglesey and back.'

'That won't be necessary. I can do it much quicker than that, using ShadowFax.'

Hergrim frowned. 'What's ShadowFax – a very fast horse[2]?'

The wizard laughed. 'No. Come into the cottage, and I'll give you a demonstration.'

ShadowFax enabled copies of documents to be sent by magic through mirrorspace from one wizard to another. It was a great boon, because apart from being almost instantaneous, it removed the need for fiddling about with tiny scrolls tied to the legs of carrier pigeons.

Inside the cottage, Gwydden produced a mirror from the bag of goodies he had brought from his lodgings in Camelot. He laid it on his desk under the window, and made a few mystic passes over it. The mirror's surface

---

[1]Which is why there are so few wizards around these days.
[2]A surprisingly common misconception.

ceased to reflect the sky and clouds beyond the window, and became suffused with deep shadow.

'Hence the name ShadowFax,' said Gwydden, and the dwarf nodded.

The wizard took a piece of parchment, dipped his quill into the ink, and wrote:

What can you tell me about a well with an eye carved on the capstone?

(Answer to Gwydden, c/o Redbrush Cottage)

He laid the parchment face down on the mirror, murmured a Latin word or two, and then turned the parchment over. 'The reply appears on the other side,' he explained. 'We might as well put the kettle on while we're waiting. The librarian's not a bad old stick, but he takes a while to find the information you want.'

Several cups of tea later, they returned to the mirror to find that the parchment had rolled itself up.

'That means we've got a reply,' said Gwydden. He unrolled the parchment, and stared at it for a long time. Eventually he said, 'Hm. Oh well, never mind.'

'May I read it?' asked the dwarf.

Gwydden handed him the parchment, and the dwarf read the following:

'Greetings, Gwydden! Well, this is a pleasant surprise! How are you? Seems an age since we last faxed. How's that little health problem of yours? I hope the ointment I recommended is doing the trick. You'll be sorry to hear that my back still plays me up – it's this Welsh climate, much too damp for someone at my time of life. By the way, you'll never guess who I bumped into last week – old Arbonidus, of all people! He's still the same, still goes round with that pet basilisk on his shoulder. Did I ever tell you how I met his sister? It happened like this . . .'

Hergrim stopped reading, and looked up. 'Does he ever actually answer the question?'

'At the bottom.'

The dwarf skipped to the end, where the close-packed writing tailed off.

'. . . *and he cut her head off with a single stroke! Boy, was she surprised! Well, I must sign off now. It's been nice chatting to you. Oh, I was nearly forgetting. That question of yours about the well with the eye engraved on the capstone – can't find anything about it, I'm afraid. Doesn't sound quite canny to me. I should leave well alone, if I were you. Leave well alone – geddit? Just my little joke. Must go now – I have to re-catalogue the books in the Transfinite Numerology section. Annoying business, there are more of them every time I look. Ciao for now.*

Trimblus (Librarian, Academy of Magic, Anglesey)'

Hergrim tossed the parchment aside with a grunt. 'So much for the biggest collection of magical books in the country. What do we do now?'

'We'll ask Mrs Tod and Macpherson. They should know something about the well – it's on the Redbrush estate, after all. Come on – we'll go up to the Hall.'

In the middle of Redbrush Park there was a lake. There was a small island in the lake, and in the middle of the island there was a Roman bath-house. The bath was no longer usable – its water supply had dried up, and it was full of dead leaves – but the inhabitant of the island didn't mind, because he never took baths anyway.

It was a pleasant island covered with grass and fruit trees, and on the south side the inhabitant had laid out a small vegetable garden. What with the fruit from the trees and the produce from the garden, and the milk from a nanny goat he kept tethered beside the bath-house, he was fairly self-sufficient. He had never been a great one for company, and he didn't miss it.

Sometimes he wrote poetry, and sometimes, when

writing poetry seemed too much like hard work, he lazed on the roof of the bath-house and watched what was happening across the lake – a relaxing occupation, because what happened was generally very little. The Hall was extremely quiet these days, with only the fox-lady and the Scottish gardener in residence, and the only excitement arose from chance encounters between the gardener and his inveterate enemies, the rabbits from the warren beyond the western perimeter wall. The inhabitant had a sneaking admiration for the rabbits, who daily risked life, limb and fluffy white tail dodging the carpet-tacks and bent nails from Macpherson's gun. He would follow their hit-and-run campaigns, and silently cheer if they managed to make off into the impenetrable undergrowth of the Forest with a lettuce or a few carrots.

Life on the island fulfilled all his requirements. It was calm, free from stress, and predictable.

Recently, however, there had been new developments. The cottage, which had been empty for some years, was occupied again, by a tall thin person in a grey robe and a short, stocky one with a red beard. They had come to the Hall once, and gone off to the cottage accompanied by Macpherson. And now here they were again, walking towards the Hall with a purposeful air.

'And now Macpherson is letting them into the Hall,' murmured the inhabitant. 'I wonder what they want? Well, never mind. Whatever it is, it can't disturb me here.'

He got down from the roof and stood for a moment contemplating the goat, whose head was bent over the lush grass, placidly chewing. 'Well, Emily?' he asked her. 'Do you miss it, eh? The parties, the excitement, the social whirl?'

The goat raised her head and looked at him thoughtfully. Then she turned her attention back to the grass.

'No, I didn't think so,' said the inhabitant. 'Neither do I.'

He smiled to himself, and went into the bath-house, where he lay down and closed his eyes. He could feel another poem coming, but it didn't feel as though it would arrive for another hour or two, and in the meantime he fancied a snooze.

'You want *what?*' said Mrs Tod, looking at Gwydden and Hergrim with a frosty glare.

'The plans to the Hall and grounds,' said the wizard. 'Especially the underground plans. Pipework, drainage, sewage. That sort of thing.'

The lady of Redbrush Hall drew her shawl round her shoulders and sat even more stiffly in her chair. 'I know nothing about such things. Really, I don't know what the world is coming to. What has happened to good manners, I wonder? When I was a girl, if anyone had used the word *sewage* to a lady, he would have been tied to the nearest post and horse-whipped. Have you no idea of decency?'

The wizard opened his mouth, then closed it again. He looked helplessly at Macpherson, but the gardener seemed to be taking a great interest in the progress of a spider that was crawling up the scullery wall, and appeared not to have heard anything.

Hergrim decided to have a try. 'Isn't there a study or a library or something, where the plans are kept?'

'The library.' With evident reluctance, Mrs Tod gave the idea a brief examination. 'Yes, we have a library. I daresay there may be something in there. Very well – Macpherson, show these two persons to the library.'

The Scot jumped slightly, and grew so pale that his face was suddenly a mass of luminous crimson freckles.

'Och, ma'am – not the libraira. Niver the libraira.'

'Nonsense, man. What's wrong with the library?'

The gardener's eyes had grown round and huge. 'Ye know verra weel, ma'am. The libraira is in the *east wing!*'

'Poppycock.' Mrs Tod straightened her shawl again with a fierce gesture of disapproval. 'What is all this nonsense you keep talking about the east wing? I grant you it may be a little chilly these days, since we no longer light fires in the bedrooms, but that's all. *There is nothing wrong with the east wing*, Macpherson, do you hear me? Don't be such a superstitious fool.'

'Superr-stitious, am I?' The Scot bridled. 'Ye know not of what ye speak. The east wing isna canny. It isna safe. It isna—' he groped for words '—it isna *nice.*'

'Hmph!' said Mrs Tod. 'No more of this nonsense. Take these people to the library. *At once.*'

The gardener stared at her hollow-eyed for a moment. Then his shoulders slumped, and he beckoned the wizard and dwarf to follow him.

They left the scullery and passed through corridors that to begin with were reasonably well-lit and swept clean. After a while, however, the passages were more gloomy, and the rooms they entered and crossed were either bare, or contained moth-eaten hangings and woodwormy furniture with mouldering upholstery. Cobwebs became more frequent, larger, and more densely tangled. The temperature seemed to steadily decrease.

As they proceeded, Macpherson walked slower and slower, and his shoulders became more and more hunched. He was muttering to himself in Gaelic, but whether his mutterings were prayers or curses was impossible to fathom. The dwarf and wizard had listened to Macpherson's protestations with a good deal of scepticism, but before long they too began to feel uneasy.

97

The chill and dampness of the east wing seemed to have something unhealthy about it, as though it had been built over a plague-infested swamp. They were relieved when at length Macpherson stopped in front of a huge blackened oak door with rusty hinges, bearing a faded plaque that said: *Library – please be quiet.*

The door was not locked, but the handle had rusted. It took all Macpherson's strength to force it to turn. He put his shoulder against the door and pushed, and it swung open with a protesting squeal.

'In ye go,' he said to the dwarf and wizard. 'I'll wait oot here. I dinna care to set foot in that room.' He shuddered, and turned his back on the open doorway.

Hergrim and Gwydden looked at one another. Now they were here, they could understand Macpherson's feelings. The east wing had an unpleasant atmosphere, and it was particularly unpleasant in the vicinity of the library.

Taking a grip on themselves, they went in.

The library was not large, but it was well-stocked. The half-light from the cobwebbed windows showed tall bookcases reaching to the ceiling and filled with dim, dust-grey volumes. The dwarf and wizard wandered into the middle of the room and stood gazing around.

'How are we going to find anything here?' Hergrim asked. 'There must be thousands of books. Is there anything to tell us what they are?'

The wizard peered up at the gloomy recesses where the bookcases met the ceiling. 'Yes, look - there are the names of subjects written up there. They're a bit hard to make out, but I think that one says *Hunting.*'

'This one over here says *Shooting,*' the dwarf announced, craning his short neck to make out the distant lettering.

'And the one on the other wall says *Fishing,*' the

wizard continued. 'Those three sections seem to account for most of the library. Evidently the Earls of Redbrush were typical English aristocrats. However, there do seem to be one or two other books.' He brushed the dust away from a group of shelves in a dimly-lit corner. 'These look like recipe books. *How to Cook Rabbit*, *The Compleat Rabbit Cookbook*, *Rabbits Stuffed and Unstuffed*, *Zen and the Art of Rabbit-Stuffing* . . . Suddenly I feel sorry for the local rabbits. Wait a minute, what's this section? *Redbrush Hall, History.*'

'That sounds like what we're looking for,' said the dwarf, peering into the shadowy shelves. 'But it seems to be empty.'

'No, there is something.' The wizard reached in, and pulled out a folder. 'Just this.' He opened it, and peered at the yellowing contents. 'There are quite a lot of papers here. We'd better take it back to the cottage, and look at it where there's more light.'

'Gwydden,' said Hergrim suddenly. He was bending down and examining one of the lowest bookshelves, which they had so far not investigated.

'What?'

'These books down here are a bit strange.'

'Strange? What sort of strange? Occult? Weird? Pornographic?'

'No. *This* sort of strange.' The dwarf straightened up, and held out a book to Gwydden. At any rate, it *looked* like a book, but as the dwarf held it in his hands, it slowly dissolved, oozing down between his fingers. In a few seconds his hand was empty except for a coating of slime, and there was a puddle of slime on the floor between his feet. The slime was dull grey in colour.

'Curious,' commented the wizard.

Hergrim was holding his hands up to his face and sniffing disgustedly. 'Ugh – it stinks.' He stiffened suddenly. 'Here – what does this remind you of?' He held his hands up near the wizard's face.

'Ye gods,' said the wizard in revulsion. 'That's horrible. Wait a minute – the well. It's the smell that was hanging round the well in the cottage garden.'

'Exactly.' The dwarf bent down again and examined the bookcase more closely. 'Whatever is causing it is worst at floor level. Two shelves up, the books are spongy, but they don't dissolve. It's as though something's coming up through the floor and attacking the paper.' He stared down at the floor. 'There must be something *underneath* the library. Something pretty revolting.'

Gwydden went to the library door. 'Macpherson?'

The gardener turned a haunted face towards him. 'Aye?'

'Does Mrs Tod know that her books are gradually turning into sludge?'

'Och, she wouldna care,' said the gardener contemptuously. 'She doesna read anything but samplers and the hoosehold accoonts.'

'But there's something very strange going on in this library. Surely she ought to be told.'

The Scot grinned manically. 'Strange, ye call it! Och, 'tis worse than strange. The east wing be under a curse! I've tried tae tell her, but she doesna listen.'

'What's underneath the library?' asked the wizard.

'The wine cellars. But we dinna use them. Mrs Tod doesna approve of wine. Or whisky,' the Scot concluded sadly.

'Has anyone been down there recently?'

The gardener shook his head. 'Not for years. Ye canna get doon there.'

'Why not?'

'*She* had them blocked off. She had workmen in, ye

ken, and laid flagstones across the trapdoor. That was before I came here.'

'Where was the trapdoor?'

The Scotsman shrugged. 'I asked her once, but she wouldna say. 'Tis my belief she canna remember.'

'Well,' said Gwydden, feeling rather defeated, 'I was going to suggest that you go down into the cellar to see what's making the books deteriorate in the library. But by the sound of it, the only way would be to take up all the flagstones in the downstairs rooms to find the trapdoor, and I don't suppose Mrs Tod would want to do that.'

'She wouldna, an' neither would I,' said the gardener, shuddering. 'I wouldna go doon under the east wing if ye gi'd me a hundred poond. Not even if it was in cash.'

The inhabitant of the island woke from his siesta, yawned, stretched, and stood up. He felt relaxed, re-freshed, and ready to throw himself into the furious hurly-burly of spondees, dactyls and iambic pentame-ters.

He scratched himself thoroughly, and went out of the bath-house into the afternoon sunshine. Emily the goat gave him an indolent stare as he emerged, and then went back to her endless chewing.

The inhabitant wandered over the grass until he came to the very heart of the island. He gazed at the small but perfect landscape that met his eyes, and gave a little sigh of contentment. Here the grass was a truly vivid green, thick and lush and sweet-smelling.

The grass dipped down to a depression filled with water -- a small pool, constantly bubbling as it was fed from a small spring. The water was clear and tinged with green – not a stagnant green, but a vibrant, healthy-looking green. Fruit trees and flowerbeds clustered round the pool, making a little scented grove.

The inhabitant bent his head, and took a long draught. As always, it tasted wonderful. He could feel it invigorating his whole body, filling him with life.

'Now *that*,' he said to himself, for the umpteenth time, 'is really water. In fact it deserves capital letters. Really Water. The real stuff.'

He raised his head, and shook himself. He was getting on in years, and should by rights have started to go grey by now, but there was no sign of it yet. He looked and felt as young and vigorous as when he had first come to the island. This, he felt sure, was mainly due to the remarkable water in the pool.

And after all, he said to himself, *it's a good thing I still feel vigorous, considering how hard I have to work. Two or three hours a day writing poetry can be a real sweat.*

Steeling himself to another exhausting session of rhyme-making, he strolled back to the bath-house in search of pencil and paper.

Back in the cottage, the wizard and dwarf sat down at the rickety table, and Gwydden pulled a bundle of grubby-looking papers out of the folder. They set to work leafing through them.

'This is pretty tedious stuff,' said the dwarf, after a while. 'It's mostly domestic accounts. *Sixteen bayles of hay, three shyllynges. Twelf hogs heddes of ale, two shyllynges and sixe pence. Ten baskettes of swete lavendere against ye smelle of draynes in ye easte wynge, a halfe-sovryn.'*

'That's a lot of lavender,' murmured the wizard absently, turning pages and scanning them. 'Hullo – what on earth's this?'

He held up a piece of parchment emblazoned with florid lettering of all shapes and sizes, and embellished with picturesque woodcuts of sylvan scenery.

'Tired of having a boring garden?' he read aloud. 'Want something to make your garden the envy of other landed gentry? Then call EBENEZER BROWN – landscape gardener to the aristocracy!!! We stop at nothing to give you a truly natural landscape!! Can't stand those almshouses? Tear them down! Hate grubby farm-workers toiling in full view of your home? Evict them! Bothered by badgers and rabbits? Shoot them! Don't delay, send a carrier pigeon today, to EBENEZER BROWN, Illegitimates' Lane, Camelot.'

'Well, well,' said Hergrim. 'Good old Culpability Brown. It's a long time since I heard anyone mention him.'

The wizard frowned. 'Culpability?'

'People called him that because if a building fell down, it was usually his fault. He was a notorious cheapskate builder and gardener. Started off in a small way, picking flowers from widows' gardens and selling them back to them as wreaths for their husbands' funerals. He ascended to the heady position of royal gardener, and was sacked when it came out that he'd been using the royal gardens for growing opium. The landscape gardening business was his last venture.' The dwarf snapped his fingers. 'Of course! Remember the initials EB over the door? He obviously built this cottage. That would explain why it's such a tumbledown wreck.'

'No doubt.' Gwydden riffled lethargically through the papers. 'There doesn't seem to be anything very helpful here. Let's tip the rest of them out and deal with them quickly.'

He upended the folder. Several more papers fell out, and also a small book. The wizard picked this up and stared at it. 'Good heavens! Another copy of *Ye Prophecies of Nostradimwit*. The Earls of Redbrush must have had wider interests than we thought.' He leafed hastily through the pages. 'Here it is - this is the prophecy. *Whenne ye shapelesse one awaykes, Ande from ye towere olde eville creepes, Goe sunnewyse from ye welle, and finde Ye grove wherein ye grene godde sleepes.* I told you it mentioned a well. Now this time, I really will try to remember it.'

'The page has gone blank again,' said Hergrim, peering over his shoulder. 'I saw it happen that time.'

'Yes. I'd better write it down, before I forget it.' The wizard picked up a pen, looked for a blank piece of paper, and failing to find one, turned over Culpability Brown's advertisement, intending to write on the back. He did a double-take. 'Here, Hergrim, look at this.'

'It's a map,' said the dwarf, looking over his shoulder.

'It's more than that,' said the wizard. 'It's what we were looking for – the plans of the Redbrush Hall estate. Hang on, let me write down the prophecy before I forget it.'

He scribbled furiously in the margin, and then they both examined the back of Culpability Brown's advertisement.

'There are two plans, side by side,' said Hergrim. 'One shows the estate before his alterations, the other after. They must have been drawn up by Culpability Brown himself. There are his initials – EB – in the bottom right-hand corner.'

'Right.' Gwydden nodded. 'Here's the cottage – only on the right-hand map. So we were right, the cottage was built by Culpability Brown. And this circle close by must be the well. But what's this line running across the map?'

They stared at the gently meandering line for several seconds.

'It's a stream,' said Hergrim suddenly. 'Look – it comes into the Redbrush grounds from the south-east, meanders through the estate, and disappears back into the Forest at the north-west corner. And it must run *underground,* because it feeds the well in the cottage garden. Then, further on, it runs past the east end of the Hall.'

'Yes, you're right. Interesting. I wonder if the stream is connected with the damp in the library.'

'What was affecting those books wasn't just ordinary damp,' said the dwarf.

'No, it certainly wasn't. Here, look at this.' The wizard stabbed the newer of the two plans with a thin finger. 'What's this big blue thing? It isn't on the other plan.'

'Big blue thing?' The dwarf laughed. 'It's a lake, of course – an artificial one. That was practically Culpability Brown's trademark – an artificial lake. Usually with an island in it. Yes, there you are.' The dwarf pointed to a small green circle enclosed within the blue area. 'An artificial island. It's even got a name written beside it – Arcadia.' He frowned. 'Now where have I heard that name recently?'

'Never mind that,' said the wizard. 'What about this well? There's nothing to say what it is, but it certainly wasn't made by your friend Mr Brown, because it's on both plans.'

'I don't know,' said the dwarf, 'but I'll bet that well is dry.'

'Why?'

'Because the only way Culpability could have fed the lake is to divert the stream via an underground channel. There's no channel marked on the plans, but the logical place is somewhere near the cottage. The well is further along the stream than the cottage, so probably the stream-bed under the well has been dry for a long time.'

'Good. So we can uncap the well, and go down inside to see what the smell is.'

Hergrim looked at him doubtfully. 'I still don't think that's a good idea. There might be anything in there.'

'Oh, don't be so wet,' said the wizard scornfully. He gazed at the plans, and his face became thoughtful. 'Wet. Yes. Hm. Now that's interesting.'

'What is?'

'Well, if you're right, and the stream is dry where it runs under the cottage garden where the well is, then it must be dry further on, where it runs near the east end of the Hall. So whatever it is that's causing the decay in the library, it can't be ordinary damp.'

'Perhaps we ought to tell Mrs Tod.'

'What – that she hasn't got damp? Anyway, Macpherson said there was no way down under the Hall. Let's see if we find anything revealing when we uncap the well.'

'You mean to go ahead with this lunatic scheme, then?'

'Yes, I do. I don't want to live next to that smell all the time I'm in this cottage. And anyway, there's the prophecy.'

'I thought you said no-one took Nostradimwit seriously.'

'Yes, well.' The wizard shuffled the papers together, except for the map, and started to put them back in the folder. 'Better safe than sorry.'

'*Goe sunnewyse from ye welle,*' read the dwarf, peering at Gwydden's hasty scrawl. 'What does that mean?'

' "Sunwise" means following the movement of the sun through the sky – going from the east to the south, and then to the west, and finally to the north. So what Nostradimwit appears to be saying is, "walk in a circle, starting at the well".'

'What earthly good would that do?'

The wizard scratched his white-haired head. 'I don't know.'

'Brilliant. And who's this *grene godde* it talks about?'

'I don't know that, either.'

'Well, I'm glad we've cleared that up,' said the dwarf sarcastically. 'Obviously a useful chap, this Nostradim-wit. Seriously, why don't we just call in the Camelot De-infestation Department, and let *them* investigate the smell?'

Gwydden shook his head. 'We're outside their area here. Anyway, they're chronically undermanned. Remember the great Rat Plague of '92? Fifteen thousand rats poured out of the sewers and overran the city, and all the CDD could send out was one unemployed wizard on a job retraining scheme.'

'He got rid of the rats, though,' said the dwarf. 'Turned himself into a giant piece of Stilton, and lured them all into a cellar which he'd previously lined with pie-crust. The whole city ate rat pie for weeks after.'

'I remember,' said the wizard with a shudder. 'I've hated rat pie ever since. Anyway, I'm going to uncap that well. You needn't come if you don't want to.'

'Oh, I'll come,' said the dwarf. 'It's got to be more interesting than gardening. When do you mean to start?'

The wizard glanced out of the window. 'Too late now – it's going dark. We'll start tomorrow, after break-fast.'

In the deepening dusk, three figures were lurking in a ditch on the edge of Redbrush Park.

'Cottonseed, stop fidgeting!' hissed the rightmost figure. 'I'm trying to reconnoitre, and you're distracting me.'

'I can't help it, Flopkin,' Cottonseed complained. 'This

stupid headband is tickling my ears. Why do we have to wear headbands, anyway?'

'Because we're the Warren Freedom Fighters. Freedom fighters always wear headbands, it's traditional.'

'But why can't we just be the Magnificent Three, like before?'

'Weren't you at the last meeting?' demanded the leader of the Freedom Fighters irritably. 'We changed the name to highlight the political nature of our movement. We are fighting against the class of the idle rich, in our historic struggle to establish a fairer and more egalitarian society.'

'I thought we were stealing lettuces from Macpherson.'

'It isn't stealing, it's redistribution of wealth. And my name isn't Flopkin any more. From now on, I'm Comrade Flopnik, Mopkin is Comrade Mopnik, and you're Comrade Cottonskovitski.'

'I don't want to be Comrade Cottonskovitski,' said Comrade Cottonskovitski in a sulky voice. 'I can't spell it. And I don't see what difference it makes, calling ourselves different names.'

'Names are *important*. Mopkin, I mean Comrade Mopnik, can't you keep the little perisher quiet?'

'Right you are, Flomrade Copnik,' said Comrade Mopnik cheerfully.

There was a sharp scuffle.

'*Ow!* Get off, Mopkin.'

'Sorry, Flomrade Cottonseed. Just following Flomrade Copnik's orders.'

'Aha!' The leader of the Freedom Fighters slapped his haunch with his paw. 'Macpherson's gone indoors at last. Come on – let's go and do a nifty bit of redistributing.'

It took Comrade Mopnik several seconds to redistribute himself so that Comrade Cottonskovitski could stand up, but then the three of them were off, scampering across the no man's land to the kitchen-garden.

'Over here, you two, and grab a lettuce.'

'Flomrade?'

'What?'

'Macpherson's coming out again, and he's pointing his gun at us.'

'Hell! OK, everyone back to the ditch! *Run!!*'

BANG!!

'Damn, damn, damn. Everyone safely in the ditch?'

'Yes, Flomrade.'

'Good. Oh, *damn!*'

A gloomy silence.

'Comrade Flopnik?'

'Yes, Comrade Cottonskovitski?'

'I'm hungry. Is it all right if I eat my headband?'

Dusk deepened into night. The Forest, wild and unkempt but basically friendly by day, gleefully swirled a black cloak round itself and became its alter ego: a place of sinister shadows and a few inadequate patches of moonlight, filled with desperate rustlings and the flapping of nocturnal wings. Occasional squeals from the depths of the leafy underworld told of weasels mugging voles, squirrels dragged from their beds and molested by stoats, and owls giving mice a free one-way ride to the top of the nearest oak-tree.

It was like this every night in the Forest. In the distant heavens, a wan half-moon and a few pale stars hung about like nervous rookie cops on the edge of a notorious gangsterland. No-one interfered with the murderous goings-on among the leaves and bracken. There was no-one who could interfere. Nature is lawless, and knows neither parliament nor judiciary nor police. But at least there was nothing in the forest that felt malevolence towards living things, not because they were enemies or potential meals, but merely because they were alive and healthy.

Or there hadn't been, until tonight.

Down one of the narrow forest tracks came *something*, a huge and shapeless something that left a stinking, glistening trail and terrified nearby animals and birds into silence until long after it had gone. Where the glistening trail lay, leaves and bracken shone with a pallid, unhealthy luminescence.

At a fork in the track, Archon paused. Making his mind up, he continued along his way.

Rounding a corner, he came at last to a wide open space. This must once have been rolling parkland, but now the area was unkempt, a wilderness of overgrown meadow sprinkled with scrubby bushes. In the centre stood a large, squarish building. Moonlight reflected faintly in its upper windows.

Not much farther now, thought Archon.

He undulated past the house. As he came abreast of the east wing, he stopped. So far, he had been following a steady signal like the scent of blood, a signal that led towards a single objective. But now the signal had split in two. One source seemed to be located in the house. The other was away to one side, among the tangled trees and bushes at the edge of the forest.

The shape-shifter wavered, turning quizzical eye-stalks this way and that.

Finally he made his mind up. Moving forward again, he drew away from the house and made for the bushes. He pushed and oozed his way through them, and suddenly came to a space recently cleared of vegetation. A low cottage stood in the centre. Some yards away, a hump of grey lichenous stone protruded from the earth.

This was the source of the attraction. Coming closer, the shape-shifter saw that the grey hump was an ancient well, its top sealed with a huge flat circular stone. He came right up to the well and waved his eye-stalks, peering at the capstone.

There was a dreadful smell lingering round the well. To the shape-shifter, it felt like coming home.

Or almost home. The capstone was an obstacle between Archon and his final objective. The capstone must be removed, and then what was under it could be released.

Archon hesitated. He could certainly remove the capstone, and that would set the next stage of the plan in motion at once. On the other hand, on the way here he had eaten a herd of cows and a pair of Shire horses, and he didn't feel much like unnecessary exertion just yet. He felt more like going to sleep.

He had waited a thousand years for this. A few hours wouldn't make any difference.

He oozed away from the well and found a secluded place where he could rest unnoticed among the rampant brambles and bushes. He settled down, and let his eye-stalks droop.

Minutes later, he was asleep.

The night passed slowly on.

Slugs, as has been noted already, tend to sleep late. It was getting on for eleven a.m. when Archon was finally roused by the sounds of hammering, levering, stone-breaking and a good deal of grumbling.

Oozing stealthily to the edge of the undergrowth, the shape-shifter saw two people labouring to remove the heavy capstone. Or rather, a stocky, red-faced, sweaty and bad-tempered person was doing the labouring, using a hammer and chisel and a crowbar, while a tall, thin, white-haired person in a grey robe was leaning on a shovel and giving instructions.

Since the two of them were saving Archon the trouble of uncapping the well himself, he settled down to watch. There was no need to eat them immediately. He could do that when they'd finished. Anyway, he wasn't hungry yet.

The capstone, which had been teetering on the edge of the well, finally fell edgewise to the ground with a dull thud, and rolled a few yards before coming to rest in a patch of nettles.

'Whoo . . . oof!' said Hergrim. He dropped the crowbar and leaned against the side of the well.

'Well done,' said Gwydden. 'I knew you could do it.'

The dwarf favoured him with a hard stare. 'Small . . . thanks . . . to you,' he panted.

'Well, someone has to direct operations. Anyway, manual labour isn't my forte.'

'How . . . conve . . . nient.'

The wizard wrinkled his nose. 'It really is awful, that smell, isn't it?' He leaned tentatively over the edge of the well, sniffed, and pulled a face. 'Ugh. Can't see anything down there, though. Just steps going down into the darkness.'

'Steps? Oh . . . damn.'

'What's the matter?'

Hergrim sat down on the wall and wiped his forehead. 'I suppose you'll want to climb down them.'

'Yes, of course.'

The dwarf made a wry face. 'It figures. In Dwarfheim we have an old saying: *Wizards rush in where wise dwarfs fear to tread.*'

'Really?'

'No, not really, I just made it up. It's a good saying, though, don't you think?'

'Very amusing,' said Gwydden drily. 'Have you got your breath back yet?'

'I think so, yes.'

'Come on, then. Let's see what's at the bottom of this well.'

Chapter Six

Archon watched as the two figures disappeared over the lip of the well. Cautiously, he followed them.

At the foot of the well, unless someone or something had disturbed it, should lie the object he had concealed there all those centuries ago.

Which unfortunately meant that the two interlopers would get there first.

Which also unfortunately meant that to prevent them making off with it, he would have to eat them, even though he wasn't hungry yet.

Archon sighed. He didn't much like eating between meals, which he regarded as unhealthy. Still, it could have been worse. The red-haired biped, though stocky, was short, and the white-haired one, though tall, was thin. Compared with the cows and horses he had polished off last night, they were no more than a light snack.

He belched, and pulled his distended stomach in as far as it would go. He would find room in there somehow.

He oozed up over the edge of the well, peered down, and then oozed down inside, following the two figures who were descending the steps in front of him.

After thirty or forty steps, Hergrim stopped. This was getting dangerous. 'Hi, Gwydden! Can't you give us a light?'

There was a pause, and then a pallid white glow appeared below – a light from Sephira, the wizard's staff. It wasn't very bright.

'Is that the best you can do?'

'Yes it is,' Gwydden called back irritably. 'You'll just have to mind your footing. Ah, good, I've reached the bottom.'

'About time,' said Hergrim, relieved.

A moment later, he was standing beside the wizard, who was peering alternately to left and right by the light of his flickering staff. They were in a broad tunnel with a rocky, uneven floor.

'The bed of the stream,' said Gwydden. 'Dry, as you said it would be.' He sniffed. 'And that smell is stronger again.' He pointed along the tunnel. 'The Hall is in that direction, and that's where the smell is coming from. Which bears out the theory that there's something unpleasant under the east wing.'

'And that's the way we're going, I suppose?'

'Of course.'

'Of course,' muttered the dwarf.

He followed the wizard down the tunnel, stepping gingerly on the broken surface of the floor. Conversation, like the stream, soon dried up. Hergrim found himself listening to the only sounds he could hear.

'My boots, a steady *clump clump*,' he murmured. 'Gwydden's sandals, *flap flap*. Wait a minute – what's that? A sort of *squish squish*. It's coming from behind us.'

He turned and looked back. They had left the well far behind, and the small area of daylight it cast on the rocky floor was out of sight. The darkness behind him was impenetrable.

'What sort of animal goes *squish squish*?' the dwarf wondered. 'A penguin wearing flippers? An octopus? I don't like it. There's something unpleasant on our trail, or I'm a goblin.'

He quickened his pace slightly, and in due course managed to come almost abreast of the wizard. 'Gwydden!' he hissed. His voice made a whispering echo that ran along the rock walls and died away.

'Mm?'

'I think we're being followed!'

'Eh?' The wizard stopped sharply and looked at him. Their faces were pale and scared-looking in the light from the staff. 'Followed? By whom?'

'No idea. Listen.'

They listened intently.

'I can't hear anything,' said Gwydden after a while. He coughed, gagging. 'Come on, let's get this over with. The air in here smells worse than a troll's armpit.'

They went on.

Archon, who had halted when he saw the wizard's light stop moving, resumed his glutinous progress. The object he sought hadn't been at the bottom of the well, after all. Presumably the stream, before it dried up, had carried it along this tunnel and deposited it somewhere.

When the two interlopers found it, that would be the time to eat them.

'Oh,' said the wizard, and stopped in his tracks.

'What?'

'We've come to a dead end.'

There was no denying it. A yard in front of them, the tunnel ended in a blank wall of bricks.

'It must be the foundations of the east wing,' said the wizard thoughtfully. 'In which case . . .'

'In which case,' the dwarf said, continuing his thought, 'the east wing was built after the stream was diverted. And something which was in this tunnel is now under the Hall.'

'Yes.' The wizard sniffed the air. 'The stench is worse than ever. Whatever's causing it must be just the other side of this wall.'

The wizard held his staff up, and they gazed at the obstruction.

'If we brought that hammer and chisel down here, you could knock a hole through this,' said the wizard. 'Probably only take a few minutes.'

The dwarf snorted. 'You don't know much about buildings, do you? You can't just go blithely knocking holes in foundations. You need props, underpinning, all that sort of thing. Not to mention picks, shovels, drills, wheelbarrows, carts, horses, ropes, pulleys, timber . . .'

'All right, scrub that idea.' Gwydden lowered his staff. 'Well, I think we've reached an impasse. We may as well head back.'

They turned, and took a few steps along the tunnel.

Squish squish. Squish squish. Squish squish.

Squelch.

'Gwydden?' said the dwarf, after a long pause.

'Yes?'

'What the hell is *that?*'

'You mean the big slimy wobbly thing with the eye-stalks?'

'Yes, that's what I mean.'

'I don't know. I think it might be *ye shapelesse one* that the prophecy talks about.'

'I was afraid so. It's blocking the tunnel, isn't it?'

'Yes. Did you bring your axe?'

'No.'

'Pity.'

'You know,' said the dwarf casually, 'this would be a pretty good time for you to come up with a spell of some sort. In fact, all things considered, I can't really think of a better time. How about it?'

'It's dangerous,' said the wizard, not taking his eyes off the slug.

'Dangerous? Why dangerous?'

'Because of Particle Escape Theory.'

'What's that?'

'Whenever a spell is cast,' the wizard explained rapidly in a hushed voice, 'it changes the particles of matter in the immediate area into other particles. However, a lot of particles take exception to being changed into something else without being asked, and they try to escape. Those that succeed can cause unforeseen side-effects.'

'Like what?'

'Like the roof of this tunnel caving in, for instance.'

'Ah.' The dwarf reflected on this for a moment. 'Yes, that could be a disadvantage.'

'Quite.'

'So what do we do?'

'We wait,' said the wizard. 'And see what the slug is going to do.'

Archon was considering the situation. Normally he would have had no problem about eating a mere two people, even between meals, but the Shire horses from last night's supper had given him a touch of dyspepsia (it was his own fault for not chewing the horseshoes properly) and he was afraid that if he ate anyone else right now he might be sick. Also he was not happy about Gwydden's staff. He had a feeling that the flame at the tip might burn the roof of his mouth.

At length he made his mind up. Turning round, he oozed swiftly back along the tunnel.

'Well,' said Gwydden, after they had waited a few

moments to see if the slug had really gone. 'Thank goodness that's over. Come on – back to the cottage. I could do with a hot bath.'

From the tangled bushes in the corner of the garden, Archon watched the dwarf and wizard climb out of the well and go back into the cottage. It was evident that he was not going to get to the object of his search by going down the well. It must be under the Hall. The question was, how was he to get at it?

There was only one answer to this question. He would have to go to the Hall and investigate.

The inhabitant of the island had had a disturbed night. This was entirely the fault of Emily the goat. At five a.m. she wandered into the bath-house and quietly ate part of the inhabitant's bed. At six a.m., just as he was getting off to sleep again, she was noisily sick over the rest of it, in which he happened to be lying at the time. At seven a.m., after a good wash, he climbed up onto the bath-house roof, where he dozed fitfully until noon. As a result of being asleep for half the night, half asleep for half the remainder, and less than half awake the rest of the time, he was never sure whether what he thought he saw happen that morning was real or just a dream.

He was looking across the overgrown park towards the old cottage. The word BOGHOLE climbed peacefully into the sky over and over again from the chimney. Then, from out of the trees, a grey shape appeared, undulating with frightening speed across the ground. It passed the lake, and came eventually to the south-west corner of the Hall. There it stopped for a moment, and, as the inhabitant watched, *changed*. It vanished from view, and a few seconds later was replaced by a white-bearded man in a black robe and a pointy hat, who knocked at the scullery door. The door was opened, and a moment later, the man in the robe went inside.

The inhabitant rubbed his eyes. Had he really seen a giant slug change into a wizard? If so, was it a slug masquerading as a wizard, or a wizard masquerading as a slug?

The inhabitant yawned. It was hard to understand what went on sometimes. Best to stay out of it, if possible.

He went back to sleep.

If, indeed, he had ever been awake.

'This is Merlin, ma'am,' said Macpherson, leading Archon into the scullery. The gardener was quite excited. It wasn't every day that so important a visitor came to the Hall.

Mrs Tod, however, was not so easily impressed. 'So you're the great Merlin, are you?' she said, gazing at her visitor with extreme suspicion through her pince-nez.

'That's right, ma'am,' said Archon. He bowed to her in what he hoped was a sufficiently respectful manner. 'Merlin Ambrosius, at your service.'

'Hmph.' Mrs Tod stared at him witheringly down the length of her long russet snout. 'I do not approve of wizards. If God had meant us to dabble in magic, he would never have given us housework.'

'Yes. Well. That is to say – mm,' said Archon. He had unfortunately never learned to hold his own in conversation, especially when people started to argue with him. If anyone disagreed with him, he usually solved the problem by eating them, after which they were allowed to disagree with him as much as they liked (not many did, his digestive processes being very efficient). Mrs Tod's sharp tongue seemed to attack him like a rapier wielded by a master swordsman – too quick and deadly to avoid. He wondered briefly whether to turn himself back into a slug and eat Mrs Tod and Macpherson on the spot, but decided against it. It would be easier to find the Hall's buried secret with their help than without it.

'I was rather hoping,' he said, 'to look round the Hall. I believe it's haunted. I'm a student of that sort of thing. Little hobby of mine.'

'Haunted?' echoed Mrs Tod, sounding like Dame Edith Evans on the subject of handbags. 'Certainly not. This is a respectable house. We have no spirits here, do we, Macpherson?'

'Och, no, indeed, ma'am,' said the gardener sadly. Spirits were a thing of the past for Macpherson, whose last dram had been consumed at Hogmanay north of the border, ten years before.

'You'd better take this—' Mrs Tod looked Archon up and down distastefully '—this *person* and show him the east wing. After which, you can go out to the garden and get me a nice lettuce to have with lunch.'

'Aye, ma'am,' said the gardener stolidly. He led Archon out of the scullery and through the same dingy passages recently traversed by Gwydden and Hergrim.

When they got to the library, Macpherson tried the door, but it refused to open. 'The dang thing's finally stuck,' he muttered. 'Aye, it's muckle warped in the frame.' He sniffed the air. 'That pong's dreadful jist here. Can ye smell it, Sir Merlin?'

Archon opened his eyes with a jerk, and wiped the blissful smile off his face. To him, the smell was sheer delight. 'Er – yes. Yes, I can.'

'It's the drains, I'm thinking,' said the gardener. 'There's mebbe a dead rabbit stuck down there.'

Archon frowned. 'Why would there be a dead rabbit in the drains?'

'Och, they're cunning wee beasties,' said Macpherson. 'They'll try anything tae steal ma lettuces. They've a warren not far frae the hoose. Mebbe they're digging some o' their nasty tunnels under the east wing.'

Archon's face became thoughtful. 'Tunnels? Really? How interesting.'

'Aye,' said the gardener gloomily. 'They keep undergroond awa' from ma gun most o' the time. Wee, sleekit, cow'rin', tim'rous little buggers, they are. One o' these days I'll catch one, an' then—' he grinned wolfishly '—rabbit pie for supper.'

'Very nice. Macpherson?'

'Aye?'

'Is there any way to get *underneath* the library?'

The gardener shook his head. 'Ye canna. 'Tis all paved o'er wi' flagstones. An' a guid thing, if ye ask me. There's somethin' muckle bad under this libraira. I dinna mess wi' ghosties an' ghoulies an' things that dinna go bump in the night.'

'Don't you mean things that *do* go bump in the night?'

'Och, no. 'Tis the things that dinna make any noise at all ye want tae be afeard of.' The gardener shook his head ominously. 'If they dinna mak' a soond, then ye dinna wake up when they creep up on ye tae suck the marrow oot o' yer bones.'

'I'm sure you're right.' *Silly old fool*, thought the shape-shifter impatiently. *If I wasn't still queasy from those horseshoes, I'd show him that the things to be really afraid of are the ones that go squelch. Anyway, it seems there's no way of getting under the Hall from inside, so it'll have to be from outside.*

Rabbits, eh? Hm . . .

'Well, Macpherson, can you take me back to the scullery, please? I really ought to be going.'

'So soon? But will ye no stay for lunch, Sir Merlin?'

'I can't, I'm afraid. I have things to attend to in Camelot. Spells, enchantments, that sort of thing.' Archon waved his hand in a manner that suggested that nothing magical could occur in the city without his personal supervision. 'When I get back, I'll report your infestation with rabbits to the Camelot Health Department. Risk of disease, that sort of thing, you see?'

'Aye, aye,' nodded the gardener. 'They're flea-ridden little beasties, right enough.'

'Quite. So perhaps you wouldn't mind telling me where exactly this warren is?'

Macpherson went to the nearest window and pointed across the Park. 'Over yonder – where the thick undergrowth starts. D'ye see?'

'Yes, I see. What's the matter?'

'Och, I was jist looking at yon sky. 'Tis a braw strange colour. We're in for a muckle storm soon, or I'm a Sassenach.'

Boadicea had been right about the weather. The cloudless blue sky had turned a nasty yellow, the colour of regurgitated fried eggs. An oppressive heat had settled over Camelot. Fat, bilious clouds squatted on top of the buildings like malevolent toads. The air was thick with bottled-up rain and constipated thunder. It was the sort of weather you only get when evil magic is brewing, or on a walking holiday in the Lake District.

It was so oppressive that it was making people in the city distinctly bad-tempered.

Uther leaned out of his bedroom window and watched the bustle and turmoil in the streets below. The cries of the street-traders were always raucous, but today they were decidedly irritable.

'Cherries! Ripe cherries!'

'Apples! Lovely juicy apples!'

'Come on, you lot! Isn't anybody going to buy these 'ere bleedin' cherries?'

'Now then, missis, wot about these 'ere apples? I can't stand here all bleedin' day!'

'You won't find riper cherries than these anywhere! Much nicer than his maggoty old apples, these are!'

'Take no notice of 'im! My apples can knock spots off his rotten cherries!'

'Mouldy, maggoty apples!'

'Rotting, slimy cherries!'

It would be a good thing, Uther thought, when the rain came.

A little later, he wandered down into the garden to see Boadicea.

The hen-woman was standing with her muscular arms folded, smoking her pipe, gazing up at the sultry yellow sky. When she saw Uther approaching, she gave him a grave and serious nod. 'The great storm be a-coming,' she said matter-of-factly.

'It certainly looks like it,' Uther agreed, joining her. 'We're in for a real downpour.'

'Oh, I bain't talking about the rain,' said Boadicea scornfully. 'I be talking about what comes after. Doom and destruction, and a great evil awakening, and terrible tribulations in the land.'

'Oh, right,' said Uther, nodding. 'Yes, you did say something of the sort once before. So what exactly is going to happen?'

'I dunno egg-*zackly*,' said the hen-woman. 'The hen-droppings don't say things egg-*zackly*. They *hints* at things. They indicates the unfoldin' of cosmic patterns. They shows you forces, and destinies, and great majestic sweeps of hist'ry.'

'Ah, I see.'

'And the weather,' said Boadicea. 'That's what I

mostly use 'em for, the weather. You can ignore cosmic forces and sweeps of hist'ry if you're a gardener, but you durstn't ignore the weather.'

'No,' agreed Uther. 'I see that. So you can't really be sure what this doom and destruction will look like? Only it would be useful, you see, if I knew what to expect, so I could make preparations. I mean, should I put the Knights of the Slightly Pear-Shaped Table[1] on Red Alert, or ought I to be getting Merlin to cast a few spells?'

Boadicea shrugged her heavy shoulders. 'I dunno. The hen-droppings be a bit ambiguous when it comes to detail.'

'Oh well. Never mind. I'll be getting back, then. Things to do, you know. Decrees to write, traitors to behead. Ha ha. Ha. Hm.' Uther turned and stumped off.

Boadicea watched the King as he walked slowly back to the castle. His head was down, and he was scuffing the ground in a preoccupied way with his feet.

'He bain't happy,' she murmured. 'And neither be I.' She replaced the pipe and glanced up at the constipated sky. 'Rain tomorrow, mebbe. An' the day after . . . who knows?'

She looked over at the hen-coops, and frowned. That was another thing. Rosemary Featherbrain was still refusing to let her collect her eggs – or egg, because there still seemed to be only the one. *Of course,* thought Boadicea, *I could grab her and lift her bodily off the nest and take the egg anyway, but . . .* But she didn't like to treat her hens like that. Hens were people. Very stupid people, admittedly, and covered with feathers, but people nevertheless.

[1]Originally the Round Table, but the carpenter was a bit careless getting it out through the workshop door.

BANG!

'All right, Comrades?' panted a voice from the depths of the ditch. 'Everyone safe?'

'Just about, Flomrade Copnik. Macpherson's shooting is getting more accurate.'

'Tell me about it, Mopnik,' said Flopkin sourly. He peered at his white tail, which had a scorch mark along one side. 'Damn. What about you, Comrade Cottonskovitski? You all right?'

From the other end of the ditch came a sound suspiciously like a whimper, and a small and pathetic voice whined, 'Stubbed my toe on a tree-root.'

'Is that all? Report properly, Comrade. What is your status?'

'I'm fed up, that's my status. My toe hurts. And I'm hungry.'

'We're *all* hungry, Flomrade,' said Mopkin. 'That's what being a freedom fighter is all about, isn't it, Flomrade Copnik? I remember you telling us that at the last briefing. *Stay hungry*, you said, *and you'll be tough.*'

'I must certainly be tough by now,' said Cottonseed mournfully. 'My skin's hanging off my bones like clothes off a scarecrow.'

'That's right,' Mopkin continued. '*Stay tough, hang loose.* I remember all your slogans, Flomrade Copnik. *A ditch in time saves three. All for one and one for the pot.* I especially liked that one you came up with when that bolshy rabbit, Robespierre, complained that the warren had no lettuce to eat. *Let them eat carrots*, you said. Wonderful, it was.'

'But we didn't *have* any bloody carrots, did we?' grumbled Cottonseed.

'That's not the point, Flomrade Cottonseed. Flomrade

Copnik didn't really mean, *Let them eat carrots*. He meant it *sym-bollickly*.'

'I'm not sure about *sym*,' said Cottonseed, 'but most of what Comrade Flopnik says is a load of *bollickly*, if you ask me.'

The leader of the Freedom Fighters bristled. 'If that's your attitude, you can get out of this ditch. We don't want bolshy whingers in this troop. This is a fighting troop, this is.'

'Oh yeah?' jeered Cottonseed. 'Who do we ever fight? All we ever do is try to steal lettuces. And *fail*.'

'Well, that's what rabbits *do*,' said Mopkin reasonably. 'Like the old rhyme says: *He who fights and runs away, lives to fight another day; he who fights and stays to die, ends up in a rabbit pie.*'

'I wish I *was* in a rabbit pie,' muttered Cottonseed. 'There might be some carrots in it that I could eat.'

Flopkin had suddenly had enough. 'Look!' he said, in a very loud voice that made the other two jump. 'You say *you're* fed up – how d'you think *I* feel? The warren made me the leader because I had both brains and courage, which, let's face it, is a rare thing in a rabbit. I wish someone else *would* take over, but there isn't anyone. Do *you* want to be leader, Mopkin?'

'Me?' Mopkin's stolid voice was filled with alarm. 'No, Flomrade Copnik. I'm not clever enough.'

'Do *you* want to be leader, Cottonseed?'

'I just want to go home,' said Cottonseed in a small, unhappy voice.

'Well, there you are. And there's no-one back at the warren who could do it – they don't know what time of day it is back there[1]. So it has to be me.' Flopkin flung

[1]Only exceptionally well-to-do rabbits, like the one in *Alice in Wonderland*, can afford watches.

his paws out in a grand, despairing gesture. 'Isn't there *anyone* who could take over this miserable, thankless task?'

His cry died away, and there was an uneasy silence. Then, from just outside the ditch, so close by that it made them all leap into the air in fright, a deep voice said, *'I'll* be your leader, if you'll have me.'

'Wh-who said that?' stammered Flopkin.

There was a rustling in the grass, and a dark shape dropped down into the ditch beside them. They shrank back instinctively, peering at the newcomer. It was a large buck rabbit, with black fur and dark, piercing eyes.

'I'll be your leader,' said the rabbit again. 'I've got brains. *And* courage. And I can save your warren from starvation. If you do as I say, you can live easy for the rest of your lives and eat carrots all day long.'

'Carrots?' repeated Cottonseed, in an awestruck voice. 'Did he say carrots?'

'Carrots, eh?' Mopkin's slow voice betrayed a burgeoning interest. 'Did you hear that, Flomrade Copnik? Carrots all day long. Sounds good, eh?'

Flopkin stared suspiciously at the bulky shape whose long ears were silhouetted against the sky. 'Look, I don't know who you are, but you can't just come barging in here and take over. Who are you, and what warren are you from?'

'My name is unimportant,' said the rabbit.

'Pleased to meet you, Mr Unimportant,' said Mopkin, holding out a friendly paw. 'My name's Mopkin. This is Flomrade Copnik, and this little chap at the back is Flomrade Cottonseed.'

'I know who you all are,' said the rabbit. 'I've been listening to you for some time. And when I say that my name is unimportant, Comrade Mopkin, I don't mean that Unimportant is my name. You can call me Comrade

Petrov, if you like. As for my warren, I don't exactly have one. I'm what you might call a nomad.'

'*All* rabbits have a warren,' said Flopkin, his voice heavy with suspicion. 'Whoever heard of a nomadic rabbit? I don't believe a word of all this.'

'If *you* don't want to believe me, that's up to you,' said the rabbit. 'But what about the rest of the warren? I think everyone has a right to hear what I've got to say, don't you?'

'I don't know,' muttered Flopkin uneasily.

'What d'you mean, you don't know?' cried Cottonseed excitedly. 'If he's got a plan for getting an endless supply of carrots, then we ought to jump at it! Let's get back to the warren now!' Cottonseed clambered out of the ditch, and sat on his haunches looking down at the others. 'Mopkin, are you coming?'

'Well . . .' Mopkin looked doubtful. 'I'd like to, Cottonseed, but I don't want to upset Flomrade Copnik.'

'Oh, Mopkin!' Cottonseed stamped his foot. 'Do you think Flopkin can give us carrots for a whole year?'

'Well, no, but—'

'So what are you waiting for?'

'All right. But only if Flomrade Copnik doesn't mind.' Mopkin turned to his erstwhile leader. 'Flomrade, do you mind if we go with Comrade Petrov to the warren, please?'

It was one of those moments when history hangs in the balance[1]. If Flopkin had made a strenuous effort to

---

[1]As the saying goes. But a balance has two pans, and presumably history is only in one pan, so what is supposed to be in the other? Geography? A-level French? That's the trouble with these old sayings - when you analyse them, they're as full of holes as a moth-breeder's underpants.

keep Mopkin on his side, things might have turned out differently. But Flopkin was tired and disillusioned and filled with *Weltschmerz*, which is even less sustaining than a limp lettuce. He wavered for a moment and then caved in.

'Oh, go to the wretched warren,' he muttered miserably. 'It's time someone else took over as leader, and I suppose it might as well be this Petrov character. He can't do any worse than me.'

'Yo!' Cottonseed chanted unfeelingly. 'Back to the warren! Back to the future! It's carrots, carrots, all the way!'

With a last sympathetic glance at Flopkin, Mopkin climbed out of the ditch, followed by the darker, heavier bulk of Comrade Petrov. Lastly, Flopkin hauled himself out and stood dejectedly alongside his colleagues.

'Right,' said Petrov. 'You lead, Comrade Cottonseed. Comrade Mopnik, you go second. I'll go third. Comrade Flopnik, you bring up the rear. And think carrots, men – carrots!'

'Yo! Carrots!' chanted Cottonseed.

They marched away into the undergrowth. As they marched, Cottonseed led them in an optimistic carrot-gathering song handed down from father to son by generations of hungry rabbits. Mopkin joined in lustily, and Comrade Petrov hummed cautiously and tried to pick up the tune as it went along. At the rear of the column, Flopkin did not sing, but trudged along in a depressed and gloomy silence.

Chapter Seven

The council chamber in the warren was full of rabbits. Archon greedily scanned the ranks of furry bodies. *They'd make a deliciously crunchy mid-morning snack*, he thought, *and I've started to feel rather peckish. But no – I need these rabbits to help me fulfil my destiny. I must try and remember that. I must also stop drooling – someone might notice.*

When all the rabbits had taken their seats, an expectant hush descended. All eyes were turned to the four rabbits standing at the front, especially Flopkin, who had been the spokesman for the Freedom Fighters on previous occasions.

Flopkin, however, stared at the floor and said nothing.

Mopkin gave him a helpful nudge. 'Flomrade Copnik, aren't you going to introduce Comrade Petrov to the warren?'

'For goodness' sake, Mopkin,' said Flopkin, turning on him with sudden savagery, 'will you stop calling me *Flomrade*? There's no such word. It's *Comrade*, you stupid oaf. You've got cloth ears and nothing between them, that's your trouble.'

Mopkin gazed at him with a hurt expression. 'Sorry, Flom – I mean Comrade,' he mumbled. 'Sorry.' He lapsed into an unhappy silence.

This was too much for Cottonseed. 'How dare you

talk to Mopkin like that, Flopkin?' he demanded, his ears bristling with righteous indignation. 'You're a tyrant, that's what you are. It's time you were replaced.'

The rabbits in the audience shuffled uneasily. They weren't used to the Freedom Fighters fighting each other. It was a worrying development. In the front row, a small rabbit kitten started to cry.

'All right, Cottonseed,' said Flopkin, glaring at him. 'Why don't *you* introduce Comrade Petrov? You're the one who's so enthusiastic about him.'

Cottonseed met his gaze squarely. 'All right, I will.' He turned to the audience. 'Fellow rabbits,' he began, a little squeakily, because this was his first experience of public speaking, 'this is Comrade Petrov. He is an Important Rabbit. He has Ideas. He will Save Our Warren.'

His words, and especially the capital letters, rang impressively around the chamber. The rabbits gazed at Comrade Petrov, who stood before them, solid and monumental, like Joseph Stalin facing the crowds in Red Square from the balcony of the Kremlin.

'Why?' said a voice.

Cottonseed looked taken aback. He peered into the audience, trying to make out who had spoken. 'You mean *how*, don't you?'

'No,' said the voice. It was coming from a huddle of rabbits near the back, but Cottonseed couldn't make out which of them it was. 'I mean *why*. Why does he want to save our warren? What about his own warren?'

'He hasn't got a warren,' said Cottonseed. 'He's a nomad.'

This revelation was met with silence. The idea of a nomadic rabbit, as Flopkin had intimated, was not an easy one to grasp.

'But what happened to his *own* warren?' the voice persisted.

Cottonseed glanced helplessly at Archon.

Archon roused himself from a happy dream in which he was eating through a warrenful of juicy rabbits, sucked in the saliva that was dribbling from the corners of his mouth, and said, 'It collapsed.'

'Why?' said the suspicious voice again.

'Men,' explained Archon. 'They built a house on top of it.'

'Oh, I see,' said the voice, sounding happier. There was a general murmur of understanding in the audience. They knew all about men – dangerous creatures, with their guns and their spades and their dogs. There was a pause, and then the voice said uncertainly, 'So how did *you* escape, exactly?'

'I was outside the warren,' said Archon. 'Hunting.'

'Hunting?' said several voices in astonishment. Flopkin, Mopkin and Cottonseed turned amazed faces towards Archon.

Idiot, Archon said to himself. *Wrong species. Hunting is something that happens* to *rabbits. Wait a moment, though. Perhaps I can use this. After all, if you're going to tell a lie, tell a biggie.* He drew himself up and stared over their heads in an even more Stalinesque pose. '*You* might call it foraging,' he said loftily. 'But *I* call it hunting, because that's how I think of it. It's time we rabbits stopped thinking of ourselves as the hunted, and started thinking of ourselves as hunters.'

'You mean we ought to carry guns and shoot lettuces with them?' said the ever-present voice. There was an uneasy sniggering in the audience.

'I *mean*,' said Archon, so loudly that the sniggering stopped dead in its tracks, 'that we rabbits have been pushed around for Far Too Long. It's Time We Did the Pushing. It's Time We Rabbits Took Over.' His capital letters resonated even more forcefully than Cottonseed's.

The warren stared at the black rabbit. They were used to Flopkin's way of rousing them ('now come on, team, let's put our backs into it and show what this warren can do') but this was something new. There was something about Comrade Petrov that made you *believe* what he said, even though the words themselves didn't seem to make much sense. The rabbits gazed at their prospective new leader and struggled to accommodate him in their mental universe.

'But how?' said the voice at the back, belatedly asking the question Cottonseed had expected earlier. 'How can we take over? Take over what?'

Archon smiled inwardly. This was the moment. He could tell from their air of rapt expectancy that he had them in the palm of his paw. Only Flopkin was still staring at the floor, as if trying to pretend that none of this was happening.

'Listen, all of you,' said the black rabbit. 'I'm going to tell you about my Plan.'

'I still think,' said Hergrim, 'that you ought to leave well alone.' He sniggered, and poured himself a second pint of Frigga's Revenge.

'If you crack that stupid joke once more,' said Gwydden irritably, helping himself to a second cup of tea, 'I'll turn your beard green and set fire to your axe. Can't you see that there may be something *dangerous* under the east wing? Pass the ginger nuts, please.'

Hergrim took three biscuits from the plate and pushed it across the table. 'That's exactly why I think you shouldn't touch it. I mean, presumably it's been there for a long time without doing anyone any harm. Surely it can stay there a while longer?'

'Well . . . I don't know.' The wizard nibbled uneasily on a ginger nut. 'That giant slug is clearly something to do with the prophecy. Maybe Nostradimwit wasn't such a lunatic as we all thought. Two parts of the prophecy have turned up – the well and *ye shapelesse one*. I don't think we have any choice – we have to try and see what's at the bottom of it.'

The dwarf sighed. 'All right. What do you propose to do?'

'Well, we can start by warning Mrs Tod and Macpherson that something unwholesome is wandering around the Redbrush Estate, and that there may be something under the Hall that needs looking into.'

The dwarf drained his beer, set down the tankard, and mopped the froth out of his beard with the edge of the tablecloth. 'Well, if you want to go traipsing over there and alarming them unnecessarily, that's up to you. Personally, I think you'd do better to let sleeping slugs lie.'

Gwydden glanced out of the window. It was starting to get dark. 'We can't do it now, it's too late. We'll go tomorrow.'

'And after that?'

'After that, we have to find this *grene godde*. Whoever he is.'

'*Goe sunnewyse from ye welle,*' said Hergrim. 'Perhaps it just means east to west.'

'Maybe,' said the wizard doubtfully. '*Is* there a path running due west from the well?'

'Not that I've noticed.'

'Me neither. Which means hacking our way through undergrowth, which surely can't be what Nostradimwit meant. I think it means something else. Perhaps I'll have a brain-wave about it tomorrow.'

Hergrim sniggered again, but the wizard pretended not to hear him.

* * *

135

'And that,' said Archon, 'is my Plan. We extend the warren by digging a tunnel under Redbrush Hall. We come up through the floor at dead of night when everyone is asleep. We capture Mrs Tod and Macpherson. And we take the place over.'

He waited for a response, but the silence in the chamber was so deep you could have dropped a skyscraper into it.

'It can't fail,' he said. 'And when it's over, you'll never have to worry about getting enough to eat again. *You* will be the owners of Redbrush Hall. *You* will control the kitchen-garden. *You* will own all the lettuces, and carrots, and whatever else Macpherson grows there.'

'Artichokes,' said someone wistfully.

'Runner beans,' said someone else.

'Swedes!'

'Parsnips!'

Parsnips, whispered the rabbits, their eyes growing large and round. In their wildest dreams they had never imagined having their very own supply of parsnips.

'And thistles,' said Mopkin.

Everyone turned and stared at him.

'I've seen 'em,' said Mopkin. 'There's a corner of the garden where Macpherson grows thistles. It's because he's Scottish.'

'Yes, but we can't eat thistles, can we?' said Cottonseed. 'Be sensible, Mopkin. We're talking about *food.'*

'Thistles *are* food,' said Mopkin. 'If you happen to be a donkey.'

'But we *don't* happen to be donkeys,' said Cottonseed irritably. 'Do stick to the point, Mopkin.' He turned to Archon. 'Go on, Comrade Petrov. We're all listening.'

'Er, well,' said Archon, momentarily distracted by a mental picture of a composite creature, part rabbit and part donkey, with enormous ears, hooves and a fluffy white tail, munching on a giant thistle. 'So what do you say? Are you going to follow me and carry out this glorious Plan? Or are you going to follow Flopkin, and carry on being hungry, scared and miserable?'

In the silence that followed, Flopkin, who at this moment was feeling more hungry, scared and miserable than he had felt in his entire life, raised his eyes from the floor and looked around. He saw row upon row of expressions that were a mixture of insane hope and pure terror.

'But,' said a voice at the back hesitantly. Flopkin thought it sounded like the one that had been heckling earlier. It sounded a good deal less sure of itself now.

'Yes?' said Archon, after waiting a little while. 'But what?'

'But we can't do it,' said the voice. It was whining a bit, Flopkin noticed. 'All this stuff about coming up under the floor and capturing the Hall. Rabbits can't do that sort of thing. Now if we were, say, weasels—'

'Or stoats,' put in another voice.

'Or ferrets,' chimed in a third.

'Yes,' said the first heckler, warming to his theme, 'if we were *fierce* animals, it'd be different. I bet weasels and stoats and ferrets could seize a place like Redbrush Hall and imprison its owners with no trouble. And I expect they could hold onto it, too.'

'Unless some even fiercer animals captured it back,' the second heckler suggested. 'Like, say, a badger.'

'Or a water rat.'

'Or a mole.'

'Or a toad.'

'Look,' said Archon, who was beginning to feel as if he had strayed into a different story, '*trust* me. It *will* work. You *can* do it. You *are* fierce.' He looked round at the scared faces. 'Or you will be, anyway, when the time comes. It's just a matter of believing in yourselves.'

Why do I have to waste my time talking this nonsense? he thought irritably. *I wish I could just eat the little perishers and have done with it. Look at them. Believe in themselves? The only thing they believe in is being shot in the behind with a barrel-full of carpet-tacks. Perhaps this was a stupid idea after all. Perhaps I'd better just dig under the Hall by myself, and risk being discovered by Mrs Tod and Macpherson.*

But it would take too long. The more of us there are digging, the quicker we'll find it, and the quicker I can put my real Plan into operation.

I'd better force the issue. We'll be here till we all starve at this rate.

'May I suggest,' Archon said, in a loud, harsh voice, 'that All of You Make a Decision. Because Time Is Short. The Moment of Destiny is Here. You Must Choose.' The capital letters reverberated round the walls of the chamber like an underground atom bomb test.

In the hush that followed, Flopkin stirred himself unwillingly. *Better get this over with,* he said to himself. *Can't fight Destiny.*

'What we usually do in situations like this,' he said, wondering as he said it just when there had ever *been* a situation like this, 'is to have an election.'

'An Election?' Archon asked, turning and staring at him. 'Is that like a Duel? A Duel to the Death between You and Me, Winner Takes All?'

'Not exactly,' said Flopkin, wishing that Petrov would stop talking in capitals, because it was giving him a headache. 'We give every rabbit in the warren a leaf, and then everyone makes scratches on their leaf to represent their choice of candidate, like it might be one scratch for you and two for me, and then all the leaves are counted, and the one with the most leaves becomes the new leader.'

Archon gazed at Flopkin, wondering what on earth he was talking about. There was only one way to become a leader, and everyone knew what it was: you killed your opponent, and then, just to make sure, you ate the most important bits of him. What was all this drivel about leaves?

Obey local customs, said a cautionary voice in Archon's head, *until they get in your way.* After all, if the Election didn't result in him being made leader, he could always eat Flopkin afterwards.

'All right,' he said. 'I want everyone in the warren to be happy with this. Let's hold an Election.'

Organising the Election took a little time, but eventually all the leaves were gathered and separated into three piles – those with one scratch (for Flopkin), those with two (for Comrade Petrov), and those which had been seriously nibbled by the voter and were therefore classified as spoiled.

Cottonseed, who had been appointed Returning Officer, was counting the votes. The tension in the warren was tremendous. You could have cut the atmosphere with a knife[1].

Finally the Returning Officer for the Constituency of Lower Redbrush straightened up and announced the result. 'Flopkin, 3 votes. Comrade Petrov, 27. Nibbled papers, 18. I declare Comrade Petrov duly elected to be the new leader of the Redbrush Warren.'

There was a murmur of excitement among the gathered rabbits, and they surged towards their new leader to clap him on the back. The surge only lasted about two

[1]Which isn't saying much, because you can *always* cut the atmosphere with a knife. It's getting it to *stay* cut that's the tricky bit.

seconds, because there was something about the black rabbit that made clapping him on the back seem positively dangerous.

'All right, you miserable rabbits,' said Petrov in a voice that was suddenly harsh with contempt. 'If you want carrots, from now on you must all *work*.' His eyes roved slowly and hypnotically over the luckless voters. They all gazed back at him, unable to move. It was as if they had all been turned to stone[1].

'There will be new Rules in this warren from now on,' Archon continued. 'Comrade Cottonskovitski will be my secretary, and he will write the Rules, at my dictation.' Archon nodded to Cottonseed, who stiffened proudly at this great honour. 'The most important Rule is that no-one will eat unless he does a full day's digging in the Redbrush Hall tunnel. I shall choose five or six rabbits to direct the digging. They will discipline anyone found shirking.'

Flopkin, who had withdrawn into a dark corner under a tree-root, nodded to himself as he listened to the unfolding drama. He knew already some of the rabbits who would be chosen to bully the others. Gloat, a fat buck who picked on smaller and younger rabbits and made their lives a misery with ear-twistings and other petty tortures. Earmite, a thin rabbit who whispered untruths and slanders to anyone who would listen. Wormcast, a dull but physically strong rabbit, stupider than Mopkin and without Mopkin's good nature.

Life in the warren was going to be far from pleasant.

But the rest of them could not see that far. They were spellbound by Petrov's dominating presence, and the promise of a golden future filled with endless carrots and parsnips.

[1] i.e., Petrified.

Could the rabbits of the warren *really* capture Red-brush Hall?

We'll only know that, thought Flopkin, *when the new tunnel is finished. Somehow, I doubt if it's going to work out quite the way Petrov has promised.*

From inside the hen-house, Rosemary Featherbrain blinked suspiciously through the open door whenever the vast malodorous bulk of the hen-woman passed by. *Not on your nelly,* she said to herself. *This egg is mine. This one stays here. This one I'm going to hatch.*

Only, she thought a little sadly, *it doesn't seem to* want *to hatch.*

It worried her. There was something not quite right about this egg. It didn't *feel* right. It had been fine when she laid it, just like any other egg. But now it felt small, and hard, and cold, like a little stone. However long she sat on it, however much love and warmth she concentrated on it, the egg seemed only to grow harder and colder beneath her. And yet she was convinced that *something* was alive inside it. She could feel it move beneath her at dead of night, when the other hens were all asleep.

It was worrying her so much that, later that night, she told the other hens about it.

When she had finished there was an uneasy hush in the coop.

'I don't like the sound of that,' said one of the younger hens anxiously.

There was a general cluck of worried agreement.

'That's what comes of trying to cheat the hen-woman,' said the oldest hen, regarding Rosemary with fierce disapproval. 'You shouldn't try to cheat her. Wiser heads than ours have set her in authority over us. The hen-woman knows best. She takes our eggs away because she knows how to look after them better than we do.'

'That's not what I heard,' said one of the youngest hens timidly. 'I heard that she takes them away to give to other humans, and they *eat* them.'

There was a horrified silence. All the hens had heard this dreadful rumour, but it was in the worst possible taste to mention it.

'That is a vile, nasty, unfounded slander,' snapped the older hen. 'You should be heartily ashamed of saying such things. Of *course* the hen-woman looks after our eggs. Of *course* we shouldn't try to hatch our eggs and bring up our own chicks. We can't *possibly* give them a proper start in life.'

'Why not?' asked the younger hen.

The old hen puffed out her chest-feathers and delivered her answer with the conviction of a knockout punch. 'Because we're all one-parent families, that's why. What sort of upbringing is that for a young chick?'

'That's true,' said a third hen sorrowfully. 'It's a crying shame, the way that rooster behaves. He only wants us for one thing, and when he's had it, off he goes. Spends all his time wandering round the castle grounds, just pleasing himself.'

'Out roosting and crowing at all hours.'

'Never takes any interest in the eggs he's fathered.'

'Never lifts a wing-feather to help in their upkeep.'

'And if you ask him to do a bit of cleaning round the coop, he just says *that's women's work.*'

'Men. They're all the same.'

There was a general rustling of feathers as the entire coop indulged in the righteous indignation common to females of every species.

'So,' said the youngest hen, 'what can we do for poor Rosemary and - and whatever's inside her egg?'

142

This was too hard for the collected feather-brains of the coop. They all turned, as one does when faced with the deep and unanswerable questions of life, to the oldest person present.

The oldest hen, who was of a deeply religious persuasion, had her answer ready.

'Pray,' she said solemnly. 'Pray for Rosemary's baby.'

In the scullery at Redbrush Hall, Mrs Tod was doing the household accounts. It was a job she hated. For one thing the ledger was big and cumbersome, and hurt her knees: a fox's knees are not really designed as a book-rest. For another, there were wriggly things living in the ledger.

There were moths in the cloth binding. There were silverfish in the spine (they lived on the glue that held the pages together; any day now the whole thing was going to fall apart). And there were bookworms. Mrs Tod no longer dared open the oldest parts of the ledger, because the bookworms had taken them over and built a small city in them. Their sleeping quarters were in years 450 to 456, there was an administrative complex in year 460, and they were currently building a sports arena in 464. Mrs Tod hated wriggly things, and she was always glad when she could put the ledger back on its dusty shelf and forget about it for another month.

But this month, she was facing something even more unpleasant than bookworms. Debts. Each month the largest outgoings were under the heading REPAIRS, and these bills had been getting steadily bigger.

Mrs Tod came to the bottom of a column of figures, added them all up, picked up a pen, dipped it into an inkwell, and wrote the final figure in grey. (She had long since ceased wondering why all the ink she bought started off red or black and slowly turned grey.) She sat back and stared at this last figure. Yes, they were definitely sinking further into the red (or grey). And there was no prospect of getting back into the black (or grey). Things were looking grey indeed. There was only one thing to be done, and it was time she took her courage in both hands and did it.

She closed the ledger, put it back carefully on the shelf so as not to dislodge any of its wriggly residents, and got a fresh piece of parchment. On it she wrote: *For Sale: Redbrush Hall. Large and desirable residence in unspoilt forest locality. Many original features – ample scope for improvement. Ideal starter home for young monarch with an interest in DIY. Offers around . . .*

She licked the nib of the pen, and stared at the ceiling for a moment. Then she wrote a figure. It was a fairly ambitious figure, but what the hell? In for a penny, in for fifty thousand gold sovereigns.

She folded up the paper, and on the outside wrote *Camelot Estates & Rentals Ltd – for the attention of Mr Smyrk.*

A few minutes later, Macpherson came in from the garden. Mrs Tod held out the letter. 'Post this, Macpherson, will you?'

'Aye, ma'am.' He took the letter and glanced at the address. His manner became less melancholy and more disapproving. 'So. Ye've decided tae sell, have ye?'

'Yes. It can't be helped. I can't afford to run this place any longer.'

'Pah!' The Scot showed his disapproval by spitting on the floor. 'If his Lairdship were here, he'd find a way tae keep the place going.'

'Well, he isn't here,' said Mrs Tod tartly. 'And even if he was, I don't see how he could work miracles. Besides, I've had enough of these draughty corridors and rickety stairs. I'm going to buy a nice cosy little cottage in one of the local villages.'

'That's all verra weel, but what's tae become o' me?' demanded the gardener.

'You'll have to look for other employment, I suppose,' said the lady of the house, shrugging her shoulders. 'I shall give you a reference, of course.'

'Reference? Pah!' The gardener spat on the floor again. 'I want more than a reference. If ye're selling the Hall, then I want a share o' the proceeds.'

'A *share*?' Mrs Tod had slipped into her Edith Evans voice again. 'You impudent man. Kindly remember that you are only a servant. I *may*, if I feel kindly disposed towards you, give you a shilling when you leave, but—'

'Pah!' The Scotsman spat on the floor a third time. 'Ye can keep yer shillin'. I want a share, I tell ye. A *fair* share.'

'Well.' Mrs Tod pulled her shawl more tightly around her thin chest, and surveyed the gardener through her pince-nez. 'I can see that if I don't give in, the floor will soon be knee-deep in saliva. Very well. Ten percent.'

'Thirty.'

'Fifteen.'

'Twenty.'

'Seventeen and a half.'

'Seventeen and three quarters.'

'Seventeen and nine and a quarter sixteenths.'

'Seventeen and – er—' The gardener furrowed his brow for a long moment, and then gave it up. 'Aye, all right. Seventeen and nine and a quarter sixteenths percent, and not a penny less.'

'Agreed. Now go and post that letter.'

'Aye, ma'am.' The gardener, his eyes alight with fiscal greed, saluted smartly and hurried away.

Mrs Tod glanced out of the window at the bilious yellow sky. 'Looks like rain,' she murmured. 'I hope the pigeon[1] will be able to get through.'

In Camelot, the weather had already broken. The sky, which had been a deep shade of congealed egg for two days, turned the colour of a burnt frying pan. The air, which had been oppressive but at least made mostly of gases, suddenly turned to water.

It rained. It rained and it rained and it rained. Then it went off to the wholesaler, got in fresh supplies, and started all over again. Very soon the rain was getting up everyone's nose[2] as much as the thundery weather that preceded it.

Snug and dry in her warm and richly scented[3] hut, Boadicea the hen-woman puffed at her pipe and watched the rain turning the castle garden into oxtail soup with green bits floating in it.

After a while she turned her attention to the floor of the hut, where several piles of soiled straw were laid out for inspection. She frowned. They were not your usual droppings, by any means. Some of the patterns were downright peculiar. She had been staring at them for half an hour now, and still couldn't make sense of them.

---

[1] The Camelot Postal Service (Airmail Division) used carrier pigeons trained to fly between their home address and the Sorting Office, a large building whose glistening white roof was visible for miles. Inside the Sorting Office, staff spent all day removing tiny scrolls from the legs of incoming pigeons and attaching them to the legs of outgoing pigeons. It was quite a good system, except for the deafening noise of cooing and the awful smell.

[2] Not, of course, literally, except in the case of several giant vampire bats sleeping upside-down in trees in Camelot Forest.

[3] Tobacco, gin, shaving cream, and just a hint of lavender.

With a sigh, she admitted defeat. She needed help with this one. Glancing through the doorway of the hut to make sure no-one was watching, she reached into the depths of her mattress and pulled out a battered book. Its front cover was missing, but the flyleaf bore the legend:

Teach Yourselfe Cloacomancy
Being Ye Ancient Arte of Divining Ye Future
by Ye Dispositione of Hen-Droppinges

Boadicea bent over the book and scanned its pages in the furtive, hasty manner of a schoolboy cribbing from someone else's essay. She peered at diagrams and cryptic notes, trying to match them with the pale blotches on the pieces of straw in front of her.

At last she found what she was looking for. She compared the shapes of the splotches on the straw with the sketched splotches in the book.

There seemed to be four main splotches: one meaning *green*, one meaning *search* or *find*, one meaning *wizard*, and a really big and impressive one that seemed to mean something like *god* or *source of power*.

Boadicea leaned back on her heels and puffed thoughtfully at her pipe.

The trouble with hen-droppings, she had long ago realised, was that they were strong on semantics but weak on syntax. Getting the basic meanings was one thing: arranging them correctly to form the right sentence was another.

There were therefore several possible ways of reading the pattern before her. It could mean *Seek out the green source of power, O wizard*. Or perhaps *Wizard, you are too green to find the source of power*. Or even, though this seemed pretty unlikely, *The wizard must search for the green god*.

Boadicea puzzled over this for some time, but in the

end she made up her mind. It wasn't really that difficult. You just needed a bit of lateral thinking.

A few minutes later, Boadicea was striding briskly up the hill towards the castle, her heavy and ungainly shape in black skirts and hobnailed boots floundering through the shifting mud of the garden. In her hands she carried several lumps of straw.

In the reasonably dry confines of the cottage, Gwydden peered out through rain-streaked windows at a jet-black sky.

'Can't go out in this,' he muttered. 'Have to wait till it blows over.'

He sat back in his chair, and ran his hands through his thin hair in a characteristic gesture of puzzlement. Surely there must be something about eyes and wells and slugs *somewhere*?

Perhaps, after all, his bookshelf would supply the answer.

He took down *The Wizard's Handbook* and began to thumb listlessly through its well-thumbed pages.

Apart from planning his abdication, one of Uther's great pleasures, at the end of a hard day's ruling, was to take a bath. Sometimes he didn't wait for the day to end, but sneaked off to have a quick bath between meetings. Which was why, when Boadicea came stomping through his apartments, she found him lying in the tub in the en-suite bathroom, his eyes closed, the loofah draped across his chest, while around him floated three rubber sea-serpents.

'Well,' said the hen-woman scornfully. 'And what time do 'ee call this?'

Uther jerked upright and his eyes opened wide. 'Sorry, Igrayne, dearest.' Then he saw that it wasn't his

148

wife, but a strange woman – assuming that someone who chain-smoked Old Bosun and sported a chinful of pine-needles could reasonably be called a woman. To be on the safe side, he repositioned the loofah lower down his anatomy.

'Ah, Boadicea,' he said. 'Nice to see you and all that, but I am, as you observe, in the bath. In such situations it is considered usual to knock.'

'Fiddle-faddle,' said the hen-woman.

Uther waited to see if she would expand on this remark, but she merely stood looking at him. She had something in her hands, Uther noticed. Lumps of soggy straw, by the look of it. The bathroom, which had been smelling pleasantly of the patchouli bath salts Igrayne had given Uther for his birthday, was rapidly filling up with the less appealing aromas of hen-droppings and Old Bosun.

'Um, well,' said Uther. 'Did you want to see me about something?'

'I asked 'ee,' said Boadicea, glaring at him, 'what time do 'ee call this?'

Uther's eye wandered helplessly round the bathroom. He had left his pocket sundial in his pocket. 'About half past three?' he hazarded.

'It be *doomsday*,' said the hen-woman, in a sepulchral and portentous tone.

'Really?' Uther looked worried. 'Already?'

Boadicea shrugged. 'Give or take a day or two. But 'tis no time to be wallowing and indulging in the sybaritic pleasures of the flesh.'

'Steady on,' said the King indignantly. 'I'm only having a bath.'

'Pah! I've no time for baths,' said the hen-woman contemptuously. 'Baths was invented by those soft foreigners, the Romans. None of *my* ancestors ever had

149

baths, and I've never had one either. That surprises 'ee, I suppose?'

'No. I mean, yes.' The King coughed. 'What exactly did you want me to do about this – er – doomsday? I'm still rather in the dark about it.'

'*This* tells 'ee what to do,' said the hen-woman. She dropped the straw she had been carrying into Uther's bath-water.

'What's this?' said the King, peering at the soggy mess floating among his sea-serpents.

'Hen-droppings.'

'What? In my bath? Ugh!' Uther thrust the sodden straw away from him with the end of the loofah. 'Really, Boadicea! Couldn't you just have *told* me?' He edged fastidiously backwards until he was right at the end of the bath. 'Well? What do the filthy things say?'

'That,' said the hen-woman, sitting down on the edge of the bath, 'be what I'm about to tell 'ee.'

It was dark and stuffy in the new diggings. The tunnel smelled strongly of sweaty rabbit. Flopkin scrabbled in the heavy loam and wondered if there had ever been a time when he was not digging this blasted tunnel. He seemed to have been doing it since he was born. Probably longer.

He stopped for a moment and wiped the dirt out of his eyes with a weary paw.

'Here, you,' snapped a voice behind him. 'Stop slacking. Dig, if you know what's good for you.'

Flopkin felt a rush of anger. 'All right, Gloat, I'm digging as fast as I can. I have to breathe sometimes, you know.'

'I don't see why,' sneered the fat buck who was standing behind him. 'Seems to me, Flopkin, that your breathing is a luxury this warren could easily do without. Seems to me that your air could be shared out amongst the rest of us. Seems to me—'

'Seems to me, Gloat,' snapped Flopkin, his hackles rising, 'that you're a fat, pompous, worthless collection of rabbit droppings.'

There was a sudden silence in the diggings. The other rabbits started to edge away from the immediate area.

Gloat moved forward slowly until his nose and Flopkin's were almost touching. '*What* did you say, Flopkin?'

'Deaf as well as stupid, Gloat?' sneered Flopkin. His tiredness had overcome his caution, and he didn't care any more. 'You're a waste of space, Gloat. You're *scroop*[1].'

The silence in the tunnel became almost tangible[2]. Then, with a ferocious yell, Gloat threw himself upon Flopkin.

The fight was brief but savage. Gloat aimed a jab at Flopkin's eye, and missed. Flopkin caught him by the ears, bit one of them in two, and then slashed at Gloat's stomach with his hind feet. He felt something give way, and a warm liquid spurted over him. Gloat screamed, and collapsed in a heap.

Flopkin got up and prodded Gloat with his foot. Gloat remained motionless. The smell of stale sweat in the tunnel was giving way to the smell of fresh blood.

This is serious, Flopkin said to himself. *If you want to get into a tyrant's good books, you shouldn't go round disembowelling his henchmen. Time to get out of here.*

He turned to face the rabbits lined along the tunnel. They cowered away from him in alarm.

---

[1]*Scroop* is the ultimate rabbit insult. Don't say it to your pet rabbit. No amount of carrots will soothe its injured feelings afterwards.
[2]Tangible silence feels like putting your hand in a bucket of cold jellied eels.

'I'm leaving the warren,' he said loudly. 'Anyone who wants to come with me is welcome to do so.'

There was a doubtful silence. One rabbit said tentatively, 'Will we have carrots?'

'I don't know,' said Flopkin shortly. 'If we find carrots, you can have carrots. If not, not. I can't promise anything.'

'Petrov promised us carrots,' said another rabbit. 'Carrots tomorrow.'

'I know,' said Flopkin. 'But when did he promise you that?'

'Yesterday,' said the first rabbit.

'Doesn't that tell you something?'

There was a puzzled silence. 'What?' said the second rabbit eventually.

'If he promised you *carrots tomorrow* yesterday,' said Flopkin, 'then you should be getting carrots *today*. So where are they?'

'But he didn't say *today*,' said the second rabbit, with the air of someone explaining something to a small child. 'He said *tomorrow*.'

'We only have to wait till tomorrow,' said a third rabbit eagerly. 'Then we get our carrots.'

'Oh, you're all idiots,' said Flopkin angrily. 'To hell with you. I'm off.'

He stumbled away towards the nearest exit. *What could I do?* he thought. *Maybe Petrov will give them carrots. All I've got to offer is sour grapes.*

'No,' he muttered. 'It's all wrong. Petrov is bad news. Oh, *scroop*.'

Two minutes later he was running through the undergrowth in the fresh air. It was raining heavily, and within seconds his fur was sodden and uncomfortable.

He came to a well-remembered ditch, and hopped down into it.

Whump. He had cannoned into something large and hard on the inside, and wet and furry on the outside.

'Here,' said a heavy, placid-sounding voice. 'Mind where you're falling, chum, there's people in this here ditch.'

Flopkin wiped the rain out of his eyes and stared. A sudden absurd feeling of relief welled up inside him. 'Hullo, Mopkin,' he said.

Mopkin stared at him. Then recognition dawned, and he said in a much friendlier voice, 'Why, it's Flomrade – I mean Flopkin. Didn't recognise you at first, under all that dirt.' He turned to someone standing next to him. 'Cottonseed, look who's here.'

'Hullo, Flopkin,' said Cottonseed. 'Isn't this terrific? The Magnificent Three together again.'

'Hullo, Cottonseed,' said Flopkin, looking guardedly at his one-time lieutenant. 'What are you doing here?'

'Oh, I had an argument with that stinking scab Earmite and knocked him down,' said Cottonseed cheerfully. 'He ran crying to Petrov, so I thought I'd better leg it. Got here five minutes ago, and bumped into Mopkin, who's legged it too.'

'Why did you run away, Mopkin?' Flopkin asked.

'Got into a fight,' Mopkin explained, a little sadly. 'I didn't mean to, Flopkin, but Wormcast was ill-treating one of the does, and it made me angry, so I knocked him down.'

'What about you, Flopkin?' Cottonseed asked.

'Same sort of thing,' said Flopkin. 'I had a scrap with that *scroop* Gloat. I killed him, I think. Anyway there was a lot of blood.'

'Yes, you've got it all over your fur,' Cottonseed said, looking him over. 'Still, the rain'll wash it off, once we get going.'

'Sorry, guys,' said Flopkin. 'We aren't going anywhere.'

Cottonseed looked disappointed. 'Why not?'

'Because we can't just desert the others, that's why not. We have to try and save the warren.'

'*You* save the warren,' said Cottonseed sulkily. 'I want to go on a quest.'

'Why?'

'Because it's heroic, and exciting, and – and *fun*.' The young rabbit stuck out his teeth in a gesture of defiance. 'When I joined the Freedom Fighters, I thought it would be fun, but it hasn't been much fun so far. I'm a young healthy rabbit, I *ought* to have fun.'

'Never mind, Cottonseed,' said Mopkin soothingly. 'Perhaps saving the warren will be fun.'

'Whose side are you on, Mopkin?' demanded the youngest Freedom Fighter.

'Flopkin's, of course. He's the leader.'

'But a minute ago you were on *my* side!'

'I know. But Flopkin's right, Cottonseed. We're the Freedom Fighters. If we don't fight for freedom, who will?'

'Quite right,' said Flopkin. 'So, Cottonseed, are you going to help Mopkin and me save the warren?'

'Don't have much choice, do I? Only I don't see how we can.'

'That,' said Flopkin, dropping into a conspiratorial whisper, 'is what I want to talk to you about. Remember Petrov's Plan?'

The other two nodded.

'Well, I've got a Plan too. Now listen, both of you.'

Chapter Eight

'Just hang on a minute,' said Uther. 'I'm trying to understand, but you're not making any sense. Ow. *Ow!* Please be more gentle with that loofah, you're scratching me.'

'Soft, that be your trouble,' said Boadicea scornfully. 'Skin like a baby's bottom. Too much easy living. Lift up your arms so I can scrub under your armpits.'

'No!' Uther made a grab for the loofah and wrenched it out of the hen-woman's muscular grasp. 'Some other time. I've been in here long enough.' He groped for a towel, wrapped it round himself and clambered out of the bath. The hen-woman politely averted her gaze as he emerged from the suds.

'Look at that,' said the King accusingly, examining his back in the bathroom mirror. 'Covered in scratches. How am I going to explain these to Igrayne?'

The hen-woman shrugged. 'Why don't 'ee just tell her that old Boadicea made them?'

'Because she's a jealous woman,' said the King, starting to dry himself vigorously. 'She might get the wrong idea.'

A strange gurgling sound filled the bathroom. At first Uther thought something must be happening deep inside the plumbing. Then he realised that Boadicea was laughing.

'I be flattered, king,' chuckled the hen-woman, removing the pipe from between her teeth and knocking it against the wall. 'It be a long time since anyone thought of old Boadicea that way.'

'Good heavens.' Uther stopped towelling himself, and stared at her in alarm. 'I didn't mean — I wasn't implying that I – I mean, you're very, er, *handsome,* Boadicea, in your own way, and perhaps if you shaved and bathed a little more often, then possibly someone, someone *else* might, might possibly, er . . .' His voice tailed away unhappily, and he flushed a deep puce all over.

'Aye.' The hen-woman looked mildly annoyed. 'Well, never 'ee mind all that folderol. 'Tis not important now. What 'ee must do, king, is see to the defence of Camelot an' its people against the comin' terror.'

'Yes, so you keep saying,' said Uther. 'But you haven't told me *how* to defend against it.'

Boadicea sighed. 'If 'ee will *listen* a minute, I'll tell 'ee what the droppings say.'

'Oh. The droppings. Right, fire away.'

'Find a powerful wizard in the Green,' said Boadicea. 'That were what the droppings said. Not that I hold with wizards as a rule, but I has to admit, they can 'ave their uses in times of desprit need.'

Uther frowned. 'In the Green? What does that mean?'

Boadicea tutted. 'Bain't it obvious? What do they call the part of Camelot where most wizards 'as their laborry-torries?'

'Laborry—? Oh, laboratories. Well, yes, the Green Light District. But I still don't see—'

' 'Tis clear enough to anyone wi' more than a hen's noddle. *Green* must mean *Green Light District.* 'Tis a shortened way o' saying it.'

'Oh, I see. To save ink, you mean. Or, well, not ink, in this case it would be to save—' Uther stopped, wondering what was the right word to use in front of Boadicea, who might technically be considered a lady.

Boadicea tutted again. 'The droppings often be cryptic. They be concerned wi' broad sweeps of hist'ry an' such. 'Tain't reasonable to expect 'em to bother wi' unnecessary words like *district*. They'm got more important things to be concerned with.'

'Ah, I see. Yes.' Uther nodded. He didn't subscribe to the broad sweep theory himself, being more of a dot-the-eyes-and-cross-the-tees man, but he respected those who did. 'A powerful wizard in the Green Light District. Well, why not Merlin? He's the most powerful wizard in the kingdom.'

'Aye. But he don't work in the Green Light District.'

'And you think that's important?'

'It be what the droppings *say*.'

'Yes, but if the important thing is to get a powerful wizard, then surely Merlin—'

Boadicea looked at him very severely from under her one enormous eyebrow. 'There bain't much point usin' the droppings, if 'ee don't take any notice of what they *say*.'

'Fair point. Okay, we'll try and find a wizard in the Green Light District. I daresay Merlin could probably recommend one. At least—' Uther's frown deepened, as he recalled the odd way Merlin had been behaving lately. 'Well, anyway, we can see what he says.'

'Well, be quick about it, king,' said Boadicea. 'Time be a-gettin' on. How long does havin' a bath *take*, for goodness' sake?'

Gwydden was coming to the conclusion, not for the first time, that *The Wizard's Handbook* was not worth the annual subscription he paid for it.

'Nothing under Eye,' he muttered irritably. 'Nothing

under Well. Nothing under Slug. Have to try the index, I suppose.'

His tone was heavy with foreboding. The index – a recent "improvement" to the *Handbook* – had been compiled by one Scabrius, a wizard with a peculiar sense of priorities, or possibly a demonic sense of humour. Many a luckless wizard, confronting a fire-breathing dragon and desperately flicking through the index for something helpful, must have boggled in disbelief at the following entry:

Dragon's fiery breath see *Beard, singed, grave risk of for careless wizards*

Which, while undeniably true, is rarely uppermost in one's mind when facing that most dreaded of magical beasts, *Draco halitosis incendii*.

Another notorious entry read:

Intelligence test see *end of index*

If the unsuspecting reader turned to the end of the index, he found a page on which was written:

It's behind you. You're safe if you don't turn round.

Scabrius's view was that any wizard who did turn round at this point must be too stupid to be trusted with a mage-staff, and that the index entry provided a useful service in weeding out idiots. Those who had turned round might have disagreed with him, but none of them had survived to make their views known.

The index contained no entries for Eye or Slug, but under Well, it said: *Well, Really* see *Really Well*.

Gwydden duly turned to Really Well, and read the following:

A charming but implausible legend states that there was once a well whose water fed the forests of England and had the power to repair any harm – frost, fire or blight – that might befall them. This remarkable well was supposedly somewhere in the deeply wooded region around what is now Camelot . . .

The wizard sat up sharply and exclaimed.

The same legend has it that the Really Well was guarded by a semi-divine personage known as the Green God. Another picturesque story is that after the Celtic gods and goddesses defeated the Fhomoire, the Fhomoire's main weapon, the hideously destructive Eye of Balor, was thrown down the Really Well by a Fhomoire called Archon . . .

'Oh good grief,' murmured the wizard. 'The Eye of Balor, and the Fhomoire! This gets worse and worse . . .'

One cannot but marvel at the poetic inventiveness of the unknown bards who dreamed up these quaint, if rather childish, tales . . .

Some time later, Hergrim came into the room to find the wizard slumped in his chair, eyes glazed, staring unseeingly out at the trickling rain.

'Gwydden?' The dwarf shook him by the shoulder. 'Are you all right?'

Gradually Gwydden's eyes refocused. 'Yes. Fine. What time is it?'

'About noon.'

'Then let's have some lunch. And then . . .'

'Yes?'

'Then I'm going to tell you a story.'

Knock, knock, knock. A hesitant sound, like a conservation-minded woodpecker trying to make a nest without damaging the tree.

'Merlin?'

A long pause, filled with tension and a certain amount of nervousness.

'I think he must be out,' said Uther, trying not to sound too obviously relieved. 'We'll have to come back some other time.' He turned towards the stairs, but Boadicea grabbed him by the collar.

'Wait,' said the hen-woman. 'Don't 'ee go skivin' off,

king. We *need* a wizard. P'raps the old Welsh fraud's having a kip. Let's go in and see.' She stepped up to Merlin's door with a purposeful air.

'You really shouldn't—' began Uther in alarm. But the hen-woman had already taken hold of the doorknob and twisted it firmly.

'Ow! That hurtth! Thtoppit!'

Boadicea let go of the doorknob in surprise. The doorknob hissed at her. 'My mathter ith out,' it lisped in a threatening tone. 'Thcram, old crone, or I will thmite thee with a thinithter thpell.'

Boadicea bristled. 'Don't 'ee be disrespectful, doorknob.'

'Thod off, fith-fathe.' The doorknob stuck out a long scaly tongue, and waggled it derisively.

Boadicea's eyebrow contracted into an angry scowl. She seized the tongue and pulled it hard.

'*Urrggghhhh!*' squealed the doorknob. 'That thmartth! Leggo!'

Boadicea let go. The tongue whisked back into the doorknob like lightning.

'Thaditht,' said the doorknob sulkily.

'When will Merlin be back?' demanded the hen-woman.

'How thould I know?' muttered the doorknob. 'He never thellth me anything. I therve him faithfully for yearth and yearth, thutting and opening the door, thtopping unwanted vithitorth – well, uthually – and what thankth do I get? Thod all. He treatth me like part of the furnitthure.'

Boadicea released Uther's collar, and turned away. 'Come on, king. We be wasting our time here. This doorknob knows nothing – it's just a skivvy.'

'Thkivvy yourthelf!' screamed the doorknob in fury. 'I hope your henth get thcurvy!'

Boadicea turned back and wagged a thick tobacco-stained finger. "Ee be more civil next time we meet, doorknob, or I'll unscrew 'ee and drop 'ee in the moat.'

'Unthcrew yourthelf, you thilly old bethom!' screeched the doorknob.

'Now that,' said Uther, as he and Boadicea descended the stairs, 'is no way to talk to a lady.'

Boadicea produced a tobacco-pouch from the strata-like folds of her skirts, and started to fill her pipe. 'Bless 'ee, king, I don't mind. Now – if Merlin bain't here, we must get another wizard. Who be the best wizard in Camelot after Merlin?'

The King rubbed his bald patch. 'Good heavens. Now *there's* a question. From what I've seen of the wizards in Camelot, if you rolled all of them into one, they still wouldn't be up to Merlin's standard. Just a minute, though. There was a fellow I met a while back – name of Gwillem, or Gideon, or something. Gwydden, that was it. He seemed reasonably competent.'

'Then I suggest 'ee send for'n,' said Boadicea. Having filled her pipe, she thrust the pouch back into the pre-Cambrian obscurity of her clothing. 'An' get they good-for-nothin' Knights ready to fight. All hands will be needed before this business be done.'

'Oh, but the Knights -' began Uther.

They had reached the bottom of the stairs. Boadicea turned and fixed him with an uncompromising stare. 'No excuses, king. This land be facin' the worst threat since the Black Dragon of Aberystwyth. Ancient evils be coming, powers be thrown down, misery and despair be the lot of every man, woman and child.'

'Yes, I remember you saying.'

'And 'tis up to 'ee to stop it. 'Ee be *king!*' She prodded Uther in the chest with her pipe, spilling tobacco down his tunic.

'Yes, I know,' said Uther, a trifle wearily. 'I'm king, and as usual, it's my job to sort it all out. I fully grasp that. Although in point of fact, I don't think there ever was a Black Dragon of Aberystwyth.'

'No, there wasn't,' said Boadicea. 'I made that up on the spur of the moment, to make 'ee see how dangerous this be. Understand?'

'Yes. Well, no, actually—'

The hen-woman waved a hairy hand. 'Never mind. Just 'ee get on with it, okay?' From somewhere in her clothing she produced a match, which she struck on the stone banister of the stairway, and applied to her pipe.

'Yes, of course. Only the Knights, you see – the Knights are—'

' 'Tis time for me to feed the hens,' said Boadicea briskly. ' 'Tis all up to 'ee, king – all up to 'ee.'

She turned and set off in the direction of the castle garden, puffs of smoke drifting above her head as she went.

'That's all very well,' murmured Uther. 'But the Knights are Igrayne's knights, not mine. What if she won't *let* me mobilise them? I think, for the moment, I'll concentrate on finding a wizard.'

'So these Fhomoire,' said Hergrim, 'were demons. And they were beaten by the Celtic gods and goddesses, who drove them out of England, into Limbo or somewhere.'

'That's right.'

'But you think maybe one of them is still around, disguised as a giant slug.'

'Not disguised. The Fhomoire were shape-shifters. He *is* a giant slug - sometimes. And sometimes he might be a man, and sometimes he might be a dwarf, and so on. He can be anything.'

'Makes it a bit hard to track him down,' said the dwarf.

'Yes. Anyway, that's not our best lead. What we should do is follow Nostradimwit – remember? *Goe sunnewyse from ye welle, and finde Ye grove wherein ye grene godde sleepes.*'

The dwarf peered out of the window at the rain. 'The sun isn't even visible at the moment. And anyway, why us? Why not leave it to Uther? He's got soldiers, and the Knights of the Slightly Pear-Shaped Table, and Merlin. They're *paid* to keep the kingdom in order. Who's going to pay us?'

'Is that all you think about?' asked the wizard disapprovingly. 'Money?'

Hergrim looked affronted. 'What d'you mean, *all*? I'm a dwarf. Money is serious business to a dwarf.'

'Well, anyway, I feel partly responsible for the fact that this slug is slithering around the place. Perhaps he was imprisoned in the well, and we've let him out. So even if we don't get paid, I feel we should do something about it.'

Hergrim shook his head. 'I think you're wrong about that.'

'About what?'

'The slug being imprisoned in the well. It was an eye that was carved on the capstone, remember.'

'Yes. And I now know what that eye represents – the Eye of Balor. According to the entry I finally tracked down in *The Wizard's Handbook*, Balor was the largest and most fearsome of the Fhomoire, and his eye was a weapon of dreadful power. Balor was beheaded by the Celtic gods, but this Archon character made off with the Eye and dropped it down the Really Well. The gods – rather lazily, if you ask me, but perhaps they were knackered after all the fighting – didn't bother to fish it out, but simply left it there. Someone must have come along later and put a capstone on the well, and carved an eye on the stone as a warning. Presumably it's the Eye of Balor that's causing the deathly smell and the damp under Redbrush Hall.'

'So what do we do about it?' enquired the dwarf.

Gwydden shrugged. 'We can't get under the Hall, Macpherson said as much. The only thing we can do is try and find this *grene godde*, and to do that we have to work out how to *goe sunnewyse from ye welle*.'

'Have you found anything in your books that explains it?'

'No.' Gwydden glanced out of the window. It was still raining hard. 'There's no point wandering around near the well, not in this rain. Let's have some strong coffee. This is a situation where I'll just have to use my brain.'

'Oh dear,' murmured the dwarf. 'We really *are* in a desperate state.'

He caught Gwydden's eye, and beat a hasty retreat to the kitchen.

At about midnight the supply of rain-clouds ran out, and the storm shrugged its shoulders and slipped away, leaving everything for miles around unpleasantly soggy. The drumming of the rain ceased, and other night-noises took over. In Camelot Forest, most of the noise came from the tree-tops, where large families of birds were trying to push each other out of the driest parts of the nest.

Macpherson lay awake in his small, spartan room, listening to the night-sounds of Redbrush Hall. There were a lot of them tonight. Mostly mice, no doubt. Mrs Tod kept setting traps for them, but however many she set, she never caught any mice. Macpherson had once suggested that she might try putting cheese in the traps, but she had merely stared at him frostily over her pince-nez and asked whether he thought she could afford to waste good food by giving it to vermin.

Scratch, scratch. Tap, tap. Scamper, scamper.

'Daft old baggage,' muttered Macpherson. He turned over and closed his eyes tight, trying to shut out the sounds, but his mind insisted on analysing them.

Scratch, scratch. That was mice, for sure.

Tap, tap. Probably a bird nesting in one of the chimneys.

Scamper, scamper. Mice again, wretched little varmints, partying in the wainscot till all hours when honest hardworking folk were abed.

Scrape.

Macpherson frowned.

Scrape.

There it went again. A hollow sound, coming from somewhere below him. The scullery?

Macpherson sat up and stared into the darkness.

Scr-rape. Scr-r-r-rape.

CRASH!

Macpherson leapt out of bed, nightshirt flapping round his bony knees, and seized his gun from its resting-place in the corner. He flung open the door and set off bare-footed down the corridor.

Just before he reached the stairs leading down to the scullery, a door swung open with an eerie creak, and a ghostly figure stepped out in front of him. It was small and white, and had huge eyes that shone in the moonlight.

'Hah!' Macpherson cried in alarm. He raised the blunderbuss and pointed it at the ghostly shape. 'What are ye, ye hideous fiend? Speak, or I'll shoot!'

'Macpherson!' snapped a familiar voice. 'How dare you point that thing at me? Put it away at once!'

The gardener shamefacedly lowered his gun. 'Och, I'm sorry, ma'am. I didna ken it was you.'

Mrs Tod straightened her white nightgown and adjusted her pince-nez, the moon flashing on them again as she did so. 'I heard a noise, and got up to investigate.'

'Aye, ma'am. I heard it too. I'm thinkin' it came frae the scullery.'

'That's what I thought. We must go down and take a look.'

' 'Tis awfu' dark down there,' said the gardener, peering down the stairs.

'Not afraid of the dark, are you, Macpherson?' said the lady fox contemptuously.

The gardener stiffened. 'Indeed not, ma'am. I was only thinking we would need a candle.'

'A good point. Wait here, while I fetch the one in my room.'

When Mrs Tod had provided herself with a candle, they crept down the staircase as quietly as they could. The stairs creaked at every step.

'Shush!' hissed Mrs Tod.

'I canna help it, ma'am. 'Tis these stairs, ye ken.'

'*I'm* not making a noise,' said the lady of the house.

'Yes, ye are, ye auld harridan,' muttered the gardener. 'Wi' that ceaseless wagging tongue.'

Mrs Tod luckily did not quite catch this. 'What?'

'Och, I was jist complainin' at the cold on ma bare feet, ma'am.'

'Great pampered Scots oaf,' was the unsympathetic reply. 'Never mind the cold. Go *quietly*.'

Macpherson sighed. 'Aye, ma'am.'

They crept the rest of the way down the stairs, and stood outside the scullery, listening at the door.

Hippety-hop, flippety-flop came from inside the scullery.

166

'What on earth is that?' Mrs Tod demanded in a stage whisper.

Macpherson nervously fingered the blunderbuss. 'I dinna ken, ma'am. Shall I open the door?'

'Yes.'

The gardener stepped past her, turned the handle, and flung the door wide.

The scullery was full of rabbits.

Every square inch of floor seemed to be covered in small, furry bodies. As the door opened, they all froze instinctively, heads turned towards the gardener and the lady fox. The light of Mrs Tod's candle flickered in dozens of wide, terrified eyes. Beyond them, a dark hole in the floor showed where, to Macpherson's amazement, the rabbits had managed to lift a flagstone and push it aside.

For a moment there was silence. Then Mrs Tod screamed. 'Vermin! Unhygienic vermin! In my scullery! Macpherson, shoot them – shoot them all!'

'Aye, ma'am,' said the gardener in a tone of grim relish. A huge rabbit pie floated before his mind's eye, and his mouth began to water. He raised his gun and pointed it at the nearest rabbit.

Next moment he let out a loud yell. The gun clattered to the floor. Macpherson hopped about the scullery on his left foot, clutching his right foot in his hands.

'What are you playing at, you Highland fool?' demanded Mrs Tod.

'Someone bit ma toes,' gasped the gardener. 'Who's that doon at ma feet?'

Three dark furry shapes were dodging round the gardener's feet as he did an impromptu version of the Highland Fling. One of them turned and rushed at the other rabbits, gesticulating wildly with his paws.

'Get out of here, you fools!' Flopkin cried. 'Before he recovers, and picks up the gun!'

But the rabbits were mesmerised. They sat on their haunches, gazing up with vacant faces at the candle in Mrs Tod's paw.

'Come on, Mopkin,' Cottonseed said urgently. 'Let's bite his other foot.'

'Right you are, Cottonseed old chap.'

'Aaaargh!' roared the gardener, as two sets of rodent teeth sank into his left big toe. He staggered sideways, bounced against the door-frame, and cannoned into Mrs Tod. The vixen shrieked, and she and the gardener sprawled in a heap on the scullery floor. The candle flew out of Mrs Tod's paws, shot across the room into the sink, and went out with a hiss.

The sudden return of darkness freed the spellbound rabbits. They bolted *en masse* for the hole in the floor. Flopkin, Mopkin and Cottonseed dashed after them, and ten seconds later there was not a rabbit to be seen.

There was a brief silence, and then Mrs Tod spoke.

'Kindly get off me, Macpherson.'

'Aye, ma'am. Sorry, ma'am.'

They disentangled themselves and stood up. Mrs Tod primly adjusted her nightgown.

'This is your fault, Macpherson,' she said acidly. 'You've let those rabbits get out of hand. I want you to get some poison, and put it down their nasty burrows. Understand?'

'Aye, ma'am,' said the gardener gloomily. 'But 'tis a pity. Ye canna put poisoned rabbit in a pie.'

'That can't be helped. See to it. Now where's that candle? I'm going back to my room. See you put back that flagstone before you go up to bed – and put something heavy on top of it.'

*　　*　　*

The rabbits listened as Macpherson dragged the scullery table across the floor and positioned it with one leg on the loose flagstone. They heard Macpherson's feet padding away, and the door closing. Then silence.

'And that's that,' said Flopkin. 'I hope you've all learned your lesson. It's lucky for you that Mopkin and Cottonseed and I were here, or you'd all be piled in the larder, waiting to be put in a pie.'

'But how did you get into the Hall, Flopkin?' asked a bemused voice.

'Through the cat-flap,' said Flopkin. 'You could have got in that way too. It would have saved all this unnecessary digging.'

'But what about the cat?'

'It died last year,' said Flopkin. 'Macpherson buried it in the shrubbery.'

'Why didn't you tell us about the cat-flap?' asked several rabbits at once.

'You never asked,' said Flopkin. 'You all seemed quite convinced that the Magnificent Three were useless, and that only the great Comrade Petrov could lead you. I hope you realise now that you were wrong.'

He paused, and listened to the delightful sound that followed this remark – the sound of a lot of rabbits mumbling apologetically that Flopkin had been right all along, and they were sorry they had ever doubted him. It would have been a moment to treasure, but for one thing. In the brief moment of struggle with Macpherson's toes, Flopkin had gained a rough impression of the number of rabbits present. There weren't enough. Half the warren seemed to be missing.

'Where are the rest of you?' he asked.

There was an uncertain silence, and then someone said, 'I think they're in the other tunnel, Flopkin.'

'The *other* tunnel?' Flopkin's tone was sharp with

surprise. 'What other tunnel? I never knew there was another tunnel.'

'I overheard Petrov talking to Earmite,' said the rabbit who had spoken. 'I think the plan was to invade the Hall using two tunnels at once, to surround the enemy.'

'Do you know where this other tunnel starts from?'

'Yes, Flopkin.'

'Take us there, then.'

The rabbits trooped down the underground passage until they came to a gap in the wall.

'This is it, Flopkin.'

Flopkin sniffed at the dark space. *It smells wrong,* he thought. *It ought to smell of fresh earth, but it smells like something rotting.*

With a *frisson* of unease, he realised that the fur on his back was standing on end.

'Mopkin and Cottonseed,' he said briskly, 'come with me. The rest of you wait here.'

It was a nearly silent trio that made its way stealthily up the tunnel towards whatever awaited them at the far end. Nearly silent, but not quite. Flopkin was sure he could hear somebody doing *something*. Was it Cottonseed? Yes, it was. Was he whingeing, as usual? No, he was whimpering, like a scared rabbit kitten.

'*Shut up, Cottonseed!*' hissed Flopkin. 'I can hear you whimpering from here.'

'Sorry, Flopkin,' said a trembly voice from the back.

Poor Cottonseed, Flopkin thought guiltily. *It isn't his fault that he's as unflinching in the face of danger as a dandelion clock in a force 9 gale. Any more than it's Mopkin's fault that he's as bright as a pitch-dark night at the bottom of a burrow.*

Rats.

As Julius Caesar used to tell his legions: Bellum infernum est[1].

When this one's over, maybe the three of us can retire. We'll have done our bit, after all, helping to build a warren fit for heroes, fighting for liberty, equality, and unrestricted access to Macpherson's lettuces. Time to hang up our headbands and go home to our loved ones, or in Cottonseed's case to his Mum.

But in the meantime, a rabbit's got to do what a rabbit's got to do. We shall fight in the scullery. We shall fight by the compost heap. We shall never give in.

This is one hell of a long tunnel. Surely we must be near the end of it now. Hard to tell, in this pitch blackness . . .

At that moment, the entire tunnel was flooded with a strange grey light.

'Are you feeling all right, Flopkin?' Mopkin enquired. 'You've gone a very funny colour.'

'So have you,' hissed Flopkin. 'It's the light coming from up ahead.'

'I don't like it, Flopkin,' whispered Cottonseed.

Flopkin silently agreed. No rabbit likes being exposed to view by a sudden light, and this light was peculiarly unpleasant. It was like being breathed on by a large dog with rotting teeth. 'Listen, you two,' he said quietly. 'I'm going up the tunnel alone to see what this weird light means. If I don't come back, you must go back to the warren and elect a new leader.'

'Yes, Flopkin,' said Mopkin and Cottonseed together, in subdued voices.

The grey light grew stronger as Flopkin went farther up the tunnel. He had the definite feeling that whatever was causing it was something he really didn't want to meet. But he was the leader, and the thing about leaders

---

[1]War is hell.

171

is, they have to lead. Even if no-one happens, for the moment, to be following.

Every now and then the light would go out, and then it would come back on again. Grey, black, grey, black, it went, like a traffic light designed for drivers with a hangover.

It was during one of the black phases that Flopkin ran headlong into something large, lumpy and not very soft.

'*Eeeeehh!*' The something squealed deafeningly in his ear.

'Who's that?' Flopkin stared into the blackness.

A voice said timidly, 'Is that you, Flopkin? We're the other team of diggers.'

The grey light came back on. In its ghastly glow, Flopkin saw a group of terrified and extremely dirty rabbits, all huddled together. The light was shining over their heads, turning their ears into silhouettes, as if they were playing the age-old rabbit game of Moon-shapes[1].

'All right,' he said briskly. 'What's going on here? Where's Petrov?'

'He's up there,' said the nearest rabbit, pointing up the tunnel. 'He told us to wait here while he went on ahead.'

'What's he doing up there?' Flopkin demanded.

The rabbits muttered in low, scared voices. 'We don't

---

[1]Played when there's a full moon. One rabbit stands at the entrance to the burrow, and the others inside the burrow have to guess the shape his ears make, silhouetted against the moon. Most young rabbits can only make two shapes – an unidentified two-leaved plant, and a rude gesture. Best at the game are older rabbits whose ears have been bitten a lot in fights – such as the world-famous Hoppy 'Doily-lugs' Whitetail, who could do the skylines of six European cities with one ear, and three mountain ranges with the other.

know,' said the same rabbit. 'We want to go home, but we're afraid he'll be angry with us.'

'I'll deal with Petrov,' said Flopkin. 'You lot go down and join the rest of the warren.'

He waited patiently until the last of the earth-stained and wide-eyed rabbits had filed past him. Then he resumed his climb along the tunnel.

We've been conned, he thought. *All that talk of capturing Redbrush Hall was just a blind. This must be the real tunnel. But where does it lead to, and what is Petrov after? And what the hell is causing this nasty grey light?*

Abruptly the tunnel stopped, and he was in a huge open space.

It seemed to be some kind of cellar. Arches of brickwork marched away on either side. Dozens of wine-barrels, covered with grey dust, were stacked under the arches.

He took all this in almost subliminally, because his attention was drawn to two shapes in the centre of the paved floor.

One was Petrov. The other was an Eye.

The Eye was unusually large, being about six feet in diameter. It squatted like a bloated jelly on the flagstones. The pupil was a grey vertical slit, like a cat's, and it was out of the pupil that the sickly light streamed.

The Eye was looking at Petrov, who was talking to it in a language Flopkin didn't understand – and didn't particularly want to, because it sounded like the sort of language you can only say unpleasant things in. The Eye seemed to understand it, however. The slow blinking of its upper lid seemed to follow the cadences of Petrov's voice.

Flopkin felt the last of his courage drain away. What *was* Petrov? Not a rabbit, despite his appearance. No rabbit could sit there so calmly, crooning to this dreadful Eye in a weird language.

It came to Flopkin that he didn't want to find out what Petrov *really* looked like.

He turned and ran, stumbling, back down the tunnel.

When he reached the other rabbits, he was breathless and almost incoherent. 'G-g—' he stammered. 'G-g-got to g-g-g—'

'Steady on, Flopkin,' said Mopkin kindly, placing a paw on his leader's trembling shoulder. 'Take your time. What's the matter?'

Flopkin breathed steadily for a moment. Then he said, in as controlled a voice as he could manage, 'We must get out of here. Petrov is not a rabbit.'

'What do you mean?' asked several anxious voices.

'He's not a rabbit,' Flopkin insisted. 'He's – something else. A wizard, maybe. Whatever he is, it's not something rabbits can deal with. We'll have to leave him to somebody else.'

He stopped speaking, and waited, desperately afraid that they would refuse to listen to him.

But the warren had had enough. Petrov's plan had not worked out as he promised, and Petrov seemed to have walked out on them. And they were afraid of Petrov, and they liked Flopkin, even if he wasn't as good at getting lettuces as they might have wished.

'We'll come with you, Flopkin,' said someone. 'You tell us what to do.' There was a murmur of agreement.

'We have to leave the warren,' said Flopkin. 'Something dreadful is going to happen, and we have to get as far away as possible before it does. Anyone who wants to stay behind can, of course.'

'We'll follow you, Flopkin,' said someone eagerly, and there was a chorus of agreement.

For the first time in what seemed like ages, Flopkin felt a surge of optimism.

'Come on, then,' he said. 'Let's get out of this tunnel.'

'So!'

The exultant syllable echoed round the wine cellar of Redbrush Hall.

'The Eye of Balor!' Archon's voice was full of triumph. 'At last – after a thousand years! The first stage of my Plan is complete! Hahahahahaha[1]!!!'

The Eye, which gave the impression of taking all this in its stride, gazed stoically at the wall of the cellar. After a moment it lowered its lid, cutting off the grey light.

'Stop that!' snapped Archon. 'I didn't give you permission to close!'

The Eye opened its lid again with evident reluctance.

'I suppose you're tired,' murmured Archon. 'After a thousand years, it's not surprising.' He yawned. 'Actually, I feel rather tired myself. The Grey Magic takes it out of you. Perhaps we could have a little rest before we go on to the next stage.' He glanced around the cellar, and his eyes lighted on the wine-barrels in the alcoves. 'And a little celebratory refreshment. What do you think?'

The Eye lowered and raised its lid, though perhaps with a certain lack of enthusiasm, since it was not going to be the one getting the celebratory drink.

In the small hours of the morning, Mrs Tod woke up. She lay staring at the ceiling, clutching the bedclothes round her chin, listening.

She could hear a noise.

She frowned, and concentrated hard. There were

[1]The insane cackle of the megalomaniac master criminal.

plenty of noises in Redbrush Hall at night – the usual scratchings and creakings, due to mice no doubt, and probably also those dratted rabbits again, she would have to make sure Macpherson put that poison down in the morning and dealt with them once and for all. But this noise didn't sound like any of these. It was a faint, distant noise that was hard to identify. It might be a large cat yowling, but there were no cats at Redbrush Hall these days. It might be a dragon roaring quietly, or possibly even a dragon being sick, but neither of those seemed likely.

Mrs Tod yawned. She was very sleepy. Whatever it was, it could wait till the morning.

She dropped off to sleep again, and dreamed that a huge savage rabbit with razor-sharp teeth was gnawing at the bedpost and getting nearer and nearer to her legs. She moaned a little and moved fitfully, but didn't wake again.

Down the corridor in his own small room, Macpherson was also dreaming, but with a smile on his face. He was dreaming of a tavern in his old home of Glenmiller in Scotland, and a huge bottle of whisky.

If Macpherson had woken up, he would have recognised the mysterious noise immediately, because it was very like one that he used to make himself late on a Saturday night, in the good old days before Mrs Tod made him go on the wagon.

It was the sound of someone very drunk, singing.

The barrels in the wine cellar had been there a long time, and the proximity of the Eye of Balor hadn't improved the vintage, but the wine inside was still drinkable, although only if your favourite tipple happened to be vinegar. Fortunately Archon loved vinegar.

He had drunk most of one barrel, and was sitting in the middle of the floor, hiccuping and yodelling. The vinegar had loosened his grip on the rabbit-shape, and he had mostly turned back into a slug, albeit a slug with large ears and a fluffy white tail.

Archon was currently singing a song he had just made up. It was coming out rather slurred, but went something like this:

That old Grey Magic has got me in its enchantment,

That old Grey Magic with which I am so extremely familiar . . .

It was a rather rough and ready song at the moment, but he felt it had potential. It just needed a bit more work.

The Eye of Balor, meanwhile, regarded him balefully. It gave the impression, without of course actually saying anything, that it rather disapproved of shape-shifting slug-rabbits who couldn't hold their vinegar.

'*Hic!*' said Archon, not for the first time. He gazed blearily up at the Eye. 'You don't 'prove of me, d'you, Eye? Hey? Well, thashall right. I don't 'prove of me either. *Hic!*'

The Eye drooped its lid in a resigned manner.

'You 'n' I,' said Archon, waving his rabbit-ears and his eye-stalks in opposite directions, 'are gonna conquer th'world. Wotcher finker that, hey? *Hic!*'

The Eye looked up at the ceiling.

'Gonna conquer th'world,' Archon reiterated. 'But not t'night. T'night we have fun. Gonna shing a shong. Yawanna shing a shong? Shingalongalongashong, hey? *Hic!*'

The Eye continued to look at the ceiling, as if hoping it would fall on them both and put an end to this.

'C'm on, don' be shy,' Archon continued encouragingly. His rabbit's ears were slowly going out of shape.

They were more like elephant's ears now. 'How 'bout a diff'rent shong? Here'sh one you prob'ly know.

A wandering slug am I,
A thing of slime and wobbles—
I ooze across the cobbles
And swallow you i-in a trice!'

The Eye closed its upper lid in despair. There was only one hope. Perhaps complete darkness would send Archon to sleep.

Chapter Nine

'So,' said Hergrim next morning, 'did you work out what *goe sunnewyse from ye welle* means?'

The wizard shook his head.

'Then what,' demanded the dwarf, 'are we standing here in the garden for? And why did you ask me to make sandwiches?'

Gwydden looked up at the cloudless blue sky. 'I was hoping I might be inspired once we started off.'

'Inspired? You? Well, I believe miracles do occasionally happen.' The dwarf sat down on the edge of the well and opened his rucksack, which contained their packed lunch and four bottles of Frigga's Revenge. 'While we're waiting, I'll open a bottle. Fancy a drop?'

'No thanks. I need to keep a clear head.'

'Ah.' The dwarf smiled cynically. 'This is *clear* as in *empty*, is it?'

Gwydden scowled and said something in Latin. It didn't sound like a spell, and Hergrim wisely refrained from asking what it meant.

There followed a deep and meaningful silence, which Gwydden filled by staring at the sky (on the grounds that that was the direction inspiration was likely to come from, if anywhere), and Hergrim filled by eating one of the packed lunches. When he had finished, he stood up and said, 'I think I'll stretch my legs now.' He stared hard at Gwydden, in case the wizard ventured any of the replies that people sometimes make when dwarfs say this[1], but the wizard was still scrutinising the heavens with an abstracted air, so Hergrim turned and stumped off. He had no particular direction or purpose in mind, but a dwarf at a loose end gets restless, which is why dwarfs get into so many fights with their neighbours.

Uther sat in his boxwood throne in the Great Hall, his chin resting on his hand, feeling as depressed as he had ever felt in his life. *Find a wizard,* Boadicea had said. That was easy enough – the Green Light district in Camelot was infested with them. He had been unable to track down the wizard Gwydden, whose lodgings had been found empty and shut up, but there had been a flood of replies to his advertisement in *Wizard's Weekly,* which ran as follows:

Anonymous king urgently requires wizard to defeat evil sorcery. Must possess own pointy hat. This is a temporary contract, caused by the mysterious disappearance of the current post-holder. Apply Royal Box 1, Great Hall, Camelot Castle.

Finding a wizard was no problem. But finding a *powerful* wizard – or even one who was reasonably competent – was like trying to find gold nuggets on the floor of a pigeon-loft.

With a deep sigh, Uther transferred his chin to the other hand, and tried hard to concentrate on what the latest interviewee for the post of Acting Temporary Saviour of Camelot from Unspecified Supernatural Evil was saying.

---

[1] E.g. 'yes, they could do with it'; 'by about eighteen inches, if I were you'; and 'why stop at the legs?' It's amazing how easily people forget that dwarfs are quick to take offence and carry large, sharp axes.

'And this spell, Your Majesty,' said the grey-robed figure, holding up a grimoire in one hand and an *Excelsior Demongrabber* in the other, both of them looking suspiciously shiny and little-used, 'is one that is known only to myself and the Great Chan of Outer Mongolia, who was kind enough to say that I was the brightest student he had ever had.'

'Ah,' said Uther. 'Jolly good. Splendid.' He hid a yawn behind his hand. 'What sort of spell, exactly?' Most of the candidates that morning had tried to turn things into gold. All of them had failed miserably, except one who had inadvertently turned his beard into straw – admittedly of a rather nice golden colour.

The candidate swelled his chest with evident pride. 'I shall now turn myself into a dragon!' he announced in a loud voice.

Uther raised his eyebrows and began to pay attention. This was different. 'A dragon? What – fiery breath and all?'

'Certainly, your Majesty.'

'I see.' Uther glanced round the room anxiously. It had never struck him before how flammable the furnishings in his castle were. 'You won't set fire to anything, I hope?'

'Of course not, your Majesty.'

'Good, good. Off you go, then.'

The candidate struck a suitably impressive pose and began to read in a deep, incantatory tone from the grimoire. His chant rose to a crescendo, he waved the staff in a mystic pass, and there was a puff of eldritch-looking purple smoke. When it cleared, the interviewee had vanished.

The staff and the grimoire clattered to the ground. A grey robe and a pointy hat fluttered down beside them.

Uther looked around anxiously. Then he looked

above him, into the rafters, expecting at any moment to see a huge scaly shape looming over him. But the room seemed to be entirely free of dragons.

'Er – hullo? Are you still here?'

There was a slight movement among the folds of the robe, and a small white mouse emerged.

'Ah,' said Uther, relaxing. 'There you are. Not a total success, hey?'

'Squeak,' said the mouse irritably. 'Squeak squeak squeak.'

Uther beckoned to a nearby guard. 'Take these things away, will you?'

The guard picked up the wizard's gear. Lastly he picked up the wizard.

'Squeak?' enquired the mouse, sitting up on its haunches in the palm of the guard's hand and looking up at the King.

'Don't call us,' said Uther, 'we'll call you. Send in the next candidate.'

The mouse, still squeaking, but in a more resigned way, was escorted from the Great Hall. Another figure entered, strutted proudly up to the throne, and bowed with a flourish. He looked discouragingly young, and his grey robe was rather too big for him.

'Your Majesty,' said the new candidate. 'I would like to show you a spell which is known only to myself and the High Magus of Persia, who was once kind enough to say that I was the brightest student he had ever had.'

Uther hid another yawn behind his hand.

'I shall now turn myself into a dragon!' The interviewee raised his staff and struck the same pose as his predecessor.

A moment later, a white mouse emerged from a collapsed pile of wizard's accoutrements and squeaked crossly.

Uther sighed. At this rate he would still be interviewing wizards when the expected Danger To Camelot walked into the Great Hall and handed him a printed card with its name on. It was time to make an executive decision. 'Very well. You've got the job. As from now, you're Acting Temporary Saviour of Camelot from Unspecified Supernatural Evil.'

'Squeak?' The mouse was evidently surprised.

'Why not? You're no worse than any of the others, and I'm getting bored. Your salary will be five groats a day. By the way, I shouldn't stay a mouse too long. There are several cats in this castle, you know.'

The mouse looked anxiously around, squeaked several times in mouse-Latin[1], and twitched its whiskers in an occult fashion. There was a puff of smoke, and a skinny young man wearing nothing but goose-pimples stood before the King.

'Put your robe back on,' said Uther kindly.

The young wizard hurriedly obliged. He picked up his staff and grimoire, and assumed as dignified a pose as someone who has recently been a rodent is entitled to.

'I feel I must apologise, your Majesty,' he said, his tone managing to be both embarrassed and pompous at the same time. 'I can't think what went wrong. The grimoire must have contained a misprint.'

'Oddly enough, I believe you,' said the King. 'However, it doesn't matter. What's your name?'

The wizard pulled off his pointy hat and executed a low bow. 'I am The Great Alfonso, your Majesty.'

'If it's all the same to you, I shall just call you Alfonso.' Uther twirled a set of imaginary mouse-whiskers and twitched his nose meaningfully.

---

[1]Mouse-Latin is like ordinary Latin, except that it has three hundred and fifty-seven different words for cheese.

The young wizard coloured a little. 'Of course, your Majesty. Alfonso would be fine. It's only a professional name anyway. My real name is Colin Higinbotham.'

He really is very young, thought Uther. *Still, I expect he'll grow into the job.* 'Well, we'll keep that a secret between ourselves, eh Colin – I mean Alfonso? Now, the first thing I want you to do is start mugging up on all the spells, incantations and general magical thingummies that might be useful when Camelot is attacked – okay?'

The Great Alfonso looked startled. 'Oh – is the city going to be attacked, then, your Majesty?'

Uther nodded. 'So the hen-woman, Boadicea, tells me.'

Alfonso's eyes narrowed. 'Boadicea? I shouldn't trust *her*, your Majesty. I've heard it on good authority that she's a witch.'

'Not a practising one,' said Uther. 'She only uses her powers for reading hen-droppings. Anyway, what's wrong with witches? Nice old biddies, mostly. Kind to cats.'

The erstwhile mouse sniffed. 'Witches aren't properly trained, your Majesty. Not educated at the Academy, like us wizards. And anyway, women have the wrong sort of brains to be good at magic.'

'I shouldn't let Boadicea hear you say that,' said Uther. 'She might think you're being disrespectful, and I've seen what Boadicea does to drunken soldiers who get disrespectful. Anyway, she *has* got second-sight, so if she says the city is going to be attacked, I believe her. So I want you to prepare our defences. Weave a spell round the city, or something.'

Colin Alfonso Higinbotham furrowed his brow. 'It would need to be a ruddy big spell, your Majesty.'

'Then you'd better get cracking, hadn't you?'

'Er – yes, of course.' The young wizard nodded

energetically. 'I shall look into it at once, your Majesty. Oh, and your Majesty—'

'Yes?'

'It might be a good idea if I had a room in the castle to use as a laboratory. More convenient than my lodgings.'

'Very well. How about the ground floor, near the kitchens?'

The Great Alfonso hesitated, in a manner that suggested that he was about to say something extremely presumptuous.

'Wizarding isn't really a ground floor sort of thing, your Majesty. You want *height*, really. And lots of windows, so you can keep an eye on star-patterns, comets, the weather, and so on. And kitchens are rather noisy places, aren't they? Wizarding needs peace and quiet. Also, if cooking odours get into the spells, they can cause unforeseen results, so—'

'A room in one of the towers, then,' said Uther, with a slight smile. He was beginning to see where this was leading.

'Well, er, that would be much better, of course. But the *best* room, obviously, would be the highest room in the highest tower, which—'

'That would be Merlin's study.'

'Oh, really?' The Great Alfonso opened his eyes so wide that his eyebrows disappeared under his pointy hat. Uther had rarely seen such an unconvincing display of surprise. 'Oh, I see. Well, do you think – I mean, Merlin apparently isn't using it at the moment, so perhaps, if it isn't too much trouble—'

Uther chuckled inwardly. He kept a straight face, however, and merely nodded. 'I have no objection. But you do realise that Merlin will probably have left a few spells around to deter unwelcome visitors? For instance,

185

I happen to know that his doorknob is decidedly unfriendly.'

The Great Alfonso smiled in a superior fashion. 'Don't worry about that, your Majesty. I passed my exam in Warding Spells at the Academy with flying colours. I shouldn't think there's anything Merlin knows about that particular branch of magic that I don't.'

Hergrim's walk had taken him to the edge of the cottage garden, marked by a line of half-rotted posts, and then across the park of Redbrush Hall. After a while he struck what seemed to be a path, and out of curiosity he followed it. It seemed to be taking a gentle curve across the park, but it was so heavily overgrown that after a while he lost track of it. He turned back, found it again, and followed it in the opposite direction. Rather to his surprise, it brought him in a roundabout way back to the well.

He sat down again on the edge of the well and opened a second bottle of Frigga's Revenge. 'Any luck?'

The wizard had stopped staring at the sky and was now throwing pebbles into a pile of leaves. He looked bored and irritable. 'Ruddy Nostradimwit – why couldn't he say what he meant? *Goe sunnewyse from ye welle* – what use is that? It wouldn't have hurt him to say *go west until you reach the third beech tree and then ask the nearest hedgehog*, would it? Or *walk along the route marked with blue crosses to the grove of elder trees?*'

'Or *follow the path made of small square stones across the park?*' suggested the dwarf, taking a swig of his beer.

'Exactly.' The wizard threw a stone at the well. 'Where have you been, anyway?'

'Following the path made of small square stones across the park,' said the dwarf. 'Fancy a drink?'

'No thanks.' The wizard frowned. 'What path is this?'

'The one that starts just where you're sitting.'

Gwydden looked down at his feet. 'Where?'

Hergrim pointed. 'See? It curves away into the under-growth. I followed it as far as I could, but then it petered out.'

Gwydden peered at the ground. 'You mean this line of stones?'

'Yes.'

'How can you tell that's a path? They're all mossy and overgrown.'

'Yes, but they're obviously artificial. You don't get small square stones laid like that unless someone lays them.'

'True.' The wizard got down on his knees and scruti-nised the stones more closely. 'These aren't stones, they're bricks. And they've been painted – you can still see a few flecks of colour.'

'What colour?'

'Yellow.' The wizard straightened up. 'You know, I think we ought to follow this yellow brick road.'

Hergrim stared. 'Why?'

Gwydden shrugged. 'I don't know. Something seems to be telling me to[1].'

'But I told you,' said the dwarf, 'it peters out.'

'Humour me,' said the wizard, favouring Hergrim with what was meant to be a winning smile.

'Huh.' The dwarf drained his beer. The weather was turning hot, and he would much rather have forgotten

---

[1] This was presumably either the voice of Gwydden's mythopoeic Jungian archetypal subconscious, or Judy Garland singing through a time-warp. (Of course it is entirely possible, since the universe is such a strange place, that these two are the *same thing* . . .)

about questing for the day and had a snooze in a deck-chair. 'All right. But I don't see what this yellow brick road has to do with Nostradimwit.'

'Nothing at all, probably. Call it serendipity.'

'I prefer to call it a waste of time,' muttered the dwarf. But he shouldered his axe, and set off along the path he had just trodden the opposite way, Gwydden following close behind.

Archon came back to consciousness with the realisation that he had drunk far too much vinegar the night before. He opened his eyes with extreme care. It was pitch black in the cellar, but that was still far too bright for comfort.

Cautiously, from the inside, he examined his shape to see what he was this morning[1]. The fluffy tail and the ears had gone, and he was back in his slug-shape. He had a thumping ache in what would have been his head if he had had one. Last night had definitely been a mistake.

'*Uuurrghhh,*' he groaned. This seemed to summarise quite accurately how he was feeling, so he said it again.

There was a sudden intolerable flash of something slightly less black than utter darkness.

'*Aaarrgh!*' said Archon in agony. 'Turn that light down!'

The Eye, which had been patiently waiting for hours for its new master to wake, closed its lid again. The beam of grey light vanished.

'Thank you.' Archon waved his eye-stalks gently for a few moments while he tried to remember the shape-shifter's cure for hangovers.

---

[1] If you accidentally knock someone down, and their first question on coming round is 'where am I?', you should call an ambulance. If it's '*what* am I?', you should drive away, very fast.

Ah, he thought. *Of course.*

There was a swirl of displaced molecules, and the giant slug vanished. Three seconds later, a two-headed troll, seven feet tall and carrying a huge scimitar, appeared in its place. The troll's right head was relaxed and had its eyes open. The left had its eyes tightly shut and its forehead knotted in pain.

With a backward sweep of his scimitar, Archon cut off his left head. It rolled across the floor and came to rest against an empty wine-barrel.

'*Aaah*,' murmured Archon. 'That feels better.[1] Eye – open!'

The Eye obediently raised its lid. Grey light shot across the cellar. The troll-head lying next to the wine-barrel groaned.

'Shut up, you,' said Archon. He kicked the head into the shadows, where it grumbled quietly to itself for a while and then was silent.

'Now.' Archon raised his scimitar and gazed thoughtfully at the green-stained blade. 'We have things to do. We must once again summon the Grey Magic.' He hefted the scimitar a few times, and brought it down in a practice swipe that would have sliced anyone standing a yard away into two pieces. 'I like this shape. I think I'll wear it for a while. Now the first thing to do is to open a door to Lochlann. Do you remember how to do that?'

The Eye lowered its lid in a gesture of assent.

'Good. Over there will be as good as anywhere.' Archon pointed his scimitar at a place in the centre of the floor some yards away. 'Focus your light there.'

---

[1]Kids – *don't try this headache cure at home!* It can be very dangerous, especially if, like most of my readers, you only have one head.

The Eye narrowed its pupil. The beam of grey light became a thin cone whose point rested on the floor.

'Good. And now the chant.' Archon raised his arms and began to mutter in the ancient language of the Fhomoire.

After a while, things began to happen. A crack appeared in the floor, and grey mist began to rise from it. The crack widened and became a jagged hole. The hole rose and widened further, like the mouth of a volcano. Something grey, wrinkled and hump-like pushed slowly up through the crater, as though the earth was giving birth to a very old baby.

'Excellent,' breathed Archon, breaking off in mid-mutter. 'Here it comes, at last!'

He resumed his muttering. The grey mist thickened. Grey slime oozed up out of the hole, and started to spread out over the cellar floor.

The hump-like object continued to rise. It looked even more like a head now, a strange bulbous head with a single sightless eye-socket. It rose towards the ceiling, above which was the ground floor of Redbrush Hall.

Grey slime continued to bubble up into the cellar.

The direction taken by the yellow brick road was curious. It started off by looping round the well, and then curved away in a wider loop around the cottage.

'It goes in a spiral, you see,' said the dwarf, pushing his way through the matted and overgrown weeds that continued without a break beyond the cottage garden. 'Outwards from the well. The curves of the spiral get bigger, and—'

'And that's not all,' said the wizard excitedly. 'Have you realised what direction this path goes in? We started off east, then turned south, then west, and now we're heading north. We're going sunwise! This must be the path Nostradimwit meant!'

'Maybe,' said the dwarf, his voice muffled by rampant hemlock and hogweed. 'But it still peters out further on.'

In the scullery, Macpherson was peeling potatoes. This was not his favourite occupation. His large hands were clumsy at handling anything much smaller than a blunderbuss, and the knife he was using was both tiny and extremely sharp. The potatoes were whites, but after his efforts they became reds. The water in the sink looked as though a school of piranha had got lucky.

'Ow! Och, ye wee skellum!'

Mrs Tod lowered her latest sampler, which showed a bored-looking youth in leather shorts drinking, smoking and playing cards. The wording underneath read: *The Devil finds work for idle Hans.*

'Macpherson! Kindly moderate your language!'

'Haud yer wheesht, woman,' said the gardener angrily. 'I wisna cussin'. Can ye no' buy a decent sized knife, ye auld skinflint?'

'That knife did very well for my mother's housekeeper,' said Mrs Tod, tight-lipped.

'Aye, it's nearly done for me, too,' grumbled the gardener. He sucked at his bleeding fingers. "Tis a muckle o' skaithin' fer a puckle bit tattie-claw.'

Mrs Tod had no idea what this last remark of Macpherson's meant, but she was not going to admit the fact, and merely tutted. 'If you'd concentrated more and complained less, those potatoes would be finished by now.'

Macpherson opened his mouth to retort, but at that moment the tap above the sink coughed like a man with bronchial pneumonia, and something grey and stinking began to ooze out of it.

'Yeuch!'

'What's the matter now?'

The gardener was staring in fascinated horror at the grey stuff. 'There's somethin' *horr-rrible* pourin' oot frae the tap!'

'What? What are you talking about?'

'Somethin' *horr-rrible!*' Macpherson repeated, staring at the slithering grey gunge.

'Show me – bring it here.'

'Och, I'm no' touchin' that stuff. 'Tis *evil* – ye can tell by the smell of it. 'Tis like *death.*'

'What rubbish.' Mrs Tod peered at him scornfully. 'Probably a carrier pigeon's fallen into the water tank again. Go up to the loft and clean it out.'

The gardener wiped his troubled brow with his hand, leaving a thin red streak. 'Ma'am, I think ye should come and see this. It's – it's *unnatural.*'

'Don't be such a credulous fool,' snapped Mrs Tod. 'Dirt is just dirt - there's nothing evil or unnatural about it.'

'This isna ordinary dirt,' the gardener insisted doggedly.

'Well, turn the tap off.'

'It *is* off!'

'That's impossible.'

'Aye, I ken.'

'Well, are you going to look at the water tank, or not?'

'Ma'am—'

But we shall never know whether Macpherson was willing to look at the water tank, because at that moment the grey substance began to ooze into the scullery from several other places as well.

''Ma'am! *'Tis comin' up through the floor!*'

'I thought I told you to weight those flagstones down!'

'This isna rabbits, ye daft besom—'

'How dare you take that tone with me, Macpherson!'

'And now 'tis oozin' through the walls!'

'So I observe,' said Mrs Tod coldly. 'And I must say, Macpherson, that when I took you on as gardener and handyman, I expected you to take better care of the fabric of this house. You should have taken steps to prevent any occurrence of rising damp.'

'*Risin' damp?* Are ye mad, woman? This isna risin' damp. This is *supernatural!*'

Mrs Tod folded her arms. 'Poppycock!'

'Och, ye silly auld—' The gardener stared round him wildly. Grey stinking sludge was steadily rising through the floor. It had already reached his ankles. The walls were disappearing under a slithering coat of what looked like grey wallpaper paste. The deathly stench was overpowering.

Macpherson came to a decision. He swiftly crossed the scullery and seized Mrs Tod. 'Forgive me, ma'am!'

'Macpherson, put me down at once!'

'Sorry, ma'am,' said the gardener, cradling his squirming employer gently but firmly in his arms, 'but this isna a place for a lady. Or for a gardener, either.'

'Unhand me, sir! Put me down and give me my sampler, this instant! What on earth do you think you are doing?'

'I'm tryin' tae find the door. Ah, there it is. Now – let's awa' oot of here, before this grey horror suffocates us!'

'*I want my sampler!*' shrieked Mrs Tod, beating her rescuer about the face with her tiny paws.

'—— yer wretched sampler,' growled the Scot, forcing open the scullery door and shouldering his way out through the dripping gunge into the fresh air.

The first word in Macpherson's utterance was unfamiliar to Mrs Tod, but from the gardener's tone she guessed that she had probably seen the last of idle Hans.

'I told you it petered out.' The dwarf had stopped at the end of the path, and was peering over the high uncut grass.

Gwydden, however, being a few inches taller, had seen the rough line of the path continuing further on, sweeping across the park of Redbrush Hall in a wide curve. He pushed the high undergrowth aside with his staff and moved in front of the dwarf. A moment later they were pressing forward again, down the smooth slope that Culpability Brown had made.

They were so busy following the yellow brick road that neither of them noticed what was happening to the Hall.

'By the sacred haggis o' the Macphersons,' breathed the gardener, gazing at the Hall from a hopefully safe distance of fifty yards. 'Will ye look at what's happening?'

'I am looking,' snapped Mrs Tod. 'And if this is your doing, Macpherson, then all I can say is, you'd better start looking for another position. And will you *please* put me down!'

'Sorry, ma'am.' The gardener lowered her to the ground. 'Och, will ye no' look? 'Tis *horr-rrible!*'

What was happening to Redbrush Hall was certainly not nice. Grey slime had oozed up from the cellars and engulfed the entire building, so that not a single brick or chimneypot could now be seen – only a grey, wobbling, jelly-like mass.

A strange noise could be heard emanating from inside the slime. It sounded to Macpherson's ears rather like a large dog chewing a marrowbone.

'Wheesht, man,' whispered the gardener, his eyes round as saucers. 'This isna canny. 'Tis foul sorcery, or I'm a Welshman.'

'Macpherson!'

The gardener recalled himself with an effort. 'Aye, ma'am?'

'Don't just stand there, you Scots oaf! *Do* something!'

The Scot turned lugubrious eyes downwards to the diminutive figure whose red fur was bristling angrily. 'What would ye suggest, ma'am?'

'I don't know, you fool. *You* think of something!'

There was a crunching of footsteps on the gravelled path behind them, and an oily voice said, 'Dear me! What an extraordinary sight!'

Mrs Tod turned sharply. 'Mr Smyrk? What are you doing here?'

'My dear Mrs Tod.' The estate agent's hands coiled round and round each other obsequiously. 'Don't you remember, dear lady? You asked me to call and value your property *vis-à-vis* putting it on the market. But my dear Mrs Tod, what on earth is happening to your delightful residence? Is it some sort of refurbishment? Are there workmen under that grey substance, assiduously renovating your stonework?'

'No, Mr Smyrk, there are not. Someone has put a curse, or a spell, on Redbrush Hall. My man Macpherson here seems singularly devoid of ideas as to what to do. Perhaps you can suggest something.'

'Ah.' The smile on the estate agent's weasel-like face grew a little strained. 'I think, dear lady, you would be better advised to call upon the services of a qualified wizard. Spells and curses are not really within my professional ambit.'

'Wizards!' Mrs Tod spat the word out as if it tasted

rancid. 'No doubt it was that wizard who called the other day who caused all this. Merlin, his name was.'

'Merlin? Dear me.' Mr Smyrk was a little shocked. 'I would be most surprised to hear that Merlin had caused anything so untoward. A most respectable fellow – for a wizard, that is. A pillar of Camelot society. He and I share the same tailor.'

'Indeed?' Mrs Tod glanced at Mr Smyrk's expensively-cut pin-stripe. 'No doubt he overcharges his clients to the same degree that you do yours.'

Mr Smyrk's smile changed from strained to glassily frozen. A professional man must expect this sort of pleasant chaff. 'Ha, ha. You jest, my dear Mrs Tod, you jest. Ha ha.'

'I never jest, Mr Smyrk.' The mistress of Redbrush Hall put her paws on her hips and looked from the gardener to the estate agent and back. 'Have neither of you any ideas? Heaven knows what is happening to my family seat under all that filthy gunge.' She waved an angry paw at the invisible building.

Uuurrr-hhukkkh!

There was an apprehensive silence.

'Macpherson, was that you?' Mrs Tod enquired frostily. She was familiar with some of the noises the gardener produced after a hearty meal.

'Och, no, indeed, ma'am,' said the Scot in a pained voice.

'I think, dear lady, that it came from the Hall,' ventured Mr Smyrk.

They looked towards the ancestral seat of the Redbrush family.

It was shrinking.

Uurr-hhhk! Huppp! Rggggh! came the noises. They sounded like giant belches. Interspersed with them were the sounds that had seemed to Macpherson like the crunching of bones. The grey jelly-like mass was getting progressively smaller.

'My *dear* Mrs Tod,' murmured the estate agent. 'That is undoubtedly the worst case of subsidence I have ever seen.'

Urgghk! Each time the grey slime burped, a little cloud of stone-dust rose into the air and hung there in the sunshine.

' 'Tis *eating* the Hall,' whispered the gardener in an awestruck voice.

'*Eating my home?*' Mrs Tod's voice was a shriek of disbelief. 'Macpherson – for pity's sake, *do* something!'

But the gardener only shook his head and continued to watch the grey mass slowly collapsing towards the earth.

'Mr Smyrk!' Mrs Tod turned despairingly to the estate agent. '*Please!*'

The estate agent looked from his client's horror-struck face to the sinking Hall, and tried to recall, from his years of professional training, what one was supposed to say in situations like this. 'Dear lady,' he murmured comfortingly. 'You need have no worries. The insurer will pay up very promptly – assuming, of course, that your policy contained the usual clause covering you against damage due to fire, earthquake, floods, and sorcerous grey slime.'

'Insurer?' Mrs Tod almost screamed. 'There was no insurer! I cancelled the policy last year. We couldn't afford the premiums.'

'Ah. I see.' The estate agent's manner suddenly changed. Mrs Tod, it was clear, was unlikely to be able to afford his services for some considerable time. His back straightened, his humble shoulders broadened and became proud, and his sycophantic smile was replaced by a coldly unsympathetic smirk. 'How very regrettable.' He took a gold-plated sundial on a gold chain from his waistcoat pocket and looked at it. 'I'm afraid I have business to attend to. Goodbye, Mrs Tod. Goodbye, Macpherson.' He turned and crunched purposefully away over the gravel.

Mrs Tod raised her paws despairingly to heaven. 'What am I to do? I'm ruined – homeless! I shall end up sleeping in a hole in the ground!' She shuddered. 'The Redbrush family haven't slept underground for generations. I shall catch my death of cold.'

'Aye, we'll all be under the groond afore long, I'm thinking,' said the gardener gloomily. 'There's a deathly curse come on the place.' He pointed a gnarled red finger. 'Look at yon monstrosity rising oot o' the slime!'

Mrs Tod looked, and let out a shriek. 'Stewed voles and hen's eggs! What is it? It's *hideous!*'

Where the Forest's only stately home had stood, another structure was now rising. It was grey, like the slime subsiding around it. It was certainly a tower, though its architect must have had either a warped mind or a warped drawing-board. Twisted and deformed, it resembled a crooked arthritic finger with a swollen top joint. In this bulbous top, presumably embedded in some kind of cavity, was an Eye. As Mrs Tod and Macpherson watched in horrified fascination, the lid of the Eye rose, and a grey light stabbed across Redbrush Park. Where the light fell, trees and grass withered and grew pale.

'What are we to do?' wailed the dispossessed mistress of Redbrush Hall.

'We canna do but one thing,' said Macpherson. 'We must go tae Arcadia.'

The lady fox frowned. 'That is not amusing, Macpherson.'

'It wasna meant tae be.'

Mrs Tod folded her arms. 'You are suggesting that I go and see *him*? After the disgrace he brought on us by leaving?'

'Aye, I am. Dammit, woman, this is no time for family feuding. Whatever differences ye may have had wi' him in the past, 'tis all pointless now. Look at yon.' The gardener pointed again at the place where Redbrush Hall wasn't. 'That was his home, just as much as yours. He ought tae be consulted.'

Mrs Tod nodded reluctantly. 'I suppose you're right.'

'Aye, I am.'

'Then let's go and see him. Though I don't see that it will do any good.'

Chapter Ten

Oblivious of the fact that Redbrush Hall had just been eaten, Gwydden and Hergrim came to the north-western edge of the park, and were confronted by a dense growth of tall trees and tangled bushes. The line of yellow bricks vanished into it.

'Now what?' said the dwarf.

Gwydden scratched his head. 'We could try clearing some of this undergrowth.'

Hergrim raised an eyebrow. 'You must be joking. It would take ten dwarfs with large axes six weeks to clear this lot.'

'Perhaps you're right. Let's see if *The Wizard's Handbook* can help.' The wizard produced his favourite grimoire from the recesses of his tunic, and thumbed through the pages. 'There's not much here. All I can find is *A spell to improve the garden by ridding it of weeds and other pests.*'

'Worth a try, I should think,' said the dwarf.

'All right.' The wizard pointed his staff at the ground in front of him and muttered a few Latin words.

The result was rather remarkable. All the sorrels, rag-worts and other plants in a long line ahead of them hoisted their roots out of the earth and walked away. Their manner was distinctly huffy, and some of the larger weeds waved their leaves at Gwydden in an un-friendly way. When they had gone a few feet, they set about digging themselves into the earth again, irritably shoving aside smaller weeds that were unlucky enough to be in their way.

Then the soil erupted, and a mole stuck its head out. It was covered in dust, and holding a carpet-brush in one paw.

'Did somebody just say *discedete omnes?*' it said, peering up with short-sighted eyes in the direction of the wizard.

'Yes, I did,' said Gwydden.

'You want me to leave? Right now?'

'No, no,' said Gwydden. 'That's all right. I was just trying to clear the weeds.'

'Oh.' The mole sounded disappointed. 'I thought perhaps you might want me to help in an adventure – boating on the river with water-rats, riding in brightly-painted caravans with toads, fighting stoats and weasels, that sort of thing.'

'No, sorry.'

The mole sighed. 'Oh well, never mind. Back to the cleaning.' It disappeared again below ground.

The yellow brick road was now visible again, curving away into the trees. They continued along it. Although at first sight the undergrowth had seemed impenetrable, they found that there was always a narrow gap through which to squeeze, although the overhanging branches made it hazardous and sometimes painful.

'There's more to this path than meets the eye,' said Gwydden.

'These branches keep trying to meet my eye,' growled the dwarf. 'Ow! That one nearly succeeded. I don't think this path was meant for people of my height.'

'No.' The wizard thrust his way through a bramble and accidentally collected a number of blackberries in his sleeves. He took them out and ate them absentmindedly. 'But it was clearly meant for *someone*. I wonder who made it.'

'Culpability Brown?' suggested the dwarf.

'Unlikely. I think this path probably pre-dates Redbrush Hall itself.'

Doggedly, they continued to follow the yellow brick road.

In the centre of Redbrush Park, where the family pile of the Earls of Redbrush had stood, there was now a tall, ugly tower. At the base of the tower was a mouth-like doorway, from which grey mist was steadily pouring. All the vegetation in a wide circle around the tower, including Macpherson's prized lettuces, had turned grey and withered. A terrible stench of decay was gradually drifting out into the Forest.

Archon was strutting round the tower, admiring it. 'Excellent!' he murmured. 'The Tower of Yrminsul! A thousand years I've waited to see this. Now for stage two.' He looked up at the Eye. 'You remember what stage two is, I hope?'

The Eye lowered its lid briefly. Slowly, like a finger crooking, the tower bent forward, until the Eye was able to focus its beam downwards, on the black doorway.

There was a distant cracking noise – so distant, in fact, that it might perhaps have come from another dimension. A few shards of stone rolled out of the doorway.

'Aha!' Archon rubbed his thick, hairy troll-hands together in glee. 'Here they come!'

A few thicker tendrils of grey mist drifted out of the entrance.

Something slowly oozed out of the doorway and stood waving its eye-stalks in the sunlight.

On the edge of the park, a female voice screamed.

*   *   *

'Mrs Tod! Are ye all right?'

The lady of Redbrush Hall opened her eyes and almost screamed a second time. A ghastly apparition hung over her, huge, misshapen and mottled with unsightly red patches. A nightmarish face.

But then, she had always known that Macpherson was far from handsome.

'Are ye all right, ma'am?'

Mrs Tod struggled to her feet and adjusted her pince-nez. 'Perfectly all right, thank you. There is no need to fuss. I was just taken a little by surprise, and I – I—'

'Fainted,' supplied the gardener helpfully.

The vixen looked at him sharply. 'Nonsense.'

'Aye, that ye did. Not that it's any wonder, considerin' yon ghastly thing that's jist come oot o' that tower.' The gardener pointed across the park. 'Och, will ye look at that? There's more o' the foul things!'

'No, I won't look.' Mrs Tod turned her face away and shuddered. 'One of them was more than enough, thank you.'

'Aye, aye,' said the gardener, looking at her with a grin. 'I wouldna want ye to faint a second time – ye might hurt your furry wee head.'

'Don't be disrespectful,' said Mrs Tod. 'I told you, I did *not* faint. The Redbrush family do not flinch in the face of danger. I had a sudden touch of the vapours, that was all.'

'Aye, we'll all have a touch o' they vapours afore long,' said the gardener, nodding towards the grey mist that was rolling out from the Tower of Yrminsul. 'Have ye seen what yon devilish stuff has done tae ma garden?'

'Any damage to your garden is trivial compared with

the loss of my house,' Mrs Tod informed him. 'And frankly, Macpherson, I consider that you are at least partly to blame for what has happened.'

The gardener stared at her in astonishment. *'Me?* Och, woman, talk sense.'

'If you had kept those rabbits under proper control—'

'Rabbits? Ye think rabbits could do *that?'* Macpherson wagged a bony finger at the bulbous tower. 'I tell ye who's done this. It's that tenant o' yours – yon skinny wizard in the cottage. Either him or Merlin. Whenever there's an unholy mess bin made, ye can bet your life there's a wizard at the bottom of it. Wizard's Brew, they call it.'

'Well, whoever's caused it, someone is going to have to pay for it. And that good-for-nothing brother of mine will have to stir himself and bring the felons to justice.'

'Aye, weel,' said Macpherson. 'Let's awa' tae Arcadia, then. That's where we'll find him.'

'Arcadia!' Mrs Tod uttered a short, barking laugh. 'An airy-fairy name for a pathetic little island in the middle of a pond. But that's my brother for you – the last Earl of Redbrush, Sigismund the dreamer. By the way, I hope you've kept the boat in proper repair. I refuse to *swim* to Arcadia.'

'Aye, aye.' The gardener nodded wearily. 'She's in the boathoose doon the far end o' the lake.'

'Good. Then let's get down there.'

The inhabitant of the island of Arcadia was unaware of what had happened to his ancestral home. He was currently sitting in the bath-house, writing poetry. This was usually his favourite occupation, but not this afternoon, because for the last hour and a half he had been trying, unsuccessfully, to think of a rhyme for 'orange'[1].

He had just decided that a spot of lunch might help the old grey matter, when he heard the splash of oars approaching the island. He felt a surge of apprehension. *Visitors?* He hadn't had visitors for . . . how long? Six weeks, was it? Or thirty years?

The inhabitant scratched his head with one russet paw. How long *had* he been on this island? He seemed to have lost all track of time, somehow . . .

A sound of voices percolated through his thoughts. Whoever the visitors were, they had arrived.

He put down his pen and wandered out into the sunshine.

Two figures had arrived at the water's edge. They had their backs to him, and were evidently having an argument. The inhabitant watched with interest.

'If you don't tie up the boat, it will float away again, and then we shall be stranded on this wretched island,' the small one in the poke-bonnet was saying.

'Aye,' the large red-haired one replied with slow patience. 'But ye see, there's naething near enough tae tie the boat up *to.*'

---

[1]In the original manuscript of Nostradimwit's prophecies, the final prophecy reads:

Whenne ye laste dayes shalle come, and fyre
   Raine from ye skies, blacke, redde and orange—
Thenne shalle ye
   ORANGE??? ye muste be jokinge!!!

Some cynics have suggested that if Nostradimwit didn't see this rhyme coming, he can't have been much of a prophet. However, the Orange Rhymers, a small but fanatical religious sect, are convinced that there would have been a rhyme if Nostradimwit had had the patience to wait for it. They have spent the last 1600 years searching for this missing word, and are confident of finding it any day now.

'Well, can't you make something?'

'Aye, I could mebbe plant a wee acorn, an' if we wait six or seven years it'll grow into a wee sapling, and then . . .'

'Don't be facetious, Macpherson. If you can't tie the boat up, then at least pull it up out of the water.'

The gardener sighed. 'Aye, ma'am.'

With much sighing and a great display of effort, the gardener dragged the small boat onto the grass. Then the two of them turned round.

'Hello there,' said the inhabitant affably. 'Welcome to my island.'

Mrs Tod glared at him. 'So here you are, Sigismund. And what have you been doing all this time? Lazing about, I suppose, and letting the place go to rack and ruin.'

The inhabitant stared at her for a long while. Then he said slowly, 'Sigismund. That's me, isn't it? And you're a relative of mine, aren't you? What was your name, now? Elspeth, wasn't it?'

'You know perfectly well that I'm your sister,' Mrs Tod said sharply. 'Just as you know perfectly well that my name is Edith. Pull yourself together, Sigismund.'

Sigismund slowly ran a paw across his skull, through his coarse red fox's fur. 'Yes, I was the Earl. That was it. The Earl of Redbrush. And I came here to – to—'

'To avoid your responsibilities,' said Mrs Tod coldly.

The Earl looked taken aback. He straightened his green smoking jacket and adjusted his monocle. 'I say, that's a bit unkind. I just wanted a spot of peace and quiet, but no-one would leave me alone. They kept wanting me to hunt rabbits all the time. But why on earth should I hunt rabbits? What have rabbits ever done to me? All I really want to do is write poetry.'

'Poetry!' said Mrs Tod scornfully. 'Stuff and nonsense.

If God had meant the aristocracy to be writers, he would have given them brains. Earls aren't meant to write poetry. Earls aren't meant to write *anything!* You should be back at the Hall, doing some proper hard work for a change.'

'Poetry *is* hard work. I've been slaving over my latest sonnet all morning. Do either of you happen to know a rhyme for "orange"?'

'Aye, I do,' said Macpherson, nodding his large head.

The fox-poet turned to him in delight. 'You do? Wonderful! What is it?'

'McSporringe,' said the gardener. 'Verra ancient Scots family, the McSporringes. Closely related tae the Scottish farming clans, the McRakes and the McSpreaders.'

'Ah.' The poet rubbed his chin thoughtfully. 'No, I don't think I can work that in, really. Not without changing the whole poem. Still, thanks for the idea. Well, and what brings you two to my little island?'

'Woe and calamity,' said the gardener in a melancholy voice.

'Oh dear. Any particular woe, or just woe in general?'

Mrs Tod let out a noise like a steam-locomotive losing its temper. *'I'll* tell you what woe!' she shrieked. 'It's our home – Redbrush Hall! It's gone!'

'Gone? You mean someone's stolen it?'

'They've *demolished* it!'

'Dear me, how unfortunate,' said the Earl. 'Well, of course these things do happen. Progress, and all that. I suppose they needed to build a road through it, or something. No doubt we'll get compensation. Have you written to the Camelot Public Works Department?'

This time Mrs Tod's noise was more like a steam-kettle having a fit. 'It wasn't people that demolished it! It was grey slime!'

'Grey slime?'

'Wizard's Brew,' said Macpherson, nodding his head with great significance.

'Magic, you mean?'

'Aye. Evil sorcery.'

'There's a tower,' said Mrs Tod, her voice so high-pitched that it hurt their ears. 'And a horrible smell. And - and - *Things!*'

The Earl wrinkled his brow. 'Things? What sort of things?'

'Horr-rrible unnatural-lookin' Things,' said Macpherson with relish. 'They're comin' oot o' the tower. Ye wouldna believe how ugly they are. Worse than what ye might see after several large drams of a Sat'day night.'

'I see.' The Earl thought for a moment. 'And why exactly have you come to tell me this?'

'Isn't it *obvious?*' shrieked Mrs Tod.

'No, I'm afraid not.'

Mrs Tod made a visible attempt to calm down. 'Sigismund, you are still the head of the Redbrush family. You must go to Camelot and insist that King Uther sends an army and destroys these *Things.* And you must insist that he rebuilds Redbrush Hall. And you must insist that he fumigates the entire grounds to get rid of any grey slime that may still be lying around. And you must insist that he provides funds to re-plant the grounds with trees and grass and ornamental shrubs.'

'An' lettuces an' carrots,' put in the gardener.

'And you must insist that he provides us with a per-manent garrison of soldiers and our own wizard to guard the Hall against any future evils of this kind. And—'

'Hold on,' said the Earl, raising a paw. 'I can see I'm

going to have to do a lot of insisting. What if Uther won't listen?'

Mrs Tod's manner changed instantly. Her impression of a steam-kettle losing its lid vanished, and she stared at her brother down her long nose with eyes like unde-frosted fish fingers.

'You must *make* him listen,' she said. 'You must make sure we get our own way.'

'But what if he won't *let* us have our own way?'

Mrs Tod folded her arms. 'Of *course* we will have our own way. We are the aristocracy. We *always* get our own way. That is what one is an aristocrat *for*.'

'Yes, I suppose it is. All right, I'll go to Camelot and see King Uther. What will you do?'

'Macpherson and I will come with you, naturally,' said his sister, 'to see that you acquit yourself in a manner befitting the Redbrush line.'

'Ah, I see.' The Earl nodded resignedly. 'Well, if I must, I suppose I must. But first let's have a spot of lunch. I've been working all morning, and I'm feeling decidedly peckish.'

Mrs Tod stamped her paw. 'Sigismund, really! This is no time to be thinking of food! You must go and see King Uther *now!*'

'But I really am rather hungry—'

'*Now*, Sigismund!'

'Oh, righto. I suppose I can always grab a bite to eat when we get to Camelot.' The Earl sighed inwardly. The idea of spending the rest of the day trying to find a rhyme for 'orange' suddenly seemed remarkably attrac-tive.

'So,' said King Bres of the Fhomoire, gazing over the green landscape of Redbrush Park with satisfaction. 'Here we are.' He was larger than the other Fhomoire,

209

and wore a crudely-fashioned silver crown where his head would have been if he had had one.

'Here we are,' chorused the rest of the Fhomoire, surging out of the doorway of the tower behind him.

'Here we are *again*,' said King Bres.

This could have been the cue for a song, but the Fhomoire had been out of circulation for several centuries, and this particular ditty wasn't in their repertoire.

'So this is England,' said King Bres. 'Still here, after all these years. Still green and juicy and succulent, and waiting to be *devoured*.'

The King of the Fhomoire made a noise deep in some part of his rather ill-defined anatomy. It sounded like the noise a gourmet might make just before sitting down to a meal in a five-star restaurant. His eyes on their long stalks waved around, taking in the green masses of vegetation. The grey mist had so far touched only the garden and the nearer half of the Park. Beyond these, the greenery was still bright and lush.

The Fhomoire had only just got up, and were still wearing their real shapes, which was why Mrs Tod had screamed and fainted. There were thirty of them, and they were all hideous and misshapen, but in thirty different ways. Each Fhomoire secretly and proudly considered itself to be far uglier than any of the others.

'Well done, Archon,' said King Bres, turning to the one-headed troll beside him.

'Thank you, sire.'

'Yes, you have done well. Even if it did take you a thousand years longer than was strictly necessary.'

'I'm sorry about that, sire, but there was this warrior, you see, with a sharp spear, and—'

King Bres waved his eye-stalks magnanimously. He was in a mellow mood. 'No need to explain. We're here, that's the main thing. By the way, that's an amusing little outfit you're wearing. Is that the fashion in England these days?'

'This?' Archon looked down at his troll body.

Trolls are not beautiful creatures. Their size and shape varies, as does their quota of heads, arms and legs, but on the whole they are large, shaggy, filthy, stupid and smelly. The average troll bears a strong resemblance to a haystack which has just been for an hour's swim in a cesspool. Compared with the true shape of a Fhomoire, however, the average troll looks like Marilyn Monroe.

'It's nothing really, sire,' said Archon modestly. 'Just a little something I ran up on the spur of the moment.'

'I rather fancy one of those myself.' King Bres vanished, and three seconds later reappeared as a bigger troll than Archon, with three arms and three heads, the middle one of which wore his silver crown. 'How do I look?' enquired the King of the Fhomoire, turning round slowly.

'Jolly good, sire – a real troll, right down to your three different-sized feet,' said Archon in an admiring tone. *Crude and overdone,* he said to himself. *That's the trouble with Bres – no subtlety.*

'I think we should *all* be trolls,' said the King. 'That way we can mingle unobtrusively with the local inhabitants. Okay everybody?'

There was a delighted gurgling sound from the rest of the Fhomoire. All twenty-eight promptly disappeared, causing a noise like a small sonic bang. A moment later they were back again. Twenty-seven had changed into large, repulsive trolls. The twenty-eighth had turned into a small cauliflower.

King Bres examined his troops with satisfaction, until he noticed the cauliflower, which was trying to hide behind the others. 'Who's that?' he demanded.

There was a certain amount of sniggering among the other Fhomoire. 'It's Cringe, sire,' said someone. 'He's forgotten how to shape-shift again.'

'Cringe!' Bres glowered at the quaking cauliflower. 'How often do I have to tell you? It's carbon electrons a half-twist *right* for animals, *left* for plants. Do it again, and this time, get it *right!*'

The cauliflower tried to execute a low bow, failed[1], and vanished, to be replaced by a nervous-looking troll. It was only half as tall as the other trolls and quite a lot less filthy and repulsive. 'S-sorry, sire,' it stammered. 'It w-won't happen again.'

'You've been saying that for the last three thousand years,' said Bres angrily. 'Look at you – look at your size and colour, compared with everyone else's – you don't *match*. You're a disgrace to the regiment, Cringe.'

'Yes, sire. Sorry, sire,' said the little troll abjectly.

'Well, you'll have to do, I suppose.' Bres turned away in irritation. He struck a pose, and began to address his troops.

'People of the Fhomoire! This is a historic moment! Once again we are in England!'

A throaty cheer went up from the assembled trolls.

'England is a green and pleasant land, lush and un-spoiled. But we are going to change all that!'

Another raucous cheer.

'We are going to turn England *grey* – the same beauti-ful grey as Lochlann, our homeland.' Bres waved a clawed hand towards the doorway at the foot of the Tower of Yrminsul, from which grey mist was continu-ing to drift.

'We will suck this land dry! We will live off its juice

[1] It is futile for a cauliflower to try and bow. They don't have the waists for it. Cringe should really have curtsied.

and its fat until there is only ash and rubble left! We will make it *our* land! And this time there are no yellow-haired, blue-eyed, so-called gods and goddesses to stop us! We have been watching England from afar, and we know that this time the land is defenceless, save for a few amateurish wizards and a king who is tired of ruling and wants to retire!'

'What about the Green God?' said a voice from the back.

'The Green God is dead,' said Bres firmly. 'We have been watching England for a thousand years, and there has been no sign of the Green God for many centuries. Now – Archon.'

'Sire?'

'We shall march to the chief dwelling-place of these humans. On the way, we shall eat.'

'Eat!' chorused the Fhomoire enthusiastically.

Archon pointed his scimitar in the direction of Camelot. 'That way, sire.'

'Excellent! Forward, Fhomoire!' commanded King Bres.

A moment later, thirty trolls were stomping across the green turf of Redbrush Park. As they tramped, they sang a traditional Fhomoire marching song:

We are, we are, we are, we are,
  we are the shapeless horde.
We can, we can, we can, we can
  destroy both bush and sward.
And when we get to Camelot
  we'll put it to the sword
If we're fee – eeli – ing gen – rous!

Behind them, grey mist continued to pour out of the tower, drifting across the park, creating a circular waste-land that grew steadily wider and wider.

* * *

Gwydden and Hergrim had been following the yellow brick road for a good half hour. The tangled trees continued to surround them at every step. The sun was now high in the sky, and even through the matted forest cover, they were beginning to feel hot. Eventually Hergrim called out, 'Gwydden?'

'Yes?'

'How much further do you think it is?'

'How much further is what?'

'How much further until we find this *grene godde*, or whatever he is. I'm getting thirsty.'

'I expect,' the wizard replied, forcing his way through a cranberry bush and pausing to fill his pockets with berries, 'that we'll find him at the end of this road. Though heaven knows when we'll find that. Oh.'

'What?'

'The path's petered out again,' said the wizard.

The dwarf came alongside him, and they both looked at the place they had come to.

It was a clearing - or it might have been, if it had been cleared a bit more. In the centre was a gigantic gnarled oak, surrounded by an area of smooth green turf. The yellow brick road ran straight up to the tree and stopped.

'Presumably it continues on the other side,' said Gwydden, looking beyond the tree at what seemed to be yet more impenetrable undergrowth.

'Good place for a rest,' said the dwarf, eyeing the soft green turf. He sat down under the oak and started unpacking the rucksack. 'Fancy a sandwich?'

'Those are *my* sandwiches,' said the wizard, sitting down beside him. 'You ate yours, remember?' He took the packet and opened it. 'Where's the cheese?'

'I ate the cheese.'

'*All* the cheese?'

' 'Fraid so.'

'Typical dwarf – no consideration for others.' Gwydden peeled back the bread and sniffed the grey paste inside. 'What's this, mushroom?'

'Yes, I made it from those mushrooms growing behind the cottage.'

Gwydden's eyes widened in alarm. 'Not the red ones with white spots, I hope? They're poisonous.'

'No, not those. The white ones.'

'Ah. That's all right, then.'

A lazy silence descended on the clearing. The dwarf drained his beer, tossed the bottle aside, and closed his eyes. Gwydden finished off the mushroom sandwiches, and then rested his head back against the trunk.

'Mustn't stay here too long,' he murmured drowsily. 'We ought to find the *grene godde* before dark. Not safe in the Forest after dark. Not safe.'

The afternoon was hot, but the shade of the tree was pleasantly cool. His head lolled forward on his chest, and his breathing grew heavy. In a few more moments, he was sound asleep. Beside him, Hergrim had already started to snore.

Side by side, the wizard and the dwarf slept under the great oak.

Several minutes passed. Then, very slowly, two of the tree's huge branches began to bend down towards them.

The grey mist spread out from the tower until it came to a small blue lake, in the centre of which was a lush green island. Here it seemed to hesitate. After thinking about it for a while, it decided to put the mysterious lake in its pending tray and sort it out later. It divided in two, circumnavigated the lake, joined up with itself on the far side, and continued its onward progress.

Beyond the Park, it came to a number of deep holes in the ground, which smelled strongly of rabbit. It investigated the holes hungrily, but they were deserted.

It passed on into the Forest, and birds and animals fled before it. But the trees and bushes could not flee, and they withered and shrivelled as the deadly mist flowed on over them.

Chapter Eleven

Colin ('The Great Alfonso') Higinbotham bounded up the stairs three at a time. He was going to get into Merlin's study! He was going to sit in Merlin's chair, and read Merlin's grimoires, and concoct something really *amazing* using Merlin's gallipots, thuribles and alembics! And then when Merlin reappeared, he would no doubt be astonished at the Great Alfonso's brilliance, and take him on as his assistant, at a suitable salary. Preferably paid weekly in gold.

He reached the top of the stairs, crossed the stone landing, and grasped the handle of the large oak door, meaning to fling it open and stride grandly into the room beyond.

'*Ow!*'

The Great Alfonso sprang backwards and leaned against the ornate stone banister, sucking his hand. He stared, outraged, at the doorknob. 'You bit me!'

'Therveth you right,' said the doorknob. 'You thould knock before entering. Didn't they teatth you mannerth at withardth' thchool?'

The young wizard's scanty ginger eyebrows came together in a scowl. 'I need to get into Merlin's study.'

'Oh yeth? Do you have an appointment?'

'I don't need an appointment. I have permission from King Uther.'

'That cutth no ithe with me, buthter,' said the

doorknob. 'Thith ith Merlin'th thtudy, not Uther'th.'

'But I *have* to get in! The kingdom is in danger, and only I can save it!'

'Oh yeth, heard *that* old chethnut before!' said the doorknob cynically. It was enjoying the situation, and saw no reason at all to cooperate. When the only power you have is the power of preventing people from doing things, you get a lot of pleasure from exercising it.

There was a moment or two of silence while the Great Alfonso examined his bleeding hand and considered the situation. There were two questions in his mind. First, did the doorknob have rabies? If so, he was in dead trouble. And second, how was he to get past this aggressive piece of door-furniture?

There was no way of answering the first question, except by waiting to see if he foamed at the mouth next time someone offered him a drink, so he passed on to the second.

'What would happen,' he said, in a conversational tone, 'if I put a spell on you?'

'Ever heard of the Thicth Theal of Tholomon?' enquired the doorknob, in a smug tone.

'Oh,' said Alfonso, somewhat dismayed. 'Merlin's used that, has he?'

'Yeth. And you know what happenth to withardth who meth with the Thicth Theal?'

'Er. Yes, I think so.'

'Of courthe,' murmured the doorknob, 'King Uther might not mind cleaning bitth of you off the wallth and theilingth for the nectht thicth monthth, tho don't let me thtop you if you're really thet on it.'

'No, I don't think I will.'

'Very withe, if I may thay tho.'

It occurred to Colin that becoming a top-class wizard might not be as easy as he had expected.

'We are, we are, we are, we are, we are the shapeless horde,' hummed the Fhomoire softly to themselves as they tramped through the Forest. *'We are, we are, we are, we are too vile to be ignored. And when we get to Camelot we'll—'*

'Hold it, team,' said King Bres, stopping. 'What's that up ahead?'

The Forest had suddenly ended. Before them stretched the fields and meadows of the broad open plain that surrounded Camelot.

In the middle distance, thatched roofs were in evidence. Smoke drifted up from several quaint and rustic chimney-stacks.

The Fhomoire shuffled to a halt. In the back rank, a small troll which was slowly turning back into a cauliflower was trying desperately to remember whether it was carbon atoms *left* or *right*, and hoping King Bres wouldn't notice.

'It's a village, your Majesty,' said Archon.

The troll with the silver crown frowned. 'A village? What's that?'

Archon sighed inwardly. King Bres had never managed to grasp the finer points of human culture. Or indeed *any* points about humans. This is what invariably happens if you regard other species merely as potential lunch, dinner and tea.

'Cottages, your Majesty,' he explained. 'Houses. Roofs, walls, doors. Streets.'

'Huh?'

'Where human beings live.'

'Ah. *Food.* Why didn't you say so? Right, team! Time for grub!'

Colin Higinbotham was beginning to feel angry. In spite of his reddish hair (which was more of a sandy colour anyway) he almost never got angry. But this upstart doorknob was trying his patience.

He had wrapped his bitten hand in his sleeve to staunch the blood. Suddenly, without really thinking what he was doing, he strode forward, grabbed the doorknob in his swathed hand, twisted it, and pushed the door open. The whole thing was over in less than three seconds. Rather surprised, he released the door-knob and looked down at two rows of fresh teeth-marks in the cloth of his sleeve.

'That wathn't fair!' hissed the doorknob. 'I wath ecthpecting thorthery, and you uthed a thubterfuge!'

'I did, didn't I?' said Colin, feeling rather pleased with himself.

'Thlime-ball!'

'Oh, you're just a bad loser,' said the Great Alfonso. He walked casually into Merlin's study, and closed the door behind him. Muffled swear-words were lisped at him from the other side of the oak panels.

So this was the great Merlin's study, he thought, gazing around.

Wow. It was really . . .

. . . empty.

No, not empty. What was that word the guy in the ultra-expensive pin-striped robe had used – the sales-man in Grimsdyke's Magic Emporium, where Colin had once gone to test-drive an Excelsior Demon-grabber[1]?

---

[1]He didn't actually *buy* one, because he couldn't afford it. He handled it covetously for a few minutes, tried a few simple illusions, and then sadly gave it back to the salesman; after which he wandered down the road to a dingy shop known as the Cheap Trickery, and bought a second-hand Wiz-o-Wand. Anyone who has test-driven a Porsche and then bought a Skoda will understand just how depressing this was.

Minimalist. That was it.

Merlin's study was minimalist in the extreme.

But expensive. It was very expensively done in black and silver, which were *the* fashionable colours for wizards this year.

Colin wandered slowly round the room, gazing at each object in reverent awe.

A big ebony chair upholstered in black chimaera-hide.

A black Axminster, into which were woven arcane silver symbols.

An ebony cupboard, its door inlaid in silver with amazingly lifelike scenes of diabolic orgies. Colin, whose upbringing had been rather sheltered, was very shocked by some of them.

An ebony desk in one corner, on top of which stood several neatly arranged and carefully dusted gallipots, thuribles and alembics. Colin nodded as he looked at these. He would make use of them in due course.

There was also a grandfather clock, apparently made out of bones.

And a row of grimoires on a shelf halfway up the wall.

Colin's fingers instantly started to itch. No wizard can resist looking at another wizard's grimoires. Glancing around him nervously, just in case this was all a trick and Merlin was hiding in the cupboard, he took down a book from the middle of the row.

Ye Elixyr of Lyfe, said the spine.

Gosh, thought Colin. *Does Merlin really have the secret of immortality and total happiness?*

He opened the book. The pages inside had been hollowed out to make a cavity, and in the cavity nestled a bottle half-full of golden-brown liquid, labelled *Auld Glenmiller Whisky*. Somewhat disappointed, but with the feeling that he now understood Merlin a little better, Colin opened the bottle of whisky and took a sip – cautiously, in case it was really some vile sorcerous substance only *pretending* to be whisky.

The whisky, however, was excellent. He took a longer sip and sighed with pleasure. Furtively he recorked the bottle and slipped it into his tunic. He closed the hollow grimoire and put it back on the shelf.

He took down the next book along, opened it, and was confronted by a title page bearing the words *Fearful Spells for Irate Wizards*, in Gothic script illuminated with woodcuts in black and red ink. The woodcuts showed imps and demons doing a variety of unpleasant things to various luckless victims, who were clearly identified as wizards by their long robes and pointy hats. At the foot of the page were printed the words *Novices beware!*

'Novices beware indeed,' muttered the Great Alfonso, feeling rather put out because he knew he was one himself. 'You don't scare me, with your stupid pictures of imps and demons.'

Next moment he all but dropped the book, because one of the imps stuck its head out of the picture, leered at him, and said in a shrill voice, 'Little boys who play with magic get their fingers burned! Hee hee hee!' It winked at him evilly and sniggered, and then shrank swiftly back into its woodcut and was a mere flat picture again.

Colin closed *Fearful Spells for Irate Wizards* hastily and put it back on the shelf, telling himself that he wasn't very irate really, and probably something a bit less fearful might be more appropriate.

He left the grimoires, and studied the final object in the room, which was Merlin's mirror.

So *that* was what it looked like. Big, smooth, oval, and (inevitably) black.

Every wizard in Camelot knew about Merlin's mirror. It was the thing, more than anything else, that made him the most feared wizard in the land, because rumour had it that using his mirror, Merlin could see everyone, wherever they were, whatever they were doing. Wizards like a bit of privacy just as much as anyone (and with more reason than most), and the knowledge that their most secret spells, not to mention their most intimate personal habits, were quite possibly being observed by Merlin made them all feel paranoid, not to say livid. It was not surprising that Merlin had many enemies but (so it was said) no friends.

And now, thought the Great Alfonso gleefully, *it's my turn.*

Seating himself in Merlin's chair, he stared hard into the mirror and said, 'Mirror, show me the danger that is approaching Camelot!'

Green lights flashed across the mirror, which lost its dull opacity and began to glow. A picture formed. It showed a group of trolls lumping along through a field. Bringing up the rear was a cauliflower, which was evidently having trouble keeping up, its legs being much shorter[1].

'Ha!' Colin rubbed his hands together. 'So - that's the danger threatening Camelot, is it? Twenty-nine trolls and a cauliflower. Doesn't seem like too much of a problem. What we need is some sort of anti-troll spell, with perhaps an anti-cauliflower clause tacked on the end. Where's my *Wizard's Handbook?*'

He produced the sorcerer's vade-mecum from inside

---

[1]If you find a cauliflower with legs in your local supermarket, don't buy it – *even if the legs are very short*. The trouble with mobile vegetables is, you don't know where they've been.

his tunic and thumbed through it. Under 'T' he found the following entry:

Trolls. Probably the ugliest and nastiest creatures in the British Isles. The rules of magic state that trolls should, logically, turn to stone in sunlight. Don't rely on this – trolls are so stupid that logic runs off them like water off a duck's back.

The best defence against a troll is decapitation (make sure you get all *the heads – some of them may be in unusual places). If faced with an army of trolls, try the Reflecting Wall (see page 149).*

'Reflecting Wall,' murmured the Great Alfonso. 'Good. Now, what about cauliflowers?'

By a strange oversight, however, the *Handbook* did not include any spells for defence against ill-disposed cauliflowers.

'Have to make do with the Reflecting Wall, then,' said Colin to himself.

He turned to page 149 and read for a while. Then, frowning a little, he stood up and went out of the study – ignoring the doorknob, which blew a sulky raspberry as he passed – and descended the stairs to the Great Hall.

Uther was sitting at his desk, writing in flowing copperplate on a large sheet of parchment. He looked up as the sandy-haired wizard entered, smiled, and waved his quill.

Excellent, thought Colin, *he's in a good mood. He'll need to be when I tell him the ingredients I need for this spell.*

'Ah, young Alfonso,' said Uther cheerfully. 'My colours have come back. That's good, isn't it?'

'Your colours, your Majesty?'

'My inks.' The King indicated the row of pots along the front of his desk. 'They turned grey a while ago, but they're back to normal now. I'm just writing an abdication speech. It's in gold, mainly, but I've put some blue bits in here and there. What do you think?' He held up the sheet of parchment.

'Er – that's splendid, your Majesty. You're abdicating, then? I didn't realise.'

'Ssshh!' Uther shook his head urgently. 'Keep your voice down – I don't want Igrayne to know. It isn't definite yet – I need to pick the right time.' His face lost its cheery expression and became a little doleful. 'Not that there ever *is* a right time. No-one to take over when I'm gone, you see.'

'Couldn't Queen Igrayne take over?' suggested Colin.

Uther looked at him aghast. 'Igrayne? Good heavens no. My wife has many excellent qualities – well, many qualities, anyway – but management skills are not among them.' The King sighed. 'No, no. I shall be here till I drop. Merlin once told me that in an ancient prophecy, the Pendragon - that's me, you know – is referred to as *rex quondam, rexque futurus*. You know what that means? *Once a king, always a king*. It's a job for life. Did you want something?'

'I've found out what the threat is,' said Alfonso. 'There are twenty-nine trolls approaching Camelot. And a cauliflower.'

'A cauliflower? Is that serious?'

'It's got legs,' said Alfonso.

'Ah.' Uther nodded. '*That* sort of cauliflower. I see. And twenty-nine trolls, you say?'

'Yes.'

'Well, what should I do, d'you think? Alert the castle guard? Ask Igrayne if we can mobilise her Knights? Call out the greengrocers?'

'There's no need for all that,' said Alfonso. 'I've found a spell. It's called the Reflecting Wall.'

'Really? Oh, that's excellent news. Well done.' Uther

beamed at him. 'I knew you'd come up trumps, young Alfonso.'

The Great Alfonso looked modestly down at his sandals.

'So what does it do, this reflecting thingy?' Uther asked.

'Well, everyone knows that trolls are incredibly stupid, your Majesty. The idea is to put a reflecting wall round the city, like a mirror. Then, when the trolls arrive, they'll see twenty-nine ferocious trolls advancing towards them, and—'

'And a cauliflower.'

'And, as your Majesty so rightly says, a cauliflower, and this will terrify them so much that they will turn and flee.'

'You really think they'll be taken in so easily?'

'Oh yes, your Majesty. Trolls are *amazingly* stupid.'

'Hm. Well, that seems okay, then. So you're off to do this spell thingy, then, are you?'

'Well . . .' Colin shuffled his feet. 'I will need some materials, your Majesty.'

'Oh, right – a shopping list, is that it? Fine. I'll write it down, shall I?' The King picked up his quill and looked at it critically. 'No, not gold ink. Green, perhaps? Yes, green is traditional for wizardry.' He selected a different quill and a new piece of parchment, dipped the quill in one of the inkwells, and looked up at Colin expectantly. 'Well, fire away.'

Colin fired away.

A blob of green ink from Uther's quill splashed onto the parchment. He had not written anything yet, but was sitting with his mouth open, staring at the young wizard.

'*How* much silver?'

Somewhat unhappily, Colin mentioned the figure again.

Uther slowly laid down his quill. 'You're not related to my wife, by any chance?'

'I don't think so, your Majesty.'

Uther passed a hand over his sparse grey hair. 'Good grief. I shouldn't think there's a tenth of that amount in the treasury. And as for all that glass . . . Well, I can see I'm not going to get my abdication speech written today. Where's the red ink? And a fresh quill – and a piece of clean parchment. Right, now then. I think it's time I promulgated a new tax.'

An hour or so later, the landlord at *The King's Head*, a dwarf by the name of Grympel, was enjoying a quiet noggin of Frigga's Revenge by himself in the bar-parlour. The evening rush would not start for a while yet, and he was not expecting to be disturbed. This was all to the good, because he was engaged in something rather delicate. He was writing a letter home.

He hefted his hammer and chisel thoughtfully, and gazed at the lump of granite in front of him[1], while trying to think of the most tactful way to say what needed saying.

Deer Anjina, he wrote at last. *I am regretful not to have rote to you erlier, but I hav bin verry bizy, wot with the hot wether and you know how peeple drink lots more in hot whether, it has been a struggel to keep up. Also I hav had hay-fever, you remember I had to giv up outdoor work such as being in the army becos of it, it is stil playing up sumthing cronic espeshly in hot wether which as I sed we hav had a lot of lately.*

---

[1]Dwarfs write most of their letters on granite. They also send them surface mail, not air mail. This is not because dwarfs are mean – though most of them are – but because the carrier pigeons have great difficulty getting airborne.

He brushed away a few fragments of stone-dust. So far so good.

I am v. regretful not to hav cum home bye now, I kno I sed I wood be home by Trollsheadmas but things hav changed. I am making a nice livving heer in Camelotte and to be perfekly frank I do not think there are the oportunittis in Dwarfheim for a dwarf of my temprament, so I wood gratley prefer to remane in sittoo as they say.

Now for the difficult bit.

Also I hope you wil not be too upsett, Anjina, I kno we livd in adjasent shacks when we were yung and peeple expekted us to get marrid one day, and you gayve me a lokk of your beerd as a keepsayke wich I shal always treshure, but peeple change you kno, and there is a ladye heer who I am seeing a lotte of recently, her name is—

At this sensitive moment, there was a sudden commotion from the public bar – the sound of breaking glass, and raised voices.

'Oh good,' Grympel murmured. 'Sounds like a brawl.' Putting the hammer and chisel down and wiping his hands, which had become damp with nervous perspiration, he went to investigate.

In the public bar, a scared-looking young soldier from the castle guard was standing next to a large wheelbarrow, which seemed to be mostly full of empty bottles. Three dwarfs, whom Grympel knew well because they were unemployed and spent a lot of time in *The King's Head,* were standing around him looking belligerent. Behind the bar, Blodwen the barmaid looked at Grympel apprehensively.

'What's going on here?' Grympel demanded.

'This *dwurgledork* tried to nick my bottle of Frigga's Revenge,' growled the largest and ugliest of the dwarfs, whose name was Nabgo.

The floor of the inn trembled under their feet, and a

little plaster drifted down from the ceiling. Blodwen let out a tiny shriek and put her hand to her mouth.

'I've told you before, Nabgo,' said Grympel sternly, 'not to use dwarf swear-words in my pub. It's an old building, and the timbers won't stand the stress[1].' He turned to the young soldier. 'Now – what's all this about?'

The soldier produced a crumpled piece of parchment from inside his tunic and held it in front of his chest like a breastplate. 'Royal c-command,' he stammered. 'New civic d-defence tax. All citizens are required to pay im-m-m-m-mediately.'

'Immediately?' Grympel frowned. 'That's not like Uther. He's usually very lenient about tax deadlines. Anyway, why do we need a civic defence tax? We've already got the castle guard, and the Knights of the Slightly Pear-Shaped Table, not to mention all those good-for-nothin' wizards. Can't that lot defend the city?'

'Yeah,' said one of the other unemployed dwarfs sceptically, 'an' defend the city from *what*? Where's the armies outside the walls? We ain't seen nothin'.'

The soldier's young face – so young that it was still liberally engraved with teenage pimples – took on an expression of timid defiance. 'Dunno. All I know is, everybody has to p-pay. In g-glass or s-s-s-silver.'

'Well, you're not havin' my Frigga's Revenge till I've drunk it,' growled Nabgo. 'An' not even then, 'cos

---

[1]The dwarfs' ability to demolish buildings by swearing has been known about for a long time. When the walls of Jericho fell down, for instance, it wasn't because of the trumpets. As Joshua was wearily trudging round the walls for the seventh time, he accidentally trod on the toe of the nearest trumpeter, who happened to be a dwarf. The rest, as they say, is History[2].
[2]Actually it's GCSE Scripture, but you know what I mean.

Grympel here gives half a groat back on the empties.'

Time for a bit of diplomacy, thought Grympel. He didn't really want to offend Nabgo. Nabgo was a fellow dwarf, and as any landlord who has had to scrub the floor in the public bar after a brawl will tell you, blood is thicker than beer (though not a lot, in the case of Frigga's Revenge). Nor did he want *The King's Head* to get a bad name with Uther, who after all was the pub's patron, even if he was a bit forgetful about settling his tab. 'Look, if it'll keep the peace, I'll give Nabgo his half groat and then you can have half my empties, okay?'

Ten minutes later, the pile of bottles in the wheelbarrow had grown considerably. The soldier looked at them with satisfaction, and then turned an expectant eye on Blodwen. 'Now it's your turn, m-miss.'

'Me?' Blodwen looked at him round-eyed. 'I don't have any empty bottles.'

'That's a s-silver locket your w-wearing round your neck, miss, isn't it?'

Blodwen's hand flew up to her sole piece of jewellery. 'You can't have this,' she cried. 'There's a picture of my boyfriend Dai in here. We're getting married next year – buying a sheep-farm in the Rhondda. He'd jilt me if I let someone take his picture!'

'Be reasonable, lad,' said Grympel. 'You can't take the girl's locket - not when it's so important to her.'

'But the tax is to be p-paid by everyone,' said the soldier. 'Everyone has to give silver if they've got it.'

'Leave Blodwen alone,' growled Nabgo. 'We like Blodwen, an' we don't want her upset. Unnerstand?'

The soldier, however, stood his ground. 'I've got m-my orders,' he insisted. 'The tax is to be paid by *all* the citizens of C-Camelot. No exceptions.'

Nabgo moved in a little closer, until his nose was almost touching the soldier's chest. 'Nah listen, you little *gruksnorf*,' he began, squinting up at the young man's pimply chin.

The floor trembled again, and more plaster drifted down. Grympel threw an anxious glance upwards, and made a swift decision. He pulled something shiny out of his tunic, and thrust it between Nabgo and the soldier.

'Here, take this, it's silver.'

The soldier took the proffered object and examined it.

'Looks like s-silver,' he agreed. 'What is it – another locket?'

'Yes,' said Grympel. He was feeling horribly guilty about this, but after all, there was no other silver in the pub.

The soldier opened the clasp, and made a face. 'Ugh – it's full of h-hair. What's this writing say? *From Anjina, ever faythfull.*'

'It's of no importance,' said Grympel hurriedly. 'Here, I'll keep the hair.'

'It's very c-coarse,' said the soldier, handing it over. 'From a dog, is it?'

'She's considered very handsome, for a dwarf-woman,' Grympel snapped. He tucked the coil of hair into his pocket. 'Now, you've got your glass, and your silver. May I respectfully suggest that you go and bother someone else?'

The major drawback with shape-shifting is that after spending a certain amount of time in a particular shape, you start to *be* that shape. It's like wearing a suit. You may, in yourself, be essentially a tee-shirt and faded denims sort of person, but after a few days in pin-stripe you will probably find yourself waving an imaginary umbrella at taxis and using phrases like 'the bottom line' and 'at the end of the day'.

At the end of the day, the Fhomoire were lying

sprawled in a cornfield a mile or so from Camelot. They had eaten three villages and a herd of Jerseys. They had also finished off a large barrel of cider which they had discovered in a farmhouse, and which the farmer and his family wouldn't be needing any more, unless they were currently managing to partake of it in the dark saloon-bar of the Fhomoire's stomachs.

Alcohol, by the way, tends to accelerate the process of becoming what you are pretending to be.

The Fhomoire were singing. They had abandoned their usual repertoire of shape-shifting songs, and were singing the troll-song. Trolls have only one song, because two would be too many to remember the words of. It dates from time immemorial, and goes like this:

Here we troll, here we troll, here we troll,
here we troll, here we troll, here we tro-oll.
Here we troll, here we troll, here we troll,
here we tro-oll, here – we – troll!

This song, with slight variations, is still sung in places where the descendants of trolls congregate.

After the umpteenth chorus of the troll song had died away on the warm night air, King Bres raised himself almost into a sitting position, and said loudly and indistinctly, 'Trolls! Listen!'

'Yuh, boss,' chorused the trolls. 'We listening.'

'T'morrer we 'tack Cam'lot.'

'Yuh, boss!'

'Th'army of Cam'lot will be smashed. Smashed! *Hic!*'

The Fhomoire cheered, a dreadful sound like a herd of rhino attempting one of the more belligerent choruses from Wagner.

'Smashed!' continued King Bres, waving all three of his fists in a bellicose gesture. 'An' then I will be Khing of Engl'nd! Hoorah! *Hic!*'

232

'Hoorah! *Hic!*' chorused the rest of the Fhomoire happily.

'Hoorah,' said a small and despondent voice.

King Bres levered his troll frame further off the ground and peered around. 'Whoozat? Who said hoorah in that unhoorahish manner?'

There was a deep sigh among the cornstalks, and a cauliflower emerged into the open.

'Cringe?' Bres leaned over his smallest follower. His silver crown had slipped rakishly over one eye. 'Whass-up wi' you, Cringe? Why aren't you drinkin' wi' th'rest of us trolls?'

'Because I'm not a troll,' said Cringe sadly. 'I'm a cauliflower, and cauliflowers don't drink.'

'Thass sad.' Hot troll-tears sprang into Bres's eyes and rolled sizzling down his hairy cheeks. 'Thass very sad. Poor Cringe. Never min', Cringe. Snot your fault. You can't help it if you were born a collyflobble an' we were born trolls.'

'But you weren't born trolls,' said Cringe. 'None of you were. You're Fhomoire, like me.'

'Nah, nah, nah.' Bres shook his three heads emphatically. 'Allus been trolls, haven't we, lads?'

The rest of the Fhomoire agreed, in a raucous mumble, that they were all ethnically pure trolls.

'No, no,' said Cringe doggedly. 'You're *Fhomoire*. It's the alcohol, your Majesty – it's gone to your heads.' He turned to Archon, who was lying nearby on his back, his remaining head staring dreamily at the stars. 'Archon – you're not a troll, are you?'

But Archon, in addition to his share of the cider, had discovered a large bottle of vinegar in the farmer's pantry, and had managed to consume it without the others noticing. 'Me troll,' Archon murmured happily. 'Me troll, you collyflobble. *Hic!*'

There was no convincing the Fhomoire that they were anything but trolls. After several minutes of listening to them explain in drunken friendly voices that they were definitely trolls because their mothers had told them so, Cringe, feeling thoroughly depressed, wandered off to another part of the field and sat looking up at the stars.

Why is it, he wondered, *that I never seem to belong? I don't think I'm a proper Fhomoire at all. Somewhere down the ancestral line, I must have got some good blood by mistake.*

The night wore on, and the Fhomoire snored in their field. Even Cringe the cauliflower eventually slept, and had a nightmare in which he was pursued by a chef waving a ladle and a bowl of hot cheese sauce.

The good citizens of Camelot slept too. So did a few of the bad ones, although most of these spent the night as they usually did, i.e. climbing up other people's drainpipes.

The list of sleepers did not, of course, include the castle guard, who famously never slept (they did sometimes close their eyes and snore, but this was purely to lull potential attackers into a false sense of security). Nor did it include a figure in a pointy hat, standing in the moonlight outside the city wall. In front of him was a large pile of empty bottles and a somewhat smaller pile of silver trinkets.

'Now then.' Colin Higinbotham leafed through *The Wizard's Handbook*. 'Page 149. Here we go.'

Ten minutes and a lot of staff-waving later, the piles of bottles and trinkets had vanished. The city was encircled by a high, shining wall of silvered glass that threw back the moonlight to the dark sky. Colin stood proudly in front of it, admiring the image it presented of a young sandy-haired wizard holding a grimoire.

'Eat your heart out, Merlin,' he murmured happily. 'If

only those stuffy old lecturers at the Academy could see this! I always told them I was a real wizard, but they put me in the bottom class with losers like Huw Jones (I wonder where he is now?). Well, I've saved Camelot from twenty-nine homicidal trolls and a cauliflower, all with a single spell. And it's a perfect job – flawless. Nothing wrong with it at all.' He gazed along the length of the mirror-wall with pride.

He felt prodigiously tired all of a sudden. 'Back to bed,' he yawned, and moved wearily in the direction of the city gate.

But the city gate was no longer accessible. It was concealed behind a two hundred foot high wall of silver and glass.

'Oh, *rats*,' groaned the Great Alfonso.

He flung *The Wizard's Handbook* at a passing bat, and sat down disconsolately on the grass.

Gwydden was having an unpleasant dream.

He seemed to be lying with his head inside a tree. This was bad enough, but it was made worse by the fact that the tree was talking to him.

'So you thought you'd have a picnic under my branches, did you?' said the tree. 'That was a very silly thing to do.'

'Please stop eating me,' pleaded Gwydden, trying desperately to pull his head out from inside the trunk. 'You won't find me very nourishing – I'm mostly skin and bone.'

The tree made a rumbling noise. It might have been the sort of noise trees make when they're hungry, or it might just have been a chuckle.

'I'm not eating you,' said the tree. 'I'm saving you for later.' And its strong, sinewy branches grabbed Gwydden by the waist and hauled him inside its trunk.

*   *   *

The Fhomoire were awakened next morning by the sound of a skylark, singing at what seemed an unnecessarily high decibel level above the cornfield. The trolls opened their eyes with great reluctance, and for some time the air was filled with the sound of groaning.

It was hangover time again.

'Heads *hurt*,' Bres complained, clutching his three heads with his three hands. 'Heads hurt *lot*.'

'Hurt *lot*,' the other trolls agreed, staggering around the field and bumping into one another like disoriented Daleks.

Somewhat nervously, because he was in imminent danger of being squashed under a huge and shaggy foot, Cringe threaded his way through the mayhem until he came to the troll with the silver crown.

'King Bres?'

'*Aaargh!* Don' talk s'loud.'

'Sorry, sire.'

'Whoozat?'

'It's me, sire. Cringe.'

'Huh?'

Cringe sighed. 'The cauliflower, sire.'

'Oh, yuh. Collyflobble. Whaddya wan', huh?'

'You've got a hangover, sire. Don't you remember the troll cure for hangovers?'

'Whuh?'

'You put the hangover into one of your heads, sire, and cut it off with your scimitar, and—'

'*Huh?*'

Cringe suddenly saw the flaw in the procedure. You had to put the hangover into the head *before* you became a troll, because if you were a troll already, you were too stupid to work it out.

'Never mind, sire. I expect it'll wear off by the time we get to Camelot.'

'Cam'lot!' The glazed expressions on King Bres's three heads acquired a touch of subhuman cunning. 'Sright! T'day we 'tack Cam'lot! C'mon, team! Off to Cam'lot!'

Lurching drunkenly like triffids with BSE, the trolls set off in what, by sheer luck, happened to be the right direction.

Gloomily, Cringe followed them.

In Camelot, the day was getting off to a rather acrimonious start. The sentries at the city gate, who usually got up at the crack of mid-morning, were slightly surprised to be woken at eight o'clock by angry voices shouting outside their comfortable sentry-house. The older sentry, whose name was Balderbreeks, sent the younger, whose name was Eric, to see what all the noise was about.

'There are people shouting,' the young recruit reported back a few minutes later.

Balderbreeks, who was filling the kettle from a tap in the wall, sighed. Young Eric was a willing lad, but he was not one of nature's geniuses. 'I *know* there are people shouting. That's why I sent you out there. What are they shouting *about*?'

'I'll go and see,' said Eric cheerfully, and went out again.

Balderbreeks put the kettle on the little pot-bellied stove in the corner, yawned, lifted his nightshirt and scratched his grey-haired stomach, and looked round for the coffee-jar.

Eric came back in, looking perturbed. 'They say they can't get out.'

'Eh? Can't get out of what? Who can't get out?'

'There's a two hundred foot high wall of something round the city, and nobody can get in or out,' Eric explained. 'The road inside the gate is clogged up with carts and donkeys and angry tradesmen wanting to get out to sell their wares in the villages, and there are angry farmers shouting outside who want to get in to sell *their* wares.'

'Is that so? A two hundred foot high wall? That sounds a bit peculiar. Someone will have to look into that.' Balderbreeks frowned around the little sentry cabin. This was starting to look serious. He couldn't see the coffee-jar *anywhere*. 'You'd better go up to the castle, and get them to send someone down to investigate.'

'I'll go now, shall I?' said Eric eagerly, turning away with the obvious intention of setting off at once.

'*Now?* No, of course not *now*. You're too keen by half, young Eric. You won't last five minutes as a soldier if you're too keen. *First in the charge is first on the enemy's bayonets*, that's what my old sergeant used to say.' Balderbreeks gave a prodigious yawn. 'There are much more important things to do *now*. For a start, you can look for the coffee-jar. And then get the frying pan out, and make us some eggs and bacon.'

Outside the walls, meanwhile, the farmers had stopped shouting because they had sore throats, and were muttering to one another in small groups instead.

'What the bluddy 'ell are they doing in there?' a burly red-faced farmer wanted to know. 'Why aren't they letting us in?'

'Balderbreeks and young Eric are probably still asleep,' said a thinner man with a long drooping moustache.

'Huh! Nice life bein' a sentry,' growled his companion. 'Nice warm sentry-box, all mod cons. They should try diggin' for grumbles an' wiggits in the frozen soil when it's twenty below of a Febry mornin'.'

'Is that what you've got in there?' asked Droopy Moustache interestedly, eyeing the burly farmer's cloth-covered cart. 'Grumbles an' wiggits?'

'Aye.' Burly pulled himself up with pride. 'My summer crop, this is[1]. Best damn grumbles an' wiggits in the south of England. Really tasty. Why, what're you sellin'?'

'Throops, mostly,' said the other, nodding at his own cloth-covered wagon.

'Oh aye? Pink throops or yeller throops?'

'Oh, pink, nat'rally,' said Droopy, with the air of a man who wouldn't be seen dead selling any other kind. 'Them yeller throops ain't nearly juicy enough, to my mind.'

'Ah, you're right there,' said Burly, nodding. 'Nothing nicer than a plate o' steamin' hot pink throops, I allus say. 'Cept possibly a plate o' grumbles an' wiggits.'

The two farmers eyed one another in a friendly and complacent way, as experts in their respective fields.

'What d'you think o' this 'ere silvery wall, then?' Burly enquired.

'Well, if you arsk me,' said Droopy Moustache, dropping his voice, 'I think there's a wizard behind it.'

'Really?' Burly stared at the wall, which was showing nothing more than the reflections of himself and his fellow agronomists. 'How can you tell that, then? Can you 'ear 'im movin' about on the other side?'

'No, I mean I think it's a wizard what *built* it. It ain't nat'ral, to my mind, a two hundred foot high silvery wall. Bound to be a wizard involved somehow.'

'Ah.' The burly farmer pulled his lower lip thought-

---

[1]As everyone knows, grumbles and wiggits grow all year round, though for some reason they only ripen on Thursdays.

fully. 'I reckon you're prob'ly right. So what d'you think we should do about it?'

'Well.' Droopy Moustache hesitated. He had an idea about this, but it was a slightly risky idea, and only the thought of his beloved pink throops withering in the sun and becoming unsaleable would lead him to contemplate such a thing. 'P'raps the wizard is around here somewhere.'

'Outside the wall, you mean?'

'Yep. An' if we find him, we can *make* him take down this blasted wall.'

'Can we? I thought wizards was a bit – you know.'

'What?'

'Well . . . *dang'rous.*' Burly coughed in an embarrassed way. A man who has fought with Mother Nature on an icy February morning and wrested grumbles and wiggits from her frozen bosom does not like to admit to being afraid of a skinny lad in a grey bathrobe.

Droopy Moustache, however, had heard more reassuring things about wizards. 'It's only Merlin who's dang'rous. The rest are hopeless.'

'Is that right?'

'Yep.' Droopy nodded with reassuring firmness.

'Oh.' Burly looked more cheerful. 'Well, no point hangin' about doin' nothin', is there? I reckon we might as well take a wander round this 'ere wall, an' see if the poxy wizard is still here.'

Colin (The Great Alfonso) Higinbotham, sleeping on the grass on the far side of the city where some elementary but, as it had turned out, inadequate prudential instinct had led him to spend the night, woke suddenly to find himself being roughly dragged to his feet by two large men smelling of sweat, earth and miscellaneous vegetables.

'Gerrup, yer poxy wizardly scum,' said one, who was built like a small barn.

'Skivin' little sorcerous git,' added the other, who was less bulky, and looked as though a ferret had lain down on his top lip and died there.

This, Colin realised, was what is meant by being rudely awakened. He blinked rapidly, assessed the situation equally rapidly, and said in a harsh voice, 'Gentlemen, if you don't let go of my arms *this instant,* I shall turn the pair of you into spotted toads.'

'Allus rather fancied bein' a spotted toad,' said the man built like a barn.

'Nice lazy life, spotted toads have,' his companion agreed.

'Yep. Nice an' cushy, like sentries.'

'Or skivin' wizards.'

'Yep.'

This is not how you're supposed to react, thought Colin. *You're supposed to blanch with fear, let go of me, and run away. Though I'm not really bothered about the blanching.*

He realised, with a sinking feeling, that this was probably not going to be a good day.

'Here he is,' said Burly triumphantly, as he and Droopy Moustache frog-marched the Great Alfonso into the centre of the group of farmers. 'Here's the bugger what built this silvery wall. What shall we do with 'im?'

There was a low growl from the mass of frustrated entrepreneurs, and unfriendly eyes bored into the hapless Colin from every direction.

'String 'im up,' said someone.

'Tie 'im to two donkeys an' drive off in sep'rate directions.'

'*Four* donkeys would be better – one to each arm and leg.'

'Or *five* – one for his head as well.'

'Or *six*,' said a particularly nasty voice at the back.

Everyone thought about this. Then everyone (there were no women present) shuddered.

'No,' said Droopy Moustache, whose face had gone a little pale, 'he don't deserve *six*. He hasn't done anythin' *that* bad.'

Colin, whose face had gone paler than anyone's, breathed a sigh of relief. 'Look, gentlemen,' he said. 'I fully understand your frustration at being unable to get into Camelot. If you will kindly release my arms and let me look at my book of spells, perhaps I can work out a way of overcoming the problem.'

There was a good deal of muttering about this. Some of the farmers were clearly none too happy about letting the wizard loose to work magic.

''Ow do we know we can trust yer?' demanded Burly, voicing the general feeling. 'Yer might turn us into spotted toads.'

Colin was about to remind Burly that a few moments earlier he hadn't seemed at all averse to this fate, but the expression on the farmer's face made him doubt whether this would be tactful. So instead he said, 'Look, what choice have you got?'

There was more muttering. At the end of it, Burly said reluctantly, 'Awright. But if any of us starts feelin' even a *bit* toadish, yer in dead trouble. There's allus them six donkeys, remember.'

Burly and Droopy released Colin's arms, and all the farmers moved off to what a layman's instinct suggested might be a safe distance.

Colin produced his *Wizard's Handbook* with what he hoped was an impressive flourish (his hands were shaking a little at the thought of those six donkeys), and opened it at a random page, which happened to contain a spell for removing bunions. He was not at all sure what to do, and had decided, for the moment, to play for time.

He struck a pose, and waved his hand in an impressive but meaningless gesture.

'Absquatulate, bunionus humungus et repulsimus,' he read out. *'Absquatulate, revoltissimus et pusillanimus carbunclus—'*

The farmers listened, impressed despite themselves. Watching a professional at work when you haven't the faintest idea what they're doing is a calming experience. It's only later, when they've gone off with your money and the tap they've put in leaks, or the light fuses, or the ceiling falls on your head, that you get homicidally angry, and by then it's too late.

Colin came to the end of the bunion spell, turned the page, and moved on to a spell for the removal of ingrowing toenails, all without pausing. How long he could keep this up before the farmers got suspicious he had no idea, but perhaps something would happen soon.

Six donkeys, said a voice in the back of his mind.

He clutched *The Wizard's Handbook* tighter.

It had *better* be soon.

Balderbreeks put down his knife and fork and pushed away his empty plate with a sigh. 'That's better. That's the *right* way to start a day's hard sentrying.'

'Shall I go up to the castle now, and tell them about the wall?' Eric asked. He was listening to the shouting outside the sentry-hut. It was less of a shout now and more of a growl, and without knowing why he felt that this was somehow ominous.

Balderbreeks drained the last of his coffee and set the mug down on the table. He scratched his unshaven chin, and cast an eye round the hut. Now where on earth was his razor? 'All in good time, young Eric. First things first. You haven't done the washing-up yet, have you?'

It was clear to Colin that his bluff was not going to succeed for much longer. There were ominous growls coming from the farming community, and they were casting evil glances in his direction.

Surely *somebody* would come to his rescue soon?

Keeping his eyes firmly on the *Handbook,* he turned yet another page and plunged desperately into an obscure spell for the removal of scropple-toe in cattle.

At that moment he felt someone pluck at his sleeve.

So this was it. Six donkeys time. He let out an incoherent moan, and turned to face his tormentors.

He found himself confronting a curious trio. One was a large red-haired man with a pale, bony face and mournful expression. The other two were foxes. One, whose expression was sharp and unfriendly, wore a poke-bonnet and a shawl. The other, who looked rather more affable, sported a monocle and a bright green smoking jacket with a number of quill pens protruding from the pocket.

'Young man,' said the fox in the poke-bonnet, peering at him over a pair of gold-rimmed pince-nez, 'I perceive from your grey robe and general air of dissoluteness that you are some sort of wizard. Kindly remove this ridiculous wall that is blocking our way. We have business with King Uther in Camelot.'

Colin looked from the foxes to the large red-haired man. He was very muscular, even more so than Burly. And behind him, the farmers were closing in. Their patience had clearly run out.

'Wizard,' growled Burly, glaring at Colin over the

foxes' heads. 'Why isn't this wall down yet?'

'*Detorquero torquerum*,' gabbled Colin desperately, waving the grimoire in front of him like a charm to ward off the evil influence of farmers, '*bovis digitum*—'

'Scropple-toe,' said the large red-haired man suddenly. 'Aye, that's it. Yon spell ye're sayin'. I recall when we had scropple-toe in the Highland cattle in Glenmiller, the local wizard used yon spell tae get rid o' it.'

'Oh, is that it?' Burly nodded slowly. 'So yer've bin tryin' to fool us, have yer? Right. Come 'ere, yer skinny little streak of pig's backside.'

He lunged at Colin and grabbed him by the sleeve.

'Six donkeys,' said the farmer grimly, and his companions echoed the refrain.

But Colin was not listening. He had stopped intoning, and was staring at something beyond them all, something that was coming towards them over the plain of Camelot.

'What yer staring at?' Burly turned suspiciously, evidently thinking this was another trick. His jaw dropped.

A group of outlandish figures was marching towards them. A not very tuneful sound of chanting preceded them. It was not loud (the Fhomoire's hangovers had improved but not entirely gone), but you could still make out the words.

'*Here we troll, here we troll, here we troll,*
here we troll, here we troll, here we tro-oll . . .'

'*Trolls!*' gasped Burly, letting go of Colin's sleeve.

'They're here,' said Colin Higinbotham, with quiet satisfaction.

Chapter Twelve

With his usual cheerful air, Eric put the last knife and fork away, and hung up the tea-towel on the nail behind the door. Washing-up was not the sort of activity he had expected when he went into the Camelot castle guard (main gate sentry branch), but he was not one to complain, and there was always the chance that he might get sent on an exciting and dangerous mission later today. Or if not today, maybe tomorrow.

'Shall I go up to the castle now?' he asked Balderbreeks, who had found his shaving tackle and was peering into a small shaving-mirror, his weather-beaten face half-obscured by a mass of white lather.

Balderbreeks turned, razor in hand, and looked round the tiny hut. Seeing nothing that currently needed cleaning, tidying or polishing, he nodded. 'Okay. But make sure you're back in time to make lunch.'

Eric saluted (carefully, because the hut was so small that an unconsidered arm movement could do untold damage), opened the door and went out.

He was instantly flattened against the side of the hut by a surging mass of red-faced tradesmen. They looked distinctly displeased.

'Awright, young Eric,' growled a scar-faced man carrying a small bag of tools and one or two pots and pans – evidently a tinker. 'What's goin' on? Why ain't you an' Balderbreeks opened the gate this mornin'?'

'But we never *shut* the gate,' Eric pointed out. 'Unless the city's under attack.'

'Well, it's shut today,' said a tired-looking man beside the tinker. He was bowed under the weight of a large basket strapped to his back. In the basket Eric could see lengths of dull grey pipe. Eric felt some sympathy for him. Being a plumber was no fun when you had to carry your own lead.

Eric peered over the heads of the jostling crowd. There was certainly *something* filling up the space between the stone towers that flanked the gateway, but it wasn't the heavy oak gate – that was in its usual place, leaning against the wall. Nor was it the portcullis which was lowered in an emergency. It was a mysterious dull black surface, which reminded him of something, though he couldn't for the moment think what.

'I don't know what that is,' said Eric. 'But it certainly isn't the gate. Have you tried pushing it to see if it moves?'

There was an uneasy murmuring among the crowd. 'We ain't touching that,' said the tinker. 'There's a feelin' of *sorc'ry* to it. We don't want to be turned into spotted toads, do we, neighbours?'

'No, we don't,' said several voices.

'Mind you,' said the plumber sadly, 'I hear spotted toads has a nice restful life.' The lead pipes in his basket clinked dully together as he tried to heft them into a more comfortable position.

'What we think,' said the tinker, eyeing Eric narrowly, 'is that it's your job to move this 'ere obstruction, see? Bein' a sentry, an' bein' responsible for the gate, an' all.'

'But I have to go to the castle,' Eric said, 'to tell *them* about it.'

The tinker's eyes narrowed still further, until he

looked as if he was asleep in an unusually aggressive way. He took half a step nearer to Eric, which was all he could manage in the space available. 'We ain't *arskin'* yer to shift it,' he said slowly. 'We're *tellin'* yer. An' there's lots more of us than what there is of you. See?'

A small grey cloud of apprehension drifted in front of Eric's normally sunny mood. 'But you can't threaten me,' he objected. 'I'm a member of the castle guard. I represent King Uther. If you threaten me, that's treason. I know that, 'cos I was reading it only last night in King's Regulations, vol V, chap IV, para VII, sub-para ix, Castle Guard, Duties and Remuneration of.'

The tinker un-narrowed his eyes just enough to leer at Eric unpleasantly. 'Yer wanna get legal, do yer? Okay, get legal. But just remember, havin' all yer arms an' legs broke hurts just as much, even if them what does it gets horse-whipped afterwards. See what I mean?'

Eric swallowed. 'Er - yes. If you let me through, I'll – er – have a look at this obstruction.'

The crowd inched aside, making the narrowest of paths for Eric to pass through.

'It's sort of rough and black,' he reported over his shoulder, running his hand cautiously over the high flat surface. 'And I can hear voices on the other side.'

'That'll be the farmers, wantin' to get their veggies to market,' said the tinker, nodding. 'They'll be mutterin' angrily, I 'spect.'

'No, they're singing,' said Eric, who had his ear pressed against the black wall.

The tinker and his companions exchanged puzzled glances. '*Singin'*?'

'Yes.'

'What are they singin'?' demanded the tinker sceptically.

Eric listened. After a while he said, 'It's a very simple song. It just seems to be three words over and over again.'

'*What* three words?'

Eric waved at them to be quiet. After a while he said doubtfully, 'It sounds like *Here we troll*. Though I can't quite see why farmers would be singing that.'

Behind him, there was a sudden loud commotion. It sounded like a panicky stampede of some sort of two-legged animals laden with clattering bags and bundles. Which wasn't really surprising.

Eric turned round to find that they had all gone. All, that is, except for the plumber's bag of lead pipes, which he had evidently dropped to speed his retreat.

'Oh,' he said, feeling somewhat at a loss.

The door of the sentry-hut opened, and Balderbreeks emerged, his chin festooned with dabs of shaving-cream. He was carrying the razor in one hand and the shaving-mirror in the other. 'What's going on, young Eric? I thought you were going up to the castle?'

Eric stared at the mirror in his superior's hand. It had its back to him, and was showing only a dull black surface.

'Now isn't that odd,' he said slowly.

Balderbreeks frowned. 'Isn't what odd?'

'*Here we troll, here we troll, here we troll,*
  Here we troll, here we troll, here we tro-oll . . .'

Colin watched, with helpless fascination, as twenty-nine huge hairy trolls and a cauliflower lumbered to and fro in an exaggeratedly tip-toed war-dance on the grass in front of the (currently invisible) city. *At least*, he thought, *they seem to be in a good mood. Perhaps that means we're safe for the moment. Perhaps we'll be all right as long as we don't antagonise them.*

Apart from the Fhomoire, there were now only the four of them – Colin, Macpherson and the two foxes – outside the walls. The farmers had fled in panic. The donkeys had kicked their carts to pieces, to give themselves an extra turn of speed, and fled after them. Piles of throops, grumbles and wiggits littered the grass.

'Young man,' said an imperious voice. 'I have waited patiently for several minutes, and you *still* have not set about removing this wall. Kindly cast one of your disreputable spells at once.'

Colin blinked, and looked down into a stern pair of pince-nez. 'Er – I don't think that would be a good idea, ma'am.'

'And why not, pray?'

'Well, because—'

'Tcha!' Mrs Tod snorted angrily. 'I can see that, like most males, you're a weak-kneed, lily-livered, disorganised poltroon. Clearly I shall have to find someone who *will* solve the problem. I shall enlist the help of those rowdy-looking fellows over there.' She turned her back on him and set off across the grass towards the lurching trolls.

'What does she think she's doing?' Colin asked Macpherson. 'Those trolls will *eat* her if she's not careful.'

The Scot uttered a gruff chuckle. 'She'll gi' 'em a muckle belly-ache if they do. Pure bile, that's what she's made of. Pure bile.'

'Now, Macpherson,' said the fox in the smoking-jacket gently, 'that's not the way to talk about your employer and my sister.'

Macpherson sighed. 'Aye, aye, I beg yer pardon, Ma Laird.'

'Who *are* you all?' Colin asked, 'and what are you doing here?'

'I'm the Earl of Redbrush. This is my gardener, Macpherson, and that's my sister, Mrs Tod. We've come to ask Uther if he could see his way to reinstating the Redbrush family seat, which has unfortunately been devoured by grey slime.'

Colin's brow furrowed. 'Grey slime?'

'Yes. The handiwork of those fellows, presumably.' The Earl gestured towards the capering trolls.

Alarm bells began to ring in an obscure part of The Great Alfonso's mind. 'But those are *trolls,*' he said. 'Trolls are just lumpish characters with a startling lack of brain and large muscles. Grey slime, that's – that's something else entirely. That's *sorcery.*'

'Nevertheless,' said the Earl, with a shrug. 'They brought grey slime with them, and it ate my house. Pity, really. Some of the family portraits weren't actually all that bad.'

Colin stared at the group of trolls.

'Oh dear,' he said softly. 'I've got an awful feeling that I may have made a mistake.'

'Well, I shouldn't worry about it,' said the Earl lightly. 'In my experience, mistakes tend to fall into two categories – those that are too trivial to make any real difference, cosmologically speaking, and those that are fatal.'

'I don't find that very comforting,' muttered Colin.

There was a sudden loud rumbling noise from beneath the Earl's smoking jacket. He put a paw to his midriff. 'Pardon me. You don't happen to know where I could get some lunch, do you? I've walked all the way from Redbrush Park on an empty stomach.'

Colin shook his head. 'You could get something in the city, I suppose, once we manage to get inside.'

'And when will that be, d'you think?'

'No idea, I'm afraid.'

'But hang on a minute,' said the Earl, 'aren't you one of these wizard chappies? Couldn't you see your way to, as it were, *magicking* some food into existence for me?'

'Wouldn't do you any good if I did. Do you know the nutritional content of magical food?'

'No.'

'Fat, zero. Protein, zero. Carbohydrate, zero. Vitamins, zero. Calories, minus several hundred.'

The Earl frowned. '*Minus* several hundred?'

Colin nodded. 'Makes you want to just lie down and do nothing for a while. In fact,' he continued, warming to his subject, 'magical food consists solely of appearance, smell and taste, or *glamour*, if you want the technical term. Unless it's made using dead leaves or stones or something, but the trouble then is that a few hours after you've eaten it, it's liable to turn back into its original form in your intestines. If it was made from stones, you get constipation like you've never imagined.' The wizard gestured around him at the piles of vegetables left by the fleeing farmers. 'Why not try some of these throops, grumbles and wiggits?'

The Earl shuddered. 'No thanks. Can't stand the things. When we get into the city, I'll see if I can find a restaurant that does traditional vulpine cuisine.'

At the moment that Mrs Tod set off towards the group of dancing trolls, King Bres caught sight of himself reflected in the mirror-wall.

He lumbered to a halt, staring. Several of his subjects bumped into him, and in a little while the galumphing had stopped, and they were all gazing in stupefaction at their own reflections.

'What dat?' King Bres demanded.

His subjects regarded themselves for a long time.

Then, as one troll, they answered him. 'Dunno, boss.'

King Bres scratched one of his heads in puzzlement. Finally light dawned. 'Them *trolls*,' he announced portentously.

The other Fhomoire peered at themselves in the wall. 'Trolls,' they agreed.

'Trolls *dang'rous*,' said King Bres. 'Better retreat.'

'Better retreat,' the rest of the trolls agreed.

The Fhomoire turned their backs on the wall, and started to move off.

A nearby cauliflower approached the King of the Fhomoire, and tapped him on the knee. 'Your Majesty?'

'Huh?' King Bres stopped, and so did everyone else. 'Who dat?'

'Me again, your Majesty. Cringe.'

'Whaddya want, Cringe?'

'Your Majesty, there's no need to retreat. Those are not *real* trolls.'

King Bres's three foreheads became even more furrowed. 'Whaddya mean?'

'That's *you* you can see in there, your Majesty.'

'*Huh?*'

Oh well, thought Cringe. *At least I tried.* 'Never mind, your Majesty. Forget I spoke.'

'Poor ol' Cringe,' said King Bres sadly. 'You mixed up, Cringe. Poor collyflobble.' He turned, lumberingly, to continue the retreat.

It looked as if Camelot was saved.

Bres took one step, and found his way blocked by a small figure in a shawl and poke-bonnet.

'You,' said Mrs Tod. 'Are you in charge of these large and unkempt persons?'

King Bres looked down at her. 'Yes, I in charge. I King of trolls. Who you?'

'I am Mrs Tod, sister of the Earl of Redbrush,'

said the lady fox. 'I want you to get me into the city.'

'City?' All three of King Bres's troll-faces looked as blank as only a troll can look. 'What city?'

'I see you are an imbecile,' said Mrs Tod. 'Behind that mirror—' she waved at the Reflecting Wall '—is the city of Camelot. I need to get in to see King Uther.'

King Bres turned slowly round and gazed at the group of trolls that seemed to be only a few yards away across the turf.

'Mirror?' he said.

He moved slowly over to the reflecting surface, and stood a foot away from it, staring at the other King Bres.

The rest of the Fhomoire shambled up and stood alongside him, all staring in fascination at their reflections.

'Mirror?' said King Bres again.

'It's the back of a mirror,' said Eric excitedly. He seized the shaving-mirror from Balderbreeks's hand, and pointed first at the dull black back of it, and then at the two hundred foot high dull black surface between the gate-towers. 'A mirror – see?'

'No, I don't see,' said the older sentry. 'Why would anyone put a bloody great mirror outside the gate? Doesn't make sense.'

'But the point *is*,' went on Eric, ignoring his superior's objections, 'that if it's a mirror, it's just made of glass and silver. We can smash it with a hammer.'

Balderbreeks looked thoughtful. 'I used to have a hammer in the hut. Haven't seen it for weeks.'

Eric looked around eagerly, and caught sight of the plumber's bag of lead pipes. 'Here – one of these will do.' He picked up a length of pipe, and walked to the city gate.

'I think,' said Balderbreeks, who was beginning to have an uneasy feeling about this, 'that we ought to report this to the castle *first*.'

'But they'll be *pleased* if we get this obstruction out of the way,' Eric said cheerfully. 'Then the farmers can get in, and the tradesmen can get out, and everyone will be happy.'

'I really think—' began Balderbreeks.

But Eric, with the single-minded optimism of youth, raised the lead pipe and with a fluid movement brought it down hard against the dull black surface of the wall.

Gwydden was becoming slightly worried. Usually after being eaten by something in a nightmare he woke up, presumably because nothing much worse could happen to him, or at any rate nothing worse had occurred to the warped imagination of the Maker of Dreams[1].

This time, however, he was just sitting inside the tree. It was dark and dank and unpleasant, but worse than that, it was boring. This seemed all wrong to Gwydden. Dreams could be either wonderful or horrible. They weren't supposed to be boring.

---

[1]The current Maker of Dreams is a gnome called Clarence. He lives in a small lighthouse off the coast of Greenland, where he makes all the dreams for the entire human race using recycled snowflakes and those glittery bits that fall off the Aurora Borealis. His favourite food is cheese, which unfortunately he can't get. If anyone else has cheese for supper, he gets mad as hell and sends them one of his nastiest nightmares in revenge. So now you know.

Clarence is two feet three inches tall, works terribly hard, and grumbles a lot.

Unless, he said to himself, *it's those mushrooms of Hergrim's. Perhaps I'm not asleep at all. Perhaps I'm on a really dull hallucinogenic trip*[1].

Well, if this trip doesn't arrive somewhere interesting soon, I'm going to ask for a refund on my ticket.

Thousands of square feet of glass shattered into fragments, with a sound that can only be compared to the shattering of thousands of square feet of glass.

The morning sun chose that precise moment to leap out from behind a cloud and fling bright sunlight across the whole scene. The shards of broken mirror became a dazzling display of cascading silver and gold. They rained down in a blinding shower of light onto the heads of the Fhomoire, burying them under a mountain of silvered glass.

When the crashing and tinkling had finally stopped, four humans and two foxes gazed with varying degrees of relief at the glazed mounds under which twenty-nine trolls and a cauliflower lay buried.

'What a nasty way to go,' murmured the Earl to Macpherson.

'Aye,' the gardener agreed. 'They canna have survived that. Cut tae ribbons, for sure.'

Mrs Tod came across the grass, beckoning to them. 'Come on, you two. We can get into the city now.'

They all trod gingerly between the motionless mounds of glass and through the open city gate.

Mrs Tod caught sight of Balderbreeks and Eric, who were staring at the debris like men turned to stone, and made a beeline for them. 'You there,' she said

---

[1]Actually *all* mushrooms are hallucinogenic, but most of the hallucinations are so dull that people mistake them for real life.

peremptorily. 'Take us to the castle. We wish to see King Uther at once.'

The older sentry stirred himself as if emerging from a dream.

'I'm not at all sure you should have done that, young Eric,' he said.

'Hm?' Eric looked down at the lead pipe in his hand. 'Well, it's left a bit of a mess, but I did remove the obstruction, didn't I?'

'Well, at least it's all over,' said Balderbreeks, who on the evidence of this remark would have been ideally qualified to be a television sports commentator.

The breeze, which had been blowing steadily from the south for most of the morning, suddenly and capriciously veered eastwards, which brought it straight in through the city gate.

Something else came in with it: a thin thread of grey mist.

Balderbreeks sniffed. 'What's that smell? It's nasty.'

'My man,' snapped Mrs Tod. 'I've asked you once already. I'm not accustomed to being kept waiting. Take us to the castle *at once.*'

But everyone else was now sniffing the air that was coming in through the gate.

'I know that smell,' muttered Macpherson. ''Tis *evil.*'

'Nonsense,' said Mrs Tod. 'How can a smell be evil?'

Macpherson's eyes suddenly widened. He gesticulated towards the horizon. 'Look! Can ye not see it comin'? We should ha' known we couldna leave it behind.'

They all looked at the skyline, even Mrs Tod.

A thick belt of grey mist was moving towards them from the direction of the Forest. It came with unusual speed, as if something more than the breeze was driving it.

Soon the first wisps and tendrils of grey were curling over the grass towards them. One of them touched the glass-covered mounds under which the Fhomoire lay buried.

The shards of glass moved slightly.

The mist thickened around the line of debris. It seemed, to those watching who were perhaps of a more fanciful disposition, to be searching. It probed among the pieces of shattered mirror like ghostly fingers.

Another of the mounds moved, sending fragments of glass tinkling down in a small avalanche.

Something slowly emerged from between the shards. It didn't look like any part of a troll. It looked more like the eye-stalk of a giant slug.

The Great Alfonso let out a despairing moan.

As the mist grew thicker around the debris, more of the slugs began to emerge.

'Aha!' King Bres shook off the last shards of glass with a rippling movement of his repulsive body. 'So! Not trolls after all! Well, you live and learn. Okay, team – let's set about conquering this city.'

The Fhomoire surged in through the city gate in an oozing, wobbling mass.

Colin Higinbotham had watched the apparent destruction of the trolls with great relief. Apparently he hadn't made a mistake after all. The trolls were just trolls, and even though the Reflecting Wall hadn't worked exactly as he intended owing to the ill-timed intervention of Mrs Tod, the trolls were now dead, and the city was saved.

Now, however, there was no getting away from the fact that Someone Had Blundered. And everyone was going to think (with some justification) that that Someone was The Great Alfonso.

Uther was not going to be pleased. In fact, Uther was

probably going to be very *dis*pleased. Uther was known to be a pretty relaxed sort of king, but Colin had an uncomfortable feeling that however relaxed a king might be, a wizard charged with defending the king's capital city who then let man-eating shape-shifters in through the front gate was likely to have a short and undistinguished future.

There was only one thing left for him to do, and the sooner he did it, the better.

Making sure no-one was watching him, he slipped away around the city wall until he was facing more or less due north.

He happened to know that King Piddle of Pittenweem still needed a court wizard. Even though King Piddle was reputed to chew cats' heads off when displeased, it was still a second chance, of sorts.

Casting a last regretful glance at the glittering piles of silver and glass - for it had been a *good* idea, as ideas which don't work so often are – the Great Alfonso set out on the long and lonely road to Fife.

Confronted with a rapidly approaching horde of flesh-devouring shape-shifters smelling of death (or something worse), most sensible people would turn and run.

This is what four of the five people standing by the city gate duly did. The two foxes melted into the shadows. Balderbreeks and Macpherson, whose instinct for self-preservation was just as strong, also dived for cover.

Eric, however, stood firm. He had joined the castle guard because of a sense of vocation. His duty as a guard, he knew, was to protect the city from enemies, and the Fhomoire were not the sort of creatures you could mistake for friends.

Eric strode forward into the path of King Bres and his

Fhomoire, struck a who-will-stand-at-my-right-hand-and-hold-the-bridge-with-me sort of pose, and said firmly, 'Just a moment, gentlemen. I must ask you for your credentials. Are you visiting Camelot for business, or for pleasure?'

King Bres scarcely slowed his advance. He oozed up to Eric and waved his eye-stalks in his face. A lipless mouth in what was presumably his head opened, and a glutinous voice hissed, *'Both.'*

'Well, in that case—' began Eric.

King Bres oozed on, cutting him off permanently in mid-sentence.

Wedged into a nearby doorway, Balderbreeks stifled a groan. *These youngsters,* he thought, *they just don't listen. I warned young Eric about being too keen. First in the charge, and all that. Quite a promising lad, really. Such a waste.*

What's worse, I'm going to have to make my own breakfast tomorrow.

In the Great Hall of Camelot Castle, King Uther was snatching an odd few minutes between appointments to write yet another abdication speech.

'Having resolved,' he wrote, *'to retire from public life, and spend my remaining years in the peace and tranquillity of a country cottage with my dear wife . . .'*

He looked thoughtfully at the last four words, and then scratched them out.

'. . . I hereby renounce my various titles, and leave my kingdom in the capable hands of . . .'

His quill came to a stop. He sighed deeply, and said, in a voice resonant with feeling, 'Oh, rats.'

The door opened, and a sentry came in. He looked distinctly agitated. 'Sire?'

'Hm?'

'There are some giant slugs approaching the castle, sire. They're devouring people as they come.'

Unhurriedly, Uther laid down his pen. 'Indeed? Who have they devoured so far?'

The sentry, who was familiar with Uther's relaxed approach in a crisis, answered promptly. 'Young Eric at the gate, sire, and Lord Porfingle.'

Uther stroked his chin. 'Lord Porfingle, eh? He was supposed to be my next appointment.'

'Yes, sire. He was on his way here in a sedan chair. They devoured the sedan chair, too, sire.'

'I see.' Uther leaned back in his chair. 'Devoured Lord Porfingle, eh? So it's not all bad news, then?'

The sentry coughed. It was not his place to acquiesce in this sort of remark about a noble personage, even when the noble personage was known to be an obnoxious old windbag. 'There's Eric, sire. He was a nice lad, was Eric, though not what you might call bright.'

'Yes.' Uther's tone was a touch weary. Why were things like this always happening in *his* kingdom? 'Where exactly are these slugs now?'

'Approaching the moat, sire. Shall I tell the guard to pull up the drawbridge?'

Uther nodded. 'Yes, but let them into the castle first.'

The sentry stared. 'Sire?'

'Can't have them wandering round the city eating people, can we? Let's get them inside the castle, and see what they want. Perhaps they just need a good square meal.'

'Yes, sire,' said the sentry dubiously. He was inclined to think that the giant slugs probably *did* want a meal, but he was worried that, rather than square, they might prefer it to be sentry shaped. However, he had a good deal of faith in Uther, who had never let him be eaten so far. 'I'll see to it, sire.'

'Good man. Oh, and take a message to the Queen, will you? Ask her if she can spare the Knights of the Slightly Pear-Shaped Table for a while, to help me get rid of some unwelcome guests.'

'Sire.' The sentry saluted reluctantly. This was almost too much. Man-eating slugs could perhaps be pacified, but Queen Igrayne had a will of tungsten steel and was distinctly counter-suggestible. He would just have to hope she was in a good mood.

When the last of the Fhomoire had disappeared up the hill, four figures detached themselves from the shadows.

'And now, my man,' said Mrs Tod to Balderbreeks, 'we are still waiting to be escorted to the castle to see King Uther.'

Balderbreeks, gazing vacantly at the grey slime that thickly coated the cobbles and marked the passing of the Fhomoire, did not reply to this. He mumbled, 'Need a cup of tea. Poor young Eric. Need a very *strong* cup of tea.' And he shuffled away towards the sentry hut.

'Well!' Mrs Tod folded her front paws over one another as aggressively as if she were making a move in a Japanese martial art. 'The service in this city leaves a great deal to be desired. I shall complain to Uther about it when I see him. Come along, you two. Evidently we will have to find the castle ourselves.'

'We don't really *need* to be shown the way,' said her brother mildly. 'You can see the castle from here, if you look up the hill.'

'That is not the point,' his sister snapped. 'We are an aristocratic family. People of our background should not have to go around *looking* at things.' She turned to the gardener. 'Macpherson, escort us to the castle.'

'Aye, ma'am,' came the melancholy reply. 'May I ask

what ye intend to do if we catch up wi' yon slimy beasties?'

'I shall give them a piece of my mind about their recent behaviour,' said the lady of Redbrush Hall. 'Come on, you two.'

'Er, Edith,' said the Earl tentatively, 'do you think perhaps, before we go to the castle, a spot of lunch . . . ?'

Mrs Tod's only reply to this was a snort.

With a grinding and squeaking of ropes and timbers, the drawbridge of Camelot castle sank lower and lower, until it bumped on the bare earth on the townward side of the moat.

King Bres and the Fhomoire oozed across the planks, leaving a sticky trail behind them. When they were all inside, the castle guard raised the drawbridge again.

A group of citizens, who had been watching from a safe distance, breathed a somewhat muted sigh of relief, and turned to go back to their shops and other businesses. They picked their way down the hill, doing their best to avoid the slime left by the Fhomoire, which stank unpleasantly.

A little grey mist blew up the hill, catching in their throats and making them cough and pull faces.

Halfway down, they passed two foxes and a human going the other way. The two parties ignored one another.

The grey mist grew steadily thicker.

In the Great Hall, King Uther rose politely from his throne as King Bres and the Fhomoire oozed through the door. Rising to greet a fellow monarch was the correct thing to do from the point of view of royal etiquette, and so Uther naturally did it. King Bres was, after all, a king, as Uther could see from his silver crown. Admittedly he was also a giant slug who ate people, but as Uther knew only too well, even monarchs have their faults.

A little grey mist blew into the hall through the doorway, bringing with it a smell of drains, or worse. Uther wrinkled his nose involuntarily, but otherwise ignored it. *How a royal guest smells is his business, not yours.*

'Ah, there you are,' he said affably to King Bres. *They're making a nasty mess of the parquet floor,* he said to himself. *Igrayne is going to hit the roof.* 'So nice to see you. Welcome to my little castle. I expect you'd all like something to eat, eh?'

'We've just eaten, thank you,' King Bres hissed through his lipless mouth.

'Oh yes, Lord Porfingle.' Uther nodded. *And young Eric,* he thought. *But I don't trust myself to mention that.* 'I – er – hope he was to your satisfaction?'

King Bres belched.

'Good, good,' murmured Uther. 'Well, and are you all staying for a while? You'll find the rooms in the East Tower very comfortable, or . . .' His gaze wandered over the wobbling mass of grey slug-flesh. '. . . or perhaps you'd prefer the cellars, where it's nice and damp . . . ?'

'We will have this room,' hissed King Bres.

'The Great Hall?' Uther raised his eyebrows. 'Well, of course, only too happy to oblige. Though I must warn you, it's not very comfortable for sleeping in.'

'Thinking of catching us off guard while we sleep?' asked the King of the Fhomoire, with a gurgle which Uther recognised, with some difficulty, as a laugh. 'I warn you, that would be rather unwise.'

'My dear fellow,' said Uther, slightly hurt. 'I hope you don't think I'm the sort of monarch who waits till his enemies – beg pardon, I mean, his guests – are asleep, and then murders them in their beds? What sort of king would do something like that?'

'I would,' said King Bres without hesitation.

'Really?' With difficulty, Uther managed not to show his disapproval. 'Well, I expect there are – er – extenuating circumstances in your case.' He hurried on, not wishing to dwell on this distressing topic. 'Anyway, as to the purpose of your visit—'

'This is not a visit,' King Bres interrupted. 'This is an invasion. We are taking over your kingdom. From this moment, *I* am king of your pathetic little country.'

Uther was not surprised by this revelation, but he had still been hoping it wouldn't turn out like this. He had also been wondering how he would react if it did. Now it had come to the point, he realised with a sinking feeling that his reaction was only too predictable.

'Well, er,' he said weakly. 'I understand what you're saying, and of course it's quite a compliment that you see my little kingdom as – er – so attractive, but when all's said and done, there are internationally recognised conventions about this sort of thing, negotiating procedures and so forth, and I really think—'

King Bres brushed all this aside with a wave of his eye-stalks. 'There will be no negotiations. As I said, this kingdom is now ruled by the Fhomoire. The first thing we will do is establish a new tax.'

'Oh, I see.' In spite of the stinking grey mist, which now seemed to be blowing in through the windows, Uther breathed a little easier. Taxes were something he understood. 'Yes, of course. Well, people in Camelot are mostly quite public-spirited, and as long as you don't set the tax higher than people can afford, a fair number of them will probably pay up. Say about forty percent. That may not sound a lot, but believe me, in a city where every citizen has the legal right to carry a sharp pointed weapon and is quite prepared to use it if they think someone is after their knick-knacks, that's a pretty good rate of collection.'

King Bres gave vent to another gurgle. 'Our tax is one that *everyone* will be able to afford. And I can assure you, our success rate in collecting it has always been one hundred percent.'

A frisson of unease scuttled along the back of Uther's neck, like a mouse with exceptionally cold feet. 'Really? Er – what sort of tax is it, exactly?'

'You might call it the *Body* Tax,' the slug-king snickered. 'We collect one hundred percent of a person's body, and put it to good use. *Very* good use. Though as I said, at the moment we're not hungry.'

The mouse on Uther's neck dug ghostly claws into his flesh. The King opened his mouth, but he could think of nothing to say that royal etiquette would allow. 'Oh – er – ah,' was all he managed, after which he lapsed into silence.

The door at the back of the Great Hall opened, and a sentry entered and hurried up behind Uther.

'Sire?'

'Yes?'

'I've been to see the Queen, sire—'

'Ah, good,' said Uther. He smiled confidently, knowing that every wife longs for an opportunity to help her husband when he is in difficulties[1].

'—and I asked her if she'd send the Knights of the Slightly Pear-Shaped Table down here to see off some unwelcome visitors, like you said, sire—'

'Yes?'

'—and if you look out of the window, sire, you'll see them now.'

_____

[1] As in the old Chinese proverb: *Wife often desires to preserve husband in pickle.*

With a burst of speed he hadn't used for a good many years, Uther darted across the Great Hall and peered out of the window into the drifting coils of grey mist.

On the hillside below the castle, a group of knightly figures on horseback were making their way down towards the city. They had a somewhat furtive air, as if what they were doing might be considered, by some ill-informed and unsympathetic people, to be less than brave.

For once in his life, Uther saw red.

'Come back, you spoilt, poncified, white-livered, good-for-nothing cowards!' he yelled, in a voice cracking with unregal emotion.

The figures on horseback turned startled faces up the hill towards him. Then, as one man, they dug their heels into their horses' flanks and spurred them twice as fast down the slope.

Uther's shoulders slumped. Dejected, he turned back into the Great Hall and gazed at the hideous mass of grey slug-flesh occupying his heartland.

'There's only one thing that can save us now,' he mumbled, 'and that's a wizard.' He let out a groan, and clutched at his forehead. 'What am I saying? Wizards are incompetent, meddling fools. If you want something cocked up, ask a wizard. And anyway, what wizard? Merlin's vanished, so has the so-called Great Alfonso, and the rest are just amateurs.'

King Bres oozed closer to him.

'Hoping for miracles, Uther?' he hissed. 'There won't be any. Do you see this mist?' He waved his eye-stalks at the choking spirals swirling in through the doors and windows. 'That is the Grey Magic. It is older and more powerful than anything your puny wizards can conjure up. It is pouring into this kingdom, seeping into the grass and the trees and the soil, devouring the life it finds there and feeding us with new strength. We are bleeding this land dry, old fool, and there is nothing you can do to stop us.' He oozed even closer to Uther, and breathed a foetid odour into the old king's face.

Uther took a handkerchief from his sleeve and pressed it fastidiously to his nose.

Well, it looks as though I'm beaten, he reflected. *My days as a king are finally over. Still, I've had a pretty good innings. Some monarchs only survive a matter of days[1]. And no royal dynasty lasts for ever. Sooner or later you have to give way to newer blood – or at any rate, blood that hasn't yet been poured liberally over the executioner's block.*

'After all,' he said aloud, 'I always meant to abdicate. It's just a pity I didn't get to read out any of my speeches.'

King Bres gurgled with laughter.

'I'm beginning to get hungry again,' he whispered, in his swamp-sucking voice. 'I think it's time to start collecting the Body Tax.'

Gwydden was finding the inside of the tree increasingly tedious. Not only was nothing happening, but he now had cramp in both legs.

---

[1] Less than that, in some cases. King Rudlan of Thule was especially unlucky. At his coronation, the four priests who were supposed to symbolically touch Rudlan's head with the Stone Crown of Thule (it was much too heavy to actually wear) inadvertently dropped it. Rudlan was deemed to have been King for the amount of time it took a large lump of granite to compress his skull and cause a fatal brain haemorrhage – about 0.25 seconds.

The next five minutes saw all the remaining members of the Thulean royal family politely offering each other the Stone Crown, while advancing cast-iron reasons why they themselves were ineligible.

Ten minutes after Rudlan's death, Thule was unanimously declared a republic.

'You're not supposed to get cramp in dreams,' he muttered. 'Or in hallucinations, for that matter. There's something wrong here.'

He got slowly to his feet, and staggered around in the dark while pins and needles threaded agonisingly in and out of his flesh.

'Ow, ow, ow,' he mumbled. And then, more loudly, '*Ow!*'

He had fallen over something. Reaching out to touch it, he discovered that it was Hergrim. He gave the dwarf's shoulder a shake.

Hergrim stirred and groaned. 'Three kippers for breakfast, mother, and six slices of toast,' he mumbled. 'I need a full stomach if I'm going to fight the trolls.'

'Hergrim, wake up!' hissed the wizard, shaking him harder.

'Mmmmm?' Gwydden heard the dwarf sit up and yawn. 'Gwydden? Is that you? What's happened to the lights? Are we underground?'

'No, we're inside a tree.'

'Ah.' The dwarf was silent for a moment. Then he said, 'Where's my axe?'

'What for?'

'So I can cut my way out, of course.'

'I don't think that would be a good idea,' muttered the wizard.

'Why not?'

Gwydden hesitated. Sometimes, if you tell people they're in a life-threatening situation and there's probably nothing they can do to prevent whatever horrible and unexpected thing might at any moment be about to happen to them, they tend, inexplicably, to panic. *And if anyone's going to panic,* Gwydden thought, *it ought to be me. I'm better at it than Hergrim. I've had more practice.*

'Hergrim,' he whispered, 'this tree is *alive.*'

'Unlikely, if it's hollow.'

'No, no.' The wizard shook his head violently, forgetting that Hergrim couldn't see him. 'Not a *tree* sort of alive. A *person* sort of alive.'

'Really? How can you tell?'

'A little while ago, it was *talking* to me.'

'What did it say?'

'It said, "I'm not eating you, I'm saving you for later".'

'That doesn't sound too promising.'

'No.'

'Have you got your staff?' asked the dwarf.

'I don't think so. I think it's still on the grass outside the tree.'

'Damn.'

There was a long pause. Then Gwydden murmured, 'This tree hasn't said anything for some time. I wonder if it's fallen asleep?'

At that moment, all around them, they heard a very deep sigh.

'I *was* trying to have a quiet afternoon nap, as it happens,' said the tree, in a booming voice that filled the hollow trunk. 'But there's not much chance of that with you two wittering on inside me, is there?'

Chapter Thirteen

'My name,' said the tree, in its booming voice that seemed to surround them in quadrophonic sound, 'is Logres. Some call me the Green God.'

'We've been looking for you,' said Gwydden. 'But we didn't know you were a tree.'

'I'm not *really* a tree,' said Logres. 'I'm just resting at the moment. Being a tree is very relaxing. People tend to leave you in peace if you're a tree.'

'Unless they're in need of firewood,' muttered the dwarf.

'Beg pardon?'

'Nothing,' said the dwarf. 'What I want to know is, why you've imprisoned us like this?'

'*Imprisoned?* Great Tir-nan-Og, I haven't imprisoned you! I've been *protecting* you. Obviously you've no idea what's been happening in the Forest while you've been asleep. Still, now you're awake, you can see for yourselves. Wait a minute and I'll let you out.'

The dwarf and wizard were startled by a sudden creaking noise. A vertical crack of light appeared in front of them, and for the first time they could see the inside of the great oak in which they had been sitting.

The crack grew wider, and thin tendrils of mist swirled in through the gap. Gwydden and Hergrim coughed violently.

'Ye gods, what is that?' demanded the dwarf in a

hoarse voice. 'It smells dreadful. It smells like – like— '

'Like the well in the cottage garden,' murmured the wizard.

'Exactly,' boomed the tree. 'Out you go, both of you, and you'll see what a mess the Fhomoire have made of my beautiful Forest.'

As they clambered out of the tree, the dwarf and wizard gazed around in consternation at the transformed Forest. Instead of the normal green, tangled profusion, what lay around them was a weird, pallid, deathly wasteland. The flourishing oaks, elms and beeches had vanished. In their places rose spindly grey monstrosities like enormous weeds, looming over their heads with a sinister, predatory air. Piles of dead grey leaves littered the ground. Cobwebs festooned the branches, their thick, sticky threads clotted with dead insects. Over everything drifted the grey mist, and the stench of death hung everywhere.

'What a dump,' said Hergrim in disgust. He reached up and touched one of the cobwebs. 'Yeugh.' He wiped his hand fastidiously on the side of his breeches, while the spider who inhabited the cobweb, having scuttled out to see what it had caught, glared at him balefully with all eight of its eyes. It was a pretty big spider, but not big enough to eat a dwarf[1], so after a moment it sulkily ran back into the shadows.

'It's like one of those fairytales,' whispered Gwydden. 'You know, where the handsome prince finds the beautiful princess asleep in the middle of a haunted wood where she's lain for a hundred years.'

---

[1] The giant dwarf-eating spider, *Arachne humungus dwarfophagus*, is fortunately almost extinct, though it is still often seen by dwarfs who have drunk too many bottles of Frigga's Revenge.

'Haunted?' said a voice behind them. 'Ruined, more like. This used to be a really beautiful place. Now look at it.'

The dwarf and wizard turned, and blinked in surprise. The hollow oak from which they had just emerged had vanished. In its place stood what could only be described as a green giant (though not a particularly jolly one).

Logres the Green God, Guardian of the Forest and probably the last genuine pagan deity residing in the Home Counties, stood nearly twenty feet tall, towering over the dwarf and wizard with his legs apart and his clenched fists planted firmly on his hips. His skin was as thick as oak-bark. In fact, thought Gwydden, it probably *was* oak-bark – as gnarled and pitted and brown as if Logres had spent the last thousand years sunbathing under a hole in the ozone layer. His face had no particular expression, partly because oak-bark doesn't smile or frown easily, and partly because his eyes, nose and mouth were nothing but deep pits of darkness, like holes made by woodpeckers. In fact at that moment a squirrel poked its head out of Logres's left ear, looked down at the dwarf and wizard in a disinterested way, and disappeared again inside the Green God's head. This put the unnerving thought into the wizard's mind that the Green God's head, like the tree he had been until a few moments ago, was probably hollow.

'Look at what those shape-shifters have done to my beautiful grove,' said the Green God, waving a gnarled and knotted arm around the clearing. 'Thousands of years I've looked after these trees, using ecologically sound methods of arboriculture, and—'

'Using what?' said Hergrim.

'I think he means sunshine and rain,' said Gwydden.

'Oh.'

'—and look what they've done to it. Completely ruined. They might as well have built a motorway through it.'

'Built a *what* through it?'

The Green God gave a deep sigh. 'Never mind. You two will be dead and buried a long time before *that* happens again[1].'

Gwydden frowned. 'Are you telling us that you can see into the future?'

'Of course I can,' said the Green God scornfully. 'I'm a god, aren't I? Well, to be strictly truthful I'm a demi-god – an elemental. But I've still got a few minor super-natural powers – and a long memory.' He sighed again, a sad sound like the wind blowing through a fence which hasn't been creosoted properly. 'Long ago, when I was only a very young god, the whole of England was covered with trees.'

'That must have been a nuisance,' said Hergrim. 'Personally I prefer mountain-tops, where the air's clean and crisp and you can see for miles. You can't get a decent view when there are trees in the way.'

'Well, you're a dwarf,' said the Green God in a dismis-sive tone, rather as one might say *Well, you're a drivelling imbecile*. 'For someone of your height, getting above things would be vital if you wanted to see anything more interesting than other people's knees.'

Hergrim stiffened. 'Yes, I'm a dwarf. And like every dwarf, I have a very sharp axe, which—'

'Er, Hergrim,' said Gwydden hastily. 'I don't think this is the time or place to start talking about axes.' He turned to the Green God. 'Logres, we were on our way

---

[1]Given that all this happened in the fifth century A.D., Logres's use of the word 'again' here is interesting, to say the least.

to find you because of a prophecy. According to this prophecy, you can defeat the Fhomoire.'

'No, no,' rumbled the Green God, his scorn suddenly replaced by alarm. He shook his head violently from side to side. With a surprised squeak, the squirrel tumbled out of his ear and landed on his shoulder. 'I can't defeat the Fhomoire. *You* have to do it.'

'But surely you're going to help us,' began Gwydden.

'No, no! I can't help. The Fhomoire would destroy me, as they've destroyed this Forest. I'm not strong enough to face their Grey Magic. I have to stay here, hidden, where they can't find me.'

'But they will find you,' Hergrim objected. 'Sooner or later, one of them will come this way, and—'

'It's no use, Hergrim,' said Gwydden. 'He's changing back into a tree.'

It was true. The Green God was growing broader and taller as they watched, his legs narrowing and sprouting roots that burrowed into the earth at their feet, his arms turning into branches, his head losing all semblance of a face and becoming indistinguishable from the rest of his body. In a few seconds all that stood before them was the same hollow tree under which they had eaten their sandwiches – the only normal-looking tree in that waste of grey, nightmarish plants.

The squirrel, perched on a thick branch which had been Logres's shoulder a moment earlier, chittered at them angrily, flicked its tail, and vanished into a crack in the trunk.

'So now what do we do?' said the dwarf.

Gwydden poked the tree with his staff. 'Logres? Are you still listening? It's no good going all arboreal on us. We want your help, and we're not going away until we get it.'

The tree remained obstinately silent.

'I think,' said Gwydden to Hergrim, 'that this might be the right moment to use your axe.'

'No, don't do that,' said the tree quickly. 'No need to get violent.'

'Ah, Logres.' The wizard smiled. 'Glad to hear you're still with us.'

'I'm not with anyone,' said the tree, a trifle huffily. 'This is your quest, not mine. I'm not going to get involved. Just think of me as your friendly neighbourhood tree, offering a broad trunk to lean against, a bit of shade if the sun gets too hot, and possibly some friendly advice, but otherwise basically rooted to the spot and therefore neutral. Okay?'

'You're a funny sort of a god,' said the dwarf. 'What sort of a god is it who turns into a tree whenever danger threatens?'

'A long-lived god,' said the tree. 'I've been around for a long time, and I intend to be around even longer. As a tree, I escape attention. I feel safe.'

'But surely,' said the wizard, 'aren't you the Guardian of the Forest? Aren't you supposed to look after it?'

'Yeah, so they kept telling me when I was younger,' said the tree grumpily. '*Logres*, they said. *We're leaving you in charge of this Forest*, they said. *It's your job to see that it flourishes and grows*, they said. *Anything that could damage or destroy it must be defeated*, they said.'

'Who's *they*?' asked the dwarf.

'Those ruddy Celtic gods and goddesses,' grumbled the tree. 'Lugh, Lir, Dana, Brigit, all that lot. Poncy crowd.'

'I thought the Celtic gods and goddesses were handsome, noble and brave,' said Gwydden.

'Oh, they all *looked* the part,' said the tree scathingly. 'Long flowing yellow hair, bronzed skins, blue eyes, and thick as two of my taproots, the lot of them. Spent all their time sunbathing on the tops of burial mounds and arguing about who had the best tan. A bunch of bimbos, and snooty with it. Treated me like dirt, just 'cos I was only a demi-god.'

'So when they gave you the job of looking after the Forest—' began the wizard.

'Just like their ruddy nerve,' said the tree, its leaves rustling in indignation. 'What gave *them* the right to give *me* orders? Me, with my own sacred grove and everything. I even had a vestal virgin, once. When I say I *had* her,' the tree went on hurriedly, 'I mean as a servant. She used to bring me flowers and cups of mead, clear away the dead leaves from my sacred grove, that sort of thing. Pretty young thing, she was. But then I noticed she was putting on weight, and her peaches and cream complexion was changing to beetroot and piccalilli. Turned out she'd been drinking most of the mead before it got to me. So I had to sack her. Last I heard, she was running a transport café for Roman soldiers in a lay-by on Watling Street. And of course,' the tree went on, puffing out its trunk and becoming pompous, 'young women these days don't *want* to be vestal virgins. They want to go out and conquer kingdoms and turn them into queendoms. I blame the Old Queen, Boadicea. If she'd stayed at home doing the cooking and cleaning, instead of going off marauding and burning and killing, which is traditionally the *man's* job—'

'Yes, yes,' said Gwydden testily. 'We didn't come here to be lectured by a male chauvinist tree. What we need is bit of help with this quest.'

'Surely the answer's obvious,' said the tree. 'There's only one thing that can defeat the Grey Magic and restore the Forest to health, and that's the Really Water.

If the Really Well is full of Really Water, the Forest will be really well.'

'But the Really Water was diverted by Culpability Brown,' the wizard objected. 'It doesn't flow anywhere near the well. It flows into that artificial lake with the island of Arcadia in it.'

'Exactly. So what *you* have to do is divert the Really Water *back* again.'

'Yes, I see,' said Gwydden. 'Hergrim, did you bring those maps of the Redbrush Estate?'

'No, I left them in the cottage.'

'Pity. Can you remember whether they showed the spot where the Really Water was diverted?'

'No, I can't.'

'Hm. So it looks as if we have to go back to the cottage. I'm not very happy about that. I don't fancy breathing in any more of that grey mist than necessary. What we need is an alternative way of finding the place where Culpability Brown put in his diversion. Er – Logres?'

'What?'

'I don't suppose, by any chance, that the dried-up stream-bed of the Really Water runs anywhere near here?'

'Possibly,' said the tree evasively.

'Do you know where it runs, exactly?'

'I might.'

'Would you like to tell us where?'

The tree was silent.

'Shall I have a go at him with my axe?' growled the dwarf.

'No, don't do that,' said the tree hastily. 'Actually, the stream-bed runs directly under my roots.'

'Aha!' The wizard smiled. 'I had a feeling it might. How do we get down to it?'

'There's a hole in the earth inside my trunk,' said the tree, with an air of reluctance. 'If you come inside, you'll see it.'

With some difficulty, the wizard and dwarf squeezed through the crack in Logres's trunk into which the squirrel had previously vanished.

'It's too dark in here to see anything,' said the dwarf. 'Where exactly is this hole?'

'Your friend's a wizard, isn't he?' said the tree. 'Why doesn't he strike a light?'

Gwydden accordingly raised Sephira, and uttered the magic words *Fiat Lux*[1]. A pale light sprang from Sephira's tip, and revealed a dark, narrow slit in the earth at the far side of the trunk's interior.

'Climb down there, and you'll be in the bed of the stream,' said Logres. He yawned. 'If you've quite finished with me, I'd like to take a nap now. You've worn me out with all your questions.'

Shortly thereafter, the inside of the trunk reverberated to the rarely-heard sound of a tree snoring.

The dwarf and wizard squeezed down into the dark hole under the tree. A moment later they were setting off, by the light of Gwydden's staff, along the dried-up tunnel of the Really Water.

In the Great Hall, King Bres had ascended Uther's throne, leaving a sticky trail all the way up the steps that led to it. Uther had moved to one side of the Great Hall, where he stood dejectedly, waiting to be subjected in due course to the new Body Tax.

'Where's my Chancellor of the Exchequer?' demanded the new King. 'Where's Archon?'

[1]An ambiguous Latin phrase. It can mean either 'Let there be light', or 'The car is full of soap-powder'.

Archon oozed forward and waved his eye-stalks in the Fhomoire's equivalent of a bow. 'Here, sire.'

'Archon, I want you to oversee the gathering of the new Body Tax. I'll give you half the team to assist.' Bres rapidly reeled off a list of names. 'Make sure you collect from our youngest and juiciest subjects first. Leave any expectant mothers, of course – we'll need them to produce babies who can be gathered in a future tax period.'

Uther, listening to this, shuddered.

Archon again waved his eye-stalks. 'Yes, sire. Er – sire?'

'Yes?'

'I couldn't help noticing, as we came in, that some of Uther's soldiers pulled up the drawbridge after us.'

'Yes, I noticed that,' said Bres. 'Not a problem, is it?'

'No, sire. After all, we're shape-shifters.' Archon vanished, and three seconds later reappeared in the form of a pterodactyl. He flapped his leathery wings experimentally.

'Very stylish,' said Bres approvingly. 'Okay, the rest of you, follow Lieutenant Archon's example.'

The Fhomoire whose names Bres had reeled off all transformed themselves into pterodactyls. The air in the Great Hall was filled with the rustle of prehistoric wings.

Bres chuckled. 'Good. Off you go, all of you, and bring us back some nice juicy taxes.'

With harsh predatory cries the squadron of pterodactyls rose into the air and flew out of the windows into the grey mist swirling around the roofs of Camelot.

Uther watched them go in dismay. Then he hung his head and gazed at the floor.

At that moment, a messenger entered the Great Hall and nervously approached Uther. 'Sire?'

'Yes? What is it?'

'It's the Queen, sire. She says her chambers are full of horrible grey smoke, and what are you going to do about it, sire?'

'Tell her I'm working on it.' As the messenger turned to go, Uther said in a low voice, 'Don't let Her Majesty come down to the Great Hall. Lock her inside her chambers if you have to.'

The messenger looked alarmed. 'I – I'll do my best, sire.'

'Good man.'

Uther watched the messenger scurry away like a scared rabbit between the lumpish grey forms of the Fhomoire. *I don't want Igrayne here at the moment*, he thought. *Not only is she just the sort of young and juicy person these characters want to levy their Body Tax on, but I can't possibly let her see this room until it's been thoroughly cleaned and fumigated.*

At the sentry-post beside the moat, Mrs Tod had encountered another obstacle to her plan to see Uther. This time it was a conscientious young sentry, who was steadfastly refusing to lower the drawbridge.

Macpherson stood gloomily beside her, staring into the moat and no doubt thinking whatever sad thoughts Scotsmen think when confronted with large amounts of a liquid which is not whisky.

Sigismund was a yard or two away, on the very edge of the moat, gazing up at the castle. Its normally lumpy outline was half-hidden in a miasma of grey mist, which lent it an unaccustomed air of mystery. Struck by the effect, he was trying to compose a poem about it, but the gurglings from his stomach kept distracting him, and the only rhymes he could think of were ones ending in '—eat'.

'For the last time, young man,' said Mrs Tod furiously, 'are you going to let down this drawbridge so that we can get in to see King Uther?'

'No, ma'am,' said the sentry, saluting her respectfully. He was very young, but he had once had a stern, forbidding old grandmother who was just like Mrs Tod (except that she wasn't a fox), and he had discovered, in an incident involving a stolen sugar mouse, that underneath her granite exterior she was a human being[1]. Since then he hadn't been in the least afraid of old ladies, however stern and forbidding.

'Young man, I *order* you to let down this drawbridge!'

The sentry saluted again, very politely. 'Sorry, ma'am. Can't do that, I'm afraid.'

Mrs Tod's eyes began to glint a peculiar shade of red. The sentry's grandmother may well have been human underneath, but Mrs Tod's grandmother had stalked the undergrowth by night and done nasty things to small animals who stayed out past their bedtime. She opened her mouth slowly in a smile that showed a great many sharp teeth. Macpherson hastily moved a foot or two further away.

'Young man,' said Mrs Tod quietly. 'Either you let down this drawbridge *at once*, or—'

With a harsh, scraping cry like the sound of several cats with their claws extended sliding down a blackboard, a posse of dark-winged shapes swooped down on them from the castle. All four ducked instinctively as the airborne Fhomoire zoomed past and descended among the roofs of the city below.

There was a cry of surprise, and a splash. The Earl had lost his balance and fallen in. With a desperate shout of

[1]He'd had to pull her hair to get her to admit that she'd taken it, but she confessed in the end. You have to watch these old ladies.

'Coming, Ma Laird!', Macpherson ran to the moat's edge and leapt in after him.

Sigismund rose majestically to the surface, trod water calmly, adjusted his monocle, and said, 'I didn't know you swam, Macpherson.'

'Och, weel, I—' said the Scotsman. His head vanished under the surface. A stream of bubbles rose in its place.

Everyone stared for what seemed like hours at the spot where Macpherson had disappeared. Eventually a shock of hair like crimson pond-weed rose from the depths and erupted into the murky air.

'—dinna, really, ye ken,' gasped the gardener, and promptly went down again.

'You two,' snapped Mrs Tod. 'What are you playing at?'

Still paddling, the Earl removed a small fish from the pocket of his smoking-jacket. He looked at it hungrily, then sighed, shook his head, and dropped it back in the water. When Macpherson's red hair came up for the second time, he seized it in his paw and began to swim to the farther bank, towing the Scotsman behind him.

'Just going to see Uther,' he called back to his sister. 'But first, I'm going to look for something to eat.'

'Come back here, Sigismund!' his sister commanded, in a tone that made the sentry raise his eyebrows and look at her with a new respect. His grandmother hadn't spoken to him like *that*. If she had, he would never have pulled her hair.

'Sorry, can't hear you,' Sigismund called back cheerfully. 'Got some water in my ears.'

Arriving at the other bank, he helped the half-drowned Macpherson crawl out. Mrs Tod watched them, fuming.

'You could – er – always swim after them, ma'am,' the sentry suggested helpfully. He had wondered whether his duties included throwing his spear at the fugitives, but on the whole felt that they didn't.

Mrs Tod fixed him with a basilisk stare. 'About this drawbridge,' she grated.

The young sentry quailed a little before the red gleam of her eyes and the white gleam of her teeth. With a sinking feeling, he realised that she was not going to give up. He needed to placate her, and he knew of only one way of placating old ladies.

Reaching into his tunic, he pulled out something white and sticky.

'Would you like a sugar mouse, ma'am?' he enquired.

In the public bar of *The King's Head*, Grympel the dwarf was having to cope with a sudden invasion of townsfolk.

He surveyed the invasion from behind the counter. They were not his usual crowd. They appeared to be a random selection of people off the street – old women, tradesmen, even a few young kids looking large-eyed and frightened.

They seemed to have brought an atmosphere in with them. Not a pleasant atmosphere, either. It was thick and grey, and smelled awful. It was drifting in through the doorway and hanging around the ceiling, and making Grympel cough.

'What's going on?' Grympel demanded of Nabgo, who had kicked, elbowed and jostled his way to the front of the crowd, and was now pressed up against the bar counter.

'Man-eatin' slugs,' said Nabgo hoarsely.

'That must be a pretty nauseating sight,' said Grympel sympathetically. 'I remember a man once asked me for a maggot sandwich. Terrible, it was – they kept wriggling off the bread. And there was this bloke used to come in here sometimes and order a caterpillar salad, complained like anything if a bit of mayonnaise got into it—'

'No, not *a* man eatin' slugs. Man-eatin' slugs. Great big slimy things. One of 'em ate Lord Porfingle.'

'Oh, good.'

'Yeah, I s'pose so.' Nabgo wiped a shaking hand over his mouth. 'Give us a bottle of Frigga's Revenge, eh, Grympel? I need somethin' to steady me nerves.'

The landlord passed the required tipple over the counter, noting as he did so that Nabgo looked distinctly scared. Grympel was a little surprised to find that Nabgo's face *could* look scared. He had only seen it look either aggressive or comatose.

More and more people were piling into the bar, and they were all wearing the same expression as Nabgo. Grympel began to feel uneasy. Normally he would have been pleased to have so many customers, but these customers didn't look as if they had come in to drink. They looked as if they had come in to hide from something.

'Can I get anyone anything?' he called out.

No-one took any notice. They were all staring at the door, while trying to get as far away from it as possible. Several people were trying to conceal themselves behind pillars. One man was pretending to be a table.

The door swung open. In the frame, surrounded by the swirling grey mist, stood a tall figure. It was hard to see it clearly, but it seemed to have a very long, thin head and enormous feet.

A deathly silence fell over the room.

'Er – yes?' said Grympel, his voice coming out unusually high and squeaky. 'What can we do for you?'

The figure stalked in over the threshold, and stood surveying them, its thin head moving from side to side. Now and then it moved its upper limbs. They sounded like great big umbrellas opening and closing.

Grympel leaned over the counter. 'Hey, Nabgo,' he murmured.

'What?'

'I thought you said slugs?'

'I did.'

'*That* isn't a slug.'

'No,' said Nabgo, with a shiver. 'I don't know what *that* is.'

'Looks like a dead crow in an overcoat,' muttered Grympel.

The pterodactyl rustled its wings more loudly, and everyone fell silent.

'I have come to collect the tax,' whispered the pterodactyl, in a voice like two bones conspiring in a graveyard.

'Oh.' Grympel remembered the lad who had come the other day with the wheelbarrow, collecting glass and silver. 'Er – that's all right. We gave, already.'

The pterodactyl's head, a nightmare version of a heron's, moved from side to side as it looked from one to another of the cringing crowd. 'I think not. Which of you is the juiciest?'

Grympel's mind went blank. 'The *juiciest?*'

'Yes.'

No-one was quite sure what the question meant, but everyone immediately tried to look as desiccated as possible.

At that moment, the door to the bar-parlour opened and Blodwen came in, carrying a feather-duster and quietly humming an old Welsh dusting song. She had been cleaning, and her face was very pink. When she saw the mass of people filling the bar, she stopped and stared. Then she caught sight of the gaunt figure blocking the doorway, and her eyes opened very wide, and her hand flew to her mouth.

The pterodactyl craned its lizard-bird neck and peered at her out of one tiny satanic eye. *'Juicy,'* it whispered, and started to shuffle purposefully towards her.

Blodwen stared at the pterodactyl. Then she looked down at her only weapon, which was the feather duster. Without even pausing to scream, she turned and fled through the door she had entered by.

The pterodactyl lunged after her, and the crowd scrambled out of its way, like the Red Sea declining an invitation to tangle with Moses' staff.

Grympel's eye met Nabgo's across the bar counter. They nodded at each other. With a smooth and prac-tised movement, each smashed a bottle of Frigga's Revenge against the counter, and they turned as one dwarf to face the approaching terror.

The pterodactyl halted in front of them.

'You leave Blodwen alone,' Nabgo growled, waving his broken bottle. 'Go back where you came from, you 'orrible great bony pigeon.'

The pterodactyl snickered. Then it vanished. Three seconds later, something grey and formless appeared in its place. It waved its eye-stalks at them. Grey mist flowed off it, filling their nostrils with its stench.

'See,' said Nabgo to Grympel, in a hoarse croak. 'I told yer it was slugs.' His eyes rolled up until only the whites were visible, and he slid down the front of the counter in a dead faint.

As if this was a signal, the crowd in the bar suddenly came to life. Realising that there was nothing now be-tween them and the door, they all piled towards the exit. Seconds later, the bar was empty except for two dwarfs and a giant slug.

The slug waved its eye-stalks, and oozed past Nabgo's body, towards Grympel.

Grympel backed slowly towards the door into the parlour, feebly waving his broken bottle.

I wonder, he thought, *whether Anjina was right all along. Perhaps I'm not cut out for the life of a pub landlord after all.*

'Well, here we are,' said Hergrim, his voice booming hollowly in the underground passage. 'This must be it – Culpability Brown's handiwork.'

By the light from the wizard's staff, they contemplated the wall of brickwork blocking their path.

'All we have to do now,' said the dwarf, 'is knock it down.'

'Er . . . ye-es,' said Gwydden dubiously.

'What's the matter?'

'Well, I can see a couple of small problems.'

'Yes?'

'First, what do we knock it down *with*? And second, assuming we *do* knock it down, how do we avoid being drowned when the Really Water rushes into this tunnel we're standing in?'

There was a thoughtful silence.

'Well, I dunno,' said the dwarf, eventually. 'But I'm getting hungry, and if I don't get lunch soon, I may just *eat* this wall.'

'There are three alternatives, as far as I can see,' said the wizard. 'Either we give up the entire quest, and let the Forest be destroyed and every living thing be wiped out across the entire kingdom, which means that you won't get anything to eat again *ever*—'

'I don't like that alternative,' growled the dwarf.

'—or we go back along the tunnel, and try to get back to the cottage to look at the plans, which means trying to find our way through that choking grey mist and probably suffocating to death—'

'—or that alternative—'

288

'—or I use magic; though of course, owing to the dangers predicted by Particle Escape Theory, that will probably bring the whole tunnel down on our heads.'

'—or *that* alternative. So. Three plans, and they're all rotten.' Hergrim kicked the base of the wall irritably with an iron-toed boot. 'Oh, *snurks.*'

The tunnel trembled slightly underfoot, and a little mortar trickled down the front of the wall.

'I don't think you ought to swear in here, Hergrim,' said the wizard anxiously. 'It's a very confined space, and the energy you release hasn't anywhere to escape to.'

But the dwarf was now feeling both hungry and reckless. 'You want that wall down, right?' he growled. 'Right. *I'll* bring it down for you. I used to do this sort of thing all the time when I was a dwarfling. Me and my friends would creep into the caves under the Dwarfheim mountains and swear black and blue until the roof started to tremble. Then we'd run out as fast as we could, dodging falling stalactites on the way. Joy-Cursing, we used to call it.'

'Sounds horribly irresponsible,' said the wizard with a shudder. 'Wasn't anybody ever killed?'

'Not many,' said the dwarf. 'Not all that many, really. Very few, on the whole. It isn't as dangerous as you might think.'

'It *couldn't* be as dangerous as *I* think,' said the wizard, looking up at the tunnel roof. 'I have a very vivid imagination. I can picture myself being crushed under several tons of rock with extreme and unpleasant accuracy.'

'You probably won't be,' the dwarf reassured him. 'If the water rushes in fast enough, you'll probably drown before you can be crushed.'

'That's comforting,' said the wizard, sounding as

comforted as a small child whose teddy bear has turned rabid and bitten it in the neck.

Hergrim squared his shoulders. 'Right. Ready?'

'No. What d'you mean, *ready*? You're not actually going to—'

'Yes, I am. I'm fed up with this quest. I want to get it over with.' The dwarf glowered at the wall. 'All right, you horrible piece of brickwork! *Frurgle! Drongo! Snyke!*'

Dust began to trickle down the wall.

'Hergrim!' Gwydden said in alarm. 'Just—'

'*Gruksnorf!*'

The wall started to bulge in the middle.

'— hang on a—'

'*Gumfo!*'

Large lumps of mortar pushed outwards and fell to the floor.

'—*minute*, can't you?!'

'*Skroot!*'

Bricks moved apart. Water started to pour through the gaps.

'Hergrim, just *wait!*'

'*DWURGLEDORK!*'

'Oh help,' said Gwydden helplessly.

With a sigh like a fat woman slipping out of her corsets, the wall disintegrated.

The dwarf and wizard took an involuntary and entirely pointless step back.

Roaring like a Scottish football crowd, the Really Water surged into the empty tunnel.

Chapter Fourteen

The giant slug had reached the bar counter. Since the counter was taller than the slug, that meant that Grympel could no longer see it.

Which is a great relief, he thought. *And it can't get at me where I am now – there's no way round. I'm safe.*

He relaxed.

Several seconds passed. Then, on the other side of the counter, two eye-stalks appeared, waving gently. Like a large grey loaf rising in an oven, the shapeless mass of the slug rose up before him, and started to ooze across the counter.

Grympel shrank back against the wall in alarm. *Of course,* he thought despairingly. *It's a slug. Slugs can climb walls. Slugs can climb anything.*

He thought of Blodwen cowering in the bar-parlour behind him. If the slug got him, it would get her next. She was going home soon, to marry young Dai. Young Dai would probably not be pleased if his beloved got eaten by a giant mollusc. It would put a real damper on the wedding.

He gripped the broken bottle tighter in his sweaty palm, and squared his shoulders. If he was going to get eaten, at least he would leave the slug with one or two stomach ulcers to remember him by.

* * *

The tunnel of the Really Water was no longer empty. A maelstrom was rushing through it, as if desperate to find something[1]. The dwarf and wizard were picked up and carried helplessly along, like balls in a pinball machine, bouncing from rock wall to rock wall, unable to breathe or speak.

Gwydden hung on desperately to Sephira. The staff's light shone eerily in front of him in the water, throwing a deep green glow over the inside of the tunnel. The Really Water, despite being only ten or so feet deep, was a rich and heady green, the colour of grass after it has been soaked by an April shower. When Gwydden swallowed some of it, which happened every few seconds without him particularly wanting it to, it tasted amazingly fresh and invigorating. He began to feel that it was almost worth having your head repeatedly banged against sharp edges of rock if you could drink this stuff at the same time.

The walk along the uneven floor of the tunnel had taken them the best part of an hour. The ride back took twenty seconds. By the end of it they were bruised, battered, and very nearly drowned. The roof, however, did not fall in, so to that extent Hergrim had been right.

Finally the muted din in their ears changed to a bubbling noise, and instead of being carried helplessly forwards, they found themselves being carried helplessly upwards.

Grey light burst around them, and their heads came out of the water. They gulped air. It was stale, unpleasant air, sickly with the smell of the grey mist, but it was still air, which millions of years of experience have shown to be generally preferable to water when it comes to breathing.

[1] A femaelstrom, perhaps.

They were in what looked at first sight like a small paddling pool, enclosed by a lichenous stone wall. Sodden and exhausted, they hauled themselves out of the water. Gwydden laid Sephira on the wall between them, and they both sat there, gasping.

The grey mist swirled above their heads. Now and then a tendril of it reached down and groped into their nostrils, making them cough and retch.

We haven't drowned, Gwydden thought, *but we may very well still suffocate.*

They took stock of their surroundings.

It was a familiar spot, even down to the giant hog-weed growing rampant nearby, and the tumbledown building from whose chimney a curlicue of blue smoke was still rising into the sky, doggedly repeating the word BOGHOLE.

They were back in the cottage garden, sitting on the rim of the Really Well, which was now filled almost to the brim with clear, green water.

'Well?' said Hergrim. 'We've done it, haven't we? So what happens now?'

Gwydden shrugged. 'Search me.'

'I thought,' said the dwarf, 'that when we re-routed the water, that was supposed to do the business. Isn't that what Logres said?'

'I thought so, yes.'

'Well, I don't see anything happening.' The dwarf gestured at the spindly grey plants and the swirling mist. 'It all looks just the same. What's gone wrong?'

The wizard stared down at the green water bubbling under their feet. He very much wanted to drink some more of it, and experience again that feeling of well-being. But though that might do *him* some good, it wouldn't restore the Forest.

'I don't know,' he said. 'You're right, something must

293

have gone wrong. Or perhaps there's something we haven't done. But if so, then I don't know what it is.'

'So we've gone to all this trouble,' growled the dwarf, 'and at the end of it we find we've been given duff information. Typical! What a complete and utter waste of time!' Fuming, the dwarf picked up Sephira and brought the staff down hard on the surface of the Really Water.

Sometimes good things can be just as terrifying as bad ones.

When Hergrim struck the Really Water, a fountain of it jetted up over their heads. It met the grey mist in mid-air, and the universe exploded.

It was as if someone had filled a room with a lethal, flammable grey gas and lit a big green match. Green fire erupted out of the Really Well, blossoming upwards and outwards like a vast green rose. The grey mist ignited and turned green. The spindly plants were transfigured into lurid green ghosts of themselves. The Forest dissolved in a holocaust of green flame.

Gwydden and Hergrim fell backwards off the edge of the Well and lay on the ground, their eyes tight shut, expecting at any instant to feel the agony of fire scorching their flesh.

After an uneventful half a minute or so, they cautiously opened their eyes, to discover a freshly-minted world.

The grey mist had gone. Overhead, the sky was corn-flower-blue, dotted here and there with fluffy white clouds like lambs newly washed in a sheep-dip and hung up to dry. All the spindly hogweeds, the gigantic and deformed plants, had vanished, and in their places stood tall and healthy oaks, elms and beeches.

The dwarf and wizard got to their feet and surveyed

the cottage garden, which was full of wild flowers.

'Terrific,' grunted Hergrim. 'All that hard work I did gone to waste – just look at those weeds.'

The wizard smiled slightly, but said nothing. He was well aware that gardeners hate wild flowers (or *weeds*, as they call them) because they're living proof that nature doesn't need gardeners, and that the whole industry of nurseries, garden centres and landscape architects is therefore a gigantic con-trick.

'Oh well,' said the dwarf. 'At least the Forest is back to normal. Let's have some lunch.'

They turned towards the cottage.

From somewhere close by, there came a deep, sonorous rumbling noise.

Gwydden raised his eyebrows. 'You really *are* hungry, aren't you?'

'That wasn't me,' said Hergrim. 'Sounds like an earth tremor. We get them in Dwarfheim sometimes, especially if someone's been swearing a lot.'

'But we hardly ever have earth tremors in England,' the wizard objected.

The earth rumbled again.

'Doesn't sound too serious,' said Hergrim. 'Just a little one, I'd say. Let's have lunch, and investigate it afterwards.' He took a couple of steps towards the cottage.

Under their feet, the earth roared like a lion whose tail has been trodden on.

The cottage collapsed like a failed soufflé. Its walls folded inwards, and its thatched roof sank gracefully to the ground, assuming the appearance of a large mat. The chimney in the centre ejected a truncated puff of smoke, spelling out the arcane word OGHOL.

A pool of green water began to form around the wrecked cottage. The roof floated on it for a while, and then sank, waterlogged. Finally only the chimney remained in view. It was emitting just two letters now, but to make up for this it was sending them out in groups of three. HOHOHO, it went, HOHOHO, as if the chimney had Father Christmas stuck down it.

The earth rumbled faintly under their feet, and was silent.

The dwarf and wizard stared at the place where their most recent home had just done a Titanic.

'Hergrim?' said Gwydden, after a long pause.

'Yes?'

'You did say that Culpability Brown was a cheapskate, didn't you?'

'Notorious for it. Why?'

'Because only a cheapskate would build an underground wall to divert a river, and then use the wall as a foundation for a cottage directly above it.'

The dwarf's eyebrows rose. 'You're not serious.'

'Oh yes. When we removed the wall, the cottage was left standing on nothing more supportive than a lot of water.'

'But surely,' the dwarf objected, 'the cottage should have had *four* foundation walls?'

'Which just goes to show how mean Ebenezer Brown really was,' said the wizard. 'What was it that lease said? *All breakages must be paid for.* I wonder how much Mrs Tod will charge us for one really *big* breakage?'

While the dwarf and wizard were watching their cottage collapse, the green shock wave of the Really Water's magic continued to spread out from its epicentre at the Really Well.

It took less than a minute to reach the edges of the Forest, turning it back into its familiar unspoiled self, in which grew, amongst other things, the oldest known species of herb[1].

Passing beyond the forest to the south and west, it met a sharp easterly in the English Channel, veered away round Cornwall, and spread out over Ireland, which shortly afterwards produced a bumper crop of shamrocks.

North of the Forest, the shock wave crossed the plain of Camelot, swept over the city, and carried on through Wales, northern England and Scotland, bringing light showers and pleasant temperatures to all parts of the British Isles by nightfall.

By the time the wave reached these outlying areas, it had grown so tenuous that no-one really noticed it.

It struck Camelot, however, while practically at full strength.

The young sentry by the moat had had very nearly all he could take. He had been verbally molested, flagellated and abused by Mrs Tod for the last ten minutes, and his self-control was crumbling. He could feel the moment of crisis approaching. He was either going to give in and shout for the drawbridge to be let down, or commit vulpicide with his pikestaff. A small, rational part of his brain, unaffected by the combined panic and adrenalin that was making saliva dribble down his chin, was laying bets with itself as to which of the two it would be.

'. . . and another thing,' the horrible red-furred old harridan was saying, 'you're much too *young* to be a sentry. You should be at school, not waving a great heavy pikestaff about. I've a good mind to talk to

[1] Thyme Immemorial.

King Uther on the unwiseness of entrusting dangerous weapons to juveniles. When *I* was a girl . . .'

The sentry closed his eyes tight. He could feel the hand that was clutching the pikestaff starting to rise. *It'll be all right,* he told himself. *I can plead temporary insanity, or unreasonable provocation. Anyone who knows her would testify on my side. And anyway, I'm probably too young to be sentenced to death.*

Through his closed eyelids, he saw a flash of green light.

He opened his eyes with a jerk. 'What was that?'

Mrs Tod stared up at the sky for a moment. Then she said, in a decided tone, 'Some child must have let off a firework. Fireworks are dangerous and frivolous. So are children. They ought to be banned.'

'What ought to be banned?' the sentry asked, against his better judgment. 'Fireworks, or children?'

'Both,' Mrs Tod told him. 'When *I* was a girl—'

'Shut up a minute,' said the sentry suddenly.

Mrs Tod gaped at him.

'*What* did you say?'

'I said shut up. I'm trying to listen.'

Mrs Tod drew herself up to her full height of two feet ten inches. 'Now look here, young man—'

'It's the King,' said the sentry urgently. 'I recognise his voice. He's shouting for help.' He cupped his hand to his mouth, and yelled across the moat, 'LOWER THE DRAWBRIDGE!'

A voice on the far side answered faintly, and a moment later, with a creak of timbers, ropes and pulleys, the drawbridge began to descend.

'And about time too,' said Mrs Tod.

In the bar of *The King's Head*, Grympel was wondering whether a few runes scratched on the bar-counter would be legally valid as a last will and testament.

He felt quite strongly that before the giant slug ate him, he would like to bequeath all he possessed to his childhood sweetheart Anjina, as some sort of compensation for the fact that she was never going to see him again. He also wanted to apologise for having given away her locket. This was quite a lot to write in the estimated 1.7 seconds he had left before the slug devoured him, but you can say a lot in a very few runes if you know how, owing to the semantic complexity (and indeed ambiguity) of most dwarf-runes.

Just as he was reaching out to scratch the rune *Grpsk*[1] with the edge of his broken bottle, a green light filled the pub, dazzling him momentarily.

Grympel blinked.

For a moment there, he could have sworn that his pub was on fire. However, everything seemed OK now. The green flames, if that was what they were, had gone.

Or had he imagined them? That was more likely. *Real* green flames were generally confined to the Green Light District, for example when one of those crazy wizards set fire to his laboratory. These must have been *unreal* green flames, though he usually only saw those after drinking too much Frigga's Revenge.

Now, what had he been doing?

Oh yes. Writing his will, and a note of apology to Anjina. And he'd better be quick about it, because that

[1]Possible translations include the following:

'Greetings / Good day / Congratulations . . .

. . . with much love / with deep respect / on having passed your exam / beheaded your enemy / drunk your way through your host's entire stock of Frigga's Revenge . . .

. . . O Fellow student / O Companion in Arms / O Beautiful Dwarf-Woman whose Beard is like Silk.'

giant slug that was squatting on the counter was about to . . .

What giant slug?

It was there a moment ago. And what was this lump of grey stone doing on the counter?

Grympel picked the stone up. It was the same dull grey colour as the slug, with a greenish tinge – though as he watched, the green tinge faded away. It was about twice the size of his fist, and very heavy, even for a stone. Almost as if it was made of something *compressed*. And quite clammy. Not slimy, exactly – not so as to come off on your hands – but still not very pleasant.

It had a sort of face etched into it. Not a human face – the eyes were too small, hardly eyes at all, more like little circles on stalks. And a wide, lipless mouth. No nose or ears.

It was sitting right where that slug had been squatting.

Very slowly, Grympel put the grey stone back on the counter and stared at it.

There was only one possible explanation. The slug had turned into a stone. And it had happened when that strange green light came and went.

Oh well. A pub landlord gets used to strange things happening in his pub. And a *good* pub landlord knows how to capitalise on them.

He rummaged under the counter and produced a reasonably clean beer-mat bearing a picture of a tough-looking dwarf holding a foaming tankard. Round the edge of the mat were painted the words *Realle Dwarfs Drynke Frigga's Revenge*. He put the stone on the mat in the middle of the counter, and regarded it with a proprietorial eye. Yes, that would do. Anyone coming up to the counter would be sure to notice it. *Ah, you've noticed that strange and interesting grey stone,* he imagined himself saying to enquiring customers. *Well now, there's a fascinating story attached to that there stone. It happened to me personally, as I was standing right here at this counter. Let me take your order, sir or madam, and I'll tell you all about it.*

Grympel smiled.

Perhaps he *was* cut out to be a pub landlord, after all.

The sentry burst into the Great Hall, waving his pikestaff in a determined manner. 'I'm here, sire. I came as soon as I heard you shouting for—'

He stopped, and stared.

'—help,' he concluded, but rather less confidently.

In the middle of the Great Hall, King Uther was dancing a jig.

Kings, generally speaking, are not supposed to dance jigs. Pavanes, sarabands and slow waltzes, yes. Jigs, reels, hornpipes and other peasant caperings, no. The reason for this is simple. Kings can only perform slow, stately dances, because otherwise their crowns fall over their eyes and they bump into their partners. If the partner is a visiting royal, this can lead to an international incident.

Uther, however, was dancing by himself in the middle of the floor, while holding his crown on with one hand.

When he saw the sentry, he turned slightly red and capered to a breathless halt.

'Oh, hullo,' said the King of England sheepishly. 'Did you want me?'

'I heard you shout, sire. I thought you were calling for help.'

'No, no. I was shouting because I was pleased. Look!' Uther waved an arm excitedly round the Great Hall. 'You see?'

The young sentry looked round the room in puzzlement. There was no-one there. All he could see out of the ordinary was a number of grey stones dotted about the floor. Singularly ugly stones, too, with what might have been crude eyes and mouths carved on them. One of them, larger than the others, was lying in the centre of what appeared to be a silver crown.

'I'm afraid I don't understand, sire.'

'They've gone,' said Uther happily. 'Turned to stone, all of them. Right before my eyes. It was the green lightning that did it, I'm sure. Green for magic. That wizard must have come up trumps after all.'

The sentry was not following this. 'Wizard, sire? What wizard?'

Uther giggled. 'Yes, exactly. I didn't think he was up to it, either. But they've all gone, and now I'm the proud possessor of a lot of hideously ugly stones.' He picked one up and scrutinised it. 'Revolting, isn't it? Here, would you like one?'

The sentry, bemused, took the proffered stone. He didn't want the repulsive thing at all, but if a king starts giving you things, you should always accept them. It might only be stones today, but tomorrow it might be gold, or half the kingdom, or a princess.

'Thank you, sire. Er – what's it for?'

'No idea.' Uther chuckled happily again. 'Put it on your mantelpiece. Tell your grandchildren about it.'

The sentry, who would be fifteen next birthday[1], blinked. *Grandchildren?*

'Tell them *what* about it, sire?'

But Uther wasn't listening. He had turned away, and was skipping across the floor of the Great Hall, humming a little tune to himself.

---

[1]Mrs Tod was quite right, he was too young to be a sentry. He'd lied about his age on the application form.

The sentry watched Uther for a moment, and then shook his head. There was no accounting for the behaviour of kings, most of whom were known to be hopelessly eccentric due to inbreeding, haemophilia and suchlike. You just had to let them get on with it. Anyway, he had a drawbridge to guard.

Hefting his pikestaff in one hand and his stone in the other, he turned to leave, and was almost knocked over by a small figure in a poke-bonnet.

Mrs Tod's legs were much shorter than the sentry's, and she had only just caught him up. She was a little breathless, but as determined as ever. She marched into the middle of the room, folded her arms, and stared disapprovingly at Uther, who was now doing a soft shoe shuffle round the throne.

'Well!' she said. 'I must say, this is a fine state of affairs. Uther Pendragon, where is your dignity? What would your father say if he saw you *dancing* – and in front of a minion, as well.'

The sentry looked round for the minion, realised it was himself, and fleetingly considered braining Mrs Tod with his stone. But no, it was too risky. Evidently she was a friend of the King. No-one who wasn't would dare to speak to him like that.

Uther shuffled to a halt and surveyed his visitor. 'Edith Tod! Good heavens. Haven't seen you for ages. How's Sigismund? How's that miserable old Scottish gardener of yours? How's Redbrush Hall?'

'It's been eaten,' said Mrs Tod. 'By grey slime.'

'Oh, bad luck. Still, never mind, you'll be able to claim on the insurance.'

'We didn't have any. That's why I'm here. I want you to rebuild it for us.'

'Good heavens.' Uther leaned against the throne as if struck a heavy blow. 'Edith, you can't be serious. Do you know how much that would cost, at today's prices?'

'Then rebuild it at yesterday's prices,' said Mrs Tod sharply. 'Don't raise frivolous objections, Uther.'

'Hmm.' The King straightened his crown and sat down slowly on his throne. 'We might manage something, I suppose. I could institute a public works programme, using unemployed dwarfs. There were quite a few of them propping up the bar in *The King's Head* last time I was there. As for paying them . . .' He stared vacantly into space for a moment. Then an idea seemed to strike him. Turning to the sentry, who was still standing at the door, he said, 'I say, you there.'

The sentry came to attention – rather awkwardly, since he was still carrying the stone. 'Sire?'

'Do me a small favour, will you?'

'Yes, sire,' said the sentry, who was familiar with Uther's democratic way of giving orders.

'Go out into the city and collect up as many of these stones as you can find. If anyone wants paying, give them an IOU.'

The sentry saluted, inadvertently striking himself on the forehead with the stone as he did so. 'Ouch. Yes, sire.' He turned and hurried away down the passage.

'What are you playing at, Uther?' demanded Mrs Tod. 'You surely aren't going to rebuild Redbrush Hall out of *these* stones? They're hideous.'

'No, I'm not,' said Uther. 'I was thinking perhaps we could open a museum, and charge people to see all these stones. The proceeds could go towards rebuilding Redbrush Hall. How does the idea strike you?'

Mrs Tod shook her head pityingly. 'It's lucky for you you're a monarch, Uther. If you had to rely on your business sense for a living, you'd starve to death in a fortnight.'

Uther looked crestfallen. 'Oh. Well, suppose I got

them carved into chessmen or paperweights, and sold them on Cheapside, how about that?'

'Do what you want with the wretched things,' said Mrs Tod impatiently. 'I have more important matters to settle. Can you organise a suite of rooms for me at a local hostelry, run by a woman of unblemished reputation, where the linen is spotless and the food wholesome and inexpensive?'

'In Camelot?' The King raised his eyebrows. 'Rather a tall order. Still, I'll see what can be done. In the meantime, why don't you stay to tea? And Sigismund, of course – is he with you?'

'He swam across the moat to find something to eat,' said Mrs Tod with a disparaging sniff. 'I told him to come back, but he pretended not to hear me. I expect he's somewhere in the castle by now.'

'I don't think he can be,' said Uther, frowning. 'Apart from the main gate, there's only one way in at ground level, and he wouldn't want to use that.'

Mrs Tod raised her bushy red eyebrows. 'Wouldn't he? Why not?'

Uther cleared his throat in embarrassment. There were some subjects he didn't feel it appropriate to discuss with a lady, even a lady fox.

'Take it from me,' he said. 'He just wouldn't.'

The Earl of Redbrush, however, was hungry enough not to care any more.

He had left Macpherson sitting on the bank above the moat, mournfully squeezing a liquid which wasn't whisky out of his kilt. The gardener was still recovering from his involuntary immersion, and Sigismund felt that he would be no help in a scavenging expedition.

Round the back of the castle, the Earl found a small culvert leading down under the castle wall. It was too small for a human being to get into, but quite feasible for a fox. It smelled pretty awful, but some vulpine sixth sense told Sigismund that if he got under the wall at this point, there was food not far away on the other side.

He got down into the culvert and started to follow it.

Boadicea had spent most of the day sitting at the door of her hut in the castle garden, smoking her pipe and watching the sky. She had read the droppings that morning, and they had been unequivocal. Today was the day. Either the kingdom was going to be overrun by nameless evil, or a wizard from the Green Light District was going to step in and save the day with a powerful spell.

Boadicea, who knew a fair bit about wizards, had sent a note that morning to Grympel at *The King's Head*. It said:

I bett you a groat to three ha'pence that the kyngdom be doomed by nyghtfalle.

An hour later, she had received a reply which said simply:

Donne.

At about mid-morning, grey mist began to fill the air. The hens didn't like it. They ran round in circles, making unhappy squawking noises and pecking nervously at each other's tail-feathers.

Boadicea looked thoughtfully at the mist, nodded her head, and went inside her hut to get a bottle of gin, which she had found was proof against most sorts of unpleasantness in the atmosphere.

Later still, she saw the pterodactyls zoom by overhead, and began to think about how she was going to get her hens away to safety.

Then the green lightning came, and the grey mist vanished. A moment later she heard Uther shout. Being closer to the window of the Great Hall than the sentry was, she recognised what the King had shouted as 'Yippee!'

'Damn,' she muttered. 'I owe that there Grympel a groat.'

She drained the last of the gin, knocked out her pipe, and reluctantly set about her daily chores, which she had postponed until now on the grounds that, with any luck, imminent Armageddon would make them unnecessary. The first thing she did was to freshen up the hens' bedding. This involved gathering together all the soiled straw from the hen-coops and rinsing the filth out of it into the culvert that ran along the bottom edge of the garden and out under the castle wall.

She watched the muck disappear along the culvert, where it would soon form a close partnership with a mass of similar muck dating back through generations of hens and hen-women. Then she turned and walked back up the garden to collect the day's eggs.

One thing she didn't notice, because she was facing the wrong way at the time, was a single large leathery shape flapping away over the city, in the direction of the Forest.

Chapter Fifteen

'The thing to do,' said Hergrim, 'is to go to the Hall. They must have something to eat there, even if it's only Macpherson's lettuces.'

Gwydden nodded. This was evidently sensible. The afternoon was wearing on, and the only other place they could go was Camelot, which was much further away.

They set off from Cottage Pond (as Gwydden had nostalgically dubbed it) towards the centre of Redbrush Park. The Really Water's magic had certainly revitalised the local vegetation. Ebenezer Brown had created his 'truly natural landscape' by ruthlessly flattening anything that blocked the view, including trees and bushes, and replacing them with neatly trimmed grass. The Really Water had largely reversed this trend. Redbrush Park was now filled with a riotous collection of cherry trees, rhododendron bushes, honeysuckle and meadow flowers. It looked and smelled delicious, but it was difficult to find anything like a direct route through it.

When they finally came to the place where Redbrush Hall had stood, they were more than a little disturbed to find that someone had apparently stolen it and put an ugly grey tower with a bulbous top in its place.

The Tower of Yrminsul was looking distinctly unwell, however. It was bent over like a wilting flower, and the eyelid of the monstrous Eye was closed.

'What *is* that?' asked the dwarf, pointing at the wizened grey edifice. 'It looks like a very old spring onion.'

'I don't know about the tower,' said the wizard, 'but that thing in the top must be the Eye of Balor.'

As if hearing its name had roused it, the Eye slowly opened its lid and swivelled round to look at them. A faint, wavering beam of light came from its pupil, and fell on the grass at their feet. The dwarf and wizard jumped back in alarm. But the light was evidently too weak to cause any damage, and the grass continued to wave healthily in the breeze. After a moment, the Eye slowly closed.

'It looks nearly dead,' commented Hergrim.

Gwydden nodded. 'It doesn't belong here. It belongs in Lochlann, the Fhomoire's land.'

'Can you send it back there?'

'I can try.'

'Okay,' said the dwarf. 'You do that, and I'll go and see if any of Macpherson's vegetables have survived.'

While Hergrim wandered away, scanning the ground for signs of something edible, the wizard produced *The Wizard's Handbook* and, after some searching, found a spell *For the Banishment of Demons and Other Not Very Nice Things*, which sounded as though it might do the trick.

He raised his staff, pointed it at the tower, and began to intone the spell.

'Ah, good man,' said Uther, looking up as the sentry staggered into the Great Hall, his arms full of grey stones. 'Put 'em on the floor with the others, will you, and let's see how many we've got.'

'Twenty-seven, sire,' said the sentry, after carefully counting. 'Plus the one you gave me makes twenty-eight. Plus the one in *The King's Head* makes twenty-nine.'

Uther frowned. 'Didn't you give Grympel an IOU?'

Embarrassed, the sentry looked down at his feet. 'Er, he wouldn't take one, sire. He said there was too much on your tab already.'

'Oh, I see,' said the King. 'Well, that still leaves us one short. Might someone have kept one, as a souvenir?'

'I don't think so, sire. Everyone except Grympel seemed only too happy to see the back of them.'

'Oh well.' Uther shrugged. 'I expect the other one will turn up. After all, one grey stone can't do any harm, can it? Not now it's no longer a shape-shifter. Now look here, young fellow, I want your assistance with something. You see all these stones, that used to be man-eating shape-shifters?'

'Yes, sire.'

'Well, I've decided what to do with them, and I want your help.'

Aha, thought the sentry. *An important task. The King has chosen me to help him rid the country of the last vestiges of a great evil.* His chest swelled proudly. 'Yes, sire.'

'Pick one up, will you?'

The sentry did so, and looked down at the misshapen grey lump in his hand. 'What do I do with it now?'

'First of all, we need this little chap.' Uther held up the smallest of the stones. It had faint markings on it like the florets of a cauliflower, and was much paler than the others, almost white. 'I rather like this one. It's got a friendlier expression than the others, don't you think?'

'Yes, sire,' the sentry agreed. It was easy to agree with this. Genghis Khan's worst scowl would have been beatific compared with the expressions on the other stones. The white one merely looked a little sad.

'Right. Now I roll the white stone across the room,

like this . . . see? And then you and I have to roll our stones towards it, and the one who ends up nearest to the white one wins.'

The sentry stared at Uther. A *game*? The old twit wanted to play a *game* with these hideous things?

Oh well. At least it was better than being slagged off by old harpies in poke-bonnets.

He rolled his stone, and watched it wobble away into a corner of the Hall and disappear behind the wall-hangings. 'But it doesn't roll straight, your Majesty.'

Uther grinned. 'That's the fun of it. Good game, isn't it? I'm thinking of calling it "boulders". Something like that, anyway. Come on, let's have another go.'

The sentry reluctantly followed his liege lord to the other end of the Great Hall, where Uther picked up the white stone and held it in his palm.

'I'm getting quite fond of this little fellow. I think I'll give him a name. Any ideas?'

The sentry sighed inwardly. *The poor old King's definitely going a bit batwise in the pigeon-loft*, he thought. *Have to humour him, I suppose.*

'How about Jack, your Majesty?' he suggested.

Engrossed in casting his spell, Gwydden did not hear Hergrim's sudden warning shout. Then a shadow fell across him, and a scream of inhuman hatred and malice tore at his eardrums. He looked up, startled.

A brown tablecloth with a huge beak and out-stretched talons was falling towards him out of the sky.

'SQUWWAAAAAKK!' screamed the tablecloth as it plunged down at him.

With the total lack of co-ordination that frequently saves the lives of unathletic people, the wizard jerked like an epileptic frog, and fell over. Too slowly, how-ever. With a scream of vindictive triumph, the pterodactyl swooped down, seized the wizard's head, and flew off with it into the blue.

Hergrim, running towards him, let out a horrified yell. '*Gwydden!*'

Gwydden sat up and blinked. 'Yes?'

The astonished dwarf skidded to a halt. 'Oh! You're all right. But I could have sworn—'

'Yes, I'm fine, thank you.' The wizard put a hand to his head. 'Oh, bother. It's taken my hat.'

The pterodactyl had discovered that the head in its claws had turned into a shabby cone of grey cloth with a battered point. It screamed in fury and tore the hat into pieces. Fragments of cloth fluttered earthwards like terminally depressed butterflies.

'That was my *hat!*' Gwydden shouted angrily. He shook his fist at the circling pterodactyl. 'Vandal!' He turned to pick up his staff, and found Hergrim staring at him. 'What's the matter?'

'I don't see,' said the dwarf, whose ashen face was gradually recovering its usual ruddy hue, 'how it could have *missed*.'

'Oh, that.' The wizard brushed ineffectually at the grass-stains on his robe. 'The whole point of a hat is to protect the head, isn't it?'

'Yes, but—'

'Obviously, it wasn't an ordinary hat,' said the wizard. 'It had a certain amount of magic woven into it, including an instruction to pretend to be its owner's head in dire emergencies, in order to confuse an attacker.'

'So what you're telling me,' said Hergrim, 'is that your hat committed suicide.'

'Just doing its job.' Gwydden squinted up at the sky. 'Oh dear. That thing's coming back again.'

The pterodactyl was circling lower and lower,

keeping a wary eye on the wizard's staff. It landed clumsily a few yards away, folded its wings, and stared at them. Its eyes were small and wicked, like marbles with evil genies imprisoned in them.

'Nasty looking thing, isn't it?' said the dwarf in a low voice. 'Big, too.' He quietly unslung his axe from the leather harness on his back. 'Ever seen one before?'

'I've seen pictures,' said the wizard. 'In very old grimoires.'

'What is it, then?'

'Some sort of dinosaur, I think.'

'*Dinosaur?*' The dwarf laughed derisively. 'Don't be a prat, Gwydden. Everyone knows that dinosaurs are just a fairy tale based on dragons.'

The wizard shook his head. 'Sorry to disillusion you, Hergrim, but dinosaurs *did* exist. A very long time ago, though. There shouldn't be any *now* – any dinosaur you find these days should just be part of the fossil record.'

'Really? Well, if this one comes any closer, we'll set the fossil record straight.' The dwarf adjusted his grip on the axe-handle, like a golfer settling down to whack the ball off the tee. 'I expect they're a lot less threatening if you chop their heads off.'

At this, the pterodactyl cocked its huge and horrible head on one side, eyed the dwarf malignantly, and said in a sly, croaking voice, 'All right, shorty. Come and try it, if you think you're *big* enough.'

Hergrim stiffened. 'Did you hear that? It's trying to insult me.'

'Don't let it annoy you,' said the wizard uneasily. 'I didn't know they could talk. It might be a magic one.'

'Come on, little man,' cooed the pterodactyl. Its voice was sandpaper pretending to be silk. 'Come and chop off my toes, if you can reach up to them.'

Hergrim let out a low growl, the sort of sound a tiger

might make if its keeper offered it milk and called it "Pussums".

The wizard laid a hand on his arm. 'Careful, Hergrim. It's just trying to get you angry.'

'I know,' snarled the dwarf, 'and it's doing a first rate job.'

'There's a dear little midget,' wheezed the pterodactyl, with a hoarse chuckle.

'Oh no,' said the wizard, aghast. 'Not *that* word.'

Hergrim's bushy red eyebrows avalanched into a furious scowl. 'WHAT did you call me?'

'Midget,' murmured the pterodactyl sweetly. 'Midget midget midget.'

Hergrim muttered something unintelligible. His breathing became ragged. His eyes slowly rolled up under the top lids, until only the whites were visible. He looked as if he was about to faint.

'Oh, not now, Hergrim,' said the wizard despairingly. 'Don't go berserk on me, *please*. I never know what to *do* when you go berserk.'

It was too late, however. Foam appeared on the dwarf's lips and dribbled down his chin. He let out a roar, raised his axe above his head and charged.

It was never going to be a fair fight.

Hergrim was in the dwarf's berserk rage, a fearsome condition which makes a warrior impervious to pain, wounds, common sense, and indeed anything much less than a nuclear warhead delivered between the eyes. A dwarf in such a mood is virtually invincible.

The pterodactyl probably knew this. That might explain why, at the instant the dwarf reached it, instead of engaging in preliminary skirmishes, it simply opened its great pelican beak and swallowed Hergrim whole.

The dwarf's battle-crazed yell resounded hollowly for a second, as if he had fallen into a deep pothole. Then there was silence. Gwydden saw a dwarf-sized lump pass down the pterodactyl's bony neck. A moment later, the pterodactyl opened its beak again and let out a dwarf-sized belch.

'Hergrim!' whispered the horrified wizard.

The pterodactyl smacked its jaws appreciatively. 'Nice bit of dwarf, that. Good strong flavour. An acquired taste, dwarfs – some people find them too pungent, especially if they haven't had a bath for a while, but I've always preferred them that way. And now, time for dessert.' The pterodactyl began to waddle over the grass towards the wizard.

Among the many variants of Sod's Law that are woven like scratchy bits of wire wool into the polyester-cotton fabric of the universe is the Principle of Unpredictable Doom, or PUD for short. This states that if you make careful plans to avoid ninety-three horrible fates, what will actually happen to you is number ninety-four, which is the worst of the lot and never even entered your head.

Gwydden, for example, had not expected that his best friend would be eaten alive by a lizard from the Jurassic Age. It therefore took some time for his emotions to decide whose job it was to react to this. They finally elected Anger, which was a bit of a surprise, not least to poor old Anger himself, who hadn't been called on to do anything for days and was having a quiet snooze in the back row.

Most wizards are calm, rational, laid back people. But occasionally something makes a wizard lose his temper completely and aim a vicious transmogrifying spell at someone who has really annoyed him. Many a wizard, driving a magic carpet and becoming involved in an argument with another carpet-driver, has angrily turned the other driver into a spotted toad, in a fit of what has thus come to be known as "toad rage".

Gwydden felt the toad rage rise up in him all at once, in a sort of splurge. A red mist came in front of his eyes, as if someone had emptied a bottle of tomato ketchup over his head. He stared at the pterodactyl with eyes that were squinting and slightly unfocused. He wanted to turn it into something more revolting than anyone had ever imagined. Worse than a big wobbly pustule oozing yellow-green slime. Worse than a politician.

He pointed Sephira at the pterodactyl, and through gritted teeth uttered a short, violent spell. It wasn't out of a grimoire. It wasn't even in Latin. It was a spell from somewhere deep inside him, consisting of a few terse syllables in a proto-language once spoken by proto-humans, before some clever dick invented stone tools and things started to get complicated. A language in which it was impossible to say things like 'Well, Jeremy, I'm glad you asked me that question', or 'the fact of the matter is this', or 'our party's position on this issue is perfectly clear', and then go on to tell a whopping great lie. It was the language of Truth. Nowadays only small children and lunatics speak it, and no-one else understands them.

It was also the language in which everything had only one name, and once you called something by that name, it couldn't pretend to be anything else.

His thin hand shaking with fury, Gwydden pointed his staff at the pterodactyl and said the first part of the spell, which included the pterodactyl's true name.

The pterodactyl changed. For a moment it re-formed itself, rather surprisingly, into a large black rabbit. The rabbit dissolved, and became a green troll with one asymmetrical head. The troll in its turn melted, and became a huge grey slug.

Finally the slug disappeared, and what took its place was something so horrible that all Gwydden's rage leaked away in two seconds flat. The rest of the spell, which would have done heaven knows what to the shape-shifter, dribbled away with it. Sephira slipped from his fingers, and he took a step back in dismay.

'Hi there,' said the shapeless shape, in a voice like sludge. 'Gwydden the Abstruse, isn't it? My name's Archon. I suppose this is all your doing, this Really Water stuff, and the Tower of Yrminsul drooping like a dying daffodil, and my friends all turned into stones? Bit of a nuisance, I'll admit. I don't mind telling you, Mr Man-Without-A-Pointy-Hat, that you're not exactly the flavour of the month with me at the moment. You've delayed my plans by several hours.'

Gwydden searched for his voice, found it hiding somewhere behind his tonsils, and croaked, *'Delayed?'*

'Delayed, yes.' The evil voice chuckled. 'Oh, you didn't really think you'd *won*, did you? I'm afraid not. My friends may have been temporarily turned to stone, but they aren't *dead*. We Fhomoire are *demons*. You can imprison us – you can even banish us – but you can't *kill* us. This Really Water stuff has impeded our progress a little, that's all. The door at the foot of the Tower of Yrminsul has been temporarily sealed, and the Grey Magic is, for the moment, trapped on the other side. But there's plenty more of it still to come – more than enough to defeat the Green God and his Really Water – and it's quite easy for me to re-open the door.'

Gwydden tried to say something, but his voice had scuttled back behind his tonsils and this time refused to come out.

'Anyway, it's been fun defeating you,' said Archon. 'And now, I'm afraid it's time to say *down the hatch.*

I would say goodbye, but of course one doesn't say goodbye to food.'

The shape-shifter oozed forward at top speed.

A grey mouth yawned in front of Gwydden. It was like a cave, except that caves generally don't drip saliva.

The wizard thought about running. He would have tried it, if he could have remembered how. You were supposed to do something with the legs, he was fairly sure.

Or he could cast a spell.

He really ought to decide which it was going to be.

And then, of course, it was too late.

It was early evening now, and eating, it seemed, was on everyone's mind.

In the Great Hall, Uther had finished his game of bowls (as he had settled on calling it) and had sat down to a supper of scrambled eggs on toast. On this occasion he had invited Boadicea to join him – which seemed only fair, since she had brought the eggs – to celebrate the defeat of the Fhomoire and the lifting of the threat to his kingdom. Neither of them were aware of what was currently happening in the Forest, which was just as well, as it would have spoiled their appetites.

In *The King's Head*, Grympel was serving his usual evening customers, and intermittently polishing the grey stone on his apron. He was also polishing up his patter, which now started, 'Ladies and gentlemen, this here grey stone is no *ordinary* stone; some say it has magical powers . . .'

A woman who ran a lodging house in Rottenapple Street was discovering that Mrs Tod was easily the most annoying tenant she had ever had. Macpherson, meanwhile, had wandered off sorrowfully in the gathering twilight, following a random route that finally took him back to the city gate. There he bumped into the grizzled guard, Balderbreeks, and joined him on his patrol. Just outside the gate, lying in the grass, they found a bottle labelled *Auld Glenmiller*, which the Great Alfonso had inadvertently dropped. The two of them retired for a liquid supper to Balderbreeks's tiny hut, from which in due course there emerged sounds of rather slurred singing.

Inside Archon's stomach, Gwydden was feeling strangely at peace. So this was what dying was like. No pain, no anguish, no worries about whether you'd remembered to make out your will correctly or left the gas on in the kitchen. Just a warm, wet, womblike interior, in which you could curl up and go to sleep.

He got himself into a comfortable foetal position, closed his eyes, and put his thumb in his mouth.

He could feel someone next to him in the stomach-womb. From a general impression of hairiness and large boots, he deduced that it was probably his great friend Hergrim. That was nice. *In death they were not divided.* A nice inscription for a tombstone. Though they wouldn't have a tombstone, of course. Pity. Still, you couldn't have everything, and it certainly was very comfortable in here.

The wetness was a bit weird, that was the only thing. It tickled, somehow. Made the skin itch. Like little teeth, almost, gnawing. But not bad enough to *hurt*, exactly.

He was drifting away now, to somewhere. He wasn't sure where. Not that it mattered. It would probably be somewhere nice, wherever it was.

No more worries for me and Hergrim, he thought peacefully. *For us, the story is over.*

*   *   *

Rosemary Featherbrain was feeling miserable. The other hens had been sympathetic to begin with, but their sympathy had worn thin, and for the past day or so they had been walking past her disdainfully with their beaks in the air.

Hens are like that. They like novelty. Rosemary's peculiar cold grey egg that moved in a mysterious way underneath her at midnight was fascinating for about sixteen hours, but then one of the other hens heard a juicy bit of gossip, and Rosemary's problem child became yesterday's news. Their sympathy turned to scorn. They decided that she was putting on airs. One sharp-tongued pullet even suggested that she wasn't a good mother, and that she ought to hand over the job of brooding to a qualified egg-minder.

Rosemary sat and gazed out of the door of her lonely little hut (no-one wanted to share with her; they had all gone off to a hen party in one of the other coops) and wondered what would become of her misunderstood grey child. Would it ever hatch? Would it be popular? Would it fulfil her private dream, and become King or Queen of England?[1]

Lost in these gloomy thoughts, she paid little attention to the wild, terrified squawking which had suddenly started in the other coop, assuming that it was just part of the evening's merrymaking.

Clouds of feathers erupted from the party coop. A crowd of panic-stricken hens shot out of the doorway and fled towards the far end of the garden. Once there, they clustered by the wall and clucked agitatedly.

On top of the garden wall, the rooster sighed and

---

[1] Not as unlikely as you might think. Ethelred II was a chicken, as he proved by refusing to fight the Danes.

opened one eye. It was always the same. Any time he was trying to have a nice quiet doze, the wretched women would start squawking. What was the matter this time?

The milling crowd of hens was directly below him. Surreptitiously, he listened to their conversation.

'What was it?' whispered one of the youngest hens, directing her question to anyone older and wiser than herself.

'That, my dear,' said the oldest hen, puffing out her chest-feathers, 'was the evil demon Sageanonion, whose name is feared by all poultry. He has the teeth of a dog, the eyes of a cat, the body of a giant cockroach and the smell of a dung-beetle.'

There was an awed silence.

'*I* thought,' ventured one of the younger hens tentatively, 'that it might be a fox.'

The oldest hen regarded her severely. 'Have you ever *seen* a fox?'

'N-no, I haven't.'

'Have you ever *smelled* a fox?'

The presumptuous youngster hung her head. 'No.'

'Well, you can take it from *me*,' said the oldest hen, looking at her coldly, 'that foxes do not smell like *that*. Nor do they have such filthy, slimy bodies.'

The rest of the hens nodded. The intruder had certainly smelled and felt *awful*.

'Are we all here?' enquired the oldest hen, cocking her head to and fro and surveying the others with a beady eye.

Since hens can't count, it took a little while to answer this question, but eventually someone said, 'I don't think Rosemary is here.'

The oldest hen tossed her head. 'Oh, her. She can look after herself. I wouldn't be surprised if it wasn't her peculiar egg that the demon Sageanonion was looking for.'

The rooster on the wall considered the situation. This was his territory, and technically it was his job to see off intruders. But Sageanonion sounded like bad news. The hens, fortunately, hadn't noticed him roosting up here. The best thing to do was keep shtum, and hope the demon would go away.

In the empty party coop, a bedraggled, filthy and stinking shape rummaged among the warm, hen-scented straw for eggs.

Those who thought they knew the Earl of Redbrush would have scarcely recognised him. After squirming through the slippery and congested culvert, his green smoking jacket and his red fur were both liberally coated with grey-white guano. His quill pens were lost, and all the words going through his head rhymed with 'starvation'.

There were no eggs in the coop. This was hardly surprising, since Boadicea had removed what there were only a little while before, and was currently, with Uther's help, finishing them off with salt and a dash of Worcester sauce. The hens considered themselves to be employed on a one-egg-per-day basis, and having produced their daily quota, were disinclined to lay any more this side of midnight.

The starving Earl emerged into the gathering darkness, and crept across the garden to the one remaining coop. He poked his head inside the door. The one hen inside seemed asleep.

Cautiously, he inserted a paw under the warm feathery body, and to his immense relief, discovered an egg.

Rosemary's eyes shot open, and she let out a squawk

of terror and indignation. She was being burgled! A shadowy figure dripping saliva and smelling strongly of culvert was after her baby! With a hoarse scream, she spread out her wings and flung herself on the intruder.

She got in a few good hard pecks, but Sigismund was determined. Clutching the egg firmly in his paws, he crawled out of the coop, dashed back across the garden with Rosemary in hot pursuit, and slipped quickly into the culvert, where he broke the egg into his mouth and swallowed the contents.

'NO!!'

Archon, in front of the Tower of Yrminsul, in the midst of an invocation that would bring the Grey Magic pouring through the doorway, let out a hoarse scream of rage and despair.

How? his mind cried in anguish. *How has someone found it - the egg in which I concealed my soul? When I find out who it is, I'll – I'll—*

But it was too late. He felt himself drying up and shrivelling, like a moth caught in a flame.

The Tower of Yrminsul, trapped in the unfinished spell, wavered in the air for a few seconds like a ghost, and then melted away into nothing.

Suddenly and violently, Archon vomited.

And carried on shrinking.

Outside the culvert, Rosemary gave a heart-rending scream of despair, and suddenly felt much, much better. A weight had lifted from her mind. What did it matter if the nasty cold thing had been eaten? It hadn't been one of her best eggs, and anyway, she could easily lay another. She wandered off up the garden, pecking in a leisurely fashion at bits of gravel.

As for Sigismund, as soon as he had swallowed the egg, he began to feel peculiar. The egg had tasted *horrible*. Just his luck to get a bad one.

He lay in the culvert, and waited. Eventually the nausea subsided, and he went off to have a bath in the moat.

Gwydden coughed, and rolled over. Where was he? Lying on the grass, apparently. And covered in some sort of – *yeugh!* – revolting grey slime.

He sat up and wiped himself down, as best he could.

The dwarf was lying next to him. He looked very pale, his eyes were tightly closed, and he had his thumb in his mouth. Gwydden shook him by the shoulder. 'Hergrim, wake up!'

The dwarf opened his eyes, retched, and shuddered. 'What happened?' he asked shakily. 'The last thing I remember was being swallowed by that overgrown turkey.'

Gwydden didn't answer, but leaned past him and picked up a grey stone that was lying in the grass. 'I think,' he murmured, scrutinising its curious markings, 'that Archon found he'd bitten off more than he could chew.'

They stood up and looked around. The Forest's riotous greenery was fully restored – all except for a nearby circle of bare earth, a few feet across.

'Where that bulbous tower stood,' said the wizard. He bent down and touched the earth with his finger-tips. 'Ice-cold. I don't think anything will grow here for a while.'

'So that's that,' said the dwarf, picking up his axe. 'How about heading back to Camelot? I've had enough of adventures for a while. All I want is a bath, clean clothes, and a hot meal.'

The wizard grinned. 'Agreed.'

With staff, axe and curious grey stone in hand, they turned their backs on the place where the Tower of Yrminsul had stood, and started walking.

Chapter Sixteen

Two people climbed the stairs of the highest tower in Camelot, and came to a heavy oak door.

'This is it,' said the one with the crown. 'Are you sure you can manage?'

'Oh yes,' said the one in the grey robe. 'I can manage all right.'

'Sorry I can't pay you at present,' said Uther. 'Only, what with one thing and another, and having to rebuild Redbrush Hall for Mrs Tod, who's a very hard person to say no to, the fact is—'

'I quite understand,' said Gwydden. 'Anyway, it was nice of you to cancel Merlin's eviction and let Hergrim and me have our old lodgings back.'

'Least I could do,' said the King, 'considering I need you to get Merlin back to his normal size.'

'Ye-es,' said Gwydden reluctantly. 'I suppose we *do* have to get him back, do we?'

Uther nodded. 'I know what you mean. He is a bit . . .' He hesitated.

'Pompous?' suggested Gwydden. 'Conceited? Arrogant? Overbearing?'

'Expensive,' said the King gloomily. 'Still, he amuses Igrayne, and it's a cardinal rule that the Queen of England must be amused. I'll leave you to it, shall I?'

He turned and descended the stairs.

Gwydden sauntered into Merlin's study, ignoring the doorknob (which sneered, 'Call yourthelf a withard? Where'th your hat, thucker?' as he passed), cast a slightly envious eye over the furnishings, and said a few previously-rehearsed Latin words.

There was a flash of green light, and Merlin appeared in the middle of the carpet, looking distinctly cross.

'You!' he said, glowering at Gwydden. 'I might have known *you'd* be involved! What have you been up to? Why have you taken so long to un-enchant me? Don't you realise there's a dangerous shape-shifter loose in Camelot?'

Gwydden chuckled. 'Don't worry. Everything's been sorted out. You're not indispensable, you know, Merlin.'

'Hmph.' England's top wizard favoured his former classmate for a few seconds longer with, if not the Evil Eye, at any rate the Less-Than-Universally-Benevolent Eye. Then he seemed to dismiss the matter from his mind. He said breezily, 'Well, well. No use crying over spilt dragon's blood. Fancy a drink?'

'Thanks.' Gwydden sat down in Merlin's armchair, and leaned back luxuriously.

Merlin waved his hand, and two whisky tumblers appeared on the table. Then he took down *Ye Elixyr of Lyfe* from the shelf, and opened it.

'WHAT!!!!'

'What's the matter?' asked Gwydden, startled.

Merlin brandished the grimoire at him, revealing the empty space inside. 'My Glenmiller is missing,' he said angrily. 'Did *you* take it?'

Gwydden's face closed up. 'Certainly not.'

'Can you prove that?'

There was a chilly silence. Gwydden stood up. 'I

think I won't have that drink after all. I've just re-membered I promised to meet Hergrim at *The King's Head*.'

'Still slumming with midgets?' sneered Merlin nastily.

Gwydden walked to the door and looked back. 'The trouble with you, Merlin, is that you spend too much time on your own in this study. You ought to get out and make a few friends. Then you might be less of a snob.'

'I've got friends,' Merlin said indignantly. 'I've got plenty of friends. They're always popping into my study of an evening.'

'Really? Who, fr'instance?'

'Well . . . Alexander the Great, for one. He was here only the other night, giving me some fascinating insights into military strategy. And Pythagoras was here on Tuesday – we had an excellent discussion about metempsychosis. And the other week I sum-moned Socrates. He was a bit grumpy – still hasn't got over that business with the hemlock – but he came.'

Gwydden looked at his fellow-wizard sadly. 'Those aren't *friends*, Merlin. Those are *dead* people. Friends have to be *alive*.'

He walked across the landing, and began to descend the stairs.

'Philistine!' Merlin shouted after him. 'My friends are the great men of history – and they accept me as one of them! Your friends are just riff-raff!'

But Gwydden had gone out of earshot.

Fuming, Merlin slammed the study door, and picked up *Ye Elixyr of Lyfe*, meaning to pour a drink. Damn. He'd forgotten it was empty.

Still, no problem.

He waved a hand, and a full bottle of *Auld Glenmiller* appeared on the table[1].

Merlin uncorked the bottle, took a sip, and smiled. *Who needs friends,* he thought, *when you're the top wizard in England?*

Three rabbits, having climbed to the top of a long slope, were gazing at a low building of grey stone.

'Looks OK to me,' said Cottonseed. 'A *good* place for a warren. It's high up, so we can see for miles around, and that squirrel we met in the woods told us there are no men here.'

'I don't know . . .' Flopkin was uneasy.

Mopkin was sniffing the air. 'Flopkin,' he said suddenly, 'I can smell carrots.'

'*Carrots?*'

All three of them sat up on their haunches and twitched their nostrils.

'Mopkin's right,' said Cottonseed eagerly. 'It's coming from over there – near that wall. Come on!' He set off at a loping run across the open ground.

'Wait!' Flopkin called after him. 'You don't know if it's safe!'

'It looks all right to me, Flopkin,' Mopkin said reassuringly.

Flopkin hesitated. The rest of the warren was waiting at the foot of the hill, exhausted and hungry after their long trek. And there didn't *seem* to be any men . . .

'All right,' he said. 'Let's get those carrots.'

---

[1]Later that day, in a small stone building in a remote Scottish glen, a man counting his stock of full bottles found he was mysteriously one short, crossed himself piously, and blamed the fairies – which was a gross slander, because all the fairies in that part of Scotland were Presbyterians, and completely teetotal.

They found Cottonseed digging furiously in the soil a few yards from the high grey wall. 'Look, Flopkin!' The youngest of the Magnificent Three triumphantly held up a large fat carrot.

Flopkin looked about anxiously. The area by the wall reminded him of Macpherson's garden. It looked tidy, as if someone had recently been digging and planting in it. But he was hungry, and the smell of carrots was delicious. Dismissing his doubts, he got to work digging.

Perhaps the squirrel had been right. After all, they hadn't *seen* any men.

Several feet above their heads, nailed to the long grey wall, was a notice – which, being rabbits, they couldn't read. It said: *Rose Hill Nunnery – all visitors please report to the Mother Superior.*

A few hours later, the nuns sat down to dinner.

'What's this?' demanded the Mother Superior, staring at her plate. 'Why are there no carrots? I specifically asked for carrots. Fetch Sister Macpherson.'

Sister Macpherson, a tall and gawky-looking nun, came over and curtsied awkwardly, while the rest of the nuns looked down at their carrotless plates in embarrassment.

'Sister,' said the Mother Superior, fixing the luckless nun with a narrow stare. 'Why are there no carrots?'

'Och, I'm sorry, Reverend Mother, but the ones that should've bin ready have bin took awa'.'

'Took awa'? What does that mean?'

'I think she means they've been stolen, Reverend Mother,' murmured the nun next to her.

'Stolen? By whom?'

'Rabbits, Reverend Mother. I saw three o' the wee things in the kitchen-garden today.'

'So we have rabbits, do we?' Reverend Mother folded her arms. 'Well, Sister Macpherson, you are our gardener. What do you intend to do about it?'

The nun brightened a little. 'Och, 'tis all in hand. I've written a wee letter tae my brother, who works for the Earl of Redbrush, and asked him tae send me his spare gun.'

'Good.' The head of the nunnery nodded her approval. 'Well, I suppose we must make do without carrots on this occasion. Carry on with your meal, sisters.'

BANG!

Three small brown shapes hopped into a ditch.

'I say, Flopkin, this is just like old times,' said Mopkin.

'Not *quite* like old times,' said Flopkin with satisfaction. They squatted down and counted their spoils.

'Six carrots and a lettuce,' said Cottonseed happily. 'I wonder why that woman in the black and white dress never points that thing anywhere near us?'

'Haven't you noticed?' said Flopkin. 'She squints. I don't think she'll *ever* aim straight.'

'Somebody might realise, and replace her,' said Cottonseed.

Flopkin nodded. 'True. But until then . . .'

'Carrots all round,' said Mopkin.

'Carrots *today*,' said Cottonseed. 'The Magnificent Three strike again.'

Flopkin stood up and stretched. It was good to be alive. There might well be rabbit pie at the end of it all, but in the meantime . . .

'Come on,' he said. 'Let's get this lot back to the warren.'

THE END

Aspire Books are available from bookshops, super-markets, department and multiple stores throughout the UK, or can be ordered from the following address:

Aspire Publishing
Mail Order Department
8 Betony Rise
EXETER EX2 5RR

Please add £0.50 PER ORDER for postage and packing, irrespective of quantity.